Brides of MONTANA

WITHDRAWN

D0920883

WITHDRAWN

Brides of
MONTANA

3-in-1 Historical Romance Collection

KELLY EILEEN HAKE

BARBOUR BOOKS
An Imprint of Barbour Publishing, Inc.

A Time to Plant ©2007 by Kelly Eileen Hake
A Time to Keep ©2007 by Kelly Eileen Hake
A Time to Laugh ©2008 by Kelly Eileen Hake

Print ISBN 978-1-68322-286-6

eBook Editions:
Adobe Digital Edition (.epub) 978-1-68322-288-0
Kindle and MobiPocket Edition (.prc) 978-1-68322-287-3

All rights reserved. No part of this publication may be reproduced or transmitted for commercial purposes, except for brief quotations in printed reviews, without written permission of the publisher.

All scripture quotations are taken from the King James Version of the Bible.

This book is a work of fiction. Names, characters, places, and incidents are either products of the author's imagination or used fictitiously. Any similarity to actual people, organizations, and/or events is purely coincidental.

Published by Barbour Books, an imprint of Barbour Publishing, Inc., P.O. Box 719, Uhrichsville, OH 44683, www.barbourbooks.com

Our mission is to publish and distribute inspirational products offering exceptional value and biblical encouragement to the masses.

Member of the
Evangelical Christian
Publishers Association

Printed in the United States of America.

Contents

A Time to Plant

Dedication

To the Creator of all things,
and for all with a spirit of adventure and a heart for the Lord.

Prologue

March, 1865

My Dearest Dustin,

It is with a heart made heavy with grief that I write this letter. After months of prayer that Hans was still alive and simply missing, we've received word that he lost his life at Vicksburg. I will never see Independence Day in the same light again, as the freedom for others has been purchased, in part, with my brother's blood.

Nor does our sorrow end there, for Papa passed on to heaven a week past. I wonder whether he would have had the strength to conquer the cholera had he not been weakened in spirit by the loss of his eldest son.

Mama is so beside herself that she's not slept since Papa died. The doctor dosed her with laudanum that she might have healing rest. I mourn with her for Papa and Hans. So much loss in such a short span of time—I fear my own heart would break were it not for the grace of God and my dreams of our future as man and wife.

Father's final instructions were to sell the house and mercantile immediately, pack all we could need, and join you on the homestead as soon as possible. It is far sooner than we'd planned, I know, but I long for the solace of your smile. This year has passed so slowly without you.

Our party is much larger than anticipated. Mama and Isaac will come with me, as Jakob is now the head of our family. She will write to Jakob herself, so you men will be receiving her solemn letter as well as mine. Mama refuses to leave the Bannings behind, as they've become more than cook and stable master and seem like family. Cade and Gilda are joining us, along with their daughter, Kaitlin, who has a surprise for Arthur when we arrive. I'm sure he'll be glad to see his wife *again after so long an absence.*

Not to worry though. I'll be bringing along absolutely every-thing we could possibly need. I'm making the arrangements for train and steamboat but wanted this letter to arrive as far ahead of us as possible. Pray that God grants us traveling mercies as we leave Baltimore to join you in the wilds of the frontier. Our party should arrive sometime in April, though I cannot be sure when. I come determined to work alongside you as helpmeet and make our spread a home.

With sincere affection,
Delana Albright

Chapter 1

April, 1865

W e've done well," Dustin Friemont declared to his partners as they sat down for the midday meal. "At this rate, we'll finish right on time." He sat with his back against the barn, flanked by his future brother-in-law, Jakob Albright, and their friend, Arthur MacLean.

"My sister comes in just over a year." Jakob batted away a few gnats. "We're running out of time."

"Not really." Dustin Friemont lifted a gloved hand to shade his eyes from the glare of the bright sun as he surveyed his surroundings with satisfaction. Majestic mountains overlooked a forest of timber, which gradually gave way to the meadow alongside a fresh creek. He knew Delana would love the land he'd chosen for their home. "We've got a tight schedule to keep, but things are going better than I'd hoped."

"Eleven months of hard labor and we've precious little to show for it." Jakob bit into a piece of jerked beef and yanked some free.

"There's 480 acres among the three of us," Dustin mused, "and in eleven months we've filed our claims and begun the work of proving up."

"Begun," repeated Jakob pessimistically, "is the right word. We don't have so much as a house raised."

"Dinna be forgettin' my smithy." Arthur MacLean flexed his powerful muscles in a mighty stretch. "A lot of work went into that."

"And a lot of work comes out of it." Dustin slapped Arthur on the back. "Without your repairs to plow and sodbusters we would never have been able to clear as much as we have."

"We have to do better this year." Jakob slurped some water. "The first year we couldn't expect to cultivate nearly enough land, but now is the time to expand. We need to raise a house for Delana. My sister is not going to live in a barn."

"Of course not!" Dustin ripped a piece of jerky with his teeth.

"Nor my wee wife." Arthur frowned. "My Kaitlin is deservin' of a real home."

"And she'll get it." Dustin brushed dust off the seat of his britches. "So enough sitting in the shade. If we've all eaten our fill of dinner, we'll get back to clearing this field."

As he worked alongside his partners, Dustin's thoughts turned to God. *Every hour spent and every ache endured is well worth it. I've been away from my Delana for so long now, Lord. It's been months since I've had so much as a letter. Please let all be well with her. I thank You for the labor that occupies my hands and distracts my heart from the distance between us. With every step I take, I clear not only the land for crops, but also the way for a new life. Please give me continued strength so I can have all in readiness for my bride. We have much to accomplish, but I know we can succeed in You. Let me prove to Delana that I will be a good provider when she arrives, Lord.*

Thirteen months. . .only thirteen more months. . .

"Only three more days." Delana answered Captain Massie's question as they oversaw the unloading of all her gear from his steamboat, the *Twilight*. "It will take three days of traveling southeast from Fort Benton to my fiancé's claim."

"And my son's," Mama added.

"I wish you the best." The gallant captain smiled at them both. "I've never seen a frontier bride with such a large entourage."

"We've come to build a life, Captain Massie." Delana surveyed the wagonloads of goods. "It will take more than this to succeed."

"It takes strong will and a stout heart," the captain agreed.

"And God's grace," Delana added. When she realized that she'd frowned at the captain for the omission, she softened her expression. "The help of gentlemen like yourself has also proven valuable."

"Indeed." Massie grinned, and Delana suspected he was thinking of the fees he'd earned for transporting so many passengers and such an outrageous amount of freight.

"Your expertise has eased our way," Delana praised. "If you hadn't advised us to purchase livestock in Kansas City, we'd have been in trouble when we found very little is available here at Fort Benton."

"Certainly not in the quantity you acquired." Massie watched as dockhands unloaded one hog, three sows, four dairy cows, thirty-five baby chicks, and two mares. "I'll be leaving you fine ladies now to attend to other matters." With that, he headed down the gangplank.

"I'm glad to see they've unloaded the oxen for the freight wagons." Mama finally tucked her wrung-out hanky into her reticule with a sigh of relief.

"Four teams of six oxen," Cade Banning confirmed. "One for each freight wagon."

"How's it going, Cade?" Delana knew he'd been below deck, supervising the transport of their precious livestock.

"Well, they know what they're doin'. I've hired four fellas who've agreed to load us up and drive the freight wagons to our spread in return for a team of mules, one of the buckboards, and provender for their journey to Virginia City. They're going to try their luck at finding gold in this territory." Cade shrugged. "I figure you will want to join Gilda and Kaitlin, to see with your own eyes where everything is."

"Where will you be?" Delana wondered aloud, anxious to keep her group together. Isaac had threatened to join the war several times since the news of Hans's death.

"Takin' young Isaac to market to purchase mules for the buckboards and see if'n we can't find a guide to the spread."

"Thank you, Cade, for keeping track of my brother in addition to overseeing that matter." Delana saw the dockhands stacking all the cut lumber into one of the freight wagons. She rushed over. "No, no, no! If you put some of that in the bottom of each wagon, it will make the load more even." The men grumbled but parceled out the lumber among the four wagons.

"What do you want in this one?" A man jerked a grimy thumb toward the freight wagon behind him.

"These trunks." Delana pointed to the teetering pile. Each one held clothing or items of a personal nature. "And this." She lovingly ran her hand over the varnished oak of her hope chest.

Kaitlin walked by, carrying a crate full of bolts of fabric. This, too, went in the first wagon. Delana's traveling writing desk and the women's sewing boxes and medicine chests rounded out the first load. The final item to find its home inside was the crate of Papa's books Delana refused to leave behind. *Papa.*

"And this one?" A tall man forced her attention to the next wagon.

"That stove." Delana gestured to the first cast iron appliance. "The other needs to be in the third." The stoves were the heaviest items they'd brought with them—and arguably the most important.

Delana directed the men, watching as pots, pans, skillets, Dutch ovens, a clockwork jack, roasting pans, baking trays, mixing bowls, and everyday dishes slowly filled the second wagon.

Gilda oversaw the third load of freight, zealously guarding the dried meat, baking supplies, canned vegetables, jars of preserves, and an array of spices. The dry goods took up a fair amount of space.

Mama hovered around the last freight wagon, watching the workmen like a hawk. Great-grandma's rocking chair, *Grossmutter's* glass dishes, and Mama's china were carefully tucked inside. The wall clock from Papa's study, and the tintype photos of their relatives rested alongside galvanized tubs, rolled up rugs, and bedding.

Cade had already seen to the three buckboards. All farming implements, tools, feed for the livestock, and the water they'd need for the trip had already been secured. With the exception of the piglets and chicks, the rest of the livestock would walk for three days until reaching the barn her fiancé and brother had built.

The sun began to set, but Cade and Isaac had not yet returned. *Lord, please let them be all right.*

Delana tamped down the fear that her younger brother had run off. *What's left of our family must stay together.*

"Isaac and Cade!" Mama's relieved cry reassured Delana. Since Hans and Papa had died, Mama had been uneasy whenever Isaac or Delana were out of her sight.

"Who's that with them?" Delana squinted but could only see the shadow cast over the third man's face by his hat brim. He stood far taller than Cade, about the same height as Dustin and with the same confident stride. . .

Can it be? Did he get my letter and travel to Benton to wait for me? Has my fiancé come to take us home? She shifted and craned her neck, trying desperately to catch a glimpse of his face.

He lifted his head, and Delana tried to tamp down the swell of disappointment. This stranger was far older than her Dustin, with a full beard and wide grin.

"Hello." Delana pasted a welcoming smile on her lips after Cade introduced everyone to Rawhide Jones.

"*Rawhide?*" Mama's tone rang with scorn, her eyebrows raised disapprovingly.

"Right you are, *Bernadine*."

The man grinned as Mama spluttered in surprise and grew red in the face. Delana realized her mother did not like this man knowing more about her than she did him. Dustin must have talked about his bride-to-be and her family to Mr. Jones. The thought pleased her.

"Glad you decided to dispense with the formalities," Rawhide continued to Mama. "Highfalutin ways aren't practical on the plains. It's good to see you've the sense to recognize it."

Mama's mouth opened and closed like that of a landed fish, but she couldn't seem to find the words. Since she'd set the tone by using his Christian name first, a reprimand wouldn't do. Rawhide's irreverent attitude apparently irked Mama, even as his compliment obviously sealed his rejoinder with the stamp of courtesy. Delana bit back her own smile.

"Though I believe I'll still call you Miss Albright." Rawhide swept his well-worn hat off his head and lowered his voice. "Unmarried young females are scarce in these parts, and we don't want to encourage unwarranted familiarity by the men. With that in mind, you can call me Rawhide, but I'll be addressing you real proper."

"Thank you," Delana murmured.

"You're every bit as lovely as your fiancé said." Rawhide turned back to her mother. "And it's easy to see who lent you her beauty."

Mama glowered at him in stony silence.

"My fiancé?" Delana laid a gloved hand on his arm. "You know Dustin Friemont?"

"Yep." Rawhide rocked back on his heels. "I know everyone within five days' travel from here. That's why Mr. Banning"—he jerked a thumb toward Cade to punctuate the comment—"has asked me to guide you to the homestead."

"*Wunderbar!* It's wonderful!" Mama, obviously recalling her priorities, deigned to give the man a slight nod. "I'm sure we can rely upon your"—her magnanimity ostensibly deserted her as she searched for an appropriate word—"knowledge."

"I know the easiest routes and the best areas for hunting along the way. Even so, this is a large group with a lot to haul." He cast an assessing glance at the newly packed freight wagons and buckboards. "It'll be a solid three-day journey if all goes well."

"Can you tell me how he and Jakob are?" Delana longed for any news of them.

"And Arthur?" Kaitlin chimed in, apparently just as eager for information about her own husband.

"They're doin' right well." Rawhide slapped his hat on his head. "For now, I suggest you turn in early. We leave at sunup."

"I can't believe it." Dustin squinted at the horizon.

"Believe it," Jakob stated with grim satisfaction, rolling his shoulders to ease the ache.

"Our first forty acres." Dustin gulped huge mouthfuls of lukewarm water thirstily before continuing. "We have five years to cultivate this much on each of our homesteads, or we won't have proved up."

"At this rate," Arthur mused, "that will mean it'll be another three years afore we've done the minimum."

"Not so," Dustin refuted. "We've done much in addition to clearing forty acres. We'll need not raise barn nor smithy this year."

Arthur brightened and slapped Dustin on the shoulder. "So long as we work together, we'll come out far ahead of those who go it alone."

"This summer, while the wheat and corn grow, we'll need to be making things ready for our brides." Dustin conjured up the image of a cozy log cabin waiting for Delana. She'd arrive at a time such as this, with the big blue sky stretching over still-snowcapped mountains and green meadows made cheerful with wildflowers.

Lord, help me have all in readiness for her. Let her look on this land with the love and pride I do. The timing is good for her to see our homestead at its finest. Let me be a good steward of the land You've given us.

Dustin dipped his canteen in the stream in preparation for returning to work. When a flock of startled birds rose from the trees ahead, he turned and snatched his shotgun from his saddlebags.

"Bear?" Jakob grabbed his own shotgun, ready to shoot if need be.

"Could just be a coyote," Arthur reasoned. "Or a mountain lion."

"Whatever it is, it could be dangerous." A predator, a dry spell, forest fire, locusts, sickness—anything was a threat to their carefully laid plans. Dustin listened intently, recognizing the sound of many horses or head of cattle. "Claim jumpers." He kept his defensive stance. No group of ranchers or fellow settlers would take his land. Whoever was coming, they'd be leaving just as quickly.

"Easy!" Rawhide rode into the clearing, and the men swiftly lowered their guns.

"What's coming, Rawhide?" Dustin heard ominous creaks and shouts amid the heavy plodding of hooves.

"More trouble than you can possibly imagine."

Chapter 2

A freight wagon?" Dustin stared in disbelief as the thing came swaying into view.

"More than one." Rawhide stooped and took a draft from the cool stream.

"They can't pass through our land!" Dustin raised his voice to be heard.

"Oh, they won't be." The older man's exasperating answer was accompanied by a mischievous grin.

"*Who* won't. . . ?" Arthur's voice faded as his eyes widened in obvious recognition of the first figure stepping onto the meadow. "*Kaitlin?*" The blacksmith rubbed his eyes vigorously before confirming the sight of his young wife. "KATIE!" He gave a mighty whoop and broke into a run. In just a minute, he was gathering his prize in his arms and spinning 'round before kissing her soundly.

It's all right. Dustin quickly began to reconfigure their plans. *Kaitlin missed Arthur and came early. It's just one woman, and it looks like she brought plenty of supplies. We can adjust. . .* His reassurances fell flat when a second freight wagon followed the first.

All right. Rawhide must have brought a really large shipment of coal for Arthur's forge. Maybe he struck an unbelievable bargain, and it'll be worth the bother of unloading so much. After all. . . He caught sight of a second figure stepping into view.

"Mama?" Jakob's disbelieving voice wavered on the too-still air before he started toward his mother.

Mama Albright? Why would Kaitlin bring Mrs. Albright all the way out here? A sudden realization stabbed his heart. *Hans must have died. She has traveled all this way to tell Jakob and to fetch him back to Baltimore to be his father's heir.* He straightened his shoulders against the loss of a big part of their work force.

We'll still be fine. Mrs. Albright won't stay long, so she's not a major concern. The thing to remember is that Delana isn't here. I still have a year to build our home into something worthy of her. If she'd traveled with her mother, she'd have led the bunch. She's always running ahead, but she didn't now. That means we'll be okay. . .

The warm sensation of deep relief vanished as the wail of an infant rent the air.

No. His mind refused to believe the message relayed by his ears. He shook his head back and forth to stop hearing the impossible sound. That failing, he gave the side of his skull a good *thunk*, which did nothing but give him a bit of a headache.

Cade and Gilda Banning walked up to where Arthur still held their daughter tightly. Dustin watched as Gilda transferred a small, swaddled bundle to Arthur's arms. The look of awe and fear on the big blacksmith's face made Dustin groan.

He desperately sought for a bright spot in what was rapidly becoming a disastrous day. A smaller man joined Jakob and his mother. *Ahhh. . .she brought Isaac to guard his brother's claim. She should have sent him alone—at fifteen he's old enough, but there's no telling what goes on in the mind of a woman. The important thing is that Delana is back in Baltimore, minding the mercantile with her father. Thank You, Lord, for giving me time to prepare for her. A proper young lady like my love needs to come home to. . .well, a house. Thank You!*

His breath rushed out of his lungs in a *whoosh* as a slight figure with golden curls and blue skirts stepped into the meadow. Dustin's heart sank as his very worst fear headed straight for him. *Delana.*

☙

Dustin. If he only knew how thoughts of him had sustained her through the arduous journey.

Dustin, she'd thought as she packed for the trip while Mama cried at leaving their home. *Dustin,* she'd promised herself when the babe cried nonstop on the train. *Dustin,* she'd held to his memory while she fought her tumultuous stomach on the Missouri River. *Dustin,* she'd searched for any hint of him during their three-day trek from Fort Benton. And now, here he was, speechless with joy at the sight of her.

"Dustin!" She threw herself into his arms, nestling close to his chest and holding him tight. "Oh Dustin. . ." The moment she'd been living for, for the past weeks, had finally come! "I'm so glad to see you." She laughed. "Even with that silly beard covering half your face."

"Delana." His deep voice, so low and private, rumbled through her.

"I'm here." Relief mixed with the joy, and tears slipped down her face as he drew back and tilted her chin upward.

"What are you doing here?" A strange gleam glinted in his brown eyes, and his mouth set in a harsh line.

"I. . .I came home," she stammered, wondering what could possibly be wrong when they were together.

"Your home is in Baltimore." He seemed to realize the effect of his flat tone and softened it. "At least, it is for another year."

"You didn't get my letter!" She pushed away from him, finally understanding what troubled him. "You didn't know we were coming." Her voice sounded small and forlorn even to her own ears.

"No, I didn't." Dustin crossed his arms over his chest but didn't break eye contact. "What did it say?"

She reminded herself of all the things he didn't know in an effort to overlook the one thing her heart knew all too well: He was not pleased to see her.

"Hans fell at Vicksburg," she began shakily and then continued with more confidence as he stepped nearer and reached for her. "Papa died of cholera last month."

"Oh Delana." He gathered her in his embrace, one hand cradling the crown of her head against his strong shoulder. "I'm so sorry."

"It's been so hard," she mumbled against the linen of his shirt. *But I don't have to be strong alone anymore. You'll stand by me and understand.*

"My poor, sweet Delana." He pressed his cheek to hers.

She pushed against his solid chest to look up against him. "Now that we're here, it will all be okay." Tears of joyous relief streamed down her face.

"How does being here make it okay?" His brow furrowed.

"Because we're together." She summoned a brave smile and reached up to cup his face. "We're all together, as a family should be."

"Honey," he took her hand away from his bearded jaw and held it in his work-roughened palm. "This isn't the place for you."

"Why not?" Delana searched his gaze. "What other place can be better than at my husband's side?"

"At your mother's, as we planned."

"But I am." She didn't understand. Surely he could see Mama right over there, with Jakob and Isaac.

"And it was good of her to travel with you." He moved to hold both her hands together before continuing, "But you'll need to go back with her for now."

"Go back?" She frowned before realizing that he didn't know Mama and Isaac and the Bannings would all be staying. "I'm so sorry you didn't get my letter, Dustin." She willed him to understand. "We're here for good. All of us."

"All of you? Where will you stay?"

Delana noticed the tightness in his jaw and hurried to reassure him.

"Cade and Gilda will claim their own land. They say they don't mind bunking in the barn until they have a place. Isaac and Mama will stay with Jakob, and of course Kaitlin and little Rosalind will live with Arthur." She nodded, encouraging him to see the practicality of the plan.

A strangled groan rumbled out of Dustin as he pulled a bandana from his back pocket and mopped his brow. He gazed at the four freight wagons, three buckboards, and everything else around him in disbelief.

"We've come prepared."

He made another one of those strangled-sounding groans, and she patted him on the arm. "I know it's a change in plans," she soothed. Allowances had to be made for his reaction. Dustin was nothing if not methodical, and she'd just waltzed into the middle of his careful plans. "I assumed you'd get my letter and know we were coming. Take all the time you need to let it sink in."

He gave a jerky nod. Silence stretched between them, and Delana waited patiently until she realized that he might take longer than she thought.

"Dear?" She patted his chest. "While you think it over and maybe talk to Rawhide about the cattlemen we hired to drive the oxen back, we ladies would appreciate a chance to wash up and such." When he didn't respond, she tried again. "Why don't you just tell me where the house is, so we can start getting settled in?"

Raucous laughter made her start with fright. She turned her head to see Rawhide laughing so hard he was doubled over.

"Oh dear!" She rushed over. "Has the heat gotten to him?" she asked Dustin as their guide struggled to draw a breath.

"No." Dustin kicked at the grass. "It's not the heat."

"Maybe we should get him to the house and have him lie down a bit," Delana worried.

"The house!" Rawhide echoed and hollered with laughter anew, tears of mirth streaming from his closed eyes.

"Yes." Delana straightened up. "You carry him to the house while I fetch our medicinal supplies. It's good that we came in time, as it's obvious some malady has befallen him."

"It sure has!" Rawhide snickered. "Women!" he gestured toward her and Mama, who'd come to stand by her side.

"Don't pay him any attention." Dustin stepped on his friend's boot. "All that's wrong with him is a busted funny bone."

"I'm not so sure. . . He needs water and rest, at the very least," Mama declared. "Let's get him inside."

"Don't you get it?" Rawhide wiped his eyes, took a few deep breaths, and continued in spite of Dustin's beleaguered sigh.

As Delana's heart sank, Dustin met her gaze with a pained look.

"We haven't built a house yet."

Chapter 3

Rawhide is laughing at me. Look at Delana—the shock and disappointment in her eyes. And Mama Albright is glaring fit to beat the sun. Everyone knows it's the man's job to provide for his family, and I've failed. She came to me, having lost the head of her household, and the house itself, looking to make a home with me. What can I offer her? Nothing. Lord, why is she here? Why could I not have received the letter so I'd have built some kind of house for her? What am I to do now?

First things first. Dustin upended his canteen over Rawhide's head, jolting his friend out of his inappropriate laughter.

"This can't be true." Delana's disbelieving whisper sent a sharp pain through Dustin's stomach.

"Yes, it's true." He squared his shoulders, praying they were strong enough for the burden now placed upon them. What he'd planned and dreamed would be a happy reunion had become a daunting reality instead.

"Oh." Delana seemed at a loss for words.

"What do you mean, 'it's true'?" Delana's mother demanded forcefully. "I cannot believe that after days on a sooty train, several more on a wavering steamboat, and three more jouncing on buckboards across the plains, we find ourselves *homeless!*" Her voice rose steadily throughout the indignant speech, ending on a note so shrill, Dustin fought not to wince.

"Mother!" Delana's shocked outrage surprised all of them. "Dustin knew nothing of our impending arrival. He never received my letter!"

Now my bride is fighting my battles for me? But what could he do but give her the curt nod she was obviously waiting for.

"And I'm assuming that Jakob never got the one you wrote to him." She looked to her brother for confirmation.

"No." Jakob looked as chagrined as Dustin felt.

"Umm. . ." Mama Albright shifted her gaze to the bedraggled fringe

23

of lace on her sleeve. "Well, you know how. . .distracted I was after your father's death. . ." Her words trailed off into an indistinct mumble.

"I only found out about Hans and Papa moments ago." Jakob's jaw clenched, and Delana hugged him before turning to her mother.

"You—you never wrote one?" Delana's quiet disbelief carried more weight than her anger moments before. She closed her eyes for a moment, drawing a deep breath. "The important thing is. . ."

"Is what, exactly?" Jakob's voice sounded oddly hollow in his fresh grief.

"Is that everyone arrived safely," Dustin announced. Delana's grateful smile spurred him on. "We're all hale of body, and now that we're together"—he clamped an arm around her waist as though to illustrate the point—"we're whole of heart, too."

In a silent but obvious show of her support, Delana snaked her arm around his middle and rested her head against his shoulder. The soft smell of lilacs drifted from her hair.

"Aye," Arthur agreed, "that we are." He cradled his babe in one arm and his wife with the other.

"We'll start building a house tomorrow." Dustin saw the men around him nod in fervent agreement.

"And we womenfolk will start supper now." Gilda bustled up to them with her apron full of provisions. "Just give us a good cook fire, and we'll take care of the rest."

God bless Gilda. Dustin managed his first true grin since they'd arrived. "It's been far too long since any of us have had a decent meal."

"Hey!" The indignant chorus came from Jakob and Arthur.

"None of us has starved," Jakob protested.

"This from the man who undercooks biscuits," Arthur snorted.

"As if you don't burn everything you put your hand to." Jakob seemed to rally from the bad news, striving to gain some normalcy. "Comes from working the forge, I guess."

"Pah," Dustin scoffed. "As though anyone could tell the difference between your gruel and your gravy, Jakob."

"I've yet to drop the stewpot and spill our supper altogether," his soon-to-be brother-in-law grinned in silent recognition of Dustin's distraction.

"And not a one of you has started that cook fire." Kaitlin prodded her husband.

"Dustin?" Delana caught his attention once again. "You'll want to go with Rawhide and Cade. We've made arrangements with the freight drivers and cattle drovers already, but I'm sure you'll need to see to the details."

"Now that I can do." Dustin straightened his shoulders, gave Delana one last squeeze, and ambled over to the menfolk.

Immediately, Cade and Rawhide were eagerly explaining the agreements they'd made. "You'll have to decide how many head of oxen you want to keep for plowin' and such," Rawhide declared. "The cowboys will leave tomorrow to take the rest back to Fort Benton. Delana bought six of the beasts—any more than that will need to be purchased. The rest of the oxen were only rented."

"More than adequate," Dustin approved. *This way the oxen won't eat all the grazing or present any danger to the women.* "What about the drivers of the freight wagons?" He glanced uneasily at the small bunch of men seated by the creek.

"They'll be takin' one of the buckboards, a pair of mules, and provender for their journey to Virginia City." Cade gestured vaguely toward one of the wagons.

"That's more than generous." Dustin refused to belittle Delana's choices. *It's beyond generous—those drivers took her in. Not that there's much I can do about it now.* He chafed at finding yet another thing outside his control.

"Your fiancée struck a better bargain than that," Rawhide chortled. "She's got backbone, your little miss."

"She dealt with the hired men personally?" Dustin glowered at Cade. The man should know better than that after working for the Albrights the past decade and a half.

"No. The men gave me their askin' price," Cade replied calmly, "and I relayed it to her. She thought it over a bit and told me it was too dear. 'Cade,' she tells me, 'please go back and tell them we have a bargain only if they all agree to one month's worth of solid labor before they continue on their way.'"

"And they agreed to that?" Dustin marveled—the labor of four men for four weeks would do a lot for their farm.

"Not exactly. They countered with one week. That scrappy bride of yours settled in the end with two." Rawhide scratched his head. "Good thing, too. Miss Albright said somethin' 'bout how she reckoned they'd be useful for building another house for the Bannings. But now it looks like you'll be needing to tackle far more'n that."

"But their services will be greatly appreciated." Dustin quickly assessed their workforce. In addition to the three men already in residence, they now had Cade and Isaac, who was old enough to pitch in. The four drivers made nine men.

I've heard tell that two men can raise a log cabin in three days. 'Course, that's without the logs peeled and the notches made exact. Ours will be better than that. Still. . .in two weeks we should be able to build two homes and not fall too far behind with our plowing. Things aren't so bad after all.

∞

Things, Delana admitted to herself, were a lot worse than when they first arrived this afternoon.

Despite bone-weary fatigue and jostled muscles, the promise of reaching their new home before nightfall had proven an irresistible lure. They'd pushed hard to get here.

Now those aches returned with a vengeance, doubled by the harsh realities they'd discovered in the wilderness—no house, no warm welcome, not so much as a good cookstove.

Lord, I undertook this journey in the faith that this is where You meant me to be. That if I was obedient and of willing spirit, we'd arrive and Dustin would help make everything all right. I cannot pretend to understand Your ways—my sight is limited to the needs of my loved ones. You know us by name, unto the number of hairs on our heads, so You know, too, the pains of our hearts. What more am I to do, Savior? Please help me understand.

She blinked back the all-too-present tears. While she waited on the Lord, there was supper to be made for everyone. She hurried over to where Gilda presided over, not one, but two large cook fires.

The men had erected a makeshift crane from which to hang the massive stewpot and laid some of the planks Delana brought along over two large boulders in lieu of a table.

"Ah Ana, love—" Gilda's smile raised Delana's spirits. "Would you help my Kaitlin with readin' the vegetables?"

"Of course." She took an armload of carrots and onions over to the "table," where Kaitlin stood peeling potatoes. They worked in silence, the only sound the rhythmic *snick-thunk* of their knives slicing through the vegetables and onto the wood planks before them.

"Your mam is good with my babe," Kaitlin observed, looking to where Mama sat with little Rosalind cooing in her arms.

"She has soft hands and a loving heart," Delana agreed.

"A grandchild would go a ways toward fillin' the space left by your da and brother," Kaitlin ventured. "I wouldna mention it during the journey, but now that you're with Dustin, 'tis time to think on such matters."

"I. . ." Delana could feel the blush rising to her cheeks. *I can only pray that it will be so. A daughter to share her childhood with Rosalind, or a son with his daddy's grin. . .* Her hand involuntarily rested on her flat stomach, and a small smile flitted at the corners of her mouth.

"There, now, I didn't mean to embarrass ye." Kaitlin put down her knife. "But 'tis the way of things. Arthur and I were scarce wed a month afore he traipsed off with your intended and left me with Rosalind to warm my thoughts."

"They came to build a new life for us."

"Aye, and now they'll be buildin' new houses, too." Kaitlin grinned. "I heard the men speakin' 'bout how they'll sleep under the wagons until a home is raised. We women are to take o'er their quarters by the barn until then."

"Did you ever imagine that your babe would spend her first night on a new land in a barn?"

" 'Twas good enough for our Savior"—Kaitlin scooped the potatoes into her apron as she spoke—"so I'll not utter a word of complaint."

"What a wonderful way to see it." Delana filled her own apron with the carrots before walking over to Gilda's stewpot.

Gilda carefully added their bounty to the lard and beef broth simmering over the flames.

"Irish stew, is't, Mam?" Kaitlin sniffed appreciatively at the laundry cauldron Gilda had commandeered for the meal.

"Aye, 'tis. Now I'll be needin' you two to cut up one of those dried haunches of venison we purchased from Fort Benton. Ask Rawhide to fetch it for ye, along with our Dutch ovens."

"Would you like me to bring our Dutch oven as well?" Delana offered as Kaitlin set off toward their guide. She looked at the three cowhands, four freight drivers, Rawhide, and their own group—quite a number of hungry men. Big as Gilda's stewpot might be, the men would eat far more.

"Kaitlin knows to bring all four, with so many men to feed who've not had a decent meal in months. We'll be makin' johnnycake instead o' biscuits this eve." Gilda carefully leaned over to add salt and pepper to the stew. " 'Tis simpler to mix and swifter to bake."

"I remember the ingredients from our lessons back home. I'll fetch them." Delana turned to go.

"Dinna forget the molasses and ginger," Gilda called after her. " 'Tis what lends the flavor!"

The three women worked feverishly for over an hour. Gilda watched the stew, adding marjoram and thyme, testing the taste, texture, and temperature time and time again. Delana and Kaitlin mixed huge batches of johnnycake batter while the Dutch ovens warmed amidst the ashes of the fires.

Delana threw herself into the task at hand, glad she'd been taking lessons from Gilda ever since learning she'd be a farmer's wife. *If there's one thing I can give Dustin, aside from responsibilities and worries, it's a good meal.* She slid pan after pan of the mixture into the useful contraptions, closing the ovens and heaping ashes on top to ensure even baking.

Soon she could feel tendrils of her hair sticking to her neck as she dashed back and forth. She knew her face would be flushed an unbecoming red, and her apron was smattered with flour. *Now's no time for vanity,* she chided herself. *Dustin will be focused on the food, not my face. A well-laden table will catch his eye far better than an immaculate dress. The smell of supper should give him more pleasure than any flowery perfume. A truly humble woman wouldn't even consider such things!*

But I am not truly humble, Delana realized, *for I wish more than anything that Dustin would look upon me and have cause to rejoice.*

Chapter 4

Dustin pitched hay from extra stalls up to the loft at a frantic pace. Three dairy cows and two horses had just been added to the barn livestock.

"It was convenient, just grabbin' hay outta them stalls instead of goin' to the loft," Jakob muttered.

"Yeah, but that's what the loft's for. We just saved time the other way." Dustin worked the pitchfork vigorously. "We always planned on having more livestock."

"I know. But the dairy cows could wander."

"Then the women would have to hunt them down for the morning milking." Dustin rejected the idea. "Besides, it's still mighty cold at night."

"And we'll be sleeping under a freight wagon tonight." Jakob sighed.

"We'll all have to make concessions for a while. And remember," Dustin reminded, "the Lord loveth a cheerful giver."

"Cheery has never really been my way," Jakob pointed out.

"Then consider this a wonderful opportunity to grow spiritually." Dustin hid a grin when his friend refused to acknowledge that statement, and they worked in silence until the new animals were settled in.

With things well in hand, Dustin figured he ought to spruce up the room where the women would be sleeping. They'd bedded down in what would eventually be the tack room. He walked over to the doorway and stopped cold.

"What's wrong?" Jakob stood beside him and groaned. "It's a good thing there are only four women." He squinted at the small space.

"And a baby," Dustin tacked on. "How did it get so filthy?"

"This place isna fit for my bride." Arthur hulked in behind them.

Dustin eyed the motley assortment of hats, boots, lanterns, knives, and laundry. "Here's what we're gonna do. Jakob, grab those saddlebags hanging on the wall and stuff everything that's not garbage into 'em, according to who owns what. Be sure to throw away any refuse."

Jakob hopped to it, stuffing the bags with the evidence of a winter's worth of bachelor living.

"What about me?" Arthur shifted anxiously from foot to foot.

"Grab all the blankets you can find." Dustin sized up the blacksmith's beefy arms. "Take 'em outside and beat 'em within an inch of their lives. That'll remove some of the grit." As Arthur hustled past him into the room, Dustin grabbed his arm. "And Arthur? Be sure to do it behind the barn, out of sight of the ladies."

Dustin tromped over to the far corner of the barn, grabbing both rake and broom. They'd need to clear out the old straw they'd tracked in. He also grabbed a handful of nails and a hammer—the gals would need something to hang their garments from. *My bride may not have a proper house yet, but she'll have a roof over her head and a clean, warm place to sleep tonight.*

While the women cooked, the men worked steadily until they'd accomplished what seemed to him a major feat: The room looked habitable. Almost inviting even. Dustin grinned as he, Jakob, and Arthur clapped each other on the back.

"I'll bet it even smells better," Jakob stated before drawing a deep breath. His eyes closed in bliss and he sniffed deeply several times.

"It's nothing special." Dustin gave the man a puzzled look.

"No, it isn't." Arthur breathed gustily. "While we've been workin', the ladies hae been cookin'."

Dustin filled his lungs with air and his nose with the long-forgotten aromas of a well-prepared, hearty meal. "Smells good," he agreed.

The sound of a ladle banging loudly on a pot jerked them into action. *Suppertime!* Dustin scrambled to be the first through the doorway, racing the others out of the barn toward the delectable scents.

The slapdash "table" bowed slightly beneath the weight of a monstrous cauldron, which emitted the intoxicating aromas of meat and seasoning. Beside it sat pan after pan of what looked like cornbread, along with blackberry preserves and butter.

Cade blessed the meal, and they got down to business.

Gilda Banning stood at the head of the table, wielding her ladle like a general with his saber. Dustin fell into line along with the others, accepting a bowl and spoon from Kaitlin with a grateful smile. He proceeded to where Delana stood. For a second, he forgot about the food, just watching her as she sliced pieces of—

"Johnnycake?" She offered him a hefty wedge.

"Smells like heaven," Dustin praised as she smeared butter on the golden bread and passed it to him. He smiled his thanks and stood transfixed by the sudden brightness in her aqua eyes as she beamed back at him. "I'd forgotten how beautiful you are," he whispered.

"Oh, Dustin." Her rosy cheeks let him know she was flattered.

"Move along, Romeo." Rawhide nudged him in the ribs. "You're holding up the line."

"Yeah!" Jakob agreed from behind him. "That's practically a hanging offense tonight!"

"You're no Stuart Granville and his Vigilance Committee," Dustin shot back as he grudgingly moved along.

Rawhide refused to let him have the last word. "And you're no Henry Plummer!"

"If I'm not like Henry Plummer," Dustin considered as he came round the table to stand alongside Delana again, "then that means I *won't* be hung." Chuckles greeted his well-made point.

"Who's Henry Plummer?" Delana asked as she served more johnnycake.

"He was a sheriff in the territory who secretly created a band of outlaws to rob miners over by Virginia City." Dustin bit into his johnnycake and lost his train of thought for a moment.

"Isn't that just a ways west of here?" Delana turned to him, eyes wide with worry as her own supper remained untouched before her.

"A good ways," he reassured her after swallowing his first mouthful. "In January, Stuart Granville rustled up a Vigilance Committee to catch the thieves. When they found 'em, over two dozen men hung for their crimes, among them Henry Plummer."

"That's horrible!" Her hand covered her mouth. "No trial?"

"Not a court for days in these parts." Dustin shrugged. "Justice was served that night."

"What awful supper conversation." Delana hugged herself and frowned. "It's not humorous or entertaining in the least. It recalls tragedy and death and evil."

"You're right." Dustin put down his bowl of stew to rub her upper arms. As far as he was concerned, the fact that he'd abandoned such good food to comfort her spoke for itself. "Forgive me, sweetheart. We've been living as rough bachelors for far too long. A gracious meal deserves decent conversation."

She relaxed and nodded. He saw to it that she got her own helping of the food and walked her over to a large, flat stone, where they sat together near Arthur and Kaitlin.

"I'm sorry," Delana murmured as she picked at her food.

"For what?"

"For coming here without your knowing. I should have waited for you to write back." Her voice quivered and she curled forward.

"It's not your fault." Dustin scraped the bottom of his bowl. "If you'd waited, you would have had difficulties with the mercantile, and it could have been weeks before you got my reply. Think of it," he said bracingly. "I never got that first letter. You wouldn't have written another for a month. Then my response would've taken weeks before you could start the arrangements, and traveling in the heat of late summer is hard on the animals and tiring for the travelers. You did the right thing." He shifted so she couldn't see his face as he added, "Even though I wish it could have been different."

∞

Delana stiffened at his words. *"I wish it could have been different."* The sentence echoed over and over in her mind, striking blows with as much force as a hammer.

He's still unhappy that I'm here. I thought he was softening, coming around to the reality of this. Lord, my heart melted when he smiled at me over by the table. And when he led me here, so we could sit together in the simple joy of one another's company, I felt more secure than I have in two months. Give me strength to prove it's right that I came. Let my hands be useful and my heart be open.

"I wish things could have been different, too," she said quietly.

I wish Hans were alive. I wish Papa had never gotten sick. I wish Mama had written to Jakob so at least one of the letters would have reached you. But most of all, I wish you would take my hands in yours and tell me you love me and can't wait until we're man and wife.

But she didn't say a word of all that. It did no good to complain, and she wouldn't have him pitying her. She wanted his admiration and acceptance, so she would make herself busy. Delana gently took his bowl and went to the stream to rinse their dishes before helping Gilda and Kaitlin clean the supper mess.

The days weren't at their full length yet, and darkness had enveloped the land by the time they finished. Arthur came up to Kaitlin after she'd nursed Rosalind beneath the privacy of a shawl.

"Let me take ye to your room for the night." He placed a huge hand on the small of her back and led her toward the barn. Not seeing Dustin anywhere, Delana hurried behind them.

Arthur led them inside the barn. A small room with four piles of fresh hay, covered with blankets, glowed cheerily by the light of a single lantern on an upturned crate. Another such crate supported a washbasin and pitcher.

"It's perfect." Kaitlin cuddled close to her husband.

"It's far from perfect," Mama disagreed as she entered the room. "Still, it's dry, enclosed, and will do for a short while."

Delana turned to see Dustin and Jakob's dark expressions as they stood across the barn. "Mama, you're tired. In the morning you'll see what a comfortable, warm place this is."

"We are blessed," Gilda declared as she stepped into the room. With that, everyone exchanged their good nights, and the men left.

"*Ja.* It's better than sleeping beneath the wagons," Mama conceded as she tested the give of the soft hay beneath their blankets.

"That 'tis," Gilda agreed. "Not that it'd make much of a difference to me tonight. I'll be asleep the moment I lie down."

"I think we all will." Kaitlin displayed baby Rosalind sleeping contentedly in her arms.

"Then we'd best say our prayers before we hit the hay." Delana had to smile as she finally understood the phrase.

The women stood close as Gilda began. "Dear Lord, thank You for giving us good weather and good men to help us on our journey. We're all here and healthy, and we've You to thank for it. Bless this night's sleep that we may arise in the morning ready to accomplish the work You've laid before us."

And help me to win Dustin's heart again, Delana added silently before raising her voice to join in, "Amen."

∽

"We're going to need more hay." Dustin surveyed the full barn.

"When will we scythe more grass if we still need to plow the clearing and build a cabin?" Arthur stopped mucking long enough to mop his brow.

"We'll find a way," Jakob promised, working faster. "At least we'll have good food and not have to waste time trying to cook it ourselves."

"That's true." Arthur brightened and grabbed his pitchfork once again. "I wonder what they'll make for breakfast?"

"It has to be better than cold biscuits," Dustin said thankfully. "And I want to tell you two that the cowboys are leaving this morning, but the freight drivers have pledged two weeks' labor."

"And I'm thinkin' 'bout staying on for a spell." Rawhide's voice came from the doorway.

"Oh?" Dustin raised his eyebrows in mute question.

"You could use an extra pair of capable hands," the older man pointed out.

"What's in it for you?" Jakob seemed suspicious.

"You mean aside from the fact I've eaten better the past three days than I have in the past three years?" Rawhide chuckled. "I aim to stick around to see you unload them wagons."

"Hey"—Arthur straightened up—"what is in all those wagons anyway?"

"I think," Dustin muttered, moving one last pitchforkful of hay into place, "the question is more along the lines of what *isn't* in all those wagons."

"Seems like your bride packed half the world," Arthur mused. "I wonder if she brought anything useful."

"She has," Rawhide smiled mysteriously. "But for now, I think there are some matters you boys need to see to right away."

"Like what?" Dustin furrowed his brow. "We'll start hewing timber after breakfast."

"Good, but you all are missin' a few things aside from a house." Rawhide raised his brows.

"We haven't installed the water pump," Jakob groaned.

"Gentlemen," Dustin said grimly, "we've got bigger problems than a nonexistent water pump."

"Like what?" Jakob's exasperated tone said it all.

Dustin groaned. "I can't believe it didn't occur to me before."

"What?" Jakob fidgeted. "What else is on our plate?"

"Bad phrase, kid." Rawhide grinned.

"Men," Dustin squared his shoulders as he spoke, "what one simple thing can we do without, but ladies require?"

"A stove?" Arthur ventured. "We can order one of those."

"They've brought that," Rawhide volunteered.

"A washtub!" Jakob shouted, pleased with finding the answer.

"Brought that, too." Rawhide leaned against a wall, watching them expectantly.

"What is it, then?" Jakob glowered at Dustin, who rubbed the back of his neck.

"We never built"—Dustin took a pained breath before finishing—"an outhouse."

Chapter 5

Delana heard a collective groan rise from the barn as she walked by. She poked her head through the doorway to see what was going on. "What's wrong?"

"Nothin'," Jakob hastened to answer. "Dustin just said something that he thought was funny, but it wasn't."

"You never were good at that." Delana smiled at her fiancé. "But what was the joke?"

"It wasn't really even a joke," Dustin admitted.

"All right, then." Delana backed up a step. "I came to tell you that breakfast will be ready just as soon as you wash up."

"That's the best news I've heard all day," Arthur told her.

"Well, it's not quite time, yet." Delana lowered her voice before explaining, "I thought you might need some extra time to shave your whiskers this morning."

"What's wrong with my beard?" Rawhide glowered at her.

"It's a very handsome beard," she soothed. "It's really more for Dustin and Jakob. See, last night Ma—" She belatedly broke off.

"Mama mentioned how bedraggled we all look?" Jakob filled in the blanks. "It was too much to hope she hadn't noticed."

"We hardly recognized the two of you when we arrived yesterday. Even after a year apart, I should know your faces in an instant."

"Mama's a stickler for those types of things," Jakob agreed. "We'll take care of it."

"Thank you!" Delana turned to leave the barn. "Something familiar will make Mama feel more comfortable."

Dustin rubbed his jaw thoughtfully. "We'll see about hunting down a razor."

Delana watched, dumbfounded, as her brother grabbed a full saddlebag from the corner of the barn and began to rummage through it. Still more curious to her, Dustin joined him in pawing through the sacks.

"Actually," she called to them, "I did think to pack a few things."

"Like what?" Dustin turned around expectantly.

"Razors, strops, combs, shirts. . ." Delana gestured vaguely. "That sort of thing."

"Can you get to them easily?" Jakob couldn't hide his interest.

"Absolutely. Just give me a moment. . ." Delana turned to leave the barn but stopped for a moment. "It might be a good idea for you to gather up all your laundry." She cast a disparaging glance at the haphazard pile of saddlebags. "If Gilda's not using the cauldron for cooking today, we could do with a washday."

She left them dumping out the contents of bag after bag, pleased she'd found something that would prove useful to the men. When she reached the buckboard where the needed supplies were held, she had Isaac take everything back to the barn.

"Gilda," she called, moving toward the temporary outdoor kitchen, "will you be using the large cauldron today after breakfast?"

"With the cowboys leavin', I suppose I could make do with my largest pot," Gilda decided. "What did you have in mind?"

"Laundry."

"Hard work, but a good idea. We'll get the men into some of the new shirts we brought and wash all their clothes. It'll keep us busy while they start work on the cabin."

"Exactly." Delana looked at her own grimy dress. "And we've some things that could use a good scrubbing ourselves."

"Aye." Gilda nodded. "Since we won't be unpacking or settling in, all we have for the day is cookin'—and a simple fire doesn't lend itself to anything too fancy."

"What're you talking about?" Kaitlin came up, toting Rosalind. "This hasty pudding looks good to me!"

"We were thinkin' on makin' this a washin' day." Gilda wiped her hands on her apron. "After the cabin's up, we'll have a lot more to keep us busy."

"True enough." Kaitlin shifted the baby to her other shoulder. "I'm desperate to do Rosalind's nappies. She's a sweet one but messy for such a wee thing!"

"No messier than a group of bachelors." Delana groaned as she caught sight of the men approaching. Jakob, Arthur, Isaac, and Dustin each carried an armful of soiled linen.

"What's so funny?" Isaac looked at Gilda and Kaitlin, who were trying to suppress their mirth.

"Women talk." Delana grinned. "Why don't you men put up a good long clothesline while we get breakfast on the table?"

"Wait. . ." Gilda looked at the heap of laundry they'd left under a tree. "A small mountain of clothes, and that's only theirs! You men best string a few good long clotheslines if we're to hang all this!"

Mama oversaw the men while Gilda had Kaitlin and Delana laying out the butter, preserves, brown sugar, and fresh milk that would accompany the hasty pudding. Soon enough, thanks had been given and breakfast began. Everyone had a bowl of the hearty cornmeal mixture and doctored it with a choice of sweeteners.

"I always did like hasty pudding better than grits." Delana sat by Dustin.

"Mmmmhmmm." His response was muffled by a mouthful of mush.

"You clean up nicely." She stroked a finger along his freshly shaved jawline and smiled as he swallowed audibly. "I've missed you," she whispered.

"I missed you, too." He mumbled the words to his bowl, as though speaking to the food.

"But if you had your way, you would've gone on missing me." She set aside her breakfast, not hungry anymore.

"Yes." His jaw clenched as he spoke. "I didn't want you here like this."

"Neither did I." Delana closed her eyes. *I wanted to have the man I love greet me with affection and excitement, like Arthur did Kaitlin.*

"We'll just have to make the best of it." He rose abruptly and pushed his own empty bowl into her hands.

There was nothing left to say as she watched him walk away.

∽

The tasty breakfast he'd just eaten churned in Dustin's stomach. For a moment, he'd thought Delana understood that he'd wanted so much more for her.

I didn't want you here this way. He'd come as close as he could to admitting how he'd failed her.

"Neither did I." Her response showed him how wrong he'd been. Instead of telling him she was happy to be here, that she loved the land and was content to wait for the modern trimmings, she revealed her

disappointment in him. She'd expected better and couldn't hide her feelings.

The only thing he could do about it was to start working— immediately. As he built their home, he'd restore her trust in him.

He saw the cowboys off with the bulk of the oxen before assembling the remaining men. The four freight hands, Cade, and Isaac had swelled their ranks, but—"Where's Rawhide?" He barely got the question out before shouts assailed his ears.

"How dare you?" Mrs. Albright was shrieking at poor, hapless Rawhide. "I am a"—her voice rose with each syllable until she shrieked the last word—"LADY!"

"Stop squawkin', woman!" Rawhide roared as he scrambled about, collecting the bits of laundry Dustin assumed Mrs. Albright had thrown at him.

"Squawking!" She spluttered before composing herself with a deep breath. "Listen to me, you unkempt brute—"

"Mama!" Delana had rushed over at the start of all the ruckus. Dustin met her there. "What on earth merits such upset?"

"That man handed me his"—Mrs. Albright raised a trembling finger toward Rawhide, delivering the last word in an appalled whisper—"*unmentionables!*"

"Here, now," Rawhide yanked on his askew hat as he broke in. "I was just givin' her my laundry. Gilda said it was washday."

"There, you see, Mama?" Delana patted her mother's shoulder. "He was just trying to keep everything orderly."

"Hmf." Mrs. Albright still glowered at Rawhide. "Since when does a man thrust his laundry into the arms of a grieving widow?"

"So you're not helping with the wash?" Rawhide cast an astonished glance from the small mountain of laundry beside them back to Mrs. Albright.

"Don't you even think of implying that I would shirk my responsibilities!"

"Make up your mind, woman!" Rawhide, having collected his scattered belongings, spoke loudly without actually bellowing. "Either you decide not to help"—he raised his eyebrows in a mute challenge and held out the clothes—"or you help your fine daughter and your friends with the laundry."

"Of course I'm helping." Mrs. Albright snatched the clothes from his outstretched arms as she all but spat out the words, "But you, sir, need to learn some manners!"

"True enough," the wily guide admitted. "I reckon you'll be helpin' with that, too." Not waiting for an answer, he turned to Dustin and rubbed his hands together. "Now, what have you decided to start with?"

"We'll be building the cabin on the cleared space nearest the barn," Dustin decided aloud. "It'll save us some time and will give the women space to plant a vegetable garden."

"And an orchard," one of the freight drivers added.

"What?" Jakob shot a quizzical glance at the speaker.

"The young miss brought saplings with her." Another man jerked a thumb toward the nearest freight wagon. "Apple trees, I was told."

"All right." Dustin took a moment to assess this new information. It would take the trees years before they yielded fruit, but planting them this spring would make it happen that much sooner. A source of fresh fruit could prove invaluable, and she'd even thought to bring his favorite.

"We need a man to dig an outhouse." Jakob gestured to the proposed site. "It has to be done today."

"I can do that!" Isaac volunteered. When some of the freight drivers chuckled at his enthusiasm, he reddened. "Better to build it now than clean it later."

"If it's all the same to you," Cade offered, "I'd like to see to putting up a water pump. It makes things easier for my Gilda when she's cooking."

"That'll have to wait until we order—" Dustin stopped when he saw the trusted friend shake his head. "Unless you thought to bring one?"

"Miss Albright thoughtfully packed one for each of us," Cade beamed as he spoke. "We have three."

"Sounds good." *One for the Bannings, one for the MacLeans, and one for Jakob's spread.* Dustin's swift tally demonstrated all too clearly that Delana had assumed he'd already have installed one for their home. He gritted his teeth and plunged ahead.

"So the rest of us need to get started chopping trees for logs and lumber." Dustin glanced at Cade. "If we don't have axes for each man, we'll work in pairs."

"We've three axes in addition to your four," Cade informed them, "and two, two-man saws."

"Excellent." Dustin looked at the four freight drivers. "Since you know each other, I'd ask you to divide into two pairs and use the saws. The rest of us will make do with axes until dinnertime. We'll be working to the west of the meadow. Make sure you spread out so no one will be in the path of falling trees. Don't take ones that are too small to be of use, nor so large they would be a waste."

With that, the men filled their canteens, unloaded their tools, and bowed their heads for the day's blessing on their labor. "Lord," Dustin began, "we thank You for granting us friends to work beside and sharp tools to work with. We ask that You grant us the wisdom to use them wisely and safely." Before chorusing, "Amen," Dustin added a silent request. *And I ask, too, that we accomplish as much as possible so the women no longer have to bunk in the barn.*

Chapter 6

"I t's a good thing we brought more than one washboard." Delana straightened up and pushed a damp curl from her forehead. "Seems like there's not a single thing from the men that doesn't need a lot of elbow grease."

"Arthur's will always be that way—smithing is such dirty work." Kaitlin scrubbed a pair of her husband's sooty breeches with vigor. "The fact that none of those men probably thought to do laundry properly the entire time they were out here complicates things."

"You should see some of the stains on this old goat's shirts." Mama worked out her ire on Rawhide's laundry. "The man can't claim to be even halfway civilized!"

"He's no old goat," Gilda laughed. "I reckon he's close as can be to my age—and yours. Hard livin' makes a man rough."

"Why he chooses to scout and guide and hunt and trap in this wilderness, with no home to call his own, is beyond my understanding." Mama rinsed the hapless shirt and surveyed her work with obvious satisfaction.

"Dustin's letters mentioned something about him being a widower." Delana frowned and tried to remember how long it had been since Rawhide's wife passed on. It was no use. She'd have to wait until she could reach her writing desk, where she kept every letter her fiancé had written her.

"Oh!" Mama gasped and stopped what she was doing. "It's a hard thing to lose your spouse." Her murmur carried all the pain of her own recent loss.

Mama didn't say anything else, but Delana noticed that she took more care with Rawhide's next shirt. *Shared sorrow deepens understanding and eases the way*, she realized. *If such a small bit of knowledge softens Mama's thoughts toward Rawhide, how close will Dustin and I become after building a home together? Lord, his words this morning hurt, but I still hope that we can settle into a good marriage.*

"...weddin'." Gilda's voice captured Delana's attention.

"What did you say?"

"Head in the clouds already?" Gilda shook her head. "And here I was sayin' how at least your groom will have clean clothes for the weddin'."

"We don't know when that will be." Delana picked up another item to scrub.

"As soon as possible." Mama punctuated the declaration by snapping a pair of Rawhide's britches until dust swirled in the air.

"Arthur told me that we don't have a proper parson." Kaitlin sipped some of their fresh water. "The wedding will have to wait on the circuit preacher."

"Do we have any idea when he'll be here next?" Delana hoped her voice didn't betray her anxiety. *How long do Dustin and I have to rekindle our love before we're joined together as man and wife? How can I marry a man who is displeased with my very presence at his side? Lord, we need time to become reaccustomed to one another. I know we're a good match, but I worry that another such change in plans will leave Dustin unsettled.*

"There, there." Gilda reached over to pat her hand. "I'm sure the lads will have your house built afore the time comes. You need not fear for your privacy."

Delana ducked her head to hide the hot blush she felt flooding her cheeks. To distract from her embarrassment, she gathered the scrubbed shirts and headed for the boiling cauldron. The heat from the fire and strong scent of lye gave a new reason for her flushed cheeks. She stirred the load with the long paddle they'd brought for that purpose, agitating the clothes so they'd wash thoroughly.

The hot work kept her hands busy while giving her time to clear her thoughts. When she returned to rinse the washed clothing downstream, she found Kaitlin nursing Rosalind.

"Here, let me help." Mama took the other side of the bucket containing the clothes from her arms. Together, they rinsed away all traces of the harsh lye before wringing them as dry as possible.

"Have we taken the clothespins from the wagons?" Delana turned to Gilda.

"They're in the bucket o'er by the wash line."

The cool, earliest hours of the morning passed by quickly, and soon it was time to start dinner.

"We'll be bakin' biscuits in the Dutch ovens." Gilda set about arranging the devices. "Thick slices of ham in the middle of the biscuits will make a hearty dinner."

"Ham sandwiches do sound good," Delana agreed.

"Crisp ham on hot, buttered bread will be simple to make in large quantity. Fresh milk alongside will finish the meal."

"How many batches will we need?" Mama looked at the Dutch ovens, then out toward the forest, where the sounds of chopping kept up.

"We'd best make plenty, so we'll have more for supper." Gilda laid out bowls and ingredients on their outdoor table. "Still more if we want biscuits and gravy later."

They mixed double batches, filling four pans for each round.

Hours later, they had a dozen batches of biscuits cooling on the table, with still more baking.

"If we do one more batch," Delana calculated, "we should have enough to last three days. Maybe we'll have a summer oven so we can bake bread after that."

"Aye." Kaitlin bounced Rosalind, who fussed a bit.

"Kaitlin," Delana called, "why don't you put her in her wicker basket for a nap?"

" 'Tis a good idea. I'll let her sleep while I slice the ham. That way, I'll keep her nearby."

The next hour flew by as they finished baking the bread. When Kaitlin stacked a heaping platter with cut ham, it was time to split the biscuits and make the sandwiches.

"Come and get it!" Delana called, ringing the dinner bell she'd unearthed from one of the buckboards.

Despite the distance to the forest and the noise from hewing logs, the men came running to wash up in the stream before receiving their food.

Delana walked about with a pitcher of milk kept cool in the stream. She poured it into tin cups as she greeted each of the workers after seeing to her fiancé first. When she reached Dustin again, he swallowed the last bite of his second sandwich, gulped down another cup of milk, and thrust the tin at her.

"Thanks," he said over his shoulder as he headed back to the forest and away from her side for the second time that day.

No matter how delicious the food tasted, Dustin forced himself to bolt it down and dash back to work. Daylight was too precious to waste a single moment. By staying on task himself, he set an example to the freight drivers as to what he expected.

The more logs they cut today, the sooner they could raise a cabin. Dustin swung his axe time and time again before he heard the sounds of sawing in the distance.

"Tim–*ber!*" He yelled before striking the last blows. With a mighty crash, yet another tree fell to the ground.

Breathing hard, he took off his hat and swiped at his forehead with a bandana. He gulped from his canteen, refreshing his parched throat as he looked over his handiwork. After the few moments he could afford to spare, he set about removing the largest limbs from the tree.

Dustin listened to every resounding crash with satisfaction as their team worked steadily through the hot hours of the afternoon. Time and again he hitched a fallen trunk to a team of oxen, driving them toward the building site. As the sun began to set, he pushed himself even harder. When Rawhide passed nearby, taking another log to the growing pile, Dustin spoke quickly, "Light's almost gone." He gestured toward the fallen tree he was stripping. "I figure the others will finish the work they're doing and call it a day."

"Most likely." Rawhide rubbed the back of his neck. "I reckon I can get this one to the clearing and fell one more, but I won't have light to strip the limbs."

"Sounds good." Dustin got back to work, determined to finish hacking off the branches and to place this log on the pile. *Maybe if the pile of logs is large enough, it will show Delana and Mrs. Albright how seriously we're taking our work and how quickly we'll finish.*

He met his goal as dusk fell and ambled wearily to the stream. As he splashed cool water on his face and hands, washing away the dirt and weariness of the day, Isaac crouched down beside him.

"I dug the hole." Isaac plucked at some grass alongside the stream. "Built a raised seat, too."

"Good." Dustin nodded approvingly until the second part of his future brother-in-law's comment sank in. "What did you build a seat out of?"

"Some of the lumber we brought." The young man shrugged. "It didn't take hardly anything."

"How much lumber did you bring?" Dustin's mind spun with the possibilities.

"A freight wagon full."

"A team of only six oxen couldn't pull a freight wagon loaded with lumber." Dustin frowned at the incongruence.

"That's what the freight drivers told Delana, so she told them to put a fourth in the bottom of each wagon." Isaac stood up. "We put lighter stuff on top so the weight was even."

Floorboards. A loft. The outhouse. Doors and shelves. It's all more than provided for. For the first time in two days, Dustin felt lighter.

"Isaac, just what did you all bring?"

"Everything," Isaac said simply.

"I know about the"—Dustin paused before ticking off the items—"lumber, livestock, and tools. You obviously brought some food and clothing. . .what else?"

"Some food and clothing?" Isaac snickered. "The girls packed more food, blankets, linens, bolts of fabric, and clothes than you could believe."

"How—" The question died a short death as Dustin recalled the freight wagons. "What else?"

"Shotguns, canteens, rope—like I said, everything." Isaac shrugged. "What more is there?"

"I'm not sure." Dustin squinted in the sparse light. "Is there anything else for the house?"

"Rugs, some furniture, and, oh yeah, windows." Isaac sounded pleased with himself for remembering.

"Windows?" Dustin echoed in amazement.

"Nine-by-nine-inch panes, wrapped more carefully than a baby." He stopped talking when he heard the supper bell. "Food!"

Dustin understood that the rest of the conversation would have to wait. As they made for the campfire, his stomach growled.

"What's for supper?" Jakob sniffed hopefully at the bubbling pot.

"Welsh rabbit," Delana answered. She presented each of them with a tin plate filled with a large halved biscuit.

"Doesn't look or smell like any rabbit I've ever seen." Rawhide seemed puzzled.

"That's because it doesn't have a thing to do with rabbit." Gilda ladled a steaming stream into his dish. "It's melted cheese and butter with spices."

"I've never understood why they call it Welsh rabbit at all." Delana handed a plate to one of the freight drivers. "But I did add some dried powdered beef for flavor and succor."

"Hot!" Isaac yelped as he took an overeager bite.

"Good," Dustin praised around his own mouthful. Several of the men grunted their agreement. *It is good, but tomorrow I'll rise early and set some snares so the girls have fresh meat. I'll do everything I can to make this easier on them.* He savored the last bite on his plate before heading over for seconds. *And if they can make something this great out of bread and cheese, what can they cook up with a few real rabbits?*

Chapter 7

"Rabbits?" Delana looked askance at the brace of hares Dustin held out. "I realized last night that we didn't have any fresh meat, so this morning I set some snares. I checked them when I knew it was about dinnertime." He looked at his catch happily. "They should make a fine supper tonight."

"Yes." Delana accepted the ties and forced a smile. *I thought he liked our cooking—he asked for seconds of the Welsh rabbit. But I suppose it just meant he was still hungry.* With a sharp pang, she suddenly knew the truth. *He believes I'm doing a poor job, so he's made sure tonight's supper will be satisfactory.*

She straightened her shoulders as she carried the six rabbits over to the area where they kept their kitchen supplies. *The corn chowder and biscuits should see him through until supper. I'll pull out all the stops tonight and show him what I can do.*

"Dustin snared our supper," she announced brightly, displaying the catch before setting it down. *A good wife supports her husband and praises him when he provides. That still holds true whether he hurt my feelings or not.*

She helped serve the hungry men before taking her own share. The sweet scent of the corn blended with the mouthwatering aroma of the bacon she herself had fried and chopped. Taking a biscuit from the depleted stock on the table, she looked around for Dustin.

I hardly saw him at all yesterday. Maybe if I sit beside him and tell him what I plan to make for supper, I can coax a smile out him before he rushes back to work.

But she couldn't find him among the others. She turned just in time to see him reach the pile of logs in the clearing. *He's avoiding me. This can't go on if we're to be man and wife.* Strengthening her resolve, she began to make her way toward him.

"Nein, liebling." Mama's soft pressure on Delana's elbow stopped her.

"He's to be my husband." *And I love him.*

"And he will, but for now he's taking some time to work everything out." Her mother's smile softened the words. "Remember that it's the man who pursues his bride, not the woman who chases the groom."

"Aye," Gilda broke in as she walked up. "I ken what you're thinkin', lass, but you followed him all the way from Baltimore. When he's ready, he'll seek your company and the love you hae for him."

"But—" Delana hung her head. *I need him to want me.*

"The relationship will work when he comes to you," Mama said firmly. "The two must meet in the middle. It's not for you to go the distance alone."

Yet that's exactly what it feels like. I came so far to be with him, but he can't leave my side fast enough. What am I to do?

"Be patient, Ana." Mama's advice was hard to hear.

"And meanwhile, keep working alongside him in spirit." Gilda began gathering dishes to clean. "Warm smiles with hot meals win men's hearts."

"I'd best be careful, then." Delana smiled wryly. "I only want Dustin's."

"And you'll get it." Mama began helping Gilda. "But for now, there are other things that need your attention."

Delana hurriedly ate a bit of her now-cold corn chowder and nibbled half her biscuit before pitching in. After they'd washed the dishes, they finished up the laundry. The momentous task had taken all of yesterday and most of this morning as well.

The afternoon passed all too quickly as Delana struggled to hasten the pace of the laundry. She scrubbed harder than she'd ever thought possible, dunked garments into the rinse water after boiling, and wrung them as hard as she could. Even so, it was hot, time-consuming work, and she despaired of finishing in time to prepare the grand supper she had in mind.

"You've been working as though the devil himself were cracking the whip." Gilda smoothed back her hair.

"I'd hoped to make a special supper tonight," Delana confessed.

"Rabbit stew?" Gilda suggested. "We baked enough biscuits at lunch to go with it."

"We had corn chowder for dinner, and Irish stew night before last. I hoped to roast the hares and make mashed potatoes"—Delana paused—"and apple cobbler. It's Dustin's favorite."

"I see." Gilda's glance let Delana know she understood exactly what the purpose of this meal was to be. "What do you say to makin' the meal but savin' the cobbler for tomorrow, when we've enough time to do it justice?"

"Sounds like a wonderful plan." She glanced toward Kaitlin and Mama, who hung the last of the laundry. There would still be enough daylight for it all to dry. "I thought that pile would never end!"

"There's some truth in that." Gilda laughed. "But next time we won't have a year's worth of grime to wash out."

"That's the best thing I've heard all day!"

Kaitlin and Mama joined them by the fire. "What are you two plotting up here?"

"Supper." Gilda looked to Delana to explain.

"We thought to roast the rabbits and serve them with mashed potatoes."

"We'll have to try that canned butter, then." Mama's tone didn't hide her doubts about the new product.

"I'm sure it'll do just fine." Kaitlin wiped her hands on her apron. "I'll just start those potatoes."

"I'll go get the spit." Delana retrieved the apparatus and set it up with Gilda's help.

"We can't use the bottle jack to turn the meat—there are too many we need to roast at once." Gilda set the hand-turned spit into place. "It's good we thought to bring more than one kind. Now we need to skin those rabbits."

"I've only seen you do that, not tried it myself." Delana tried not to grimace at the grisly prospect.

"I'll skin the first one so you get the idea." With that, she hung the first rabbit above the hock, placing a basin under it, and set to work. After the bleeding, careful skinning, and dressing, the rabbit was ready to cook.

Pushing back a wave of nausea, Delana imitated Gilda's actions. She tried to carefully remove the skin from the meat, only to find the task far messier and much more difficult than it had seemed. By the time Delana finished preparing her first rabbit, Gilda had finished two more.

"You'll improve with practice," the cook encouraged her after a side-long glance at the decidedly mangled pelt Delana presented. "By the time we butcher hogs in the fall, you'll be an old hand at things like this."

Delana forced a cheery nod. *I'll prove to Dustin that I'm ready to be here. There are many things I can do to aid my husband-to-be. The first time is always the most difficult whenever I try something new. Dressing game will get easier.*

They alternated between basting the meat and rotating the spit for even roasting. As they worked, Mama boiled the cleaned, peeled potatoes for mashing. Since Rawhide indicted her, Mama had made an impressive effort to do her share.

It's good for her. For both of us, really. It takes our time and keeps us from thinking about lost love. Papa left this world physically, and Dustin has distanced his heart. In Baltimore, we'd be in mourning, but here we have purpose.

Delana watched eagerly as Dustin took his first bite of the roast rabbit. She ignored the approving grunts of the other men in anticipation.

"Mmmmmmm." He closed he eyes as though to prolong the taste.

"I'm so glad you like it!" Delana beamed.

"It's delicious." His smile warmed her until he turned it to Gilda. "Gilda's cooking has always been excellent."

Gilda! Delana fought to keep the smile on her face.

"Delana's as much to thank as I am." Gilda nodded encouragingly. "It was her idea to roast them instead of make a stew."

"Good idea." Dustin barely spared her a glance. "I saw the skins drying—you obviously took great care with them, Gilda. Don't be so modest."

"Ah, but Delana skinned and dressed nearly as many as I did," Gilda explained. "She's a talented cook."

"I see." Dustin swallowed visibly, and Delana watched in dismay as he put his fork down.

⌒

Dustin's appetite dwindled as he imagined Delana skinning the rabbits. *I should have skinned and field-dressed them myself. I was in such a hurry to work on the house that I ruined my gesture. Instead of making this evening meal easier for her, I made her work harder.*

"I should have taken care of it myself." Dustin frowned at the sumptuous meal, now a vivid reminder of how he'd once again failed his bride.

"Why? We're capable of handling it." Delana's chin was raised. "I know I wrote to you about how I cooked with Gilda."

"Of course!" Dustin belatedly realized he'd offended her and tried to clarify. "I just assumed you learned in a real kitchen, with a fancy stove and such."

"Fire is fire," Delana gave a slight huff. "And game and fowl need be dressed before cooking no matter where that fire is."

But it would have been easier for you if I'd thought to do it myself. Even better, if you had a stove and such to work on.

"The house will be ready before you know it." He stuffed more food into his mouth so he wouldn't have to say more.

"We see you work day in and day out." Mrs. Albright bustled up. "You men have many log piles there."

"Yes, you do." Delana seemed to soften with the reminder of how much work he'd put into building their home. "How's it coming?"

"We've hewn and stripped enough trees and taken them to the building site. We're nearly finished peeling the bark so there will be a snug fit between the logs." He finished with pride, "Your summer oven is ready now."

"How wonderful!" Delana's delighted smile made him sit a bit straighter.

"We couldn't work so fast had you not enlisted the labor of the freight drivers," he complimented her. "And the lumber in the freight wagons will be more than enough for a raised floor and loft." He watched as her eyes took on a pleased sparkle. *Good, she deserves to know that her forethought eased the way for both of us.*

"And Isaac is awfully proud about his outhouse." Arthur sounded amused. "We've been sure to let him know how much we appreciate his efforts."

"Don't be forgettin' my Cade installed the new pump." Gilda rested her head on her husband's shoulder. "Laundry will be far simpler next time!"

"I'd say that in three days you ladies will be sleeping in a real house," Dustin ventured.

"Well. . ." Delana's hesitation made the back of Dustin's neck prickle.

Does she not have faith that I'll provide well for her and our family? Have I not shown how far I'll go to give her all I can? When I say it shall be done in three days, I mean it!

"What?" Dustin's voice sounded tight even to him.

"Gilda and I were thinkin' that it would be worth extra time to have everything we'll need." Delana's words sparked his ire.

"Of course you'll have everything you need," he gritted. "Just tell me what it is."

"A root cellar. Gilda and I have read how animals can burrow into a family's root cellar and eat everything they put up!" Delana's brow furrowed with worry. "We wondered if it wouldn't be wisest to dig the root cellar below the house, so there'd be less of a chance that would happen. It would be easier to access come winter, too."

"Ah." Dustin relaxed a bit. "I see you've given this some thought. The reason we wouldn't build a root cellar beneath the house itself is that it makes the cabin more difficult to heat in winter. A large, cold space directly beneath the house would compound a harsh season."

"That makes sense." Delana seemed disappointed. "So what will we do?"

"When we dig out the root cellar, we'll line it with stones to block burrowers." Dustin smiled. "We'll have plenty of stones after clearing our fields." Jakob and Arthur chuckled at that.

"Enough for a smokehouse, too?" Gilda's question gave him pause.

"We dug a cairn near the barn. That saw us through the past winter." Dustin rubbed his jaw. "But we'll need a smokehouse this time around. We'll see to it." He looked at the ladies speculatively. "You've done a lot of thinking about storing provisions. Is there anything else you'll need?"

"We can hang the milk and such in the stream to keep cool, so we don't need a springhouse," Gilda decided. "So there's nothing else that's a necessity."

"A root cellar and smokehouse to join the outdoor oven." Dustin looked to where the freight drivers were already bedding down for a good night's sleep. He'd hoped to raise two cabins while they had the extra hands, and who knew how long Rawhide would stick around?

We'll have the cabin in three days. They've already been here two, and there will be two Lord's days as well. If we raise another cabin in four days— with Isaac and Cade helping it should be quicker the second time around— we'll have three more days' labor. I need at least one day to help catch up on plowing and planting. In two days we could dig the root cellar and build the smokehouse with so many hands to share the work.

"We'll see to it." He announced his decision.

And we'll take a day between the cabins to build Delana's root cellar. It will be used immediately. I want her to know that her needs are a priority. With God's help, I'll always see them well met.

Chapter 8

The next morning, Delana rose bright and early. She'd slept better than she had in weeks.

Good morning, Lord! I want to share my joy with You. I confess that when I first arrived and Dustin seemed so cold, I struggled not to lose heart. He inhaled his food and walked away from me when I yearned for closeness. Last night, when he stopped eating because I'd dressed the rabbits, my heart sank. I thought he didn't believe in me, couldn't imagine me as capable of the tasks I'll need to assume as a farmer's wife. But the more we spoke, the better I felt. Dustin listened to me and asked for my opinions. Finally, we're beginning to work together as I'd thought we would as soon as I arrived. I should have waited patiently on Your time, Lord. I know things will be better now. Thank You for Your many blessings!

After her morning time with God, Delana began her chores. She had all three dairy cows milked before she heard the other women stirring. Delana walked with a light step to build up the cook fire and start the coffee.

"Mornin'." Gilda was the first to join her. "And what were you fixin' to make for breakfast?"

"Have we enough biscuits to just make gravy?" Delana thought of the fresh milk she'd just put in the stream to keep cool. It would taste wonderful after warm gravy on flaky biscuits.

"We've only the canned butter, and we'd best save that." Gilda rummaged among their supplies. "Bread pudding takes no butter and would taste a treat. I've only ever made it with bread, not biscuits, but I don't see why it won't work."

"Perfect!" Delana started cutting the leftover biscuits into small squares while Gilda pumped and heated water.

They coated the pudding dishes with lard, added the squares to be moistened, and turned their attention toward mixing the batter.

"I'll fetch the milk and eggs." Delana headed for the stream, leaving Gilda to measure out the vanilla and sugar. Returning, she saw Kaitlin and Mama had come out just in time to help dole out the mixture and pop the puddings into the Dutch ovens.

While they baked, some of the men mucked out the barn, while others worked to finish peeling the logs. By the time the puddings had cooled and Delana set out fresh cream, everyone was ready to eat.

Dustin said grace. "Dear Lord, we thank You for the food that smells so good." He took an appreciative sniff before continuing, "And for the able hands who prepared it. We ask that You keep watch over us as we do the work You've given us. Amen."

Delana watched happily as the men, led by Dustin, made short work of their breakfasts. Her joy increased when he stopped beside her before going to work.

"Today we'll notch the logs and build the foundation." He patted her on the shoulder, giving her a smile before he moved on.

Dustin's bit of attention caused Delana to hum later as she washed dishes alongside the other women. "We'll be able to bake real bread today," she all but sang the words. "Dustin told me the summer oven is ready."

"We must churn butter." Mama looked to the rope holding the buckets of milk in the cool water.

"We'll need it to make apple cobbler." Delana stacked the dishes and carried them back.

With that, they settled into the same routine they'd used two days ago, working alongside one another to speed the process.

"I still canna believe we've gone through so many biscuits in two days!" Kaitlin pinched some dough into shape after they'd been working awhile.

"We'll make enough loaves of bread to last three." Gilda put the first four loaves in the ovens.

"We filled each oven five times over before." Delana waited for the next batch of dough to rise. "So this time we'll do seven. . .no, eight would be best."

"Aye, best finish it all at once." Kaitlin dusted some flour off her apron. "When the cabin's up, we'll need to spend our time planting a good-sized garden."

"With the way Rawhide eats, we'll have to plant double!" The small smile on Mama's face belied her words.

"I was under the impression he decided to lend a hand while we were in need." Gilda headed toward the fire.

"I hadn't thought of that." Mama stopped mixing for a moment then stirred more forcefully. "That'll save us some work."

"Don't be so sure." Delana hadn't missed the flicker in her mother's eyes. Rough though he was, Rawhide had pulled Mama out of her deep grief and made her concentrate on the present. "I've no doubt he'll be a frequent visitor. Where else can he get so much good food?"

"He is a wily one," Gilda chuckled.

They settled into the rhythm of baking, and by the time Gilda pulled the last golden-brown loaves out of the ovens, they needed to start dinner.

It's a lot of work, Delana admitted to herself as she repinned a few errant wisps of her hair, *but there's satisfaction to be found in a job well done and pleasure in good company. I might even miss the way we cook out here once the house is up.*

∽

Once the house is up, they'll be able to cook over a stove the way ladies should. Dustin finished notching the first end of his umpteenth log. I'll build a large table the same day we dig the root cellar. Delana will lack for nothing.

"Eleven pairs of hands make this go fast." Jakob took a swig of water from his canteen. "We'll be finished by dinnertime."

"I hope so." Dustin looked around and saw that his future brother-in-law was right. They were working at a mighty pace. "We'll be able to lay the foundation and floorboards this afternoon, with time to spare."

"If all goes this well tomorrow," Cade fanned himself with his hat as he joined the conversation, "we'll have the cabin up and sealed with a day to spare."

"Not quite." Dustin wiped his hands on his bandana. "The roof joists will take some time, as will the loft inside. Any time left over should be put to helping the ladies settle in."

"We sure brought enough stuff to haul in." Isaac swiped a hand across his forehead.

"If you keep shootin' the breeze," Rawhide grunted from a short ways behind them, "we'll never get this thing up."

Dustin didn't speak with anyone again until the final log was fully peeled and notched.

"Good job," he congratulated them all. He was just beginning to wonder whether they had enough time to begin the foundation before—

"Dinner!" They all heard the bell and took off at the same time.

The warm, yeasty scent of fresh-baked bread tickled Dustin's nose long before he reached the table. After he said the blessing, he swallowed spoonfuls of the savory chicken broth, using a third piece of the soft, pillowy bread to soak up what his spoon couldn't reach.

He sighed with satisfaction when he'd finished and patted his stomach. When Delana came to collect his bowl, she giggled.

"What's so funny?" He handed her his spoon, too.

"The way you're sighing and holding your stomach, anyone would think you had a tummy ache but for the pleased grin on your face."

"A good midday meal after a hard morning's work is more than worth appreciating." He stood up.

"It's good to hear you say that." The quiet pleasure in her voice caught his attention.

"Why?"

"You've all but inhaled your food at every meal then hurried away again just as fast."

"I wanted to keep on schedule building our home," he explained. "My rush never meant I didn't enjoy what you put on the table."

"I wasn't sure." Her admission felt like a punch in the gut.

For a year I put my heart and soul into clearing the land she stands upon. I was to have thirteen more months to see to the niceties, yet she arrives far in advance. By attempting to rectify our lack of a house, she feels as though I'm not letting her know I appreciate her. Every single thing I do is to provide for our family, but she somehow interprets it as neglect. What more am I to do?

"Now that you are sure I like the cooking, I've got to get back to work." He jammed his hat on his head and stalked back to the building site.

In the heat of the afternoon, they swiftly built the foundation and affixed the wooden floor he knew Delana would want. A dirt floor couldn't be kept clean and invited bugs into the home—an unpleasant truth he and the guys had discovered out in the barn.

When that was done, they all took a moment to admire their handiwork and drink some water. The sun had not even begun to set, so they had a couple good work hours left to begin building the house.

"Let's divide up into pairs," Dustin directed. "It'll take four two-man teams to maneuver the logs into place." He joined up with Rawhide, Jakob with Arthur, and the freight drivers paired up as they had when sawing the trees. Dustin turned to Cade and Isaac. "We'll be needing the pulley system for the higher logs. You're both good at that sort of thing—why don't you rig it up until one of the men needs to be relieved?"

"Sure." They headed off to get some rope.

Privately, Dustin was glad they wouldn't be called upon to lift the heavy logs. *Cade's older than Rawhide but not used to life out here. Isaac is young but overeager and not yet at full growth. Either of them could easily hurt himself with this kind of work, and I'm thankful for the other things they can accomplish more safely.* Not that he'd ever tell either one—it'd be insulting.

By the time they'd laid the first six rows of logs, fitting them by the notches in the corners, Dustin had reason to praise their progress.

"We'll try to finish this stage before noon tomorrow. That way, we'll not be doing the hardest work in the heat of the day." His announcement was met with fervent agreement from all the men.

"We have it ready!" Isaac and Cade showed the clever pulley system they'd set up. "It's counterweighted so the logs won't tip it over," Isaac explained.

"It'll be a great help from here on out," Dustin approved. The thought of hefting logs any higher than they'd already managed made his back twinge. The walls already stood as tall as his head, and they each needed another five logs if there was to be room for a loft.

"Progress will be slower tomorrow," Jakob assessed.

"Perhaps not." Dustin grinned. "Isaac and Cade's hoisting system will speed things up. I'm sure we'll finish the basics tomorrow." And in another day, Delana will have a real home.

Chapter 9

I t's amazing how much you've done," Delana perched next to Dustin on a boulder by the barn.

"Just wait until tomorrow." Pure masculine contentment underlay each word. "We'll have it up entirely."

"We'll be moving in tomorrow night?" Delana jumped up in excitement.

"No." His curt tone made her stiffen. "The structure will be up, complete with roof and loft, but there won't be time to settle in until after the next day."

"Let me fetch some dessert. While we enjoy it, you can tell me exactly what else needs to be done." She couldn't imagine what more would complete their house. She walked over to where Gilda was already dishing up the fragrant cobblers. Delana grabbed a dish. "This should have them smiling," she reveled.

"You and your beau seemed quite cozy whilst you ate your supper." Gilda dished up a chunk and kept repeating the action as she spoke. "Why don't you take these two plates and relax a bit? Kaitlin's comin' to help me pass these out."

"I don't think it will be too difficult to find the recipients." Delana tilted her head to where Isaac and Arthur were already edging near. Laughing, Gilda shooed her back to Dustin's side.

"Here you are." Delana presented the treat to Dustin with a flourish.

"Apple cobbler!" Dustin clutched the plate greedily. "I thought I was imagining the scent!" He breathed in the sweet cinnamon aroma before taking a bite. "Mmmmmm. . ."

"It is pretty good," Delana judged after sampling her own piece.

"Best thing I've tasted in a year," Dustin said fervently. "I didn't know you brought apples."

"Of course I brought some! I know apple cobbler is your favorite."

Dustin paused between bites long enough to mention, "Except for apple pie."

Delana laughed. "Or any type of apple dessert."

"I'll never say no to an apple." Dustin savored the last bite of his dessert before eyeing her plate speculatively.

"Here." Delana switched their plates to give him the last morsel. "But supposedly, thinking that way got Adam into trouble."

"Oh no, you don't." Dustin would have looked dignified if it weren't for the flake of crust on his chin. "The Bible never says it was an apple." He waved his fork at her. "Don't malign the fruit unless you have the facts."

"Fair enough." Delana stacked the plates but stayed beside him. "So what do you plan to do after tomorrow?"

"We need to cut out areas for windows and the door, install both, and then seal the walls." He paused. "Otherwise it will provide precious little protection from wind and rain."

"I see what you mean." She realized the gaps between the logs needed filling. Delana put a hand on his warm forearm. "You've thought of everything."

"That's what Isaac, Cade, and Rawhide say of you." Dustin chuckled. "It was good thinking to bring along the cut lumber and bricks for the summer oven."

"But not the windows?" She arched a brow.

"They'll let in light and make our home more cheerful." He paused. "But it would be foolish to install all the panes you've brought."

"Why?" She withdrew her hand and frowned. Packing the glass had been even more difficult than packing fresh eggs in barrels of cornmeal.

"Large windows put us at risk—they're too easy for a bear to crash through."

"Oh." Delana shuddered at the image he painted. "How small will they be?"

"Four panes per window." Dustin held his arms in the air to demonstrate the size. "We'll put one on either side of the door."

"What of the other walls?" She didn't have a clear picture as to what their home would look like from the inside.

"The far wall"—Dustin gestured left—"will have a loft coming halfway into the cabin. It will sleep Gilda and Kaitlin now, and someday. . ."

"Children," Delana breathed. *He's thought of our babies, too!* The thought elated her.

"You and Mama Albright will sleep in the nook underneath." He paused, cleared his throat, but didn't say what Delana knew they were both thinking.

"What of the kitchen?" She eased the awkwardness.

"We'll put the stove in the far right corner." Dustin framed the area with his hands as he spoke. "I'll build shelves on the wall beside it, and a sturdy table and benches, too."

"You don't want windows near the beds or stove, so the house will remain warm even in the dead of winter." Delana came to the conclusion slowly. "Well, I brought enough glass for three times that." She smiled at his astonishment. "Mama doesn't know, but I brought extra so she and Jakob could enjoy the light as well. The Bannings brought enough for one window in their cabin and in Arthur and Kaitlin's."

"Even so, there will still be gracious plenty left." Dustin looked out at the fire. "When we build homes for the Bannings and Arthur and Kaitlin, we'll put them to use."

"What a wonderful idea!" Delana tucked a lock of hair behind her ear. "Each of their homes can have two windows, just as ours will!"

"That's more than they planned on," Dustin observed.

"I like that idea far more than extra windows in our own home." Delana turned to him. "Can we keep it a secret until the time comes?"

"As a surprise?" He flashed a conspiratorial grin. "They'd enjoy it even more that way."

"And so will we." She reached her hand toward his, sighing softly when he wrapped it in his. His warm smile warded off the chill of the deepening night. "So will we."

⚭

With her sweet little hand nestled softly in his own, far larger, rougher one, Dustin resolved once again to protect her. Her hands aren't as soft as they were in Baltimore. He rubbed his thumb across her palm and smiled when he felt her slight shiver.

It amazed him how much these delicate hands had taken on since she arrived. *She doesn't stand over a stove to cook; instead she labors over heavy pots in an open fire. The meat here doesn't come from a butcher, neatly skinned and dressed, but from our own land.*

In Baltimore, she had Gilda to cook for her. She learned in order to prepare herself for life on a farm. Delana packed everything up and led her family across civilized America to join me in the wilds of the frontier.

"You've done well." He stood up, pulling her to her feet. "It's cold out here, and we've more than earned a night's rest."

"Good night, Dustin." She stood very close, her hand still in his. Her eyes, large and luminous in the moonlight, seemed vulnerable. The chill reddened her cheeks, and he could see the faint mist of her breath between slightly parted lips.

It would be so easy to slide my arm around her back, take one step closer, and kiss her. He struggled with the impulse. *She's just lost her father. It's been a long, hard day, and she blushed when I spoke of the sleeping arrangements.* He forced himself to step away from the woman he loved. *My fiancée deserves my respect and understanding.*

"Good night, Delana." As she walked away, he went to make his bed on the cold, hard ground.

When he awoke the next morning, Dustin stretched before scooting out from under the freight wagon. The first night he'd slept out here, he'd sat up too fast and cracked his head.

He pulled on his boots, scratched his prickly jaw, and realized no one else was awake yet. After giving serious consideration to lying back down for a little more shut-eye, he tugged on his boots, grabbed his razor, and took off for the stream. After cupping some of the fresh water to his lips, he looked around at the quiet beauty of the morning.

Lord, You've helped us accomplish more than I dared hope we could in a short period of time. Thank You for that. I ask for Your guiding hand as we finish the cabin today, and that all of the men remain safe. Amen.

He got off his knees and began walking to the barn before he realized he couldn't start mucking out the stalls—not while the women still slept inside. Dustin turned his attention toward the cabin but knew he couldn't lift the heavy logs on his own.

Some of the ends of the logs, left over from when they cut the beams to size, caught his eye. He strode to them and began comparing the sections too thin for the eighteen-foot-long walls. After much consideration, he selected four thick branches, each roughly three feet tall. He braced the longer one, marked it, and began to saw down the others to make table legs. When he had the four sections even, he stopped and checked to see what everyone else was doing.

The women were stirring—Delana had already toted pails of milk to the stream. The men had risen as well. Cade and Isaac stood testing the ropes of their hoist. Dustin set aside the wood. He planned to make supports for the kitchen table out of the sturdy logs, but for now he needed to go about the morning tasks.

As soon as all four women were out of the barn, he and Jakob mucked it out and replaced the soiled hay with fresh. They found Rawhide overseeing the men; Isaac and Cade strapped the selected log into the ropes while the other men prepared to pull them taut. Dustin and Jakob hurried over to watch the log be lifted quickly and smoothly.

"Ease up!" Rawhide directed as the log swung high into the air—far too high for its intended placement. The men slowly fed back a length of the rope until the log hung over its mates. Dustin and Jakob each held an end of the notched log and fitted it into place before detaching the ropes.

"It works!" Isaac puffed out his chest.

"Let's get another one ready." Dustin helped wrestle the next log into the rope harness. In a remarkably short period of time, they'd laid the seventh layer of the walls before the breakfast bell rang.

Dustin found himself gobbling his oatmeal as though he'd not eaten in months. *"You've all but inhaled your food at every meal and hurried away again just as fast."* Delana's quiet words echoed in his mind, and he set aside his impatience to linger over the morning meal.

Delana kept busy pouring milk and wouldn't meet his gaze. He didn't have so much as a chance to smile at her before the other men were putting down their bowls and looking to Dustin. He drew on his work gloves and led them back to the cabin. There, he became distracted from Delana's strange behavior as the cabin grew before their eyes.

The joists took longer, as did the rafters and support beams for the roof. One false move would be disastrous with the angled slope. Using the ladders from the barn, they finished the paneling for the roof. The bark peeled from the logs created rough shingles that the men nailed into place.

"We've come a long way." Jakob clapped a hand on Dustin's shoulder.

"After dinner we'll measure and cut out segments for the door and windows," Dustin planned aloud. "At this rate, we'll have all of them installed before the night's out."

"Good." Arthur came to stand beside them. "This will be the last night my wife and babe sleep in a tack room."

"Yes." Dustin took a deep breath. "It's good to be ahead of schedule." *For the first time since Delana arrived, things are within my control.*

Chapter 10

K aitlin!" Delana watched in horror as her friend tripped. Kaitlin curled around her baby as she hit the earth. Delana reached her side a moment too late.

"Ro–sa–lind," Kaitlin panted, the air knocked from her lungs.

"It'll be all right." *Lord, please let her be all right.* Delana took the crying baby and unwrapped her blanket. She felt the soft down of Rosalind's head before gently probing chubby arms and legs. "No bumps or broken bones," she told Kaitlin as Rosalind began to suck her thumb.

"Praise the Lord." Kaitlin winced as she sat up. Bracing herself on one hand, she peered at the ground. "I stepped in a gopher hole."

"Don't get up!" Delana shifted the baby over her shoulder.

"Let me take a look at you," Gilda clucked over her daughter. She pushed Kaitlin's skirt up to press on her daughter's ankle. When pain made her hiss out a breath, Gilda resigned herself to the worst. "We'd best take your shoe off afore it isn't possible." She set about undoing the laces of Kaitlin's half boot.

"I've just wrenched it." Kaitlin tried to stand up again.

"Where did you fall?" Mama put out a hand to stop her.

"Right here." Kaitlin sounded confused.

"No, no." Mama tried again. "What part of you fell?"

"I wrenched my ankle and pretty much went sprawling, so. . .all of me, I suppose."

"She means what part hit the ground first," Delana clarified. Mama usually had no trouble with English, but occasionally she'd arrange the words as though it were German.

"I twisted to shield Rosalind, so this shoulder." Kaitlin gestured to her left. "Ouch!"

Mama gently pressed around the area, and soon it was evident that more than Kaitlin's ankle was bruised.

"Here." Delana slid the baby into Gilda's arms and looped Kaitlin's right arm around her shoulders. Soon, Kaitlin was standing on her good ankle, and Delana supported her as they hobbled back to the barn.

Mama fetched the medicine bag and followed. Using some cool water from the stream, she fashioned cold compresses.

"You rest awhile." Gilda smoothed back her daughter's hair. "We'll leave Rosalind with you, and maybe you can both sleep a bit. I'll wrap the ankle in a while."

"Not that I have much choice," Kaitlin commented wryly as she lay down.

"Try to enjoy the chance to take it easy." Delana winked at her. "Praise God it wasn't more serious."

"Amen to that." Gilda clasped her hands together.

"Ana, why don't you stay with Katie?" Mama said.

"It's about time to start dinner," she pointed out.

"Gilda and I can handle making the potato soup." Mama put her hands on her hips. "We've a ready supply of fresh milk and plenty of butter after yesterday afternoon. Surely we can boil some potatoes without you two."

"Don't forget all the bread we baked yesterday morning." Gilda nodded. "You two can chat awhile. If you want to keep yourselves busy, that pile of mending might call to you."

"I'll just fetch our sewing boxes and be right back." Delana traipsed out to the wagon and rummaged around until she found the two wooden boxes. *Soon, all our things will be in our house—not out here in these old wagons.*

"Socks or shirts?" Delana began pulling items from the pile. "It's amazing how hard these men have been on their poor clothes."

"Always have been." Kaitlin laughed. "I'll take the socks. Arthur mentioned he hadn't gotten but one pair back after washday, so I'd wager most of these are his."

"Don't be so sure." Delana poked a finger through a hole in the toe of one sock and waggled it, much to Rosalind's delight. "There are far more here than one man could claim."

"Then we'd best get to it. Blisters put a man in a sore disposition." The two women threaded their needles and began darning.

"There's hardly any sock left to this one!" Delana held up one with more holes than fabric.

Kaitlin sighed. "Put it in the rag pile."

"What's the matter?" Delana stopped stitching and looked at her friend in concern. "Do you hurt?"

"The ankle twinges," she admitted, "but 'tis my pride botherin' me most."

"It could have happened to any one of us. We all cross the meadow several times a day." Delana patted Katie's knee. "No need to fret."

"Yet I'm the only one who managed to take a tumble." Kaitlin gave a rueful smile. "The men fell trees and lift the logs all day, coming back with nothing more damaging then a few splinters."

"Thank God they're all hale and well." Delana resumed stitching. "But I'll venture to say none of the men go about their tasks while carrying a spirited babe."

"True enough." Katie brightened and picked up a sock. "Rosalind can be a handful. Ma says she has my mischief."

"She'll need it." Delana looked at the babe. "It takes courage and grit to live here."

"In the wilderness, or outnumbered by men?" Katie wondered aloud.

"Both!" They shared a laugh before a contented silence fell. Too soon, Delana's thoughts turned to Dustin.

Last night we spoke and laughed like we used to. When we said good night, I thought I saw a gleam in his eyes. . .but he didn't kiss me. I'm his wife-to-be. Why does he shy away?

"What has you frownin' so?" Katie had stopped darning to watch her face.

"Nothing of any great import." Delana tried to shrug off her unease.

"Oh no, you don't. You canna listen to my frettin' over a turned ankle and dismiss whatever causes you worry." Kaitlin gave her an arched look. "Out with it."

"It—it's of a personal nature," Delana murmured.

"So it has to do with Dustin, does it? I thought you two looked cozy last night, yet you didn't go near him this morn."

"He talked to me of how he'd build our home, and what it would look like inside. I hadn't felt so close to him since Baltimore." Delana tied off the last stitch and put down another sock.

"But. . ." Katie coaxed. "Don't be lookin' surprised. 'Tis obvious that's not the end of it."

"When everyone was busy getting ready for bed, he took my hand and held it in his." Delana remembered the reassuring warmth of his strong clasp. "He stood up, pulling me with him. It seemed like such a right moment, with the moonlight shining through the leaves and our hands still linked. . ."

"The right moment for a bit of affection, you mean." Katie smiled. "You're engaged, soon to be man and wife, and reunited after a long absence. 'Tis only natural."

"My thoughts were much the same as he looked into my eyes and stood so close. . .but he stepped back and said good night." Hurt welled up at the memory. "I thought we were past his disappointment at my early arrival—which was awkward enough—but now I wonder if he wants me to wife." The words came in a rush, as though they couldn't be true if she spoke them quickly enough.

"Now then, you might be confused about him pulling away, but don't doubt he wants you." Kaitlin leaned forward intently. "No man works every minute of the day to build a house for a woman he doesna love."

"Yet it wasn't until last night we managed to spend any time together at all. It's as though he's too busy. . ."

"It's his way of showing he intends to provide for ye. Look at the works of his hands as though they were sweet words."

"It would be easier to do so if he held me close instead of pushing me away." To her horror, her eyes grew misty.

Kaitlin spoke slowly, tactfully. "Had you ever shared a kiss before he set off for the frontier?"

"Twice, once when we became engaged and again on the day he left." Delana's cheeks flushed at the memory of his strong arms around her, his warm lips pressed against hers in silent promise.

"Wait." Kaitlin's voice pulled Delana from her reverie. "You've been apart an entire year, with naught but letters to bind your hearts. He knows you're grieving the loss of your father and brother. . .he honors you by taking it slowly."

"Perhaps." Delana turned back to her mending, but her thoughts grew more tumultuous. *But perhaps I'd rather be loved than honored.*

⌒

"Where's Delana?" Dustin squinted but didn't see her anywhere when he answered the dinner bell.

"And Katie?" Arthur wondered.

Gilda wiped her hands on her apron. "They're in the barn after a wee accident this morn—"

Dustin took off toward the barn before she finished and knew from the thundering footsteps behind him that Arthur had the same idea. Dustin paused to open the barn door when they reached it, and Arthur rushed past him.

"Katie!" he bellowed, kneeling and gathering his wife to his chest.

"Delana?" Dustin rushed to her side but didn't see anything amiss as his fiancée dropped her mending in surprise.

"Yes, Dustin?" Her brow crinkled as she looked at Arthur hugging Kaitlin close.

"Gilda said there was an accident." Dustin peered at Delana intently, his gaze taking stock from the crown of her head to the soles of her dainty shoes. "Are you all right?"

"I'm fine, and so is Kaitlin." Delana raised her voice and added, "Though that was before a blacksmith came in to smother her."

"Ease up," Dustin cautioned Arthur as one glance showed Delana's assessment to be true. In his relief, the burly blacksmith had pressed his wife to his chest so tightly Kaitlin could hardly draw breath.

"What happened?" Dustin demanded, willing his heart to beat at a normal pace. When he thought Delana was hurt, he'd been all but unable to breathe himself.

"Kaitlin took a spill today," she calmly explained. "She had the quick wits to curl around Rosalind so the baby wasn't hurt."

"I stepped in a gopher hole and turned my ankle." Kaitlin ducked her head in embarrassment.

"And here it is, wrapped up tight wi' you sitting to gie it a rest." Arthur gave a deep sigh of relief. " 'Tis thankful I am you suffered no worse."

"She'll have a bright bruise on her shoulder as well." Delana's news made the churning in Dustin's gut grow worse. "But she'll be fine, and the baby has no injuries. A few days rest"—she broke off to share a grin with Kaitlin—"while we finish all your mending will see her put to rights."

"That's my girl." Arthur gave Kaitlin's uninjured shoulder one last squeeze before rising to his feet. "I'll bring you and Delana some dinner so you don't have to stir yourselves." He grinned at Delana. "I trust you to see to it she gets in no more trouble."

"I make no promises."

Dustin scowled darkly as he and Arthur left the barn. *I was a fool to think I had things in hand.*

"Quit your glowerin'." Arthur stopped walking after glimpsing Dustin's expression. "All is as well as it can be—spilled milk and all o' that."

"Hardly. Kaitlin could have harmed a lot more than her ankle when she fell. What if she had hit her head on a stone, or the babe took most of the impact?"

"The Lord was watchin' o'er my wife and child this morn," Arthur agreed. "It does Him no service to dwell on the evil He didn't let befall us."

"Open your eyes!" Dustin squared his shoulders. "This was nothing less than a solemn warning. Women and children do not belong out here—it's far too dangerous."

"I wouldn't go so far." Arthur frowned.

"I would. What if it had been a snake hole? A single angry bite and we could have lost either of them." Dustin crossed his arms. "And that is from a mere stumble. At any moment, they could walk beneath an old tree and be crushed by a widow-maker. Remember the day they first arrived and we worried a bear that came to challenge our claim? There are mountain lions, too. We're not so far into warm weather that a snap blizzard couldn't destroy us. Remember the June freeze Rawhide told us about?"

" 'Twas a year afore we e'en arrived. You're dealin' in ifs, Dustin."

"A man has to," he responded grimly. "Any one of a dozen things could harm our women out here—and we don't control a single one of them." The very thought made his blood run cold.

"Then what do you suggest? We keep them bundled up in the barn for now and locked inside the house once it's finished?" Arthur scoffed. "Life on the frontier is an adventure we knew Kaitlin and Delana would share with us sooner or later."

"Later, after we had a house, when we could be close to them more often and be on hand should the need arise." Dustin clenched his hands into fists at his sides. "Like today."

"We'll have the first house tomorrow," Arthur pointed out. "If that's what troubles you, 'twill na be an issue for long."

"And the baby? The wilderness is no place for an infant." Dustin shook his head. "They shouldn't be here."

"They're our women. Of course they should be here."

"No. We're honor bound to protect them, and right now we've too much to accomplish." Dustin took a deep breath before announcing his decision. "They must go back."

Chapter 11

"D inna be daft, man!" Arthur rolled his eyes.

"I'm not." Dustin tugged his hat brim lower on his forehead.

"You most certainly are, makin' a mountain outta a gopher hole," Arthur scoffed. "There are gopher holes anywhere."

"Think, Arthur!" Dustin had to talk some sense into the burly blacksmith. "It's the least of the perils here."

"Aye, so I canna fathom why you're bent sideways o'er it."

"They've scarcely been here for three days, and already Kaitlin is injured. The babe would easily have been harmed as well."

"Anything that pains my wife pains my heart." Arthur's brow furrowed. "I'm that sorry her ankle hurts her, but such a thing isna so dire as to take her from my side."

Dustin jumped on his words. "The next thing could be. So many things could cost a life."

"I dinna mean her passin' on," Arthur growled. "I referred to your cockamamie plan of sendin' them away. I lived without my wife for a year, and I wouldn't bear her absence again after so short a reprieve."

"Isn't it worth missing them if it keeps them safe?" Dustin kept pressing. *Next it could be worse. Next time it could be Delana.*

"Nay, you've the wrong of it. 'Twas na right to leave my wife 'tall, but 'twas necessary. I missed the birth of my child." Arthur crossed massive arms over his barrel of a chest. "I'll not miss Rosalind's early smiles, nor any of the sweet firsts that lie ahead. She'll be crawling, then toddlin' and talkin' to her da in the blink of an eye. I would share those joyous moments with my bonny Kaitlin."

"But they'd be more secure back in Baltimore."

"How so? They've no home, no business, and no men save Cade, who's now a grandda, and Isaac, who's barely more than a whelp." Arthur gestured to the freight wagons and buckboards to illustrate his next

70

point. "They sold everythin' and spent that money on passage here and supplies to carry us through. Where would you have them go, alone and without means?"

"I . . ." Dustin pondered the situation. *Delana, Isaac, and Mrs. Albright have funds—although it would be like them to pay for the Bannings and Arthur's wife to come. Their home is gone—she gave up everything to come here. How can I turn her away after she's journeyed so far to reach my side? The war rages on, with more battlefields and horrors each day. At least here, she is away from all that.*

The thought of Delana coming into contact with jaded soldiers made his blood run cold. *Which is safer—a civilized place in the midst of a savage war, or a wilderness isolated from human ugliness but full of other dangers?*

Faced with the weight of his lack of options, Dustin heaved a sigh and said the only thing he could. "We'd better eat some dinner and get back to building the cabin."

"Aye." A grin broke out across Arthur's face. "We do what we can and rely on God to o'ersee the rest."

"It's harder than it sounds," Dustin grumbled as they walked toward Gilda's pot.

"Keep faith that the Lord cares for us, and remember"—Arthur cracked his fingers loudly before bestowing his final pearl of wisdom—"The most difficult things can be the most rewarding."

༄

Delana and Kaitlin watched the men leave the barn before bursting into laughter.

"Oh," Kaitlin gasped. "They stampeded in here like panicked cattle!"

"And if Arthur held you any tighter, you would've fainted from lack of breath." Delana's giggles subsided. "It's wonderful to see how much he loves you, rushing in here and holding on like he'd never let go."

"It's a good thing he did!" Kaitlin straightened her skirts. "Did you notice Dustin came running, too? I suppose Mam didn't tell them which one of us was the poor unfortunate."

"Maybe." Delana brightened. The intense gaze Dustin leveled as he looked her up and down had made her breath hitch. He'd made absolutely sure she was all right.

"Why don't you go ahead and help them bring in dinner? I don't think the chances of them carrying all that food without spilling someone's soup are very good."

"You're probably right." Delana headed toward the barn door and found it partly open. She reached to push it fully open but stopped as he heard Dustin's voice ring out.

"We're honor bound to protect them, and right now we've too much to accomplish." There was a brief pause and Delana debated whether to tiptoe away or fling open the door.

"They must go back." Her fiancé's pronouncement stopped her in her tracks.

Is he talking about us? Delana bit her lower lip. *He couldn't possibly be thinking of sending us away!* Panic whirled about her as thickly as the dust motes dancing in the sunlight. As she stood frozen in shock, the men kept talking.

Daft is right! She silently applauded Arthur as he told Dustin that he was "makin' a mountain outta a gopher hole." The phrase made her smile, but the meaning broke her heart as the man she loved argued to send her packing.

The difference between Dustin's line of thinking and Arthur's stalwart defense of his wife's presence staggered Delana. *Dustin wants me as far away as possible, but Kaitlin's husband fights for the privilege of having her by his side. Why can't Dustin feel that way about me?*

Afraid to move for fear of their hearing her, she cried silently as Arthur passionately declared he would share the joyous moments of life with Kaitlin. Even in the face of such devotion, Dustin never stopped pressing to have his way.

Lord, I let myself believe Dustin loved me and wanted me to wife. Here he is, turning away from me in the face of something so small as a wrenched ankle. The love between a man and a woman is to be as Your love for us—a thing pure and strong in spite of the obstacles we face. Dustin speaks of peril and wanting to spare us from danger. Doesn't he realize that his words and actions are the greatest threat to my happiness?

While she sought the Lord's wisdom, Arthur talked sense into Dustin. She finally heard her stubborn man capitulate—but only after Arthur pointed out that there was no home to send her back to. With heavy heart and hunched shoulders, Delana returned to the tack room.

"What happened?" In spite of her ankle, Kaitlin managed to scramble upright and throw her arms around Delana.

"D–D–Dustin wants to send us away," she blubbered into Kaitlin's collar.

"Over a wrenched ankle?" Her friend's astonishment made it all the worse.

"He's using it as a pretext." Delana's sobs wouldn't stop. "Dustin doesn't want me here. . ."

"Now, I'm sure that's not so." Kaitlin's crooned words held no comfort.

"I heard him and Arthur." She sniffed and tried to stop crying. The men would be back with dinner soon.

"You listened in?" Kaitlin stiffened with disapproval.

"No. I was about to push open the door when I heard Dustin say he'd send us away. After that, I couldn't move. . ." Delana wiped her eyes with the back of her hand. "I kept thinking about how much effort I put into packing, how long the journey was, and how hard I've worked to prove I'm ready. . .all for nothing."

"And is he still set on this foolish plan?"

"Arthur talked some sense into Dustin's thick skull." Delana helped Kaitlin back down to her mattress.

"Then there's no permanent harm done." Katie cocked her head to the side. "Did you hear him say why he wanted us to leave?"

"Something about how gopher holes are the least of the dangers out here and that we'd be safer back home until they were ready to take care of us." Delana glowered at the memory. "As though we're Rosalind's age."

"There, you see? 'Tisna that he doesna want you—'tis that he wants you to be safe." Kaitlin shrugged. "Mam says men oftimes get such silly notions stuck in their heads. We women have to be patient and clever enough to get past it."

"And if I feel neither patient nor clever?" Delana sat back down.

" 'Twill pass. Think on all you've done up to now, Delana." Kaitlin gave her an encouraging smile. "You're plenty clever and certainly capable. We'll just have to ask God's help with the patience."

"And meanwhile? What do I say when Dustin walks back through the door?"

"You thank him for bringing your dinner and smile as prettily as possible." Kaitlin winked. "And I'd mention some of those things you're always saying about how beautiful the mountains are or how the clear blue sky makes you feel as though heaven is nearer to this place than any other. 'Twill put him in mind of the blessings you enjoy here."

"It doesn't sit well to not tell him what I overheard." Delana squirmed. "It seems..."

"It seems to me as though the place to protest was by the barn door." Kaitlin leaned close. "Glowerin' at him now willna change anything except prove to him you're unhappy. 'Twould be a different matter were he still set on sending us back, but he's already decided not to. When the time comes, you'll speak with him about the way he's made you feel."

"When the time comes," Delana repeated thoughtfully. Kaitlin's advice made good sense.

"I don't know what time you're talking about"—Dustin's voice preceded him into the tack room—"but the food has come!"

"And plenty of it." Arthur stooped a bit to fit through the doorway.

"Oh my." Delana jumped to her feet and relieved Dustin of two of the hot soup bowls he clutched against his chest. "You're lucky you didn't burn yourself. Who carries four bowls of soup?"

"The man who isn't toting two platters of fresh bread and a crock of butter." Arthur carefully passed the food to Kaitlin before plunking down on the floor.

"I brought the preserves!" Mama came bustling in, and the room seemed very small indeed.

"Mama?"

"Well, I couldn't very well leave two young women alone with two young men in our sleeping quarters!" She seemed shocked by the very thought.

"You forgot baby Rosalind." Delana gestured to where the child lay beside Kaitlin.

"And that we're already wed," Arthur put his arm around Kaitlin's waist.

"But we're glad to see you," Delana broke in to avert Mama's next comment.

"And the preserves!" Dustin added some to the slice of bread and butter he then passed to Delana.

"I wondered where everyone went." Rawhide shadowed the doorway and looked at the indoor picnic.

"Join us." Mama's invitation surprised Delana, but she held her tongue.

"There's no place for a man like me here."

"Such nonsense." Mama waved away what she probably thought was false modesty. "You asked me to help you with the manners, and I tell you to sit down."

"There's no place for me to sit," Rawhide clarified, eying the slice of bread Arthur was slathering with butter.

"Sit where you stand." Mama held up a thick slice of the warm bread. "Butter?"

"Yeah." Rawhide somehow tucked himself half inside the doorway, half out.

"Yes, please," Mama corrected. She smeared butter and blackberry preserves on the slice and held it just out of reach until Rawhide caught on.

"Yes, please," he echoed plaintively. He stuffed the treat in his mouth almost as soon as he touched it.

"And now what do you say?" Mama was clearly angling for a thank-you.

"Mmmmmff." Rawhide took another huge bite and grunted. "Good."

The men guffawed while Delana and Kaitlin tried to smother their amusement.

"Thank you," Mama corrected.

"You're welcome?" Rawhide seemed to think she was thanking him for the compliment.

"I—" Mama shrugged. "It's a start."

Delana looked at where Dustin sat tickling baby Rosalind. *Dustin's a bit rough, too.* He caught her watching and smiled. *But it's a start.*

Chapter 12

T he men hastily fell into line, effectively blocking most of the cabin from view. Dustin stood with his back squarely against the door as the women advanced. He didn't even try to hold back his grin. *Thank You, Lord, for the perfect timing. We finished the loft just as Gilda rang the dinner bell. The cabin is ready for them now.*

"Up you are to things." Mrs. Albright's gaze darted from Jakob to Dustin to Rawhide.

"That means she thinks we're up to something," Jakob translated. "She's always right when she says that."

" 'Tis glad I am we won't disappoint her." Arthur stared fixedly at Kaitlin.

"You have to admit we've never ignored the meal bell before," Dustin gloated. "Since we couldn't bring the cabin to the cooks..."

"You brought us to the cabin." Delana reached him first. "After keeping us far away for the past four days, you intentionally ignored the dinner bell." She raised on her tiptoes and craned her neck, trying to see around the line of men. "It'd serve all of you right if your food burned."

"It won't, will it?" Dustin's grin slipped.

"Nay." Gilda chuckled.

"Can we see it or not?" Delana tapped her foot impatiently.

"It's finished." Dustin straightened his shoulders and took a step forward, closing the distance between them. "And you'll be the first to see it." With a sudden move that made her gasp, he swept her into his arms. He tucked in his chin until his forehead touched hers and rumbled as quietly as he could, "Since you'll be sleeping in our home before we live as man and wife, I plan on carrying you across the threshold."

Delana wound her arms around his neck and looked up at him, eyes big. When he straightened up, she nodded enthusiastically, catching her lower lip in anticipation. Arthur nudged the door open for them. Dustin angled his shoulders as he stepped inside, careful not to bump his precious armful against the doorframe.

Still clasping her to his chest, he kicked the door shut, strode to the center of the cabin, and turned in a slow circle to show her the entire space. Her excitement fed into his, and he wanted to show her every inch of the place. Careful to keep her encircled in his arms, he set her on her feet.

"It's breathtaking," she marveled, still drinking in the sight of their new home.

"So are you." He waited until her eyes widened then bent to steal a kiss.

A soft sigh whispered across her lips before he felt their warm softness. He threaded his fingers through her silky blond hair, heedless of the small pins he dislodged. He savored the moment before reluctantly pulling away. His hand still twined in her lustrous curls, he smiled and gave her the product of all his hard work.

"Your home."

∞

"*Our* home," Delana corrected softly. An odd gleam flickered in Dustin's eyes before he nodded, but she attributed it to the extraordinary moment. She lightly pulled away from him to explore the house.

The Franklin stove that had stood on display at Papa's mercantile now graced the far right corner of the cabin. She ran her fingers over the iron scrollwork on the oven door.

"We'll be able to make apple pie now." She turned and smiled at him. "And apple crumb cake, too." Going back to her exploration, she admired the shelves Dustin had already installed near the stove.

"These will hold all the dry and canned goods. It was so clever of you to put them in right away." A few more steps and she stood in front of the first sparkling window. She cupped her hands as though to capture the cheery sunbeams streaming through. "I brought fabric for curtains. We'll make them up tomorrow—oh."

"It's the Lord's day," Dustin affirmed.

"Monday, then." She passed the door and second window, standing in the recessed alcove beneath the loft. "It's cozy here," she praised, proud of herself for not blushing at the site where their marriage bed would soon be placed. She grasped one of the supports of the ladder leading to the loft.

"Here." Dustin took her free hand in his and curled it around the other support. He stepped back, his hands securing the ladder but his head turned as she climbed up.

"It's so roomy!" She could almost stand at her full height at the tallest point of the roofline.

"Growing room." Dustin poked his head over the top rung, but didn't join her farther in.

So our children won't be overcrowded as they grow. Delana beamed at him as she pronounced, "It's perfect."

She climbed down the ladder, and cheers erupted as they opened the door. Soon everyone crowded in.

"I want to show you one more thing." Dustin grasped her hand and led her outside toward the small woodpile stacked against one wall. As they turned the corner, she spotted it.

"A table!" He'd chosen well-matched plank logs and sanded them to form a smooth surface atop four sturdy table legs.

"So you'll have a real kitchen." He braced both palms on the table and pressed downward to show how solidly it stood.

"Is there anything you didn't think of?" She rubbed her hand over his shoulder.

"If there is, I wouldn't know it." He grinned. "But I'm sure we'll find out about it sooner or later."

"Let's go have our last meal in the meadow," Delana invited. "We'll have supper in the house."

"Trying to bribe me into hauling everything inside?" He quirked a brow.

"Absolutely." With that, they headed toward the old cook fire one last time.

Delana's impulse was to eat as quickly as possible so they could start moving in. To her dismay, everyone else seemed ready to settle in for a well-deserved rest. She busied herself by cleaning the dishes but chafed to settle into the house.

"You seem anxious," Mama noted. "Why, when all is in readiness?"

"It's not. The men have built the house, but I've yet to do my part." Delana twisted her hands in her apron. "There's so much to do, I can't stand just sitting here!"

"Of course you cannot stand and sit at the same time." Mama looked puzzled. "But if you want to work, we'll start and the others will join us when they're ready."

"Let's start taking some of the kitchen supplies." Delana grabbed two pans, and Mama took a sack of potatoes. Together, they tramped toward the cabin. After Delana deposited the pans on the stove and Mama set down the potatoes, they walked outside to find Dustin and Jakob bringing the table around the corner.

"Ah, the table *ist gut.*" Mama nodded her approval.

"We'll need you to direct us as to where things are." Dustin backed through the door, still holding one side of the table.

"I'll consult with Cade and Isaac—they helped load the wagons." Delana took Mama's elbow, and they walked back. *Neither of us will step in a gopher hole today. Now that the cabin's ready, I'll hear no more foolish talk of sending us away.*

"We'll be unpacking, then?" Cade had already begun hitching a team of oxen to the second freight wagon. Dustin and Jakob had taken the first wagon to the cabin that morning in order to install the impossibly heavy iron stove.

"Yes." Delana peeked in the freight wagon and found it held more lumber, the saplings, and the second stove. "Wait, Cade." She walked over to the third wagon, which contained some of the furniture and linen goods. "We'll need this one today."

Soon both of the necessary wagons stood by the cabin, and Isaac unhitched the oxen and led them to pasture.

"We should unload the larger and heavier items first," Dustin reasoned. "Everything else should come later."

"The heavier items are packed farther down," Delana pointed out. "We loaded things so the wagons would be evenly weighted. The smaller items, dry goods and kitchenware, can be placed on our table or the shelves."

"Right." Dustin nodded. "Then we'll take in the larger pieces."

Gilda and Cade oversaw the unloading of the wagons while Delana and Mama went inside to shelve provisions and direct placement.

"Please lean that rug over by the stove for now." Delana pointed to the corner. The stove hadn't been lit—moving in this afternoon would make it hot enough work without the added warmth.

"We'll need nails to hang the pans and pots," Mama observed as she neatly stacked them on the table.

"Let's put the trunks atop one another, here." Delana gestured to the side of the table as clothes and linens were brought in. "Place the bolts of fabric atop them. Mama, they'll be reaching the china soon."

"I'll go see to it that they take special care." Mama bustled out of the room, and Delana could hear her through the open door and windows as she directed "Gently! These belonged to my grandmother."

Delana smiled and remembered how they'd wound heirloom quilts around the fragile pieces of glass and crystal before surrounding the china with tightly packed straw.

As men carried in pieces of the bed frame, Delana pointed them to the alcove. Dustin stomped his boots outside before coming in to attach the carved headboard and baseboard. It took three men to maneuver the surprisingly heavy feather-stuffed mattress through the door and into place. When they'd finished, the bed nestled cozily near the far corner opposite the stove.

"Please put that at the base of the bed," Delana suggested to Dustin as he and Jakob carried in her hope chest.

"The washstand goes beside the bed," Mama directed as she followed Isaac inside.

"Under the window," Delana decided as the men carried in a petite cherrywood desk. They placed her writing lap desk atop it and set a box of books beside it.

A pretty chair with turned out feet sat against the wall. She'd fetch her sewing case from the barn later.

Isaac scrambled up the ladder and positioned the bedding passed into the loft. Arthur carried in Rosalind's cradle and frowned at the ladder.

"Kaitlin will sleep in the big bed." Delana had him set the cradle nearby. Her friend couldn't climb the loft ladder with a freshly wrenched ankle, and it would be simpler to have the mother and babe on the ground floor anyway.

"Over here." Mama had Delana's wooden dish cupboard sandwiched against the wall by the kitchen window.

"That's the last of it," Delana proclaimed.

"There's a lot more." Arthur gestured toward the wagons.

"We brought furnishings and such for the other cabins as well." Gilda patted him on the shoulder. "They'll be accounted for later."

"Let's unload what's left of the lumber and consolidate the rest into one wagon." Dustin looked over both of them. "We'll dismantle the other freight wagon for more lumber. There's plenty of daylight left to begin work on the second cabin." He turned to smile at Delana. "We'll leave you women to settle in."

"Exactly." Delana nodded at him. "And we'll still have supper ready, come the evening."

"I can hardly wait." Dustin put a hand to his stomach.

"You'll have to." She laughed and shooed him to work.

Arthur carried Kaitlin to the chair and carefully set her down. He nudged the cradle close by her before taking his leave.

"All right, ladies." Delana shut the door, and Gilda rolled up her sleeves. "We've got work to do."

Chapter 13

"A hhh," Dustin exhaled a deep breath. "A good day's progress, to be followed by a fine night's meal."

"Something sure smells good—and we're still yards away from the house!" Arthur's stomach grumbled. "Not that I'd be too choosy, mind."

"What do you think they've been doing in there all afternoon?" Isaac rubbed the back of his neck as he trudged along. "We carted everything in hours ago."

"We'll find out." Dustin stopped at the shut door and gave a light knock. "Good evening, ladies!"

"One moment!" He heard the flurry of skirts come close, and he stepped back from the door to let Mrs. Albright, Gilda, and even a limping Kaitlin come out.

"Come in, Dustin!" Delana's cheerful voice brightened the already well-lit cabin.

"What's for sup—" The word died on his lips as Dustin stepped fully into the cabin and saw the full extent of what the women had done.

A blazing fire danced in the stove, warding off the chill of nearing nightfall. Woven rugs in differing shades of blue warmed the hardwood floor beside the bed and under a chair. Blue gingham curtains fell in soft folds over both windows, their color echoed in the thick quilt and feather pillows covering the bed. Fresh white towels hung over the back of the washstand, which held a cobalt blue washbasin and matching pitcher. Above the chair hung a sampler he knew must be the work of Delana's hands. In soft blue on clean white she'd stitched his favorite verse: *"Faith is the substance of things hoped for, the evidence of things not seen."* Everywhere he looked, he saw the thoughtful touches Delana had used to make the house he built into a welcoming home.

"What do you think?" Delana's soft voice came from beside him.

"It's true what they said." He smiled and wrapped an arm around her shoulders. "You thought of everything."

"I tried."

"The thought you've put into our home pleases me, Delana." His gaze met hers. "You made each thing my favorite color"—he cupped her cheek in his palm and clarified—"the same sweet blue as your eyes."

"Ohhh." Delana's soft sigh and flushed cheeks made him want to steal a kiss, but he realized everyone was crowded around the still-open doorway.

"If you're finished, there are some of us who've worked up an appetite." Rawhide's hopeful voice broke the tender moment as Delana laughed.

"Come in and sit down." As everyone trouped in to sit on the benches he'd made for the table, Dustin remembered how hungry he was.

"Potpie?" His mouth watered at the sight of an individual pie on every plate.

"Yes." Delana sat on the bench at the right side of one chair, waiting for him to take his place at the head of the table. Out of consideration for her sore ankle, Kaitlin sat on a stool pulled up on the far side.

Dustin took his place with a sort of humility he'd never expected. *I'm the head of this household.* The thought—and accompanying responsibility—both pleased and staggered him.

"Let's join hands and pray." Dustin held Delana's delicate hand in his right and began to thank the Lord for the blessings around him, finishing with, "And, Lord, know that there is always a place for You in the home You've seen fit to give us. Amen."

"Tomorrow's Sunday—that means we rest." Isaac shoveled a forkful of pie into his mouth.

"You deserve it." Mrs. Albright patted her youngest son's shoulder. "You've worked hard and accomplished a lot."

Now that she's lost her eldest, she dotes on her youngest son. The coddling can't continue long, or it will spoil the boy. Dustin pushed his own fork into the golden, flaky crust on his plate.

"Delicious," Arthur put Dustin's thoughts into words.

"Good company and fine food fill this house." Dustin looked around him. "There's not a thing I can think of to improve this meal."

"Perhaps a few of the raspberries I saw this afternoon." Isaac took a gulp from his cup of water.

"Oh?" Dustin had noticed Isaac's disappearance. He reasoned that the young man needed some time to grieve for the deaths in his family—away from the women.

"A little ways past the south bank of the stream," Isaac clarified. "Plump and bright red in the sunshine."

"What a wonderful find!" Delana refilled her brother's cup.

"What say we have a picnic dinner tomorrow and go berry picking in the afternoon?" Gilda smiled at the thought. "The one who picks the most wins his or her favorite meal the next day—provided it's within reason."

"I'm in," Arthur volunteered.

"Sounds like a fun way to spend the day." Delana closed her eyes. "I do love fresh raspberries and cream."

"We can do much with berries," Mrs. Albright added. "Come winter, we'd be glad of some preserves and such."

"I look forward to that." Dustin thought of all the tasty treats the raspberries would make possible. *Picking raspberries will be much easier than felling trees, though with no sweeter reward.* He looked at Delana, bright and animated as she chatted with the guests at their table.

"What would you do on the Lord's day before we came?" His fiancée turned to ask him.

"Take care of the necessary things as usual, play horseshoes—"

"I'd love a rousing game of horseshoes." Isaac's smile faded as Dustin gave him a stern look over his interruption.

"I see no reason why that can't be part of our picnic!" Delana rubbed her hands together. "Maybe I'll try it, too. I like a challenge. I've heard that the most difficult things can be the most rewarding."

Dustin snapped his gaze from Arthur to Delana. *That's the same thing Arthur said to me when we spoke of sending the women home. But what could the significance be?* Her sweet smile revealed nothing. *Ridiculous to think there's a connection. It was good advice then, and it's doubtless been given many times.* "Then we'll do it together," he told her.

"I'd be grateful for your guidance and expertise." Her eyes sparkled. "Though I might damage your standing."

Dustin couldn't resist boasting, "My reputation can handle it."

"Listen to him speak as though he's the champion," Jakob scoffed. "A happy throw every now and again doesn't tell of perfected technique."

"It tells of skill," Dustin rebutted.

"If it's skill that tells the measure of the man," Arthur enjoined, "then you'll soon see me standing tall."

"You're unparalleled at throws so far they seem impossible, but you overshoot those nearer to the mark. We take one step back after each throw to make the competition more interesting," Dustin explained their unusual rule to Delana.

" 'Tis always better to surpass the mark than fall short of it." Arthur winked at his wife. "So I'll take that as a compliment."

"And I'll take it as my first lesson." Delana smiled up at Dustin. "I look forward to many more."

∞

After a morning devotion led by Cade, Delana began preparing a picnic dinner.

Kaitlin sat with her at the table as they set to plucking four of the scarce supply of chickens they'd brought for eating. They carefully stowed the feathers in a sack between them to stuff a mattress later.

"Fried chicken and biscuits will put smiles on their faces." Gilda crumbled leftover bread into fine crumbs.

They dressed, cleaned, and cut the chickens into pieces before sizzles sounded in the kitchen.

"The men are with the horseshoes." Mama packed the biscuits, butter, and preserves into a basket. "Practicing."

"It should be a day to remember." Gilda set another piece of crispy chicken on the platter.

"I hope so." Delana set out a few of the blankets the men wore out over the past year. "The weather's lovely, and everyone is in good spirits since the house is up."

"A good night's sleep didn't hurt." Kaitlin chuckled. "The house is an improvement for us, but the men like the tack room in the barn far better than the bare earth."

Delana stacked buckets for raspberry picking. "It was so clever of Dustin, Jakob, and Arthur to clear the area where the three claims meet."

"Mmmmhmmm." Kaitlin picked up Rosalind, who'd begun to fuss. "The cleared land provides perfect places for our cabins, so we're close as can be."

"And our claim will follow." Gilda covered the full platter with a cloth and set about filling the next one.

"Ist gut to have friends for neighbors." Mama smiled at Gilda and Kaitlin.

" 'Twill be just as good to have neighbors for friends." Kaitlin smiled back.

When the chicken was crispy, the dishes washed, and everything packed for the picnic, they called the men and set off. Delana spread the old blankets under the shade of a grove of trees. From where they sat, everyone could see tantalizing red glimpses of the wild raspberries hanging in their brambly bushes.

"I love fried chicken." Isaac brandished a drumstick and set to with enthusiasm.

"I know." Mama passed him a biscuit.

"You know, I'd thought to ask for fried chicken after I win the raspberry-picking contest." Jakob took a bite and chewed thoughtfully. "Time to start thinking of something else."

"Let me know what you come up with," Rawhide directed. "I'll take it into consideration when *I* win that contest."

"No matter who picks the most berries," Dustin remarked, "every one of us will win a delicious dinner so long as these women are working the stove."

Was it just three days ago I told him I wasn't sure he liked my cooking? How strange it is that it seems like we've been here so much longer than six days, yet the time doesn't drag on. We pack so much into every day out here that we experience more to remember. Pleased with the thought, Delana stood up. "Who's ready to stop planning their win and start picking those berries?"

"I'll stay here." Kaitlin cuddled a now drowsy Rosalind. "It's best not to wake her, and my ankle isna ready for me to go gallivantin' around yet. But pick plenty for me!"

"We will," Dustin promised her as he grabbed Delana's hand and gently pulled her toward the grouping of raspberry bushes. Isaac saw them edging over and loped past them.

"The race is on." Delana looked at their entwined hands, loathe to let go. Still. . . "I'm going to need my hand if I'm to have any chance!"

"Just remember," Dustin stopped speaking as he raised her hand to his lips for a kiss that sent shivers down her spine. "This hand belongs to me and will soon wear my ring."

She squeezed his hand. "I never forgot."

Chapter 14

Dustin cast a furtive glance toward Delana's fourth bucket then at his own, which was only his third. Happily, he'd perfected a way of evening the odds and had been employing it for the past half hour or so. He couldn't have gotten away with it if they could simply fill the buckets with berries. Their harvest was too fragile—the bottom berries would be crushed if they put more than a few layers in the bucket.

He waited until she straightened up to take a few steps away from the already-plucked area she'd harvested. He pounced. Snitching another plump red berry from the top of her bucket, he bit into the sweet fruit.

"What are you up to?" Alerted by his sudden movements, Delana turned and narrowed her eyes.

"Picking raspberries," he said blithely. Dustin stooped to add more of them to his own stash—and to hide his grin. This wouldn't be nearly as much fun without her, so he wasn't about to have Delana finish before him. *I wonder how many times I can do that before she notices that her pail should be much heavier.* He bent to gather another handful and had more difficulty than when he'd started. *More importantly, how many raspberries can I eat before I pop?*

"Do you remember the woman who obeyed the prophet Elijah? She poured out her small supply of oil, only to find that, though it should be gone, her jar didn't empty no matter how many times she poured out the oil?" Delana gestured toward her pail. "I think this bucket is the opposite of that. No matter how many berries I put inside, it never becomes full."

"Oh?" Dustin struggled not to laugh at her disgruntled expression.

"Although," she mused, glancing at her pail as she added another handful of raspberries, "it doesn't even feel heavier."

"Maybe we could work something out." Dustin moved his pail closer to hers. "If we move some of your berries into my bucket, it would have as many berries as it could hold without crushing them. Then I could carry yours while we fill it." *Even better, you'll stand closer to me.*

"It looks about equal," she decided after scrutinizing his crop. She began transferring some of hers to round out his pail. "There." Delana handed him her lightened load.

He edged closer as they redoubled their efforts. With their teamwork—and the bonus of him not sneaking a raspberry every time her back was turned—their pail filled rapidly.

"We work well together." Dustin lifted their harvest for her inspection, stepping so close he imagined he caught a whiff of lilacs from her.

Delana tried to stand but toppled from the unexpected burden of Dustin's boots on her pooled skirts. "You're stepping on my dress!" As she lost her balance, his arm shot out and snaked around her waist.

"Gotcha." With her pressed to his side, Dustin wanted to taste her sweet lips in the afternoon sunshine. He contented himself with offering her a raspberry. "I'd say we deserve a little reward."

"Mmmm." She savored the luscious fruit before selecting another. "Here's one for you—if you've any room left in your stomach."

"I did put away a lot of that fried chicken," Dustin agreed before accepting the proffered fruit.

"Ah." Delana raised a brow. "I thought you might be full from all the raspberries you've sneaked."

Dustin stopped chewing and gaped at her. "You knew?"

"Of course I knew." She giggled. "I thought it was funny, how you'd look so pleased with yourself every time I turned back around."

"What gave me away?" He set down the pail.

"The juice on your chin." She reached up to brush it away with her fingertips.

Dustin held his breath at the softness of her touch. *Lord, this day of rest has made me anxious to finish my work. The second cabin must be built before the circuit preacher comes.* Delana put her hand on his forearm, bracing herself as she lifted their harvest.

And, Lord? Please let the preacher come soon!

⌒◯⌒

Delana rubbed her thumb across fingertips still tingling from their brush with Dustin's slightly stubbled chin. He'd made her want to giggle as he boyishly filched her raspberries, but the slightest touch reminded her he was all man.

"Arthur beat us," she noted as they left the wild patch.

"No matter." Dustin waved the loss away. "He's pounding the stake for horseshoes. Now the fun really begins."

"Hmmph." Delana pretended to be affronted. "So berry-picking with me wasn't fun?"

"Oh, I enjoyed it," he assured her, "but it's the prospect of teaching you to play that I'm looking forward to."

"So am I, but Mama disapproves. She says horseshoes are for men."

"The game is played by men," Dustin agreed. "Still, what reason is there not to let a woman try? It's not a dangerous sport."

"So you would agree that I shouldn't participate were it more dangerous?" Delana gave him a sideways glance. "Women are capable of more than some men think." She waited for his answer, wondering if he sensed its import.

"I never underestimate a woman." He caught her free hand in his and squeezed gently. "You've proven you're a force to be reckoned with."

Thank You, Lord! He sees that I am strong enough to live and work alongside him. The house was a turning point in his way of thinking, I believe. Now we're a team, the way it should always be.

"We're both stronger when we work together." She squeezed back.

"I'll catch the rabbits, and you'll cook them." Dustin smiled, but said no more.

"You muck the stables, and I'll milk the cows." She needed him to see that their partnership extended beyond one simple instance.

"I'll clear the land and turn the soil, while you plant the garden," he caught on.

"I'll make preserves out of the raspberries we picked together." She set the pail down by Arthur's.

"Yes." Dustin set his beside hers. "I've built the oven where you'll bake the bread."

"You wear through your socks, and I'll darn them." Delana frowned. "Actually, that doesn't seem quite even."

"I'll find a way to make it up to you." The gleam in his eye made Delana move a step closer.

"Come on, you two!" Isaac set down his half-filled bucket and hurried toward Arthur, who checked to see that the stake held fast.

The closeness of the moment shattered, Delana strove to recapture the lightheartedness they shared by the berries. "How about *I* find the way, and you still make it up to me." She tapped her index finger to her chin. "It bears thinking on—we've already darned and stitched a pile of your clothes."

"That sounds ominous." Dustin led her over to the cleared area where they'd play the game. "Maybe I'll have to keep you distracted."

"Good idea," she teased. "You can start by teaching me to toss this." Delana casually leaned over to pluck a horseshoe from the grass and moved around to find the best pitching spot.

"Steady, now." Dustin's warm hands curled around her shoulders, giving her support. "Move it from hand to hand to get a feel for its balance before you toss it."

Delana transferred the piece of curved iron from one hand to the other, testing its heft. "Is there a way you hold it when you toss?"

"Yes, though different people do so differently." His hands moved down her arms to cover her own. He adjusted the way she held the horseshoe. "You draw your arm back, like so." He carried her through the motion as he instructed. "Sight your target and judge the distance, and then tense to give it all your strength and control."

Delana tried to control the wild galloping of her heart, all too aware of his broad chest at her back, his strong arm guiding hers. *I've never felt so safe and so jumpy at the same time.*

When he took his hand away, the horseshoe slipped through her suddenly nerveless fingers to the ground. The warm spring day felt unexpectedly cool as he stepped away to retrieve it.

"If it were possible to use both hands, I'd have you try that since you're so dainty." Dustin frowned in thought. "But you don't get the same range or accuracy."

"Let me try with one hand a couple of times." Delana tried to ignore the way Arthur, Rawhide, and Isaac quickly distanced themselves from both her and the stake. She pulled the horseshoe up and flung it toward the stake. Or rather, she meant to throw it toward the stake. It landed embarrassingly wide—and short of the post.

"This time," Dustin suggested as he handed her the next one, "try it with your eyes open so you can aim."

She tried again but gained nothing save a rapidly tiring wrist. Disgruntled, she turned to Dustin. "You said something about using both hands?"

"Yes, but you'll recall I mentioned it worsened aim." Dustin gave her an infuriating grin. "To tell the truth, you can't afford to lose any ground."

"She can't get any worse." Rawhide blew a sour note on a blade of grass. "Let her give it one more try, then the real contenders can start the competition."

"Give it everything, liebling," Mama rooted for her, throwing Rawhide a dirty glance. "Show them what the Albright women can do!"

"Right!" Delana, surprised that her mother suddenly seemed to support her horseshoe endeavor, put on a good outward show, but inwardly groaned. *Mama really shouldn't have made the Albright pride rest on this. Lord, I know it's too much to ask that I ring this horseshoe around the post. All the same, I'd ask You to guide my hand so that it comes closer this time!*

Abandoning all pretense at good form, Delana clutched the horseshoe in both hands, braced her feet shoulder width apart, and gave a mighty underhand heave as she shut her eyes.

Clang! The blessed sound made her open her eyes. The men gaped at her accomplishment.

"Yes!" She tugged on Dustin's sleeve. "Did you *see?*"

"You hit the post and glanced off," Dustin marveled. "Who would've thought. . ."

Mama put her hands on her hips. "I did. *Mein* liebling can do anything she minds."

"You mean anything she puts her mind to, Mama." Jakob grinned.

"Ja." Mama agreed before shaking a finger at her son. "But you mind your Mama."

"Are you going to compete?" Isaac asked Delana.

"I've had enough for today." She started walking toward Kaitlin. "After all, it's better to surpass the mark than fall short of it."

Chapter 15

With a feminine audience on hand, the men competed more fiercely than usual. Dustin, determined not to be outdone by Delana's throw, took his sweet time eyeing the distance.

"It ain't movin', and the women are the other way," Rawhide burst out after a while. "No reason to stare that long."

Dustin ignored both the scout and the giggles coming from the shade. With a deep breath and a quick prayer, he launched the horseshoe toward the post.

The resounding *clang* and subsequent whirring as the horseshoe spiraled down the post brought a triumphant smile to his lips. "Now there's a reason to stare."

Walking with a bit of a self-satisfied swagger, Dustin helped himself to a dipperful of cool water as Isaac tried his hand. The youngster's toss listed too far left, and he threw his hat to the ground in disgust.

The late afternoon whirled by in a flurry of *whooshes* followed by satisfying *clangs* or disheartening *thumps* as the horseshoe hit the ground. Dustin earned most of the former, earning him a smile from Delana and scowls from the other men.

"I knew you would win." Delana's confidence made him walk a bit taller.

"I'm sorry to see the sun setting." Isaac's lament made Dustin realize how quickly the day had gone by.

"We have a lot to do tomorrow," Dustin agreed. "The second cabin will go up faster than the first."

"It only took you five days to build ours." Delana's brow furrowed. "That's already so speedy!"

"True." Arthur gazed into the distance where his cabin would be the next structure on the horizon. " 'Tis simply we'll be more skilled at the work. Then, too, we built your summer oven in that time."

"I'll cherish the day." Kaitlin's soft smile bespoke a woman looking forward to settling in her own home.

The women gathered the blankets while the men toted the pails of berries. The night's chill would keep them fresh without the benefit of a springhouse.

After a substantial supper of biscuits and gravy, the men trooped off to catch some sleep. Dustin reached the tack room just before the others. Still basking in the contentment of the day, he set his lantern on an up-turned crate.

"I can't believe she hit that post." He kicked his boots off and prepared to go to bed. The straw-filled sack mattress seemed soft as fluffy white clouds after sleeping on the unforgiving ground. Dustin hoped the extra blankets he'd left with the freight drivers would help make them more comfortable.

"Lucky shot," Isaac grunted. "My sister was smart to stop when she did."

"On second thought," Dustin mused, "I believe it. My Delana has spirit and determination." He settled back and added, "Not to mention a good teacher."

"Her toss had nothin' to do wi' your teachin'." Cade shook his head. "I never heard you tell her to grab the thing and heft it blindly, with both eyes closed."

"I was right by her. She aimed before she closed her eyes." Dustin set the record straight.

"Call it what you will." Rawhide pulled up his blanket. "The thing I can't believe is that Arthur picked the most raspberries."

Recalling the prize, they all turned to stare at the victor, who nonchalantly pretended he didn't notice the attention.

"What did you choose?" Jakob looked suspiciously at Arthur, who was whistling. "It wasn't that sheep's stomach thing you were telling us about before, was it?"

"He wouldn't do that to us," Dustin broke in. He looked at Arthur's cat-with-the-canary grin and thought twice. "Would you?"

"I dearly love my haggis," Arthur drew out his response, "and well my Kaitlin knows it." He plumped his pillow and turned over without saying another word.

"Oh no, you don't." Dustin aimed his own pillow at the blacksmith's head. "We don't have any sheep, so that couldn't be it even if you were that ornery."

"You should try haggis before you judge it." Cade sounded aggrieved. " 'Tis a traditional Scottish dish."

"I'll make you a deal," Jakob yawned. "You don't make me try it, and I won't judge it."

"Pah." Cade rolled his eyes. " 'Tis good for the likes of you. Puts hair on your chest."

"Douse the lantern and quit yammerin'," Rawhide grumbled.

"I'll second that," Arthur yawned.

"You'll get no sleep until I've got peace of mind." Isaac nudged Arthur with his elbow. "I'm not trying any mystery dish."

"This much I'll be tellin' ye, and no more." Arthur sat up and glowered at the lot of them, his burr thick with fatigue. "I chose Kaitlin's favorite dish as she couldna pick the berries wi' her sore ankle."

"Ah." Cade nodded and drew his blanket over his shoulders.

"What's Kaitlin's favorite?" Isaac and Jakob turned to Cade and voiced the question as one.

"I'll be honorin' Arthur's choice." Cade stretched and smiled. "Though I will say that my daughter's as true a Scot as her husband."

Dustin, Jakob, and Isaac groaned loudly.

"Hush up," Rawhide groused at them. "Whatever it is, it will fill your bellies when they're empty. Even the women will have quit running their mouths and turned in by now. Let's get some shut-eye." With that, he snuffed the light, plunging the tack room into darkness.

"Men, Cade's going to tell us his daughter's favorite dish before he falls asleep," Dustin stated cheerfully. "Because he has only one other option."

"Oh?" Cade challenged.

"Yep." Dustin didn't bother to smother his chuckle. "Otherwise I'll tell Gilda what you said when you first got here."

"What did I say?"

"That you didn't think you could have made it one more day, traveling with a passel of women," Dustin reminded him gleefully. Silence stretched so long he began to wonder if the older man had fallen asleep.

"Cinnamon buns." Cade's quiet answer brought a smile to Dustin's lips.

Cinnamon buns, Dustin thought as his eyes drifted shut and rest claimed him. *I can almost smell the. . .*

Scents of cinnamon and sweet icing in the kitchen made Delana think of Christmas. One of her earliest memories was of Mama making the dough for *apfel borogie*, a special pastry she served every Christmas morning. She rolled it flat, filled it with apples seasoned by cinnamon and nutmeg, and then braided the outer strips of dough into a soft woven strudel.

The recipe matched the dough for cinnamon buns. Mama made extra and slathered it with butter, sugar, and cinnamon before rolling it into a spiral. Then she sliced the rolls and baked them. Though she never told Mama, Delana always chose her cinnamon bun before they even made it to the oven. Without fail, Hans would swipe that exact bun from the platter before Delana even finished icing them.

Her girlish memory took on the pain of loss. *I'll never bake him another cinnamon roll. Hans will never spend Christmas with us again.* The fragrance filling the kitchen filled her with grief as well. Cinnamon memories of Hans had her blinking back unexpected tears.

"Hans?" Mama, who shared those same memories, had obviously recognized the sheen of tears in Delana's eyes and came to wrap her in a warm hug.

"I miss him," Delana sniffled. "Papa died before I could understand that Hans will never come home." *And I wouldn't let myself think of it even then. The effort to keep everyone together and get us here took all I had.*

"It is right that we miss them." Mama's clasp tightened. "God's children are missed long after He takes them home. Hans and your Papa are with the Lord—it is hard for us, the ones who stay behind."

"Yes." Delana pulled away and patted her hair back into place. "But we have Jakob and Isaac to think of now."

"And Dustin." Mama smiled softly. "Isaac says nothing of joining the war since we came here."

"I know." Delana drew a relieved breath. Isaac's determination to avenge his brother's death had caused her and Mama many sleepless nights during the journey. She thanked the Lord once again for Cade, whose keen eye and tactful maintenance had ensured that Isaac didn't attempt the foolish venture.

"There is empty place in the heart," Mama commiserated. "But we fill the days and God loves us through them."

"You're wise, Mama." Delana gave a slight smile. *Thank You, Lord, for bringing her so far from the grief-stricken woman who wouldn't speak for three days after news of Hans's death, and mourned so deeply she couldn't sleep after her husband's passing. Now, Mama comforts me. You've given her strength when I could no longer carry us both in grief.*

She planted a kiss atop Mama's dark blond hair, now threaded liberally with white. "We'd best get this batch in the oven. Kaitlin and Gilda will be back with the cream from last night's milking any moment."

"Ja." Mama took the pan while Delana wiped the tabletop with a kitchen rag.

"Here's the cream." Kaitlin entered the cabin with a slight limp, her mother right behind her.

"I've sliced some of the raspberries and added a bit of sugar for sweetness." Delana placed the large bowl beside Kaitlin, who added cream. Its cool whiteness took on a pink tinge from the juicy berries as she stirred gently.

With that done, Delana got up to pour milk into the tin cups, leaving Kaitlin to sit and drizzle icing on the finished buns.

"It's so sweet that Arthur chose your favorite," Delana told her friend.

"Yes, though he might not deserve so much credit." Kaitlin took on an almost impish air. "They're one of his favorite treats, too."

"He's very clever." Gilda bustled over with the last tray, sliding it far enough away that Kaitlin wouldn't burn herself on the still-hot edge.

"Talking about me when I'm not around?" Rawhide stuck his head through the door. "And you say I need manners."

"Ja, you do." Mama motioned for him to come inside. "Thinking you're the only clever man here—such arrogance!"

"Ha!" Rawhide waggled his brows. "So you do think I'm a clever man."

"I think you're more a difficult one."

"No, just hungry." Rawhide swiped a finger full of icing from the bowl she carried past and received a whack on the back of his hand for his efforts. He jerked away in surprise before grumbling, "No one can tell me that was ladylike."

Delana smiled as she watched them bicker. Rawhide's needling brought out Mama's strong will. Whether the ornery man knew it or not, he'd helped Mama in the midst of deepest grief.

The men shouldered into the cabin, eagerly sniffing the fragrant air around them. After the blessing, it seemed Delana had hardly taken three bites before all the cinnamon rolls vanished from the table. *Even after we made two extra batches!* The berries and cream didn't last much longer, but the men were all smiles as they set back to work.

"I've never seen food disappear so quickly!" Gilda tsk-tsked as she piled dirty dishes.

"Here." Delana pressed a cinnamon bun, the one without icing, into Kaitlin's hand. "I saved one for Arthur—a reward for his good choice."

"Thankee." Kaitlin wrapped it in a cloth napkin and tucked it in one of her apron pockets. "I'm sure he'll enjoy that."

They finished tidying up after the morning meal and turned their attention to the surfeit of berries they'd gathered. Even after this morning's meal and yesterday's playful tasting, they had a generous supply.

Gilda began boiling a load of them down, adding a little sugar. When the mixture was thick, they'd spread it on sheets of paper to dry before rolling the preserves for storage.

"Let me get these out of the way." Delana took the raspberries she'd combined with white vinegar and placed the bowl at the other end of the table. Adding some of this sweet syrup mixture to a pitcher of water made a refreshing drink, almost like lemonade, only with raspberries. "I know it takes a couple of days to make it, but I love raspberry quencher."

"I hope it turns out well." Kaitlin tucked Rosalind into the cradle and limped back to the table.

All four women sat around the table, paring knives in hand, and began to halve a large pile of raspberries. Slowly, the sliced berries, layered generously with sugar, filled one of their largest stewpots. By the time they'd finished, Delana's entire hands were stained red. She covered the berries and sugar, pushing the pot over by the raspberry quencher mixture.

"We'll boil that and make jam after dinner." Gilda checked on the mixture boiling at the stove. "This is ready to spread and dry."

"The fruit leathers will be useful during winter." Mama placed paper on the table. "When boiled, they're as wonderful in pies and such as when they were fresh. Some say even better."

"Hard to imagine." Delana popped a raspberry into her mouth and savored its tart sweetness.

"Someday you'll see for yourself." Mama gave her a knowing smile. "Most things get better with age."

Chapter 16

F our days later, Dustin waited outside the second cabin as Arthur gave Kaitlin the tour of their own home. This cabin was built as the mirror image of Dustin and Delana's, with a stone fireplace taking up most of one wall instead of a stove.

Something moved on the horizon, capturing his attention. Dustin squinted but could only make out a lone rider approaching at a steady pace. Normally, he'd assume it was Rawhide, but his friend stood beside him. Dustin strode toward the approaching figure. "Parson Booker."

"Looks as though you've been keeping busy," the visitor observed as he dismounted.

"We have indeed, and so have you. It's been too long since you came." Dustin grinned. "What news from the civilized world?"

"Last week this was officially declared the Montana Territory." Preacher Booker clapped him on the back. "The first step toward statehood."

"Good news, indeed! And I've some news of my own to celebrate." Dustin grasped the reins of the parson's mare and walked her over to where everyone began streaming out of the cabin. "My bride-to-be arrived a little less than two weeks ago."

"Looks like she brought a few friends." Parson Booker raised his eyebrows at the gathering crowd.

"I'll take his horse to the barn." Rawhide led her away, freeing Dustin to draw Delana forward.

"Preacher Booker, this is Miss Delana Albright, my fiancée." Dustin went on to introduce Mrs. Albright, Isaac, and the Bannings. Arthur presented Kaitlin and Rosalind.

"Nice to meet all of you." Though the preacher smiled, he seemed uneasy. "Had I known the population increased so, I would have come sooner."

"You're welcome here anytime," Dustin assured him. "We're glad to see you."

"I ran late in Virginia City." The preacher's brown eyes filled with regret. "A mining rights disagreement—I stayed to see three men buried."

"I'm sorry to hear that." Dustin removed his hat, and the other men followed suit for a moment of silence.

"How long you will stay?" Mrs. Albright glanced at Delana and Dustin. "We have much to plan."

"I'm to officiate at my sister's wedding in Charleston." The preacher gave a heavy sigh. "I catch a steamboat at Fort Benton in three days."

"But Fort Benton is three days away!" Delana burst out. "You will miss your sister's wedding unless you leave tomorrow morning."

"Yes." Preacher Booker looked at Dustin. "Is there any reason why the wedding should not take place today? I've no notion when I might return. It could be months, and I'd like to see you two settled in God's sight before I leave."

"Excuse us." Dustin ushered a speechless Delana into the new cabin for a moment of privacy. He braced her with a hand on either shoulder.

"Today?" When she found her voice, it emerged in a squeak.

"Today." He answered the question firmly. "We've waited for one another an entire year, Delana." He tilted her chin, meeting her troubled gaze. "Your father asked you to bring the family here to provide you the support a husband can supply. The security *I* will give you."

"I know." Delana nibbled on her lower lip. "I had thought to have more time. . ."

"We've a life full of sweet moments before us." He cupped her cheek with his palm. "I'm anxious to begin it."

"Oh Dustin." Her bright blue eyes swam with tears. "I'll not keep you waiting. I'd always thought my father would walk me down the aisle. I'd meet you in a pure white dress and veil, carrying a bouquet of flowers. Now there'll be no aisle, nor a wedding gown, but those don't matter. I just wish Papa was here."

"He wished this for us." Dustin gathered her in the circle of his arms as she shed a few tears. When she leaned back and offered a watery smile, he knew she was ready. "Let your unbound hair be your veil, and put on the blue dress that matches your eyes. You'll wear all the promise of the beautiful Montana sky as we wed."

"I'd like that. It speaks of limitless possibility." Delana nodded.

"What could be more fitting?" She smoothed her skirts while he opened the door.

"Come, come." Mrs. Albright ushered Delana toward their cabin, followed closely by Kaitlin and Gilda.

As soon as the door closed behind them, Dustin sprang into action.

"Arthur!" Dustin angled one of his friend's benches out the door. "Would you grab the other?" He took his bench to an old bur oak just yards away from the cabin he'd built for Delana. He set it down beneath the high arcs of the branches, and Arthur followed suit.

"What else can we do?" The blacksmith looked around for inspiration.

"Actually," Dustin was seized with sudden inspiration. "There is one thing. . ."

∽

Delana winced as Mama ruthlessly twisted her hair into a too-tight upswept knot. "Dustin asked me to wear it down." She gratefully pulled away from the brush her mother wielded like a bristly weapon.

"I will put your lilac oil in the wash water." Mama hurried away.

"Here." Kaitlin pressed something into her hand. "I wore it on my wedding day. 'Twould honor me if you'd use it on yours."

Delana stopped running the brush through her golden curls to look at the hairclip resting in her palm. An intricately looped design, delicately worked in silver, caught the faint light coming through the windows. "It's beautiful." She reached out to hug her friend.

A knock sounded on the door. Delana's heart thudded. *It's been only a few moments. I'm not ready yet!*

"The groom asked me to deliver summat." Arthur's words galvanized Delana to stand before her mirror. She caught a few locks in the lovely clip, leaving the rest of her hair to tumble down her back. Her head felt oddly light.

"Dustin wanted you to have these." Arthur held out a small posy of wild blue hyacinth. "He said his bride would have a bouquet to match her dress."

"Oh." Tears welled into her eyes as she held her bridal bouquet. *Dustin did his best to make this the wedding of my dreams.* The delicate flowers she held were worth more than any amount of gold. *This is a symbol of his love.*

When Arthur left, Delana slid out of her work dress and cleansed

100

herself with the cool, lilac-scented water. She slipped into her blue dress and looked around at the home Dustin had built for her.

When next I step into the house, I'll be a wife. Delana took a deep breath. *Lord, the time is short, so I'll be brief. Thank You for Dustin, and please help me be a good wife to him. Be with us this day and throughout our marriage. Amen.*

"I'm ready." She smoothed her skirts one last time, took the bouquet from her mother's hands, and stepped outside.

Jakob waited outside the door, tucking her hand into the crook of his arm. "You look beautiful, Ana. Papa would be proud."

Delana blinked back tears at the sweet words. *Papa would be proud that we are all here, together. If only he could be here to share this moment with us.*

Everyone waited under the bur oak tree, seated on the benches but looking over their shoulders to watch her progress. Isaac sat beside Mama, Gilda with Cade, and Kaitlin with Arthur, who held Rosalind in the crook of one arm. Rawhide and the freight drivers filled the other bench.

Delana knew they were all smiling, sharing her joy, but she had eyes only for Dustin. He stood straight and tall in his Sunday best, his gaze fixed upon her. Jakob led her toward Preacher Booker.

"Who gives this woman to be wed?" The preacher asked, his voice rich and solemn.

"I do." Jakob grasped her hand, guiding her to Dustin's arm.

Delana clutched her hyacinth bouquet as her brother gave her away. She smiled into Dustin's brown eyes. " 'I am my beloved's, and my beloved is mine.' I'm ready now."

⌘

Dustin stood before Preacher Booker, watching Jakob walk Delana toward him. He drank in the sight of his bride, radiant in the soft blue with her golden curls cascading around her sweet face. She held a small bouquet of the blue wildflowers he'd picked as she came to him.

After this day, Delana will be my wife forever. The thought overwhelmed him as Jakob placed her small hand on his arm, symbolically giving her over to Dustin's care.

" 'I am my beloved's, and my beloved is mine,'" he repeated to her before turning to the parson. *Mine.* Preacher Booker's words seemed to be coming from a far distance, but somehow Dustin echoed the proper vows at the right time.

Just as the sun set, the preacher pronounced them man and wife. Dustin gathered Delana in his arms and silently promised to begin this marriage the right way. All coherent thought fled as he kissed his bride. When he reluctantly let her go, he blurted out the first thing that came to his mind. In the flickering light from the lanterns, he asked his beloved, "Are you hungry?"

"What?" Delana sounded surprised. "Not right now—oh!" Her answer faded to a gasp when Dustin scooped her into his arms.

"Good." Amid the cheers of their family and friends, he carried his prize to their home. For the second time, he carried her over the threshold.

Delana kept her arms circled around his neck, her head nestled against his chest. "Dustin?"

"Yes?" He gently kicked the door shut and stood there in the dark, waiting to hear what she had to tell him.

"I love you."

"I love you, too." He carefully set her on her feet and held her close. "The wedding might not have been what you imagined, Delana"—he paused to kiss her softly before adding—"but I promise you this: Our marriage will be all you hoped for."

Chapter 17

Two months as a married woman had agreed with Delana. That, along with the secret knowledge she held in her heart, made the prospect of Independence Day bearable.

Tomorrow will mark one year since Hans fell at the Battle of Vicksburg, and still this terrible war rages on. The anniversary of his death will be a difficult remembrance, but my joyous news will help keep Mama from sinking into her grief. Delana pressed her hands against her still-trim tummy and smiled.

Lord, thank You for the many blessings You've given me. On the same night Dustin and I began our life together, You created the precious life growing inside me. Please keep my baby safe and let the child give Mama a reason to rejoice tomorrow on a day of mingled sorrow and freedom.

With a full heart, she moved down the garden row she was weeding. *I've said nothing even to Dustin of my hopes, unsure until so recently that I carried our child. Tonight, when it's just the two of us in our home, he'll hear the news first.* Delana finished pulling the weeds from her section and went to fetch a dipper of water. The cool liquid refreshed her.

"Nein! Oh, nein." Mama's anguished cry had Delana running toward the henhouse.

"Mama?" She skidded to a stop next to her tear-streaked mother.

"Isaac!" Mama clutched a piece of paper filled with the spiky writing of her youngest son. She thrust it toward Delana, her face ashen as she repeated, "Isaac!"

Delana put one arm around her stunned parent and scanned the hastily written note:

Mama,
I have gone to fight the Confederates who took Hans's life. You
and Jakob have a cabin now, and Delana and Dustin are married
and settled. You don't need me to help take care of you, so I go to

help win this war for Hans.

Love,
Isaac

∞

Delana awoke to find herself lying on the bed she shared with Dustin, who stood beside her.

"Are you all right?" He squatted to be at eye level and smoothed a hand over her hair.

"I think so." Delana's hands went to her stomach. "Oh Isaac." Tears stung her eyes.

"Jakob and I will search for him." Dustin straightened up. "With God's guidance, I'll bring him home."

"Thank you." Mama stood at the foot of the bed, wringing her hands. Her gaze fixed upon Delana, she didn't speak again until Jakob and Dustin headed to the barn.

"How far along?" Mama's soft question had Delana hugging her middle.

"Two months." She closed her eyes, dismayed to find her joyous news become another concern.

"We already loosened your stays." Gilda shook her head. " 'Tis not good for the babe, you being cinched in."

"Promise me," Delana croaked out the words, "you won't tell Dustin."

" 'Tis not our news to tell." Kaitlin's brow wrinkled. "Though it willna be kept hidden for long."

"I know." Delana looked at the three women around her. "It only needs to wait until Jakob and Dustin bring Isaac home."

If Dustin knew I carried his babe, he wouldn't leave me. Right now, the most important thing is that he finds my brother and brings him home. Oh Isaac. . .

∞

When he found the boy, he would hog-tie him and sling him over the saddle so the kid couldn't run off again.

Dustin's jaw clenched. How could Isaac do this to Delana and their mother? Four fruitless days of searching hadn't brought a satisfactory answer. With Jakob headed in the opposite direction, Dustin had only his own rage for company.

Lord, Delana has already lost one brother and her father in such a short period of time. I understand Isaac's grief over Hans's death, but a headstrong fifteen-year-old will be in his grave before he witnesses justice. All Isaac can accomplish by this foolish plan is breaking the hearts of his mother and sister. Please let me find him, Lord. I can't bear the thought of going home empty-handed.

Sleep claimed him for the night after he finished his prayer. Despite exhaustion from four days of hard riding, memories of Delana's tear-filled eyes plagued him through the night.

He awoke feeling no more rested than when he'd made camp. Dustin tried to pin down a course of action.

He'd traveled due east in case Isaac had been fool enough to try crossing the wilderness on horseback. The boy would run out of provisions—if he were lucky and had no other troubles.

I rode hard. Either Isaac pressed on, keeping a frantic pace to stay ahead of me, or he didn't come this way. I pray Jakob overtook his brother on the way to Fort Benton. He reached for the saddlebags he'd left lying next to him. If he chased after Isaac even one more day, Dustin wouldn't have the supplies to return home himself. *I'll return home with nothing to show for the days lost.* Stomach growling, Dustin rummaged in one of his saddlebags.

His fingers closed around a bag of beans, but the back of his hand brushed against something warm and. . .furry? Dustin snatched his hand out of the bag. *Raccoon. Lucky thing this one's still sleeping. It would've clawed my hand and arm to bits were it awake.* Dustin stood up, stepped back, and shook the contents of the bag onto the ground. Out tumbled coffee, a fork and pie tin, a few bags of beans, some jerky, and a small gray. . .kitten?

Awakened so rudely, the tiny cat opened its mouth and made a piteous mewling sound. The furry bundle crouched low to the ground, light green eyes looking at Dustin hopefully.

"What are you doing out here, cat?" Dustin hadn't come across anyone for four days. He gently scooped the little scamp into his hands and looked it over. "You're no wildcat."

In response, the kitten rubbed its head against his fingers. When Dustin stroked the softness of its fur, the little cat's chest rumbled with a raspy purr.

In that instant, Dustin knew he wouldn't be coming home as empty-handed as he'd thought. There'd be a furry addition to his and

Delana's home. He found the thought oddly soothing.

I may not be able to bring her brother home safe and sound, but she'll have something cuddly to comfort her a tiny bit.

"Let's make some breakfast." He held his new friend in one hand and reached for some jerky with the other. "Now, what am I going to name you?"

∽

Delana stepped away from the heat of the boiling wash kettle, bearing a shirt on the long paddle. She tipped it into the bucket of rinse water and closed her eyes.

It's so hot. She placed the tip of the paddle on the ground and used it to brace herself as she mopped her forehead. Although she'd not kept down the few bites of toast she'd managed to swallow that day, her stomach churned.

She stretched, turning slightly to ease the kink in her lower back before rejoining the others at the stream. She saw something from the corner of her eye and snapped to attention.

Shading her eyes, she squinted and could just make out the figures of men approaching on horseback. One, two. . .three! Dustin and Jakob had found Isaac!

"Praise the Lord!" She snatched up her skirts and hurried to meet them. After six days, they'd come home. "Isaac!" Her little brother rode between Jakob on the left, and. . .Rawhide. The third man wasn't Dustin.

"Where is my husband?" she blurted out as soon as the trio reached her. She was vaguely aware of Mama, Gilda, and Kaitlin bustling up beside her.

"We split up to cover more ground." Jakob swung out of the saddle. "He headed due east."

Still disappointed that Dustin hadn't returned with them, the knowledge that no tragedy had befallen him allowed her to breathe again.

"Mein Isaac!" Mama all but smothered him in a tight embrace before stepping back and giving him a rough shake, berating him in a flood of German before she hugged him once more. "Never do this again."

"I won't." Isaac squirmed from her grasp and stared at the toes of his boots.

"We're glad to have you home." Delana spoke past a lump in her throat.

When the horses were lodged in the barn, Mama herded everyone into the cabin she shared with Jakob and Isaac.

She had the men sitting at her table in no time, each with a cup of milk and some ginger drop cookies.

"Where did you find him?" Mama sat between Isaac and Jakob. "Fort Benton?"

"Rawhide found him." Jakob shook his head. "They told me he'd bought passage on a steamboat that had left forty minutes before I even arrived."

"You?" Mama stared at Rawhide. "You brought my son back to me?"

"Yep." Rawhide swallowed another cookie. "I was in town on business and was surprised to see Isaac there. When I found out what he was up to..." He shrugged.

"Rawhide talked some sense into me," Isaac finished. "Said it was a powerfully foolish plan. Told me my death wouldn't win the war—just make the rest of my family grieve." He looked down at his cup. "I didn't want to put you through that sadness again. I just felt like I had to do something so Hans's death mattered."

"So I told him that instead of shedding blood, the best thing he could do to honor his brother's memory was prove him right." Rawhide wiped his mouth with the back of his hand, but Mama just pushed another plate of cookies toward him.

"Rawhide says men like us, who make our own way and live by the work of their hands, show that America doesn't need slaves to be successful. Hans fought so that all people can have the right to build their own lives.

"I aim to help us prove up and make the farm a success and show that Hans was right—real men don't live off the work of others."

Tears of joy slipped silently down Delana's cheeks as she listened to her little brother. He wasn't so little anymore. Rawhide had done what she and Mama couldn't—talk to Isaac man-to-man. He'd been making his own way far longer than Jakob, and with the weight of experience behind his words, Rawhide had gotten through to Isaac. She couldn't begin to express her gratitude.

"Rawhide." Mama broke ties with propriety and reached across the table to take both his hands in hers. "Thank you for taking my baby boy and giving him back to me a man. I can never repay so much joy."

"Well, Bernadine..." Rawhide stared at their intertwined hands before gazing into her eyes. A slow smile spread across his face as he suggested, "You could always marry me."

Chapter 18

With a heavy heart and an empty stomach, Dustin returned home. Not even the sight of the three cozy cabins could distill the weight of his failure. He stabled his horse before heading toward his house with the benefit of light from a barn lantern.

He knocked at his own door, dreading what would come next. Delana peeked around the blue gingham curtains, and her eyes widened with happiness as she caught sight of him. Dustin hated the thought that her joy at seeing him would dwindle away when she heard he had not found her brother.

"Dustin!" She swung open the door and flung herself into his arms. Warmth seeped from the cabin into the unexpectedly cold night as he held her close.

He followed her inside but didn't sit down as she busied herself at the stove.

"You must be famished. Let me warm a few biscuits and whip up some gravy."

"Wait." The pressure of his hand on her arm turned her to face him. "Isaac is not with Jakob and your mother." He broke the bad news as gently as he could.

"Did he decide to sleep in the barn with Rawhide?" Delana's lack of concern made his chest ache.

Her faith in me is so strong that she can't imagine I didn't find her brother. She thinks she's fixing supper for her triumphant husband, but I have to tell her the truth.

"Delana, I didn't meet Rawhide or find Isaac at all." He waited for her shoulders to slump.

"Then they weren't in the barn?" She shrugged as though the motion would carry away the bad news.

"No. I don't know where either of them is, Delana." He searched her

108

face for any hint of understanding.

"Neither do I, but I'm sure they'll turn up." She patted his shoulder and smiled brightly. "I'm so glad we don't have to worry anymore!"

Dustin pinched the bridge of his nose, drew a deep breath, and tried again. "I didn't bring Isaac home."

"How could you?" Delana's brow crinkled in puzzlement. "Rawhide found him at Fort Benton and talked sense into him."

"He's home?" Dustin asked incredulously.

"For two days now. Jakob was so relieved to find the pair of them. . . Now that you're here, everyone is happy again." She put her arms around him and pressed her cheek to his chest.

"Everyone's happy." Dustin closed his arms around her, relief overflowing his thoughts.

"Well, almost." Delana leaned back and tucked a shock of his hair behind his ear. "Rawhide asked Mama to marry him, and she hasn't said yes yet."

"Rawhide and *your mother*?" Dustin thought of the unlikely pair and shook his head.

"Not yet." Delana drew away to warm some biscuits in the oven. "But I think she'll say yes eventually."

Dustin sat down to mull this over. He drew off his pack and remembered the kitten. "I did bring a little something back for you."

"Oh?" She blinked. "What did you find in the middle of the wilderness?"

"Just a little *Paket*." Dustin named the kitten the German word for package, hoping to heighten Delana's curiosity.

"A package on the plains?"

"Of sorts." Dustin lifted the flap on his saddlebag, and the kitten thrust his head out to mew sleepily.

"A kitten!" Delana scooped the fur ball into her arms, looking at her present in astonishment.

"He crawled into my pack one night." Dustin grinned as Delana rubbed her cheek against Paket's soft fur.

"However did he wind up out there?" She wiggled her index finger, and the kitten playfully batted at it. "He's so small!"

"Perhaps a family headed for Virginia City lost him, though I'm not really sure. He's old enough to have been weaned." Dustin stood alongside her and ran a finger down the kitten's nose. "I thought he'd make a good addition to our home."

"I love him." Delana raised on tiptoe to give him a peck on the cheek before handing Paket to him.

"It's a relief to know everything's back to normal." Dustin took a huge bite of the biscuits and gravy she set before him.

"Not entirely," Delana hedged.

"Oh." Dustin swallowed. "Except for Rawhide and your mother." He still couldn't wrap his mind around the idea of those two as a couple. "We're one big, happy family." He fed Paket a bit of biscuit.

"Yes, we are." Delana took his left hand in hers and sat beside him. "And we're about to get bigger." She placed his hand on her abdomen.

"A babe?" His mouth suddenly dry, Dustin gulped down some water. "You're expecting a child?"

"Yes." Delana nodded happily. "*We're* expecting our first child."

"When did you. . .when will it. . ." Dustin took a deep breath.

"I believe we conceived on our wedding night," Delana answered his half-spoken question.

That was in May. Dustin did some rapid counting. *June, July—she's two months along. August, September, October, November, December, January, February. . . Oh no!*

"You'll give birth in February." He closed his eyes at the prospect.

"Soon after Christmas," Delana affirmed. "Isn't it wonderful timing?"

"No!" The crestfallen look on her face made him soften his response. "We'll be snowed in, Delana. There are no doctors, no midwives. . .no help at all."

"We'll be just fine." She put her hand to her stomach and gave a soft smile. "Women have been having babies since long before doctors."

And dying from childbirth for just as long. Dustin thought of his own mother. Neither she nor his younger sister had survived the ordeal.

"You won't." He made the decision. "Come September, I'll take you and your mother to Fort Benton. You'll get the help you need, and I'll come back for you after the spring thaw."

"What?" Disbelief was written on every line of her face. "You'd send me away?"

"There is no other choice."

"Yes, there is." She wrapped her arms around herself. "You could love me and stay beside me as I bring our child into the world."

"Not possible." He dismissed the notion. "Unless I leave with you in September, I'll be snowed in. If I go with you, I'll be stuck at Fort Benton until the thaw in March or even April. That's seven months or perhaps up to eight."

"Yet that's what you'd have me do." Delana's lower lip began to tremble.

"That's different." He had to make her understand. "If I leave for seven months, I forfeit our claim. One of the conditions of proving up is that I stay here over six months out of a year."

"It's months from two different calendar years," she insisted.

"But we made our claim the April before this last. Our second of the five years runs from until April third again." Dustin stood up. "I can't go with you."

"I won't go without you." Delana made a wide gesture with one arm. "I don't want to leave our home at all!"

"You must—for your sake and the babe's."

"I'm not ill or frail." Delana planted her hands on her hips. "There's no reason to think there will be complications."

"And there's no reason to assume there won't be!" He belatedly realized he'd gotten louder and modified his tone. "There's no sense in denying the possibility."

"Just as there's no purpose in allowing fear to rob us of this joy." Delana glowered fiercely. "Our child was conceived in this house and will be raised in it. It's only natural that the birth take place here as well."

"Not in the dead of winter." Dustin's jaw clenched as his wife refused to see reason. "As the head of this house, I've made the decision. You will go to Fort Benton in September, and I'll hear no more of it tonight."

The next morning, Delana crawled out of bed without having slept. She pressed a cool, damp towel to her aching head before dressing. Moving quietly so as not to wake Dustin, she set about making breakfast. She looked at the array of food and couldn't imagine eating anything. Delana hadn't suffered morning sickness for a fortnight but knew she'd be able to keep nothing down this morning.

He'll change his mind. He has to change his mind.

She set about making breakfast, ignoring the familiar sounds of Dustin waking up until he stood beside her.

"What's for breakfast?"

"Gruel." She handed him a bowl. *If he wants to act like a little child, he'll eat like one.* The idea held a sort of poetic justice.

He downed his breakfast without another word passing between them, then stomped to the barn.

Delana looked at the thin, yet lumpy mixture and made a moue of disgust. He'd eaten it without a word of complaint.

I'm the one who's guilty of being childish. Shame flooded her. *I'm a married woman, soon to be a mother, and yet I allowed myself to be petty. But I don't want to leave my friends and family and be all alone during my first Christmas as a married woman. He'd have me tucked away at Fort Benton when I should be helping gather the harvest and putting up the fruits of our garden.*

Rosalind's first birthday will pass without me seeing her first steps or hearing her first words. What if Rawhide convinces Mama to marry him in the late fall, and I'm not here to wish her wedding blessings? Her heart cried out at the very thought.

"No," she told Paket, firmly stating the syllable and sitting down. "I won't go." Delana slipped to her knees. "I can't."

"Lord," she whispered, rocking gently back and forth, "I cannot leave my husband and home to bear a child in a strange place. The truth remains that I cannot change Dustin's mind about it either. Wives are to submit to their husbands, I know. But what if our husbands are making the wrong decisions?"

She thought of the time not long ago when she wanted nothing more than to have Dustin make the difficult decisions. "After Papa died, the thought of getting here, of being with Dustin, saw me through. I felt that if we were together, it would all somehow work out. Dustin would be strong for me, and things wouldn't be so hard."

Though she'd wept silently through the night, it seemed she had still more to cry as tears welled in her eyes. "We're here together now, but it's still so hard, Lord. I never questioned my faith in Dustin, my belief that he would do right by me and my family. Now I realize that I can't rely on my husband to spare me from all the pains in this world. I should never have put him on that pedestal in the first place. Dustin's strengths are to complement my own, not carry my burden.

"I ran to a man when I should have run to You. Yours is the strength beyond all measure to support us when we stumble. Yours is the love whose perfection forgives our frailties and carries our burdens." Peace flooded her as she acknowledged the truth.

"I put my faith in You, where it belongs, and trust that You will guide Dustin to see that he can't ease his fears by sending me to Fort Benton. Only trust in You can do that."

Delana rose to her feet, dried her tears, and went to ask her husband to pray about his decision.

Chapter 19

"What's this I hear about you proposing to Mama Albright?" Dustin found Rawhide in the barn.

"Depends on what the person said when he was talkin' to you." Rawhide leaned against the wall while Dustin mucked.

"Delana mentioned that you asked her mama to marry you." Dustin halted and leaned on his shovel.

"That's about the long and short of it." Rawhide scratched his beard.

"What made you do a thing like that? You've always been the most independent man I ever knew."

"Independence has its rewards, but a man can only stand his own company for so long." Rawhide grabbed a shovel. "Me being such an interesting fellow, I just managed to hold out longer than most."

"Why Mama Albright?" Dustin couldn't think of a tactful way to pose the question. "You two seem an unlikely couple."

"Why not Bernadine?" Rawhide stopped shoveling to glower at Dustin. "She misses her husband; I've gone through missing my first wife. We've got plenty in common. Both of us understand the value of day-to-day companionship."

Dustin winced as he thought of the long months when Delana would be at Fort Benton. Rawhide had a point about the companionship.

"I'm no expert," Dustin hedged. *Now there's an understatement. I can't even get my wife to a doctor when she's going to have a baby!* "But it sounds to me as though you're talking from the head. Are you just being practical?"

"A man doesn't take on a woman like Bernadine Albright to be practical." Rawhide's statement defied contradiction. "I sure didn't choose her for the sake of convenience."

"Then why did you spout off all that about commonalities and companionship?" Dustin raised a brow. "What's the core of it?"

"Ah." Rawhide drew a deep breath. "There comes a time in a man's life when surprises are few and far between. Challenges that used to bring achievement seem hollow with no one to share them with. Now, Bernadine"—the older man chuckled as he spoke—"she's a surprising challenge."

"You wouldn't be looking for a merry chase, only to lose interest when you've caught your prize?" Dustin folded his arms across his chest. If he thought for even one instant that Rawhide was toying with his mother-in-law, the old wanderer would have a few acres less to roam around in.

"Nah, Bernadine's special. Sure, when I first met her I thought she was an uppity, too-starched kind of woman, but she's proven me wrong. The woman lost her son, husband, and home in a few short weeks. Instead of wailin' over it, she's pitched in around here." Rawhide took on a kind of goofy grin. "She's got a sparkle in her eye, brains in her head, and spirit in her soul. Life will never be dull if I can convince her she has room in her heart."

"In that case you might think of asking Jakob's blessing before you ask her again."

"What kind of a rascal do you think I am?" Rawhide seemed affronted. "I got that before I tried it the first time!"

"How will you set about convincing her to say yes?" Dustin wondered if he could borrow any tactics to appease Delana.

"I figure I've got a mighty fine start, seein' as how I led her out here, helped build the cabins, and brought her son back to her in one piece." Rawhide leaned the shovel against a wall. "Then there's the fact that, with the freight drivers gone for over two months, I'm the only eligible man for her in these parts. Those are good odds."

"Can't hurt." Dustin didn't bother to hide his grin. "Assuming she wants to remarry."

"Now don't go throwing a wrench in the works." Rawhide shook a finger at him. "I'll pay her court: say nice things, pick her some flowers, weed her garden, and anything else I can think of."

"I can think of something that couldn't hurt." Dustin's eyes narrowed speculatively. "You could escort her and Delana to Fort Benton this winter and see that her daughter delivers her grandchild safely."

❧

"Delana!" Kaitlin came rushing toward her.

"What is it?" Delana stopped and waited for her friend to catch up.

"I dinna want to bear tales," her friend worried, "but I overheard Dustin say something I know would upset you. You should be forewarned."

"Did he mention his plan to send me to Fort Benton for the winter, by any chance?" Delana patted Kaitlin's arm. "I already know. Why don't you come for a walk with me? We might find a patch of wild mint for a pitcher of tea."

"Mam's with Rosalind, so I dinna see why not." Kaitlin fell into step beside her. "I'm surprised to see you so tranquil. When last he spoke of sending you away, it seemed so devastating. Aren't you going to fight this decision?"

"I already have." Delana sucked in a breath at the recollection. "When I shared my joyous news, he immediately calculated that the baby will come sometime in February. Instead of sharing my elation that we'd have another wonderful event after Christmas, he spoke of our isolation and the harsh winter."

"Oh, that's a pity." Kaitlin shook her head. "Did he say naught of his pleasure at being made a father?"

"Not a word." Delana twisted her handkerchief. "His thoughts were for doctors and midwives. That's when he concocted this outlandish scheme to send me to the fort."

"This canna be allowed. When is he fixin' to send you?" Kaitlin huffed. "We'll need time to change his mind."

"I already told him I didn't want to leave. Reminders of my good health did not sway him, nor the prospect of a seven- or eight-month separation. He doesn't heed my wishes."

"Oooh." Kaitlin's eyes scrunched in anger. "How can you not be affected by the way he ignores your words?"

"Believe me"—Delana grimaced ruefully—"I was affected. Enough so that I made him lumpy gruel for breakfast. He ate it without a word of complaint. When he left for the barn, I dissolved into tears. Only then did I do what I should have long before—pray."

"So you've the peace of the Lord about you," Kaitlin surmised. "That explains it."

"Confiding in God all my hurt and disappointment made me realize I hadn't turned to Him as my rock since Papa's death. Dustin has agreed to pray on the matter, so I need to trust that the Lord will soften Dustin's heart on this issue." Delana grinned. "Failing that, surely the

Almighty can work on his hard head!"

"I dinna envy that task." Kaitlin giggled. "Arthur can be the same way when he gets ahold of some strange notion."

"It must have something to do with being male," Delana mused. "Rawhide may not have proposed to Mama again, but he hasn't backed down either."

"Since when is loving your mother a strange notion?" Kaitlin gave her a soft nudge.

"That's not the part I take issue with." Delana headed toward a small hill filled with lush plants. "The way he just slipped his proposal into the conversation was all but guaranteed not to sit well with Mama."

" 'Twas sudden." Kaitlin thought a moment. "Do you think she would have him if he wooed her properly?"

"I hope so." Delana thought of the times Rawhide had coaxed a sparkle into her mother's eyes. "And I think we'll find out soon enough. Yesterday he asked me what her favorite wildflower is."

"That's better." Kaitlin stopped and sniffed the air. "The scent of mint freshens the breeze." She turned toward the soft wind and walked west.

"Here it is!" Delana bent to pick a few sprigs. The invigorating scent grew stronger as she gathered. "I've had a craving for mint of late and plucked my first patch bare." She placed one of the silver-green leaves on her tongue, letting the flavor refresh her.

"You should plant some in the garden so it's right at hand." Kaitlin carefully dug up one of the plants, roots and all.

"Summer is late to be planting anything," Delana said, "though it can't hurt to try. I'll be making a large batch of tea with these. It will be ready tomorrow."

"We should gather more while it's plentiful and dry some." Kaitlin filled her own apron pockets. " 'Tis good for the stomach, they say."

"I've heard that before, though I don't know much about herbs." Delana straightened. "It's something I would like to learn about."

"Mam knows a bit. She'll tell you to take a tea made of red raspberry leaf every day for the last month or so until you come to term." Kaitlin fell into step with Delana. "I took it when I was close to birthing my Rosalind."

"What does it do?"

" 'Tis good for the womb and eases the way for childbearing." Kaitlin smiled. "Scotswomen have used it for hundreds of years."

"I'll be sure to remember that." Delana stepped around a fallen tree. "It's fortunate that raspberries grow here!"

" 'Tis wonderful how the Lord provides."

"Yes." Delana put a hand over her stomach, thinking of the child within. "We are blessed."

∞

"Nein." Dustin widened his stance, refusing to let her pass. "Women who are expecting children do not ride horses."

"Then let's look on it as a marvelous surprise not to be expected, but anticipated." When Delana tried to sidle around him, he picked her up by the waist and set her outside the barn once again.

"It's too high," he protested. *She has to know it's not safe. What if she falls?*

"I'll choose a short horse," she promised. "It's not as though I'm planning on climbing a tree."

He crossed his arms over his chest. "Don't get any ideas."

"I'm only in my fourth month, darling." Delana laid a hand on his arm. "Staying active is the best thing I can do for me and our child."

"Uh-uh." Dustin shook his head. "If you feel the need to move around, go for a walk. Just not in the forest." He suddenly thought of Kaitlin's wrenched ankle. "And not alone."

"Anything else?" His wife scowled at him, and Dustin bit back a smile. She was about as intimidating as a fluffy chick.

"Don't wander too far," he added, just for good measure.

"Would you like to hammer a post into the ground, attach a short rope to it, and tie the other end about my waist?" She jabbed him in the chest. "I'm not a child. I'm just carrying one!"

"Exactly." He turned the words around on her. "Everywhere you go, so does our baby. Would you let a baby get up on a horse? Or climb a tree? Or wander about in the forest alone?"

"It's not the same, and you know it." She gritted her teeth. "And don't act as though you're being reasonable. You won't let me climb the ladder to the loft or stand on one of the benches to reach the top shelf."

"Those are both reasonable." He mentally patted himself on the back for his vigilance.

"You won't let me build a stool—the bench is the only thing I can use." Obviously exasperated, she bunched the fabric of his shirt in her hand.

"Now, be fair." Dustin winced as she caught some chest hair in that grip. "I wouldn't let you build a stool even if you weren't pregnant."

"You're impossible!" She let him go and turned to stalk away, the little gray cat trailing behind her.

"I love you, too," he called after her, rubbing the sore spot on his chest. *How can* she *accuse me of being unreasonable?*

Chapter 20

"BERNADINE ALBRIGHT," Rawhide rode along the western edge of their property, bellowing with all his might. "I'M FIXIN' ON HAVING YOU TO BE MY BRIDE, SO I'M ANNOUNCING MY INTENTIONS TO ONE AND ALL."

Of the entire Montana Territory, Delana mentally tacked on. She watched as Mama released the handles of the wheelbarrow, a dull *thunk* sounding as it hit the ground. She saw her mother's eyes widen in shock before narrowing in anger.

"Foolish man!" Mama's full skirts made her look as though she sailed on the grasses of the plains as Rawhide kept on hollering at the top of his lungs.

"I'VE PURCHASED THE LAND ALONG YOUR WESTERN BORDER, FREE AND CLEAR. YOU'LL SEE THAT I AIM TO SETTLE DOWN WHERE WE CAN BE CLOSE TO YOUR CHILDREN."

He has to see her coming. Delana knew that Mama in a temper was practically impossible to ignore. *He'll stop shouting at any moment. There, he's stopped now. . .* Her thoughts slowed as her step quickened. *He just drew breath to keep right on bellowing. If the man has a lick of sense, he'd—*

"Rawhide Jones," Mama commanded, "turn that horse and ride off until you're fit for polite company."

"NO!" Rawhide's shout made everyone wince, and he cleared his throat. "Not possible, Bernadine."

"You've made a fool of yourself, riding this border and shouting like a man who's taken leave of his senses." Mama shook her index finger at him. "And after I already told you I'd not remarry with my husband not even a year gone. The very idea!" She huffed. "Scandalous."

"So long as I have your attention." Rawhide leaned forward and, instead of riding his horse away as quickly as it could carry him, swung out of the saddle to stand toe-to-toe with Delana's outraged mother. "Mark my words, Bernadine Albright, I'll wait for you to grieve your first husband. I'll wait for you to see past my rough manners. Whenever you decide you want me, know that I'll be here."

"It will be a long wait." Bernadine shook her head. "I loved my Otto." Tears thickened her words. "He cannot be replaced."

Delana fought between the urge to comfort her mama and the obvious need for the two stubborn souls to reach some kind of understanding.

"I respect that." Rawhide's reply seemed solemnly sincere. "No one will ever be like my Fredericka. . .and that's as it should be."

"Ja," Mama whispered her agreement.

"But there are many things left here to share." Rawhide's gesture encompassed the mountains, forests, and meadows around them. "I'll wait if it means I can share these joys with you."

Mama didn't say another word.

"Of course," Rawhide began as he swung back into his saddle, "I figure I might have to pester you every so often—just so you know I'm still here. Besides"—he grinned—"a man can get mighty hungry during a long wait."

Waiting can be so difficult. Delana sighed. The heat of the sun beating down upon her did little to warm her heart.

The first of September seemed every bit as hot as the summer months before. Even so, Delana feared change in the wind. She and Dustin hadn't spoken about Fort Benton since the night she'd told him he was to become a father.

Lord, he promised to pray about it and listen for Your answer. I've waited on You and trusted that whatever decision Dustin came to, it would be the right one for our family. Now it's coming to the time when I need to know what to prepare myself for. If it is Your will that I leave, then it must be for the safety of our child and I will go. I cannot pretend to understand Your ways. . .but I need time to be able to say good-bye to my husband and home, friends and family.

Mama noticed her preoccupation, but Delana couldn't explain it. This was something between a husband and wife. What mama thought bore no consequence; the matter belonged in the Lord's hands.

Since the only thing Mama thought could be distracting her daughter was the baby, she took to telling birth stories at random moments.

This morning Kaitlin happened to mention an unfortunate yearning for pickles.

"I remember my sister Hildegarde going into labor. She demanded pickles during the early hours. Her husband got them for her, and she ate so many we couldn't see how they fit. Later, she upset her stomach." Mama grimaced. "She would never eat another pickle."

Delana grimaced. Some stories just shouldn't be told. For all her attempts to be encouraging, Mama made her even more uncomfortable.

The only person whom she could talk to about her uncertainty was Kaitlin.

"Surely Dustin would have told me if he changed his mind? He'd let me know." Delana drummed her fingers on the side of the bench. "Last he told me, I'm going."

"Maybe since he hasn't set you to packing, he assumes you know you're not." Kaitlin frowned. "That didn't come out right, but I meant to say that he would have you preparing for the journey if you were still to leave."

"Unless he hasn't made the final decision." Delana stood and paced around her kitchen. "I know I said I'd trust the Lord's will. . .but I had thought to know what it was!"

"You're a stronger woman than I." Kaitlin's eyes grew sad. "I missed my Arthur so much while I carried Rosalind. I missed his strength. I wished I coulda held his hand. . ." She shook her head. "Carrying a babe is a wondrously frightening time. Your husband should be with you to help."

"He hovers too much as is," Delana grumbled. "I can hardly step foot outside the door!"

"I ken he frustrates you with his fussin'." Kaitlin smiled wistfully. "All the same, I see it as a measure of his love. No man hovers unless it's love."

"I think you're right, but for now it's exasperating. I've no way of knowing if he'll send me away or keep shadowing my every move."

"Well. . .you could pack a few things," Kaitlin said. "To prepare your-self if he persists with his cockamamie plan."

"Now that's an idea." Delana considered it. "If I pack, it shows Dustin that I trust the decision he made so many weeks ago. On the other hand, if he's changed his mind, he'll tell me so! Either way, at least I'll know what we'll be dealing with."

With her plan made, Delana resolved not to waste any time putting it into motion.

September has arrived, Lord. I know that I have to send my wife away, but I can't imagine spending so many months without Delana. Her safety and that of our child come before lesser desires. The time when I must say good-bye draws close, and I have yet to tell her.

I've prayed and waited to see whether I would experience a change of heart. Even after all these weeks, I know my responsibilities haven't changed. Still, I dread telling her. She's been so patient, never pushing me to finalize my decision. I know Delana feels strongly that she belongs here, but I cannot in good conscience allow her to stay. Emotions don't take precedence over logic.

All the same, Lord, I'm asking for Your help in facing my wife.

Chapter 21

You look like a man with a lot on his mind." Arthur brushed bits of straw from his shirt as he stepped out of the barn.

"Tonight I need to tell Delana I'm sending her to Fort Benton through the winter." Dustin let loose a heavy sigh. "She's not going to like it."

"I see." Arthur leaned against the doorframe. "Kaitlin mentioned something like that might be on the wind."

"Oh?" Dustin frowned. "I never spoke with her about it." *I'd hate to think Delana was taking a matter to others that should remain between us and the Lord.*

"She overheard you make a comment to Rawhide several weeks ago and asked Delana about it." Arthur raised a thick black brow. "Would you take kindly to a few well-meant words from an old friend?"

"Depends on what those words are." Dustin bristled at the idea of being told how to handle his marriage.

"I'll tread carefully, then. All I can share is my own experience—you take from it what you will."

"Fair enough." Dustin relaxed his rigid stance. Arthur wasn't one to use his words lightly.

"You'll recall that I wasna wi' my Kaitlin when she carried our wee Rosalind." Arthur waited for Dustin's nod before continuing. "I dinna know she expected our child when I left her in Baltimore."

"And if you had?" Dustin opened his canteen. "What would your decision have been? To leave her, to take her into an isolated wilderness, or to forfeit the future of your family altogether?"

"That I canna say, as I was never put in that position." Arthur folded his arms across his massive chest. "I dinna favor any of those choices, just as you see no perfect solution to your own dilemma."

"This much I've considered on my own." Dustin took a swig of his water. "I've thought on it often."

"I'd expect no less. But I'd count myself a poor friend to both you and Delana if I dinna tell you how deeply I regret missing that special time. My Kaitlin couldna lean on me when she dinna feel well. I canna go back and give her the comfort she needed when I was miles away."

Arthur's remorse sliced through Dustin. *Delana will go through the same thing if I send her to Fort Benton.* He shook his head. *What am I thinking? There is no if—it is the safest place for her and our child.*

"Since Kaitlin stayed in Baltimore, she had all the resources and help she'd need were she or the babe in danger." Dustin referenced his main reason for the decision he'd made. "Delana will have the same help to ensure she and our child are safe."

"That's a powerful reason to send her," Arthur admitted. "But the state of a woman's heart affects her health. What if she needs your love and support more than the science of a doctor?"

"There's no way to know that." Dustin dismissed the notion. "Besides, she carries my love wherever she goes."

"Did that knowledge stop you from missing Delana during the year you spent apart?"

No. I thought of her every day, wondering if all was well with her, if she would be happy here with me. But such musings do no good.

"The knowledge that I did what was best for our future eased the sacrifice."

"And if you werena certain that was best for your family's future— as Delana isna sure?" Arthur's quiet words tore into Dustin like sharp daggers.

"It will only be a short time."

"Seven months away from your wife isna significant?" The blacksmith shook his head. "We both know 'tis not true."

"What would you have me do?" Dustin clenched his fists. "Allow her to stay at the risk of her life and the life of our child?"

"Pray." Arthur walked up to him, placing one large hand on Dustin's shoulder. "I would have you pray."

"I have. My decision remains."

"Dustin, let me ask you something." Arthur stayed by his side until he assented. "When you prayed, did you ask for the Lord to reveal His will. . .or did you ask Him to support yours?"

With that, his friend left Dustin to his own thoughts.

There is nothing I will not do to protect my family—even unto being without my wife through the long winter. He began to walk toward home. *How dare Arthur question my obedience to God! I've asked Him time and again to help Delana realize what must be done.*

The thought stopped him in his tracks. *Lord, is it possible that I've prayed for You to do my will instead of me seeking Yours? Every time I've come to You it has been to ask for what is best for my family.*

"But I've asked for what *I* think is best." The realization staggered him even as he spoke it aloud.

Lord, I ask Your forgiveness for my shortsightedness. Please give me a sign. . . something to show me what You would have me do. I'll not say a word to Delana until I'm certain of Your will.

Delana took her valise from her trunk that very night, determined to end the matter once and for all. *Whether the answer is what I hope for or not, it will be settled.*

Dustin gave her an astonished look as she plopped it on the bed and began adding hankies, a nightgown, and her cloak. Two dresses followed the other items. Paket, now almost double the size he'd been when he'd arrived, tried to wriggle into the valise. Delana fished him out and set him on the bed.

"What are you doing?" Dustin's deep rumble sounded behind her.

He's going to tell me I'm not going, that I shouldn't be packing! Delana calmly folded a blanket and placed it inside. "I'm packing." She held her breath and waited for him to tell her to unpack.

"All right." The weight of those two words made her shoulders stoop for a moment. "Since you've changed your mind. . ."

"I didn't change my mind." Delana turned to face him. "I'm trusting you. Though I must say, I thought you'd come to a different conclusion."

"How so? This is the best way to see that you and our child are well cared for." Dustin drew her into a hug. "I pledged before God and man to protect you and care for you all the days of my life."

"I thought of other things," Delana admitted. "Yet I know you prayed over the matter and feel led to choose this path. I will follow you."

"I asked the Lord for a sign as to whether you should go or stay." Dustin tilted her chin. "Your trust in abiding by the decision you thought I'd already made ended the matter. The moment I saw you pack, I knew what we were to do."

"No!" Delana pulled away and shut the valise with a sharp snap. *My desperation for a decision can't push him toward the wrong one!*

"I couldn't know whether you didn't speak of it because you felt the matter already settled, or if your silence meant it was no longer an issue." She struggled to remain calm. "After so much time, I expected to have you tell me clearly once and for all."

"So you're not ready to go to Fort Benton, although it is the safest decision for you and our child." Dustin sank down onto the edge of the bed. "Why can nothing be simple?"

"I was ready to honor the path the Lord revealed to you." Delana sat beside him and reached to take his hand in hers. "That changes if you don't have a peace about this decision."

"What I don't have peace about is upsetting you." Dustin rubbed his temples. "You will be protected to the best of my ability—what more is there to consider?"

"Do you want me to tell you what I think?" Delana spoke quietly, hoping her husband would choose to hear her. "Whether my thoughts sway your decision or not, I'll be satisfied to know that you considered them." *Lord, please let him say yes!*

"You are my wife." Dustin met her gaze squarely. "The hopes of your heart are things to be shared. Tell me."

∞

Whatever concerns she has, I'll do my best to alleviate them before seeing her to Fort Benton. Delana honors me as the head of our home by accepting my decision; it is good that I should honor her views in return.

"I think of living without you for seven months." Her eyes shone with unshed tears. "How can I not share each day with you when our child grows within me?"

"It is a long time," he conceded. "Try to understand I think of sharing years with both of you once you are safely delivered of our son or daughter." He rubbed his thumb over the sensitive skin on the back of her hand. "I'm willing to trade a few months to safeguard our life together."

"I remember Psalm 128: 'Thy wife shall be as a fruitful vine by the sides of thine house.' Our family is multiplying as we are instructed, but you consider sending me away from our home."

"We'll raise our child here, along with any brothers and sisters the Lord sees fit to give us." His reassurances seemed to have little effect.

"The scriptures tell us that children are the heritage of the Lord, and the prophet Ezekiel exhorts a mother to be joyful with her children." Delana looked down at their joined hands. "That joy is halved when we're apart. How can my heart be full when my child takes me away from the man I love?"

Dustin sucked in a sharp breath. "I love you, and I'll miss you while you're gone. Remember, though, that I will come for both of you. We do this to ensure our family is whole."

"And if it is best for the child, is it best for our marriage?" Delana bit her lip before continuing. "A husband is told to cleave unto his wife, and also to live joyfully with her."

"I am joyful when I am with you." He smoothed her hair with his palm. "A few months won't take that away."

"And what of Matthew's warning about man and wife—that what God hath joined together, let no man put asunder?" She paused a moment. "Are we not dividing ourselves when it is unnecessary?"

"I believe it is necessary." He drew her into his arms, though she suddenly stiffened and went absolutely still. "Are you all right?" He fought to remain calm. *What if, in my determination to be sure she stays healthy, I push her toward illness?*

"The baby. . ." Delana's voice held wonder, not pain. "He just kicked."

"Where?" Dustin flattened his palm over her stomach, trying to feel the force of a tiny foot.

"Kaitlin and Mama are right. . .it's as though a butterfly just fluttered beneath my ribs." Delana took his hand in both of hers. "You won't be able to feel him, yet. Not until he's much bigger."

"I'm going to miss it." Gloom invaded the cabin as Dustin realized this was something he couldn't share with her.

"Oh," Delana gave a tiny gasp. "There he goes again." Her eyes shone with happiness. "I can feel him moving!"

"Him?" Dustin wondered if she even knew she'd said it.

"A son." She nodded. "Somehow, I just know our firstborn is a son."

"A son," Dustin repeated, humbled. "Our son."

"Yes."

"When will I be able to feel him?"

"It will be months still before the time comes." She cradled her abdomen lovingly. "All things in God's time."

"All things in God's time." The words knocked the air from Dustin's

chest. *God chose to give us this baby now—He timed it so our child would be born in winter. Just as he brought Delana to me a year in advance. I've tried to create a timetable, and God moves things along at His own pace. It's beyond my control.*

"You're not going to Fort Benton." Dustin cuddled her close. "God gave us the child now, and I have to trust His plan. It's just like my father's favorite verse."

"What verse is that?" Delana smiled up at him.

" 'To every thing there is a season, and a time to every purpose under the heaven.' Seasons change, time goes on, and God guides us away from our own plans. My father knew this, and he always claimed the third chapter in Ecclesiastes spoke to the farmer in him." Dustin stood, drawing his wife to her feet along with him.

" 'A time to plant. . .' " She looked at her tummy and smiled.

" 'And a time to pluck up that which is planted,' " Dustin finished. "We'll gather the sweet harvest together."

Epilogue

April 1868

"We did it!" Dustin's words made Delana leap into his arms.

"You have the deed?" She tried to rummage through his pockets.

"Right here." He handed it to her. "One hundred and sixty acres, free and clear to Dustin Friemont."

"You worked so hard." Delana rested her hand on his arm. "I'm so proud."

"We worked hard. I couldn't have done it without you." He rubbed his thumb across the sensitive skin at the base of her neck, making Delana shiver.

"Five years and one hundred and twenty acres cultivated." She smiled up at her hardworking husband. "The Homestead Act meant we only needed to plant on forty."

"Our home is worth the effort." He looked over her shoulder. "Our family deserves it."

"Daddy!" Brent raced up to his parents, his little sister's shorter legs churning at a furious pace to keep up. "You're back!"

"I sure am." Dustin stooped to embrace their children.

"Good to see you!" Arthur clapped him on the back as he stood up.

"From the smile on your face, I see you've officially proven up." Jakob and Isaac joined the group.

"It is wunderbar." Mama beamed at them.

"This deserves a celebration!" Gilda and Kaitlin each held two fresh raspberry pies.

"Good news always does." Rawhide looked at Mama. "But good news can always be added to."

"Rawhide," Mama spoke so softly Delana almost couldn't hear her.

"Bernadine." He stepped closer, clasping both her hands in his. "Your worth is beyond rubies—certainly deserving of a man's patience. I waited as you grieved for your first husband. Then I waited as you devoted your-self to your handsome grandbabies. I've held out for the three and a half years since you first turned me down, knowing your need to help your children establish themselves. Now they have. It is time to think about your own happiness—and mine." He sank down on one knee before her, never releasing her hands. "Bernadine Albright, will you marry me?"

"Oh Rawhide." Mama's eyes sparkled with unshed tears. "It's about time you asked me again."

A Time to Keep

Dedication

To God, first and foremost, and to my critique partners and editors,
without whom this book would not be what it is today.

Prologue

Scotland, 1876

Fifteen-year-old Ewan Gailbraith sidestepped yet another muddy puddle in a Scottish thoroughfare. *"Be my braw lad and take good care of your mama for me, son."* His father's words echoed through his mind. *"I'll find good work and send ye the fare to come join me in America."* Ewan stubbornly trudged on in the face of the unseasonable downpour.

"Da left us nigh on a year ago." The lad aimed a fierce kick at a hapless rock as he neared his destination. "Surely this week we'll hae another letter." He drew up short at the old tavern banged together from a motley lot of old boards and prayed that old Ferguson would have an envelope for him.

He swung open the lopsided door. For once his arrival was unannounced by the creaky old hinges, now too waterlogged to protest. Ewan stomped his worn boots on the threshold to dislodge the worst of the mud and then bypassed the hearty welcome of the roaring fire in favor of approaching the tavern owner at the bar.

"Mr. Ferguson," he addressed, drawing up to his full height, "hae you any word from my da this day?" He clenched his teeth as the barkeep looked him over, as much to stop them from chattering as from biting back angry words at the miserable man who drew out his answers as long as the voyage to America.

"Aye." The man reached beneath his scraggly beard, into the pocket of his coat, and drew out a much-handled brown packet. He placed it on the weathered face of the bar and slid it toward the youth.

"Thankee." Ewan manfully resisted the urge to pounce upon the package, instead calmly nudging it off the bar and into the safety of his own threadbare pocket. His hand lingered over the small coin inside before drawing it out, placing it carefully on the bar, and turning away.

"You should warm yoursel' by the fire afore ye step outside again!" the barkeep's wife called to him.

Ewan hesitated, reluctant to waste even a moment before bringing his mam the news from his father, but saw the wisdom of the woman's words. He'd be no good to Mam if he caught a chill and couldn't work. He grudgingly moved toward the warmth of the flames, holding his hands toward the heat. He kept ignoring the curious gazes of the old timers who probably hoped he'd open the envelope before them all and give the town some new gossip to chew over.

He waited until he felt reasonably warmed, if not dry, and headed back into the gray rain. His long stride covered the soggy ground quickly in a bid to stave off the cold on his journey. With each step he took, the packet thumped against his side—a weight that would either ease his burden or add to it. Which would be the case, he knew not. 'Twas not his place to open the envelope before bringing it to his mother. His restless hands clenched at his sides as he neared their small, well-thatched cottage.

"Ewan!" Ma swung open the door and pulled him inside, clucking like a hen as she drew off his jacket and wrapped his hands around a warm mug of water. "I couldn't believe you'd taken off in this weather! What was so important it could not wait a day or two?"

Ewan jerked his chin toward the sopping wet jacket she started to hang on a peg by the door. "It has come, Ma." He watched her blue eyes widen in hope and surprise before her fingers deftly searched his pockets and withdrew the packet.

"Do ye ken what it holds, son?" She turned the envelope over in her hands as though loath to open it.

"Nay. I thought 'twas best we open it together." He put down the mug and walked over to his mother, placing his arm around her shoulders as he towered over her.

At his silent nod, she tore open one side of the envelope and drew two smaller ones from the packet. She opened the thinner of the envelopes first. They stood in silence as they each drank in the strong, sure strokes of his father's hand.

Ewan let loose the breath he hadn't known he'd held. Da was fine and well in America, and he sent his love and hopes that they'd all be together soon. Ewan gave his mother's shoulder a firm squeeze. She then slit open the other envelope to find a significant amount of money. "Oh Ewan!" Tears of joy ran down his mother's tired face as she looked up at him. "He's well, and we're that much closer to joining him! Why, in another six months or so, we'll have enough to pay both our passages to America."

Ewan looked at his mother's smile and saw the lingering sadness in her eyes. Fine lines had sprung up around her eyes over the last few months and now gave away the disappointment she tried to hide. With each month her husband had been gone, Imogene Gailbraith had lost a bit more of her joy. In another six months, or even an entire year, Da would not recognize this slight woman as the beloved wife he'd left in his son's care.

Now's the time. 'Tis the right thing to do.

"Ma," Ewan began, taking her chilled hands in his own, "I've given the matter much thought, and I've come to a decision. . ."

Chapter 1

Montana Territory, Autumn 1887

L ook out!" Brent Friemont practically shoved Rosalind MacLean off the path as he rushed to plunge a bucket into the stream.

Rosalind gasped to see the normally fastidious young man's clothes all askew. "What's wrong?"

"No time." He hurried past her with the now-brimming bucket. Rosalind turned. Whorls of smoke were rising atop the maple trees.

"Fire!" Quickly she filled the unscrubbed pot, still dirty from the morning meal, with water and raced up the path after Brent. Water sloshed over her skirts and bare feet as she went, but she paid no heed. When she reached the line of trees, her suspicions—fueled by the acrid scent of smoke tinged with something even more unpleasant—were confirmed. Someone had set fire to the outhouse.

When she reached the site, several men were already fighting the flames. Dustin Friemont and Isaac and Jakob Albright had obviously rushed over at the first sign of trouble. She handed over the heavy pot with relief. It hadn't been easy hauling it up the hill. She drew in a deep breath and promptly began sputtering. *Not the smartest idea I've ever had,* she admitted to herself when she rushed once again to the stream. Before long, they'd managed to douse the flames. All that was left was a heap of sodden, smoldering wood—and a lingering stench.

"What on earth happened?" Isaac turned to Brent, outrage written plainly across his handsome features.

"I. . .er. . ." Brent avoided his uncle's gaze only to find Rosalind staring at him in befuddlement. The young man blushed bright red and mumbled something almost incoherent.

"What?" Isaac had plainly missed the whispered confession.

"I was trying to smoke a cigar." Brent spoke more loudly this time, though he seemed no less embarrassed.

"You were *smoking?*" Dustin Friemont roared, having just come upon the scene in time to hear his son's confession.

"In the *privy?*" Isaac's disbelief more closely mirrored Rosalind's.

"Yes." Brent stared at the wreckage in misery. "I knew better than to try it at home, Pa."

"You would've done well to take that caution a step or two further." Isaac grimaced. "Smoking near anything made of wood is foolish."

Rosalind stepped in. "I think he's learned his lesson." When she caught Brent's adoring gaze, she wished she'd remained silent.

Brent Friemont, a little less than two years her junior, had taken to giving her cow eyes whenever she so much as glanced in his direction. Since she was one of the few single girls in the area who wasn't his younger sister, Rosalind couldn't really blame him for his notice. Then again, she really couldn't encourage him either.

Dustin doled out the punishment. "He'll have learned his lesson once he cleans up this mess and builds a new outhouse."

"What happened?" Rosalind's dad stared at the charred mess. Mam, followed by Brent's mother, came hard on his heels.

Most days, Rosalind considered the proximity of their homes to be a blessing. When her mother and father had settled this land with the Friemonts and Albrights, they'd agreed to build their homes and barns on the strip of earth joining their properties. She'd grown up with Brent and, later, Marlene. Their parents, Delana and Dustin, lived within spitting distance of her family home. Two generations' worth of each family, all with homes on the same three acres of land.

Not too long ago, it had been three generations on each side. Rosalind looked toward the small cemetery where they'd buried Bernadine, Rawhide, and her Grandda Cade. The only one left was Rosalind's grandmother, Gilda Banning, who'd moved in with the MacLeans when Grandda passed on.

Any way Rose looked on it, she couldn't help but feel all of them were one big family. She knew that her family and Brent's hoped for a match to officially unite them. Try as she might, she couldn't fathom it. Brent seemed as much the scapegrace younger brother to her today as he had when he'd slipped wriggly tadpoles down the back of her dress on his sixth birthday.

Marlene ran up. "Oh Brent. *Now* what did you do?"

By this point, it seemed as though everyone had gathered at the scene of the crime. Rosalind looked at the familiar faces with fondness, and a part of her wished she could make their dream of a marriage come true. However, that part was drowned out by the loud, insistent voice demanding that she be true to her own heart. Marriage was a lifetime commitment—a commitment she simply couldn't make to the young man who'd just burned down an outhouse.

"Clean it up and build a new one?" Brent's voice jerked her back to the current problem. "Maybe I should take the opportunity to dig a new one altogether." Anyone who knew Brent could see that the idea of touching the filthy, smelly heap in front of him was enough to make him turn green.

"Good idea." Rosalind's da clapped him on the shoulder. "Clean up this mess and create an entirely new outhouse. Nice to see a man take responsibility for his mistakes and make amends."

Brent rubbed his shoulder sullenly, obviously unwilling to utter another word that might land him more work. One by one, all slipped away to tend to their own chores until Brent was left alone with Rosalind and his sister.

"I'm sorry, Brent." Marlene gave him a commiserating glance even as she looped an arm around Rosalind's shoulders and began to walk away. She bit back a snicker before she added, "This whole thing really stinks!"

She and Rosalind hurried away, failing to hold their giggles. They stopped when they were out of Brent's sight to talk about the contretemps.

"That wasn't very nice, making fun of your brother," Rosalind pointed out.

"There are worse things." Marlene gave a meaningful glance backward before wrinkling her nose. "I just don't understand what goes through his head sometimes."

"Nor do I. Though I wonder"—Rosalind plucked a late-blooming wildflower and twirled it between her fingers—"if others say the same about us."

"Who knows?" Marlene stretched and thought for a moment. "I'd probably say everybody reads us like we're open books."

"Surely not." Rosalind dropped the tiny flower and looked at the wide blue Montana sky that stretched ahead of them, broken only by the mountain peaks in the distance. "Human beings, like life, are never that simple."

"This life is simple," Ewan Gailbraith announced to the young man he'd be showing around that day and training for the remainder of the week. "You work hard, keep your mouth shut, an' help others when you can. Don't waste money or flash it around, stay away from Hank's chili, and don't start anything. Only other advice I can give you is to take care o' your tools and they'll take care o' you."

"Yes sir." The wiry lad twisted his hat in his hands. "I don't mind honest work, so long as it's for honest pay."

"As a wheelwright, you'll be paid well for your skill." Ewan smiled. "In a couple of years, you'll hae enough saved to start a life anywhere you like. That's what most men do."

"Is that what you're planning to do, Mr. Gailbraith?"

Ewan gestured toward a freight car. "That's where we keep the raw materials." *When and where will I leave the railroad and begin my own life?* He kept talking business in an effort to distract himself from the question he refused to answer. "We build makeshift forges when and where we need them as the railroad builds from town to town. For the first week, you'll be transporting finished items and presized strips down to where the track is being laid. It won't be too much longer before we hae to set up the forge farther down."

"I thought there was a small town a little ways farther down."

"There is. Saddleback is where we'll set up our next base. We'll be continuing the main line an' beginning an offshoot running through there, so you can count on staying there awhile. You'll end up trying your hand as farrier before long, I'd warrant."

"I apprenticed with a farrier for the last year." The young man sounded a bit more confident now.

"All to the good. I do both jobs myself." Ewan stopped for a moment and spoke more carefully. "Now, if you were apprenticing, why didn't you see it through?"

"My master drank too much one night and fell in the horse trough. I found him the next morning."

"Overfond o' t' bottle, eh?" Ewan gave the youth a measuring look. "There are some here who share that weakness. You seem a bright lad, but I'll offer you this warning: Don't indulge in drink, gaming, or some o' the loose women who follow the railroad. Any one of those vices will take your money and leave you feeling ill. I don't tolerate that sort of behavior from my men. Understood?"

"Yes sir." The fellow stood a little taller. "I never held much stock by those ways myself."

"I'm glad to hear it." Ewan turned and continued walking. "Honest values and hard work will take you farther than the railroad itself ever can."

Chapter 2

"The railroad will take this town and build it into a city." Rosalind could practically have danced upon the words she spoke to her father. He didn't respond while he ate the mid-morning snack she'd brought to his smithy. "Think of it—the workers who lay the rails are not so far off. I heard that they'll have reached us before the week is out."

"I'm thinkin' on it more an' more wi' each passing day, Rosey-mine." Da wore an expression she'd seen before only when he looked at his son. Pride tinged with regret for what could have been.

She and Luke were the joys of her father's life, but Da had hoped to pass on his trade to his son. With Luke's weak lungs, he would never stand at his father's forge, carrying on an age-old family tradition. Yes, she knew well the wistful gleam that crept into Da's eyes as he spoke of the progress of the "iron horse." But what could he possibly regret when they'd be linked at long last to the world beyond Saddleback? What opportunities lay at the other end of those rails?

"Da? What is it, exactly, you've been thinking on?"

"Sit down wi' me for a moment, lass." He gestured to a bench in the corner and sat down heavily. " 'Tis time and past for us to speak on a few matters."

"Da?" Worry sparked in her heart at the lines on her father's brow.

"Don't fret so, Rosey-mine. 'Tis nothing so dire as you may imagine." Her father drew a deep breath. "It seems to me as though 'twas only yesterday your ma came out here to join me. Her showing up wi' you in her arms was the sweetest moment of my life. I remember it so clearly. But I look on the memories which filled the passing years, and I know better. I see the stamp of time on your lovely face, Rosey, and can't deny that you've become a woman grown. If I were honest, I would say that I've known it for quite some time now."

Dread thudded in Rosalind's heart. Surely Da wouldn't tell her she must choose a husband and move on? Aye, most lasses wed long before their twenty-third year, but couldn't he see that it wasn't the right time for her?

"You are a beauty, just like your mother." Da's sudden smile brought a welcome rush of relief. "But with that beauty comes danger. A lovely lass without the protection of a husband can be a target for evil men."

"Da!" Rosalind burst out, desperate to stop his flow of words. "I know everyone expects me to make my choice soon, but I can't! Not when all I've ever known is this small piece of the world and the familiar faces on it! The railroad will give me the opportunity to see a bit more, meet new people, afore I settle down. Would you deny me that chance?"

"Nay, Rosey-mine, I wouldn't. Your ma and Delana cherish hopes that you'll choose to wed Brent. Nay, don't speak now." He held up one massive hand as though to ward off her alarm. "'Tis your choice to make, daughter, but to my way of thinking, Brent 'tisn't the man for you. If he were, you would hae settled on him long ago."

Rosalind nodded, half ashamed at the admission she'd be letting down her mother but half relieved that her father understood and accepted her decision.

"I'll hae no part in shoving my lassie out of our home and into the arms of a man she doesn't love as deeply as I cherish your ma. And, were I to be completely honest, I don't know what we'd do wi'out you." Her father's grin made Rosalind's own smile falter.

Here, then, was the heart of the matter. Da knew she longed to explore the opportunities the railroad would bring, but he was reminding her of her responsibilities here at home. She helped Ma with the garden, cooking, housework, and sewing when she wasn't taking meals to Da or watching over Luke. If she followed her own dreams, she'd be leaving her family behind—and they needed her. Rosalind struggled against the sense of confinement pressing in upon her. She'd never abandon them, no matter what it cost her. She opened her mouth to assure her father that he could rely on her.

"What I mean to say is that we love you dearly, Rosey-mine, and I mean to warn you about the changes the railroad will bring." Her father's serious expression bore into her.

"Oh, I already know much of what to expect." Her enthusiasm rushed to the tip of her tongue. "'Twill bring many people—farmers, traders, railroad officials, and more—to our small town. The number of families will swell, and our ability to send goods and receive modern niceties will increase dramatically. Should we want to visit Fort Benton or Virginia City, 'twill take naught but a fraction of the time we'd spend on horseback to arrive there and journey back. New friends, adventures just a ride away, and shorter waits for everything! The railroad is a marvel, Da. 'Twill change everything." *And I can hardly wait!*

" 'Tis glad I am to hear you've been thinking on the matter so seriously." Da nodded his approval. "Is that all you have to say on it, or will you be able to tell me of some o' the drawbacks the railroad brings along with all that shining opportunity?"

"Drawbacks?" Rosalind felt her brow crease as she considered this. "I suppose 'twill be awkward meeting new people and drawing them into our small community, but we'll all be the better for it, Da. And along wi' the opportunity will come more work for you—the more people, the more demand for your smithy, I know. I wouldna like to see you o'er-worked." She gave him a stern glance.

"Nor would I," he agreed, a grin teasing the corners of his lips. "Though the work and pay will bring benefits as well—medicine for Luke, some of those newfangled laundry contraptions for your mam, delicious treats for us to sample at the general store. . ." He paused until he caught his daughter's eye. "And fine, fancy young men to turn a pretty lass's head."

"Oh Da." Rosalind tried to ignore the heat rising to her cheeks.

"Now, you wouldna be trying to tell your old da the thought hadna crossed your mind?" His teasing made the blush deepen.

"I—" Rosalind's response was mercifully cut short by an interruption.

A tall, burly man stood in the entryway, powerful shoulders blocking out much of the day's light. Even though Rosalind couldn't see his shadowed features, she knew this wasn't one of her neighbors. It seemed as though the railroad—and the changes to come—had arrived.

∞

Ewan blinked, trying to adjust his vision to the dimness inside the smithy. Slowly, he began to take note of the way things were set up. He liked what he saw.

The stone forge stood about forty inches high and forty inches square—large enough for big work and deep enough for the fire to most efficiently use the air from the great leather and wood bellows. He'd seen from the outside of the structure that the forge's chimney boasted a brick hood to carry out smoke and fine ash.

The anvil and slag tub stood close enough at hand to be immediately useful, but with a good, clear working space around them. The front and sides of the forge held racks and rings to hold hammers, tongs, chisels, files, and other tools. This in and of itself was not unusual; the fact that the tools had been put in their proper place immediately after use was. Most blacksmiths heaped their tools on the lip of the forge, having to quickly dig out the needed implement from beneath several of its fellows before continuing work.

Altogether, it was a well-built, well-stocked, and well-kept smithy far above and beyond what he'd expected to find in the depths of the Montana wilderness. Ewan tamped down an unexpected spurt of longing. It had been a long time since he'd worked in an honest smithy; instead lugging a cast-iron patent forge from work site to work site. The only advantage of a patent forge, in Ewan's opinion, was the mobility so highly prized by the railroad.

"Will you be needing anything, now?" The resident blacksmith, a tall man who spoke with the lilt of home, stepped in front of Ewan.

Ewan shook himself free of the unbidden memories before speaking. "Perhaps." He looked around frankly, nodding in admiration, before continuing. "I'm Ewan Gailbraith, and I work wi' Montana Central as their head blacksmith. I step in to help wi' a bit o' the work of farrier and wheelwright." Ewan allowed his syllables to boast of his own Scottish heritage. "We had some men decide to stay back at Benton, and I find myself a bit shorthanded as we make our way toward your town."

At the approval Ewan demonstrated for the smithy's workshop, the man seemed to thaw a bit.

"Now, then, that's a shame." The smith's eyes held a spark of interest. He gave an assessing look in return for Ewan's own appraisal.

"We're miles away from here, and the company will be moving t' make camp in this area any day now." Ewan noted the flicker of unease that crossed the older man's features as he quickly glanced over his shoulder to the corner of the shop.

It didn't take much to see what concerned the man. A lovely lass stood in the corner, her demure pose belied by the avid interest on her face as she listened to their conversation. Within the darkness of the smithy, the colors of her braided hair and lively eyes were shadowed, but there was no hiding her lithesome shape and obvious intelligence. Ewan caught himself before his glance could become rude and resolutely returned his focus to the blacksmith.

"'Tis good to know when we can expect the chaos ahead." The blacksmith thrust his hand toward Ewan. "Arthur MacLean, blacksmith of Saddleback."

"I'd a suspicion." Ewan grinned and returned the man's firm grip as he pumped his hand in welcome.

"This is my daughter, Rosalind." Arthur gestured toward the lass, and she stepped forward with lively grace.

"'Tis grand to meet you, Mr. Gailbraith."

Ewan noted a pair of bright blue eyes framed by a riot of fiery curls. "And you, Miss MacLean." Intensely aware of her father's scrutiny, Ewan greeted her with all the formality a wary papa could require, even as he tried to hide his astonishment. Why had no one seen fit to warn him or the other supervisors that this small, out-of-the-way settlement held at least one pretty, unmarried female? This would greatly complicate things, as the workers saw precious few women along the work trail.

"Now that you've been introduced to Mr. Gailbraith, run home and tell your mam to be expecting a guest for dinner." Arthur MacLean folded his arms across his massive chest. "For now, he and I have some business to discuss."

Ewan refused to give in to the urge to watch Rosalind MacLean leave the smithy. He waited in silence until he could be sure the girl was out of earshot.

"Mr. MacLean," Ewan spoke before her father had the chance, "before we discuss smithy business, I would like to have a word about your daughter." He waited for the man's leery nod. Obviously, Arthur MacLean was a man who liked to have all the facts before he made a judgment. That boded well.

Ewan searched for words to put the matter delicately. Finding none, he plunged forward. "In large cities, men who so choose may find. . . companionship. However, it has been long days since we were at such a place. Lonely, less-than-civilized men will be descending upon your town by the dozens, and I will plainly tell you that I have fears concerning the well-being of your daughter."

"As do I." The man uncrossed his arms and rubbed the back of his neck. "We've another young lass or two in the area as well. The only men they've ever known, they've grown up with. This is a small town filled wi' friends and extended family. None of the girls has any notion of how to handle strange men."

"I'm certain that you are able to protect your own, sir, but I hope that I may trust you t' warn the others of your community t' be diligent about watching o'er the misses." Ewan gave the man a meaningful glance. "I'll give the men a stern talking-to and set up what measures I can."

"I'll be taking your word on that, Mr. Gailbraith."

"Please, call me Ewan."

"Ewan. And you're to call me Arthur." MacLean gave a decisive nod. "Now that we've reached an agreement concerning what I deem the most important matter we could discuss, let's get down to business."

CO

"Mam!" Rosalind rushed into the house. "Da sent me to tell you we'll be having a guest for dinner!"

"A guest?" Luke piped the question first.

"Aye. A Mr. Gailbraith, smith for the railroad. He came to Da's shop just now. He was still there when I left." Rosalind rushed about, tidying the flowers in a cracked mug, polishing a spot on the ornate metalwork of the stove grate, whisking dishes onto the table. "I'll pop in a batch of biscuits from the dough I made this morning. They should be finished in time."

"Such a flurry," Mam marveled as she stirred the stew. "Is there aught you should be telling your mam before this important visitor walks through our door?"

"He's come to offer Da work, I think." Rosalind slid the biscuits into the bread oven. "And he brings news that the railroad men will be here any day!"

"I see."

Rosalind stilled as Grandmam caught her by the wrist and addressed her brother. "Luke, would you please go to the springhouse and fetch some butter and milk?" Once he was out of sight, she turned her sharp gaze upon her granddaughter.

Mam was the one who spoke up. "Rose, there's something we'd been meaning to speak wi' you about. 'Tis a delicate matter, but the time has come upon us sooner than expected." Mam had the same long look Da had worn scant minutes ago.

"Yes, Mam?" Rosalind wondered if it had to do with the same topic. *I hope it doesn't. Lord, I'm not ready to tell her my decision against Brent.*

"From all your talk, I know you are thinking that the railroad will bring many wondrous things—and so it shall. Yet the men who will build the rail line may not be so very wondrous, daughter." Mam paused meaningfully. "You've been sheltered here, surrounded only by friends and family. Now, strangers will begin to arrive in our midst—men who may not be as honorable or God-fearing as those you know. You must hae a care, Rose, not to become enamored wi' them or fall prey to any unscrupulous tricks. Be wary of these strangers, and guard your heart and mind, as well as your physical self. Do you understand me, Rose?"

"Aye, Mam." Rose nodded faintly. "Such dark thoughts about our fellow men though! It puts a caution into my heart to hear you, who I've never heard say a harsh word over any soul, warn me so."

"See that you take heed. From now on, you are not to walk anywhere on your lonesome. You will hae your father, brother, myself, or someone known and trusted by us in your company at all times."

"Mam!" Rosalind couldn't stop the dismayed cry. *I already take Luke wi' me almost everywhere I go, and I'm always at the house or the smithy. The only moments I hae for my own thoughts and dreams seem to be while I'm traveling from one place to another. I didn't think they could clip my wings any further! Oh heavenly Father, I don't see how I'm to bear it!*

"I know 'tis a sacrifice on your part, made necessary through no fault of your own, dear." Mam rubbed her hand down Rosalind's back. "Lovely young women usually learn to take such precautions at a far earlier age. You've had more freedom here than most."

Freedom? I've lived in the same small area my entire life! Until now my whole world consisted solely of Saddleback. Now, at my first opportunity to see anything different, I'm pulled ever closer to the bosom of my family. She paused, trying to see it from their view. *Da warned me. Mam and Grandmam did the same. . . .*

Lord, is this Your way? Parents protect their children, and though I feel I'm no longer a child, I know that they ask these things for what they deem my own good. Your Word tells me to honor my father and mother, and so I shall.

"I'll not go anywhere unescorted, Mam." The very words seemed to constrict her, but Rosalind knew that to struggle against her parents' wishes would only make them tie her still more tightly.

"I'm glad to see you being so sensible, Rose. 'Tis a sign of your maturity. Someday, not too far off, you'll hae a home of your own, and our little chats will be about how to rear your little ones." Mam, stirring the pot once again, had her back turned to Rosalind and so could not notice her daughter's expression of worry. She kept speaking. "If this man is a smith, he'll have a hearty appetite. Best see if you can slip in one more batch of biscuits, dear."

Rosalind smoothed back the irrepressible wisps of curls around her face before pulling the fragrant golden biscuits from the oven.

"Smells wonderful." Da's voice preceded him and Mr. Gailbraith, giving them last-minute warning.

"It does indeed," Mr. Gailbraith agreed, taking off his hat as he entered.

"Ewan Gailbraith, this is Kaitlin, my bonny bride." Da put a loving arm around his wife's waist. "And her mam, Gilda Banning. This is my son, Luke, and you've already met my daughter."

"'Tis pleased I am to make your acquaintance, Mrs. MacLean, Mrs. Banning." He gave a slight bow to Mam and Grandmam. Then, turning in Rosalind's direction, he nodded his head and said, "Good to see you again, Miss MacLean." With a smile, he greeted Luke, pumping his hand heartily.

Rosalind busied herself, refusing to show any undue interest in the man now sitting at their table. The light of day revealed his hair to be deepest ebony, and his smiling eyes glinted green. A strong jaw squared his face and framed a ready smile. All in all, he was even more handsome than she'd supposed. This, then, was the first stranger in their midst.

He doesn't seem dangerous at all. There is something in him, aside from his broad shoulders and arms made thick from hard work, to remind me of Da. Perhaps this is the reason Mam warned me—I do not make a practice of seeing darkness in another. I know nothing of this man yet would be liable to trust him already. His very ease of manner and handsome appearance must make him every bit as dangerous as Mam fears these men may be. Now that I've been warned, I'll be sure to watch myself around him. For all I know, he's a threat.

Chapter 3

Miss Rosalind MacLean, Ewan decided, was a serious threat to his peace of mind. Standing near the window with the sunshine pouring a golden blessing upon her fiery locks and creamy skin, she delighted his eye and dismayed his heart. What red-blooded man among his workers would be able to resist such a siren? The light blue skirts of her dress swayed gently as she brought a basket of perfectly baked biscuits to the table.

No, no, no. Please, Lord, tell me she didn't bake those biscuits. Show me that she burns any morsel of food she tries to prepare. When she speaks, let her be missing a few teeth. At the very least, let her be clumsy enough to knock things over! When she gracefully set the hot biscuits down and gave him a soft smile full of perfect teeth, Ewan despaired. It took him a few moments to regroup with a few more cheery thoughts.

Perhaps she laughs like a donkey, eats with poor manners, or displays signs of becoming a nag. Maybe she isn't usually so clean as today or is content t' shirk her chores. She could have harsh words for others or be one o' those babbling women who causes men to shudder. There are still numerous off-putting faults she may possess to discourage suitors.

One-half hour, one blessing, two bowls of stew, and three lighter-than-air biscuits later, Ewan leaned back. He watched as Rosalind MacLean graciously cleared the table, leaving a bewitching scent of roses and the silvery chime of her laughter as she passed. She'd been respectful to her parents, kind to her brother, welcoming yet reserved toward him, and maintained neither silence nor continuous chatter. Ewan stifled a groan, masking his discomfort by patting his almost-too-full stomach.

"'Twas a delicious dinner, and I'm much obliged t' you all. I haven't eaten a meal so grand in ages."

"Will you be leaving, then, so soon?" Arthur sounded genuinely disappointed.

"I've work to attend to, and I'd not want to be holdin' anyone else from theirs." Ewan eyed what seemed a veritable mountain of dirty dishes.

"You can't make the time for some coffee and a bit o' shortbread, Mr. Gailbraith?" Rosalind's clear, cool voice washed over him.

"I *am* powerful fond of shortbread," he admitted. "And I wanted to ask about something before I left."

"Yes?" Arthur's undivided attention seemed overly intent. "What can we tell you?"

"When and where is Sunday meeting held hereabouts?"

"It moves around," Luke MacLean said.

"Oh?" Ewan smiled at the lad. Had Arthur not already mentioned his son was twelve, Ewan would have estimated the slight lad to have reached only eight or nine years. Perhaps his small stature explained his absence from the smithy. He'd need to gain more height and breadth to do a blacksmith's work. "And where would a man be finding it come this Lord's day?"

"That'd be at the Friemonts' place, just north of us." Kaitlin passed him a mug of strong, hot coffee as Rosalind placed a plate of shortbread on the table.

"We meet at nine o'clock sharp," she advised. "Now, the Albrights hae the largest house hereabouts, but all the same we'll be on benches under God's own Montana sky. If you're late, you won't manage a seat."

" 'Tis glad I am to hear that you're a God-fearing man, Gailbraith." Arthur gave him a hearty clap on the shoulder. "If the railroad brings more like you, I'm thinking we'll hae no need t' regret its arrival."

"I can't speak for the others." Ewan felt the need to be honest. "They're rough men. They all work hard, eat as much as they can, as fast as they can, and seek diversion where they may. Some have been following the railroad for so long they can't be held to the same standard as city folk."

"All men should be held to the standard of God," Rosalind spoke up. "So long as they're honest and treat others as they'd like to be treated, we'll get along fine."

Ewan's heart sank. *How can she be so naive? I just warned her that they're hard men who lack manners and don't care for niceties. There is no way to be plainer wi'out being too blunt for delicate female ears. Lord, please see to it that her parents discuss the matter wi' her!*

"Unfortunately," he began cautiously, "the law of the railroad camp seems t' be more along the lines o' every man for himself. The men hold certain loyalties to their work crews and such, but in the long run, they'll take what they want as long as they think they can get away wi' it."

"We'll all be sure to keep that in mind." Kaitlin sent her daughter a meaningful look, and Ewan rested more easily.

"How came you to be out in the Montana Territory?" He reached for a piece of buttery shortbread that melted almost as soon as he tasted it.

"Ah, now there's a story for those romance novels my daughter has a way of sneaking." Arthur's words made Rosalind blush as pink as the flower for which she was named, but it seemed only Ewan had noticed. "I trekked out here o'er two decades ago wi' naught but a pair of friends and a heavy load of determination."

"Aye. Naught else on account of him leaving his bride behind wi' her folks." Kaitlin's glance held more love than reproof, but the revelation that Rosalind's father had left his wife to travel across America struck a horribly familiar chord. The shortbread turned to sawdust as he tried to force it down his throat, and he slugged some coffee to wash it down. The bitter memories were harder to swallow. As long as he lived, Ewan would never understand how the promise of a new land could call a man away from his loved ones, leaving them alone and unprotected. *That's not fair,* he amended. *Arthur left his wife with her parents, so she wasna alone.*

"Imagine my surprise when I discovered I was wi' child." Kaitlin beamed and hugged her daughter close. "Our own wee lassie came into this world loud and strong. She would hae made you proud, Arthur."

"She already has, Katy-me-love. My only regret 'tis that I could not share the moment." Arthur's smile dimmed. " 'Tis a petty sorrow in the face of so many blessings, but one I will take to my grave regardless."

"Now, Da"—Rosalind left her mother's side to kiss her father's cheek—"you may not hae been there for my first months of life, but your provision and love hae seen me through the years."

"Ah, I love you, Rosey-mine, just as I loved you when I caught my first glimpse of you being held in the arms of your mam, fresh from traveling thousands of miles to my side." He patted his daughter's delicate hand. "The Lord safely delivered two blessings that day."

"How wonderful for you," Ewan choked out, his own loss harsher in the face of their shared love. "So many never make it t' the promised land or to the waiting arms o' their loved ones."

"Too true." Rosalind's eyes held a compassion that seemed to sear his soul. "What of you, Mr. Gailbraith? Where is your family while you follow the railroad to provide for them?"

"I cannot say where my da is, the Lord took my mam o'er a decade ago, and I hae no wife." Ewan, aware of how gruff his voice sounded, summoned a semblance of a grin. " 'Tis good to see that you value what you're so blessed to have."

He shoved away from the table and strode to the door, plunking his hat on his head. "Thank you for your welcome and hospitality, Mrs. Mac-Lean. I've much work to finish this day, so I must be going. I look forward to working wi' you, Arthur. Mrs. Banning, Luke, Miss MacLean." With a tip of his hat, he walked out without a backward glance.

∽

"Mr. Gailbraith seems nice enough," Rosalind ventured as she and her mother cleared the dinner table. Luke had volunteered to go to the Albrights' place and see about arranging an apple bee. The tree branches drooped, heavy with the weight of ripe fruit, but Rosalind felt the weight of unanswered questions.

"Aye." Mam's short agreement made Rosalind relax for but a moment. "*Seems* is just the right word to be using to describe him."

"His manners 'tweren't off-putting, he showed Da proper respect, and he asked after Sunday meeting." Rosalind stopped wiping down the board. "What concerns you?"

"What type of man does not know where his own kith and kin lay their heads?" Mam stoked the fire with more vigor than was strictly necessary. "A good son looks to his father in his twilight years, and that's a fact."

"We cannot know his reasons, Mam. There could be a perfectly good explanation." *Why am I defending the man? I've barely met him, and yet he's the first new man in town. Will Mam be so suspicious of everyone, or is it Mr. Gailbraith in particular?*

"Will you be telling me that a man with an honest explanation would all but bolt from the table?" Mam shook her head. "There's something amiss there."

"Mayhap." Rosalind went silent as she gathered the trenchers and pot to scrub by the brook.

"Be sure to fetch Luke afore you make your way to the stream."

"Yes, Mam." She stopped at the threshold when she thought of

154

another question. "Is there aught else you find to dislike about him, or are we to be wary simply because he's not our neighbor?"

"I've already spoken wi' you, Rose. A young miss cannot be too careful around men, especially strange ones." Mam shooed her out the door, but Rosalind caught the statement made under her breath. "Particularly ones as handsome as Mr. Gailbraith."

Ah, so I'm not the only one to notice his fine looks, Rosalind mused. *And I suppose Mam saw the dark storm in the deep green of his gaze when he spoke on his family. No mother, no wife, no father in his life. 'Twouldn't surprise me a bit if 'twas pure loneliness as made him pull away, after hearing all about our happy family. It takes strength of a different sort than a blacksmith usually needs to live such a solitary life.*

"Rose!" Luke's voice made her look around sharply. Her little brother loped down the path toward her, cutting her search short.

"Hello, Luke. I've come to seek your escort to the stream."

Her brother caught on to her joke and replied with an exaggerated bow. "Of course I will escort you, miss." He took the heavy pot from her hands and walked beside her, the top of his head barely reaching her elbow. At twelve years, he should have come close to his petite sister's shoulder.

Rosalind shoved the worry aside and listened to her brother's uneven breathing, noting a hint of a wheeze creeping into the sound as they passed the hayfields. "How are you?" She tried to keep her tone light.

"Now then, you wouldna be fussing o'er me, would you?" He teased a smile on to her face. "Surely not, on account of how you know of my hay fever. 'Twill ease when we near the brook."

And so it did. The harsh, raspy sound Rosalind so dreaded had faded away by the time they knelt by the cool, clear water. She watched as her brother scooped up some damp sand and scrubbed enthusiastically.

To those who didn't know of the difficulties Luke suffered from hay fever, running, smoke, and cold weather, it would be all too easy to see a healthy young boy. In truth, Luke's weak lungs made it so he could never take up blacksmithing, run with other children, help with the haying, or play overlong in the snow. At those times, his fight to breathe was nothing short of terrifying for those who loved him. And love him she did. Rose would do anything to see her brother happy and healthy.

"Hey!" Luke glowered at her in indignation, his scowl made comical by drops of the water she'd just splashed him with. At her grin, his anger disappeared, replaced by a crafty gleam. "Rose, if you mean to splash someone, you really should try to do a better job."

"Oh, now?" Rosalind shot to her feet, thinking to back away before her brother could retaliate. Too late. She blinked and sputtered after he doused her with an impressive splash. She planted her hands on her hips and glared at her brother. "And who's to say I meant to splash you, Lucas Mathias MacLean?"

"Ah." Luke didn't look at all repentant as he gave his thoughtful reply. "Then I suppose it serves you right for your carelessness."

Rosalind, unable to think of a suitable rejoinder, gave in to her brother's logic. "Why, you may have a point."

"Most usually I do."

"In that case, may I suggest you work on the virtue of humility"— Rosalind gathered the wooden trenchers—"so that others don't think poorly of you when you use your intelligence."

"Yes, Rose." His downcast eyes and soft voice made him the very picture of a humble young man—until he peeked up at his sister. "How was that?"

She couldn't help but laugh. He joined in. Still laughing together, they started for home. Rosalind's merriment dried up when they passed the freshly cut hayfields and Luke's breathing grew raspy once more.

Chapter 4

"This is the patent forge supplied by the Montana Central Railroad Company." Ewan gestured toward the heavy equipment. "Thank you again for letting us set up near your forge. 'Tis a good location for the work we'll be doing in the area, and 'twill simplify things whilst we work together."

"Aye, 'tis no trouble." Arthur circled the "portable" forge, a monstrosity of cast iron. "Grand, the way you don't have to build a new forge every time you pick up and move. Comparatively, this sets up right quick."

"True enough," Ewan agreed. "But no one will convince me that a good stone or brick-built forge 'tisn't the very best to work wi'."

"I'll not even be tryin'." Arthur straightened up. "All the same, 'tis an incredible piece of modern machinery."

"Sure as shootin'." The young man named Johnny cast a fond eye on the forge. "She's a beaut, that's what I say."

"There's work enough to go around." Ewan looked to the makeshift hitching posts where dozens of horses were tied, waiting to be inspected for shoeing.

"Let's get to it." Arthur walked confidently over to a chestnut mare, running his hand over her withers and crooning for a moment before inspecting her hooves, one by one.

While Johnny worked to make the fire hot enough to temper iron, Ewan began with a tall bay. *Not a day too soon.* The gelding's hooves had overgrown the shoe by a long shot and would certainly begin to crack painfully if let go any longer.

He removed the too-smooth shoes one by one, cleaning each hoof before trimming it down. He fetched one of the shoes Johnny had heating over the fire and set it on the hard wall of the hoof, cautiously using hammer and tongs to shape the pliable metal to the best fit possible before nailing it in place.

Ewan worked efficiently, his job made simpler by Johnny's aid. All the same, he remained careful to soothe each horse and keep a wary eye on the back legs as he worked. Many a blacksmith, overconfident in his expertise, had become careless. Such men received a harsh kick to the ribs or skull and were often fortunate to survive at all. Ewan noted approvingly that Arthur showed the same awareness and appropriate caution. Things were going well.

"What say you to a bite of dinner?" Arthur spoke up only after Ewan had finished shoeing a strawberry roan. "My wife and daughter packed enough for all of us."

"Aah!" Johnny straightened out. "I was beginning to fear you'd hear the rumble of my stomach between the blows of the hammer."

They settled in the shade of a large tree whose leaves, in bright shades of orange and deep red, covered the ground more than the branches. Arthur passed around cold bacon sandwiches and apples.

"How long have you worked wi' the railroad, then?" Arthur took a mammoth bite, almost halving his first sandwich.

"Just started a few days back." Johnny swallowed audibly before he reached for his canteen. "Ewan's been training me."

"Is that so?" Arthur eyed Ewan speculatively. "And how long has it been since you enjoyed the comforts of home?"

"Too long." Ewan shifted against the tree trunk, finding a less lumpy resting place for his shoulder. "Years, in fact."

"Years, eh?" Arthur savored a sip of cool water before popping the rest of his sandwich in his mouth and reaching for another. "Were you ever wi' the Northern Pacific Railroad Company?"

"Aye." Ewan frowned as he polished off his first sandwich. "I moved on after I realized the company didn't share my priorities."

"The Last Spike Snub?" Johnny stopped eating to stare at Ewan. "Is that whole mess what made you decide to leave?"

" 'Twas a symptom of the overall problem, aye." Ewan sampled his apple. The crisp fruit gave a tart but sweet flavor. *Tart and sweet, the same combination offered by old memories.*

"I heard tell of that about three years ago, but I don't know the details." Arthur poured some water into his cupped palm and combed it through his hair. "I'd like to hear your version of it."

" 'Twas a raging fiasco, to tell the truth." Ewan closed his eyes, remembering the upswell of righteous anger against the company. "I know that the men had been pushed to finish the tracks before the worst of winter hit. When the two lines were ready to be joined, the owners of the company arranged a grand occasion to announce their success in bringing the railroad as far as the Montana Territory."

"That much I know," Johnny affirmed. "What I don't understand is how a happy event upset so many people."

" 'Twasn't the meeting of the railroads that caused problems," Ewan clarified. " 'Twas the way the company treated its own guests.

"Several important people, wealthy, powerful, of great renown, were invited to meet at the Helena depot. These particular guests were transported to the site in the finest railroad cars o' the Northern Pacific. Sumptuous dining cars, Pullman sleeping compartments, and more were provided for these favored few.

"The bulk of the guests, however, weren't so fortunate. Dignitaries, people prominent in only the Montana Territory, and large landowners were also invited but left t' find their own transportation. They waited in the cold for the delayed train full of the other guests to arrive. At long last, the ceremony began."

"So they were upset that they weren't given the same treatment." Arthur mulled over his thoughts. "Since they were already in the Montana area, it stands to reason they would need to arrange their own transport."

"Sounds to me like some uppity folks got their noses out of joint over nuthin', if you ask me." Johnny rolled his eyes. "Can't imagine such a fuss over something so minor."

"That wasn't the end of it," Ewan warned before continuing. "Once the event actually began, only those who had traveled on the train cars were allowed inside the pavilion area t' hear the speakers. Everyone else was made to crowd in behind the platform, straining to hear. Even worse, the majority o' the seats inside were empty."

Ewan noted Arthur's darkening frown and nodded. "After the speeches were made and the spike driven in, 'twas time to dine. Everyone expected a grand feast after traveling miles to celebrate the occasion and waiting for hours in the cold. Many had daylong trips home t' look forward to."

"Stands to reason," Arthur proclaimed. "After being treated so poorly, they deserved some reward for their trouble, particularly as invited guests."

"And so they expected." Ewan paused to let that sink in. "The final blow was that only the train passengers, warmly ensconced in the new dining cars, were allowed t' take part in the feast. The multitude of guests—those who had traveled so far to bear witness to this historic occasion, waited patiently through delays, and suffered a grievous slight throughout the ceremonies—were told to go home. Precious few of those guests had even thought t' bring food, and a great many went hungry that day."

"Shameful." Johnny's jaw clenched. "I knew that a lot of people felt like it was a waste of time and that they'd been insulted, but I never knew the exact particulars. I don't read all that much, truth be told."

"Out here the news comes slowly. When we heard about it, there were far fewer details." Arthur turned his level gaze to Ewan. "You were right to sever ties wi' such people. It speaks to the strength of your character."

" 'Twasn't as though I were the only one who left." Ewan shrugged. "And I'm of the opinion that Montana Central hired me more for the strength of my arm." With that, he got to his feet. "Let's get back to work."

∞

"It'll never work." Rosalind flopped down in the barn's fresh, fragrant hayloft. Isaac had walked Marlene over. The two girls had finagled permission to snatch some leisure time, since they saw each other far less often now.

"Sure it will!" Marlene settled in next to her. "It feels as though we've hardly even seen each other in the past fortnight! Both our families have watched us with eagle eyes since the railroad men started lurking around."

"Wi' good reason. Some seem like good men, but others give me an uneasy feeling," Rosalind admitted. "Besides, it won't last forever. The railroad will hae to keep steaming along eventually."

"Do you really want it to take all the eligible young men away with it?" Marlene sat up straight. "Our very first opportunity to make new friends and meet men who aren't our neighbors, and it's all but snatched from us!"

"I'm not going to do it." Rosalind sifted a few smaller pieces of hay between her fingers. "I won't say I'm going to meet wi' you while you say you'll meet wi' me and we both hie off to find adventure. No matter how you try to justify it, 'tis dishonest and unsafe."

"You're right. Besides," Marlene huffed as she settled back into the hay, "we'd be found out before long, even if I could actually tell an untruth like it was nothing."

"If nothing worse happened," Rosalind reminded her best friend, glad to see her letting go of the rash idea. Usually they saw eye to eye despite their seven-year age difference, but occasionally, Marlene's youthful exuberance got the better of her. "Although, I've had a few thoughts of my own. . . ."

"Do tell!"

"There is one way I can think of that will allow us to be useful, see each other regularly, and spend a bit of time with the railroad men in a protected setting." Rosalind paused until her friend nudged her arm.

"Out with it, Rose. You can't keep me waiting up here forever, and we need to work out the entire plan!"

"Our fathers wouldn't argue if we took in laundry and mending to earn some money. We're of the age where we'll be setting up our own homes soon." Rosalind shared a conspiratorial glance with Marlene. "Or if that idea doesn't tickle your fancy, I should think we could talk a few of our family men into making some rough picnic tables for us to run an outdoor café. We could use the summer oven and an open fire to make home-cooked meals for all those bachelors."

"That," Marlene sighed, "is surely the most brilliant thing I've ever heard you say, Rosalind MacLean. No one could possibly object to such a worthwhile—and profitable—endeavor!"

"And I prefer almost any chore over laundry," Rosalind added.

"Me, too. I love the feel of clean clothes and sheets, but it's such monotonous, long, hot work, no matter what the season. Soap making is almost as bad." Marlene grimaced, then seemed to realize she'd gotten away from the important topic. "We'll have to convince our parents that we'll finish our own chores. How do we manage that?"

"We'll still milk the cows, gather the eggs, and help wi' breakfast in the morning. If we suggest that everyone eat the dinner we make, our mothers won't have to make any." Rosalind spoke the thoughts aloud as they came into her head. "We'll still help wi' supper and do our sewing in the evenings at the hearth. I suppose that leaves doing the weekly laundry on Saturday as the big problem. We could close down that day and the Lord's day—and only run the outdoor diner five days a week."

"Five days a week sounds good to me." Marlene gave a sly smile. "The men we're interested in will come to Sunday meeting anyway."

"Exactly." Rosalind let Marlene think she was simply bored and boy-crazy. *No one needs to know that I'll be saving the money I earn so I can travel on that railroad someday.*

"Let's go talk to Aunt Kaitlin now!" Marlene scrambled down the ladder in record time, looking up at Rosalind expectantly.

"You can't seem overly excited," Rosalind cautioned as she descended the ladder. "If you're too eager, they'll think it a whim and shut us down before we even open. We hae to present it in just the right way— thoughtfully and reasonably. Show them we're aware of the responsibility we'll be taking on and we're ready for it."

"When did you get so wise, Rose?" Marlene smiled and linked arms with her. "First, we convince your mother, then my mother. With them on our side, our fathers will surely consent!"

"That's the plan." Rosalind smoothed her hair back. "Men are the heads of the household, but women are the hearts, and every sensible person on earth knows which of the two is stronger."

Chapter 5

"Hae they gone daft?" Ewan rubbed his eyes but found no relief. "Do you see that? Tables and benches they've set up o'er near a summer kitchen?"

"I see it." Johnny didn't sound as though he disliked the sight at all.

"They're not planning on selling dinner. Surely they know better." Ewan thumped a moonstruck Johnny on the upper arm. Johnny's eyes still followed the little blond's every movement.

"I'm afraid not." Arthur's voice, heavy with misgiving, sounded behind them.

"I aim to be first in line," Johnny planned aloud, receiving glares for his enthusiastic support of the womenfolk.

"How did this come t' be?" Ewan struggled to maintain a calm demeanor. *Did I not speak wi' the man scarce three days past about keepin' the townswomen clear o' the workmen? This'll set the cats about the pigeons before I can so much as blink!*

" 'Tis the honest truth, I'm not all too certain." Arthur's brow furrowed in puzzlement. "I came home to find my favorite meal on the table, and Rosey talking about how she wanted to contribute to the growth of the community, and my sweet Kaitlin sayin' as how 'twas a good opportunity for the girls to learn the value of hard work in a business setting."

"And you said 'twas a foolish idea?" Ewan felt a sort of sinking in the region of his stomach at the older man's sheepish look.

"I said I'd hae to think on the matter, and the next thing I knew, Kaitlin left the table and came back with a fresh rhubarb pie and the sweetest smile you ever did see." He gave a rueful grin. "The next thing I know, I'm making benches."

"Good man," Johnny approved over Ewan's groan. "If I could say so, sir, I think you made a very wise choice. Excellent."

"We'll see." Ewan tried to think positively. *Lord, is there any possibility You could make the men so distracted by good, homemade food that they'll ignore any other. . .attractions?* He glanced over to where Rosalind and— what was her name? Arleen?—spoke animatedly, creamy cheeks flushed with excitement and effort.

Lord, I can see I'm coming to the right place for help. 'Tis gonna take nothing short of a miracle.

Refusing to dwell on it, Ewan worked so single-mindedly that the morning all but flew by. He'd just set down a pair of tongs when Johnny yanked his arm and practically dragged him over to the table nearest the makeshift kitchen. Left without a choice, Ewan plunked down.

The rich, hickory smell of that pot of pork and beans doesn't tempt me in the slightest. Those steaming trays of sweet golden cornbread aren't enticing in the least. I'm here only because 'twould be rude to leave.

Ewan kept a litany of protective statements running through his mind, trying to convince himself that he wasn't pleased as punch to be the first man sitting at the table, with Rosalind smiling at him and ladling out a hearty serving of beans.

"Smells wonderful," he praised. "Such a clever idea to set up an outdoor diner where you'll have customers in droves." *Fool. And to think, I thought less of Arthur for giving his blessing. At least the man had a wife and daughter trying to convince him, and he made it all the way to dessert! I haven't even taken my first bite.*

Determined to stop himself before he said anything else, Ewan filled his mouth with pork and beans. *Mmm. Meaty, filling, slightly sweet, and perfectly cooked.* He closed his eyes and took another bite before he realized Rosalind and the other girl were watching him and Johnny expectantly.

"Good," Johnny grunted, making short work of his bowl and slathering a piece of cornbread with butter. "Best thing I've tasted in months."

The girls' faces lit up at the verdict before they turned to hear Ewan's opinion.

"Best pork 'n' beans I've ever had," he admitted. Rosalind practically beamed at his compliment, and Ewan accepted the truth. When Rosalind MacLean set her mind to something, whether it be her father's permission, a thriving business, or his own grudging approval, she found a way to get it. If he wasn't so busy savoring his piece of cornbread, Ewan just might have to think about how disturbing that was. He took a second piece, just for good measure.

"Well then, I think we're ready to open." With that, the blond girl rang the dinner bell loud and clear. Hungry workers came sniffing around in hopes of some good food. They were delighted to find it in plentiful supply. Word spread quickly, and soon the benches at the table creaked with the weight of satisfied customers.

Ewan's good mood evaporated as he took stock of the hungry eyes following the girls' progress around the tables. A few watched the saucy sway of Rosalind's skirt with more interest than they showed the food she placed before them. The only thing that helped Ewan's uneasiness was the knowledge that the girls' fathers were keeping close guard on the situation.

When the men finished clearing every morsel, they exited en masse, leaving soiled tables full of dirty dishes and cornbread crumbs in their wake. Even the girls' families left without offering to pitch in. Ewan frowned to see the amount of work the girls had before them. They looked anything but upset.

"We did it!" The girls chorused as they hugged.

"We might even need to make more tomorrow, just in case the men tell a few of their friends," Rosalind added.

"Word will spread," Johnny broke in. "Tomorrow will be a mad rush to get a spot at one of your tables. You'll be turning customers away in droves before you know it."

"It'd be a good idea to have your fathers and brothers—men you trust—overseeing a table each to make sure no fights break out." *If you can't beat 'em, join 'em.* "Things could get ugly if you're not careful."

"We hadn't thought of that." The blond—Marlene, Johnny had told him—showed signs of worry on her pretty young face.

"Dustin, Da, Isaac. . . I don't think Brent is formidable enough to control a group of grown men, and Luke certainly can't. That's only three, and we have five tables." Rosalind bit her lower lip. She looked so delicate. Ewan knew he was sunk when she turned her brilliant blue eyes toward him with a speculative gleam. "Would you and Johnny consider helping us out in return for your dinner five times a week?"

"Absolutely!" Johnny grinned at Marlene. "Anything we can do to help, you just let us know. We'll take care of it."

"I'd be glad to pitch in." Ewan looked down at Rosalind. "And I'd still be more than willing to pay for your cooking. 'Tis worth far more than the asking price as is."

"You'll not pay for a meal at these tables, Mr. Gailbraith," Rosalind declared, unknowingly giving him a reminder that he had no right to be thinking of her as "Rosalind." She was Miss MacLean to him, and that was how things should be.

"I'll not argue the point, Miss MacLean." He gave her a polite smile. "At the moment, my stomach is far too full for me to gainsay you."

"Perfect." She clasped her hands together and turned to her friend. "Marlene, we did it. Everything worked out!"

As Ewan and Johnny walked back toward the forge, the afternoon's work stretching ahead of them, Ewan couldn't hold back one last doubt. *We'll see what happens tomorrow.*

◌

"I never thought I'd see the day when I saw the use of your mother's o'erpacking, Marlene." Rosalind set aside another clean plate. "Wi'out all these dishes, we'd be in a pickle."

"Be sure you tell her that last part." Marlene swished another one through the clean water. "It'll make her feel even better about helping convince father to agree to this venture."

"I did fear Da might take back his agreement when he saw that bunch of hungry men swarming all around our new benches." Rosalind massaged the small of her back for a leisurely moment before returning to the task at hand. "Praise the Lord all went well today. Had the slightest thing gone wrong, that would hae been the end of it."

"Well, it's only the beginning"—Marlene scrubbed a particularly stubborn splotch of dried food—"which means we have plans to make and supplies to purchase before long."

"Aye. We should start by deciding what we'll be cooking for the rest of the week." Rosalind paused to consider what would be simplest to make in vast quantities. "Maybe shepherd's pie?"

"Agreed. Why don't we make it a policy to have some kind of soup or stew as the main dish every other day?" Marlene pushed back a few straggling locks of her golden hair. "With enough variety, the men won't complain. It's the simplest thing to make for so many. . .and hearty enough for working men."

"Let me think a moment." Rosalind ticked off types of stew and soup. "There's Irish, corn, and beef stew, and potato, parsnip, and split pea soup. . . . If we add a pork bone to Scotch broth, that will serve.

Along wi' pork 'n' beans, Welsh rarebit, and biscuits with gravy, we'll hae enough simple recipes to see us through."

"Exactly." Marlene rubbed her hands together in anticipation. "We'll need to stock up on all the vegetables we can buy and see about having the men slaughter another hog to keep us in provisions. We'll need cornmeal for johnnycake, flour for biscuits and bread. . . . How soon do you think we can persuade one of the menfolk to take us to the general store?"

"Soon, I hope, though we've already asked for their help at the tables every dinner. 'Tis glad I am to have enlisted the aid of Mr. Gailbraith and his friend. They'll help smooth things along."

"Johnny," Marlene murmured absently, dreamily swirling her finger in the sandy pebbles lining the brook.

"What?" Rosalind turned a gimlet eye on her friend. "When did you become familiar enough wi' the man to call him by his Christian name? Surely you hae not given him leave to address you so."

"I should say not." Marlene snapped back to attention. "He calls me Miss Friemont as is right and proper, but he invited me to call him Johnny. I haven't done so to his face," she added hastily at the warning glint in Rosalind's eyes.

"See that you don't. Mam says a young miss can't be too careful around strange men, no matter how affable they appear. Using each others' first name signifies a familiarity inappropriate between the two of you." Her warning delivered, Rosalind sank back on her heels and admitted, "Though I've had to remind myself of the same thing when I think on Mr. Gailbraith."

"Ooh!" Marlene squealed and abandoned the dishes altogether. "I knew it. I just *knew* it! You haven't so much as cast an interested glance at any other railroad worker."

"That's simply untrue." Rosalind grinned. "I gave that one man an interested glance when he claimed he owned the entire railroad."

"That's not the type of interest I'm meaning, and you know it, Rose." Marlene shook her head. "I meant the kind of interest that makes a woman's eyes widen and her knees go weak."

"Sounds to me as though such a hapless woman wouldn't withstand a terrible fright."

"You know what I mean." Marlene shot her friend an exasperated glance. "The type of feeling that makes you want to call Mr. Gailbraith by his first name."

"Rubbish." Rosalind waved the notion aside. " 'Tis only that 'Ewan' seems to suit him far better than his surname."

"And you're in a position to know such things since when? Best come out with it, Rose. You've seen the handsome blacksmith quite often since he began working near your father. Don't pretend you haven't looked forward to seeing him around and perhaps exchanging a friendly greeting."

"I—" The intended denial stuck fast in Rose's throat. *If I were to be honest, I do look forward to Ewan's—Mr. Gailbrath's—warm smile and cheery wave.* Could his resemblance to Da while working over the forge be the only reason, or had a different sort of fondness crept into her heart over the past week?

"Aha!"

Rosalind realized her awkward pause had not escaped her friend's notice.

"I thought as much," Marlene crowed, sobering quickly when Luke popped into sight. "Luke's coming." She welcomed Luke brightly. "Come to lend a hand, have you? Well, we've plenty enough dishes to tote back and pack inside the crates." She leaned back toward Rosalind to give a whisper. "Don't think that this conversation is over, Rose!"

I was afraid of that.

Chapter 6

E wan strove mightily to attend to his work, focusing on the iron he'd heated to a glowing red and now manipulated into the proper shape. Trouble was, he couldn't help but notice Rosalind MacLean, along with Luke and their blond friend whom Johnny seemed to have taken a shine to, riding past his forge in a buckboard and then heading into the small mercantile.

'Tis early in the morning. You've no call to be letting your mind wander from your work, Ewan Gailbraith. He sternly forced himself to concentrate on the task at hand and finished reshaping the implement before cooling it in the tempering bath.

A fine job, if I do say so myself. He gave a mighty stretch and glanced toward the general store. *'Tis no quick trip for a peppermint whim. The lasses hae been in there a goodly amount of time. Perhaps they're browsing as women are apt to do.*

He looked to his next task. 'Twould take the better part of the morning to repair the broken wheel. Montana Central needed an official wheelwright to repair the wagons that carried loads of supplies away from the train cars and to the more remote areas where workers cleared the land and made ways through forest and rock. As it was, the work fell on his shoulders. He found it useful to know many skills, but he'd learned an unpleasant truth. The more kinds of work a railroad man was able to do, the more he'd be called upon to do. Whether he'd been hired on to do the task wasn't a big part of the equation.

Learning to do every scrap of work possible was how I helped support Mam after Da came to America. Any trade that involved working wi' iron, I turned a hand to.

"Ewan?" Johnny's hesitant tone caught Ewan's attention at once. Blacksmithing was good, honest work, but a simple mistake could cost a man dearly.

"Aye?" He quickly surveyed his new friend and found nothing visibly wrong. The tension in his shoulders eased.

"I'm finished with this bit." The younger man gestured toward the whorls of steam rising from the tempering bath as it cooled the heated metal within.

"Good." Ewan bit back a grin as Johnny cast a furtive glance toward the general store down the road. It appeared he wasn't the only one who'd noticed the ladies' destination this morning.

"And it occurred to me that I could use"—Johnny's brow furrowed—"an. . .er. . .well, this place could certainly use a few. . ."

"A few. . .what?" Ewan crossed his arms over his chest, delighting in his friend's awkward ploy to see the girls in the shop.

"Pounds of fresh-ground coffee!" His triumphant pronouncement made him nod sagely. "You know, to keep up our strength throughout the day. Nothin' like a pot of hot, strong coffee."

"Like this one?" Ewan hefted the pot keeping warm by the forge and made a show of peering around. "Seems as though we've a goodly enough supply to see us through the week." He put down the pot and nudged a sack with the toe of his leather boot.

"Oh." Johnny's face fell. "Right."

"Although"—Ewan decided to finally take pity on the poor fellow and give his consent—"it seems to me that you can never have too much coffee on hand. We might well invite Arthur over for a mug or two."

"Only neighborly!" Johnny untied his heavy, soot-stained leather apron and had it over his head in record time.

"I could do wi' a bit of a break, myself," Ewan admitted, pulling off his thick work gloves. *And seeing some of the pretty things on display at the store would be a welcome change.*

Together, the pair made their way to the general store.

"Good placement they've set up," Johnny noted. "Smithy's in the middle of the village, and the store's nearby, but far enough away not to catch most of the ash."

"Wi' the railroad, this place will flourish into a thriving city before too long." Ewan shrugged off a vague discomfort at the notion. This place—with its endless skies, fresh air, mountains full of good pine, and tight-knit community—wouldn't maintain all its current charm in the face of progress. The thought saddened him, even as he told himself the railroad would ensure the survival of Saddleback.

"I hope it doesn't change too much," Johnny said, unwittingly echoing Ewan's own thoughts. "I'd hate to see the place turned into one of those crowded, gritty modern cities I've seen too many of."

Ewan gave a terse nod in reply as they stepped through the mercantile doors. A welcoming coolness settled around him as he made his way further into the well-insulated shop, wending his way past farming implements, seeds, buckets, sacks, rope, and various examples of leatherwork.

"Here we go." Johnny stopped in front of the large grinder but kept his head turned toward the back counter.

"Mr. Mathers!" The girl called Marlene greeted Johnny with a charming smile before giving Ewan a sedate nod. He didn't miss the way she nudged Rosalind with her elbow while doing so.

"Mr. Gailbraith." Rosalind's acknowledgement, while friendly, bore a hint more reserve than that of her friend's.

"Miss MacLean. Miss Friemont." He took stock of the mound of merchandise dominating the counter. "I'd be happy to lend a hand."

"Thank you." Her smile deepened, and a tiny dimple flittered in her right cheek. She got prettier every day.

"Welcome," Johnny jumped in. "We wouldn't let you little ladies haul a load this big."

"I'm glad to say we won't be carrying it farther than the wagon outside," Rosalind smiled. "Though 'twas such a lovely day for a walk, we gave a thought to leaving it behind."

"Although, it is an awful lot of things, isn't it? Somehow it seems heavier when it's right in front of you than when you just write it down on a list." Miss Friemont pressed a hand to her heart. "Your help would be greatly appreciated. We remembered a few things not on our list once we got here."

"Must hae been quite a list." Ewan raised an eyebrow.

"Indeed." Rosalind pulled a piece of paper, filled with handwriting, out of her sleeve and squinted to read the tiny script. "Though I think we've all the supplies we could possibly need for the diner. Except for the vegetables." She turned to the shopkeeper. "We'll be needing to take a look at your carrots, parsnips, onions, and potatoes before we tally it all up." She headed for the large crates holding the produce.

Johnny's smile, if possible, grew wider as he dug his elbow into Ewan's ribs. "Looks like we can count on delicious dinners for the rest of the week, at the very least! I hope they make mashed potatoes—they're my favorite." He whispered this last.

"We'll be sure to consider that, Mr. Mathers." Rosalind's promise proved Johnny's whisper had carried a bit too far.

"Of course," Miss Friemont agreed with a twinkle in her eye. "After all, we want to keep our favorite customers happy."

∽

Rosalind sucked in a shocked gasp at Marlene's blatant flirtation with the two railroad blacksmiths. Such forwardness! And yet, her disapproval was tinged with another, darker emotion she recognized as envy. *How can she be so at ease around these men?*

She relaxed when she saw a hint of rebuke in Ewan's—Mr. Gailbraith's—eyes. *So 'tis not just that I'm socially awkward. Such saucy comments are too volatile for even Mr. Gailbraith.*

"We want to make sure our cooking keeps bringing patrons to the outdoor diner of course." Rosalind diffused the tension Marlene remained oblivious to. "And we especially appreciate your willingness to try the dishes before we open every afternoon."

"Not as much as we appreciate your fine cooking." Ewan's—Mr. Gailbraith's—smile gave a sense of warm sincerity, and Rosalind could tell he knew exactly what she'd been trying to do when she spoke up.

To cover her sudden awkwardness, she turned her attention back to her long list. "Mr. Acton, if you'd let me know what we've collected while I check it off my list, 'twould greatly ease my mind."

"Of course," Mr. Acton agreed as he added bushels of vegetables to the order. "Vegetables, eggs, flour, cornmeal, sugar, brown sugar, baking soda, molasses, beans, a wheel of cheese, vanilla extract, cinnamon, nutmeg, salt, pepper, and coffee. Is there anything left on your list, Miss MacLean?"

"Wait a moment. . . ." She looked at all the crossed-off items one last time. "Salt pork." Rosalind glanced up to find the railroad men both looking as though the very mention of that much food caused a corresponding emptiness in their stomachs.

"If I may ask, Miss MacLean," the blacksmith ventured, "what are you planning on for today's dinner?"

"You'll hae to wait and see, Mr. Gailbraith." Rosalind shifted closer to the counter. "Though, if you had a request, what would it be?"

"After the pork 'n' beans and shepherd's pie, I'd gladly tuck into any dish you set before me." His smile reached up to brighten his green eyes.

"Though I must admit I bear a certain fondness for Irish stew."

"As do I, Mr. Gailbraith." She watched as the shopkeeper tallied their order.

"Seems we have a lot in common." His voice lowered so only she could hear, and the deep rumble sent a thrill down her spine. "Scottish heritage, smithing families, and now favorite dishes."

"Here you are." Mr. Acton claimed her attention as she completed the transaction.

"Luke!" She called him away from the corner where he'd been admiring a few fancy toys. "We're ready to get going."

"Then let's head off." Ewan shouldered the heaviest load with manful ease. "For a man never knows what may lie ahead."

Is it my imagination, or was he looking at me as he said that? A giddy little bubble filled her heart at the idea, only to swiftly deflate as she remembered her mother's words—a woman could never be too careful with a strange man. *What lies ahead could be dangerous.*

That sobering thought cast a cloud over the beautiful day.

Lord, You hae written that You love a cheerful giver, and Ewan lends a hand without thinking about it. How can I meet his selfless generosity wi' suspicion? Return distrust for help so freely given? And yet, Your Word tells that we are to seek wise counsel. How to behave around a man so strong and good-natured as Ewan, 'tis certainly beyond my own experience. If 'tis possible to join caution wi' caring, 'tis what I must do, though I cannot see how the two align. I've not the time to dwell upon the matter just now, but 'twill be in my thoughts. I ask for the wisdom to see and follow Your will.

"Oh!" Marlene's gasp caused Rosalind's gaze to follow hers. The modest buckboard, loaded down with their many purchases, was filled to bursting. Even the narrow bench up front for the driver held one of the crates of vegetables.

" 'Tis a small matter," Rosalind assured her. "Luke may drive it ahead, and we'll follow on foot."

"And what of dinner? We haven't the time to walk for a half hour before unloading the wagon and beginning." Marlene's voice came out low and rapid. "More time has passed while we were in the store than we planned for."

"Ewan and I are glad to come along," Mr. Mathers pronounced loudly, his eyes fastened on Marlene's upset expression. "We'll unload everything."

"Thank you!" Marlene seemed all but ready to hug the man, and Rosalind swiftly linked arms with her to avoid that catastrophe.

Luke drove the buckboard back to the outdoor oven that was the hub of the diner, and the other four followed more slowly on foot.

"Oof!" Marlene suddenly lurched forward, dragging Rosalind away from her thoughts and toward the hard-packed dirt.

Rosalind jerked her arm back, attempting to compensate for Marlene's lack of balance. The maneuver was successful, and neither of them landed facedown in the dirt, though Marlene seemed to feel the incident to have been very traumatic.

"I tripped over a root, just there!" Marlene pointed to a bare, even patch of earth, and Rosalind's eyes narrowed in suspicion. Marlene must have noticed, because she hastily swayed the tiniest bit to grasp hold of Mr. Mathers's arm. "Perhaps it was a rock that moved. Oh, I think I've turned my ankle." Her light lashes fluttered as though valiantly holding back tears, and Rosalind immediately regretted her uncharitable thoughts.

"Are you all right, Marlene?" She tried to loop Marlene's arm over her shoulders, but her friend pulled away and clung to Mr. Mathers instead.

"I'll be fine," she asserted a bit breathlessly as the young man slipped a supporting arm around her waist. "Yes, that's. . .better."

"I'd be glad to help you walk the rest of the way, miss." His offer couldn't have come any quicker, and he seemed loathe to let go of Marlene anytime soon—a fact Rosalind noted warily.

"How gallant of you," Marlene breathed, leaning gracefully against his stalwart support. "I'll be fine in no time at all. Usually I'm far more nimble." She cast her gaze to Rosalind, obviously expecting her friend to back her up on this.

"Yes," Rosalind agreed drily. "By far."

"Well, if Miss Friemont is up to it"—Ewan's voice had the vaguest hint of doubt—"we'd best continue. Miss MacLean?" He politely proffered his own arm to Rosalind, as was proper.

"I think 'twould be best." She tucked her hand in the crook of his arm, feeling the warmth of his strong muscles through the thin cambric of his everyday shirt. Suddenly feeling slightly out of breath herself, she gulped in the fresh mountain air in what came out as a sort of heavy sigh.

"Don't fret," Ewan patted her hand comfortingly. "Your wee little friend will be fine, of that I bear no doubt at all."

"Of course," she murmured, looking at the couple slowly making their way before them. Although Marlene leaned against the support Mr. Mathers so readily offered, her step showed no sign of an injured ankle.

Rosalind bit back a comment.

"To my way of thinking," Ewan said, his deep rumble soothing her ire, " 'tis simply an example of something I was taught long ago."

"Oh?" Rosalind quirked a brow, wondering what wisdom the handsome blacksmith would share with her. *A man like Ewan Gailbraith must know all sorts of things I wouldn't.*

"Sometimes," he bent his head closer to hers and spoke with a conspiratorial grin, "when it serves a purpose, people seem worse than they truly are."

Chapter 7

E wan hefted a bag of flour into the old smokehouse the girls were using for storage. When he returned for another load, he was caught by the sight of Rosalind as she untied her sunbonnet and drew it off.

A soft breeze tickled the springy tendrils around her face while her hair caught the sun's light and burned with a brightness bold enough to warm a man's heart. He quelled a surge of disappointment when she dutifully donned the bonnet once more to conceal her crowning glory and protect her fair skin.

Lord, You truly hae made everything beautiful in Your time. 'Tis struck I am to see the loving stroke of Your hand around me, and the bearer of Your stamp so unaware o' it. Beauty is one thing; beauty wi'out the stain of pride gives even more pleasure.

"Are you certain?" Johnny, eagerly bringing Miss Friemont some cool water, sounded genuinely anxious. *Young pup.*

"Certainly." Marlene pointed the dainty toe of her boot downward, then flexed it upward, causing the frills of her petticoat to froth over her ankle in a flagrantly feminine display. It worked, too. Johnny watched the motion, transfixed.

Ewan rolled his eyes. *If I didn't know any better, I'd say the minx had "tripped" on purpose to garner more attention. But surely no woman would use such an obvious ploy. . . .* He saw her laughing charmingly at something or other a besotted Johnny had said. The girl certainly had her eye on the lad. *Would she?*

He carried more sacks to the converted smokehouse, after taking a moment to clear his head. When he got back to the unloading Ewan practically bumped into Rosalind as she came out of the tiny structure. Ewan quickly stepped back, getting a firmer grip on the goods he held lest they topple upon her pretty little head.

She gave him a ghost of a smile and sidestepped, obviously concerned with getting the work done in time to begin dinner. The tip of her braid bounced against the slim curve of her back as she walked the few steps to the wagon and reached up.

Now, there is a woman who wouldn't need to resort to petty wiles to catch a man's attention. She carries herself like a lady.

And she was carrying another sack back toward him. While she'd continued working, he'd stood and stared like an imbecile. Ewan swiftly deposited his load and strode past her to gather the last of the items. He cast an irritated glance to where Johnny still paid court to no-longer-maimed-but-not-helping Marlene.

"Oh no." He felt Rosalind's small hand press against his forearm where he'd rolled up his sleeves at the same time he heard her sweet, clear voice.

He almost dropped what he carried. "What's wrong?" He craned his neck to look down at her upturned face. Ewan watched in fascination as her cornflower blue eyes widened and her mouth opened in surprise at the unexpected intimacy of the moment before she yanked her hand back as though the brief contact had scalded her as it had him.

"I—I put those things aside so we could use them today." She looked toward the summer kitchen. "They need to go over there."

"Fine, then." He smiled, then looked at the bounty in his arms as his stride covered the short distance. Among other things, he held a modest crate filled with potatoes, onions, and carrots. A small sack held some precious spices, most likely salt and pepper. He cast a glance over his shoulder to see her exiting the old smokehouse with a piece of meat. He squinted to see it—lamb.

She's making Irish stew, just like I asked. The realization flooded him with unexpected warmth. *Pretty Rosalind wi' the dancing braid and twinkling eyes wants to show her thanks for our help, and she found a circumspect way to do it. Aye, the lass is every inch a lady.*

Yes, he'd do well to keep a watch over Rosalind MacLean—and it wouldn't be a hardship to do so.

∞

"Don't worry!" Rosalind turned Marlene away from where she stood staring at what seemed an impossible apple harvest.

Bushel upon bushel of the fruits filled the barn, emptied of its usual occupants to make room for this new purpose. Tart, yellow-green apples sat apart from their sweeter, deep red cousins, the bounty almost overwhelming.

All right, Lord. Truth be told, 'tis overwhelming. Every year the apple trees Delana brought here yield more and more fruit. Give us hearts grateful for Your provision, rather than thoughts of aching shoulders.

"This will take days!" Marlene frowned. "We'll have to shut down the diner."

With a pang, Rosalind realized she wouldn't see Ewan—*Mr. Gailbraith, Mr. Gailbraith, Mr. Gailbraith,* she reminded herself harshly—until Sunday meeting. Which was, if she recalled rightly, to be held in this very barn.

Can we finish the work wi' only Mam, Delana, Marlene, Grandmam, Mrs. Parkinson, and the Twadley girls? She stared at the abundance of apples once more. *Surely not. And the men work at harvesting this time of year. 'Twas good of them to help pick the apples!* Rosalind sighed.

"I've an idea." Marlene whirled around giddily. "I'd warrant we could get the men to do it."

"Marlene! Your father, brother, and uncle hae more than enough to do in the fields. And Da works all the day long, too. We'll not shirk our fair share."

"So serious, Rose!" Marlene giggled. "I meant the men who come to our diner. What if we announced an apple bee? We'll have music and laughter and some supper to make the time go by."

" 'Twould be doable if we were to double whatever we make for dinner." Rosalind thought about it. "And to sweeten the deal, we could promise them apple cobbler wi' dinner later in the week."

"Now you're thinking!" Marlene scanned the open working space in the barn. "We'll bring in the benches for folks to sit on and our tables to hold the food. Mr. Twadley will bring his fiddle, and Luke's a whiz at playing the spoons. Brent would like the chance to show off with his harmonica."

"We'll hae an apple paring contest wi' the prize to be a fresh apple pie the next day." Rosalind thought of how best to make sure the work got done. "The men can take the pared apples to the cider press afterward. If enough men show up for the bee, we can get most of the work done in one evening!"

"Oh," Marlene spoke smugly, "they'll come. Just you wait and see. Tomorrow night, there won't be room enough for all the men who want to help."

The next afternoon, all the women of the town came from miles around to lend a hand. Soon, the wooden tables groaned under loaves of bread, pans of johnnycake, plates of biscuits, crocks of butter, platters of chicken, and two massive pots of Marlene and Rosalind's thick, creamy potato soup.

The diner benches lined the working area, with buckets and crates placed everywhere for the apple peels. Every hog in town would be well fed. Paring knives lay in rows; thick, brown string waited to hold apple slices for drying; and the cider press stood ready a short distance from the barn. Barrels next to heaps of straw were ready to cold-pack the fruit destined for the root cellars.

The men would come straight after the workday, and they'd work by lantern light until eyes drooped. With the barn doors thrown wide open, they'd carefully placed lanterns so as not to risk a fire.

The women took their places by the doors, closest to the waiting apples, as the men trickled in. Rosalind marveled at the difference in how they worked.

The women deftly turned their apples, sliding the paring blade smoothly beneath the skin to slick off the peel in one long rind of curlicues. The men attacked the apples as though whittling, moving the knives in short jerks to send shaved bits of peel flying into the buckets.

"I once heard," one of the Twadley girls confided to Rosalind and Marlene, "that if you peel the whole skin into one strip and toss it behind you, whatever shape the peel falls into on the floor represents the name of the man you'll marry!"

"What fun!" Marlene's hands moved with more cautious determination as she worked, though she kept her gaze fixed firmly on the men entering the barn. When Marlene straightened, her hands going still for the barest moment, Rosalind looked to the doorway.

There, his powerful frame gilded by the lantern light, stood Ewan. His broad shoulders all but blocked the smaller man who stood at his side.

Rosalind felt her breath hitch as Ewan stepped farther inside, his gaze passing over the barn's occupants and coming to rest on her. He dipped his head in acknowledgement before walking over to take a seat next to her father.

Mr. Mathers, much to Marlene's delight, made a beeline toward her.

She none too subtly scooted over to make room for him to plunk down, leaving Rosalind clinging to the edge of the bench.

Discomfited and not eager to examine why, Rosalind put down her knife and the apple she'd just finished paring. She dropped the long peel into the bucket behind her as she left for a drink of water.

Marlene's hastily smothered gasp made her turn around. There, obviously having missed the bucket, sat Rosalind's long apple peel, its curls resolutely shaped into an unmistakable letter *E*.

Chapter 8

F or pity's sake, Johnny." Ewan laid down his hammer as he caught his assistant giving him yet another odd look. "If you hae something to say, come out wi' it already."

"I— Oh, nothing." Johnny turned his back to Ewan.

"We're men. Quit shilly-shallying about and looking at me as though I've grown a second nose or sommat equally interesting. You're twitching more than a horse wi' pesky flies. 'Tis distracting."

"What do you think of Miss MacLean?" The younger man now wore a cautious, crafty expression Ewan found to be even more off-putting than the furtive glances.

"She's a fine lass." Ewan shrugged and said no more. *Pretty as a fiery sunset spreading o'er a blue sky, God-fearing, hardworking, deeply loyal, intelligent, kind. . . The list goes on. I won't be telling any o' that to Johnny though.*

"I see." Johnny sounded more subdued, disappointed even. "It's just that Marlene told me that she—Miss MacLean, that is—she got a sign last night at the apple bee. And—"

"Johnny!" Ewan bit out the name. "You're clucking like a gossipy hen, you know that?" *I don't want to hear about Rosalind getting a love-token from some other man. She deserves better than the fellows I've seen hereabouts, and that's that.*

"Fine." He sounded a bit huffy as he tossed a few last words over his shoulder. "If you don't want to know that she returns your high opinion of her but is too proper to say so. . . ."

Ewan froze as Johnny's voice trailed off, tantalizing him with the thought that Rosalind might have noticed him the way he'd noticed her—the way he'd kept noticing her since the very first time they met.

"Oh?" He struggled to keep his tone neutral as he sought more information, but Johnny gave a shrug and said no more. "And this is leading to what?" he finally prompted more explicitly.

"Surely you don't expect *me* to say anything." Johnny inspected a piece of iron, obviously decided it wasn't ready, and thrust it back into the forge. "I don't want to sound like a. . .what was it?" His brow furrowed as he repeated, "A gossipy hen, right?"

"I may hae been a wee bit hasty," Ewan admitted grudgingly.

"I'm glad to hear you realize that." Johnny, his lips firmly set, refrained from saying anything more. His silence was deafening.

"Johnny!" Ewan roared at long last. "Just tell me whatever 'tis that seemed so important naught but five minutes ago!"

"Marlene is of the opinion that Miss MacLean thinks highly of you." Johnny stretched to get the cricks out of his muscles. "More highly of you than any of the men who've been sniffing around her lately. Marlene reckons her best friend has eyes for you, Ewan. I aimed to see if you returned her interest."

"Aye," Ewan admitted aloud for the first time. "She's a rare woman. But I'd hae no thought of courting her, you see."

"No, I don't see." Johnny gaped at him. "A pretty young lady who cooks like an angel and seems to like you above other men, and you have no thought of seeking her out? You're daft!"

"Now, Johnny—" Ewan stopped his protest before he uttered it. *Maybe he's right. How long hae I been thinking about settling down? And here the Lord brings me to the MacLean doorstep, where beautiful Rosalind is ripe for marriage.* "That may bear thinking on."

"Too right, it does." Johnny picked up his tongs once more. "I've already decided to speak with Marlene's father. Come spring, I'll have enough seed money to start my own spread. And in a year, I'll have a threshold to carry my bride over."

"You don't think you're being a bit hasty?" Ewan chose his words carefully, aware of the strength of Johnny's infatuation.

"I just said we'd wait a year before Marlene and I will wed."

"So you plan to settle down and want to see others do the same, eh?" Ewan couldn't resist teasing his friend just a mite.

"Something like that. You'd make a good neighbor, and Marlene wants to stay close to her friend." Johnny picked up his hammer. "Could work out to be a real good setup."

"Could be."

Ewan mulled over the information for hours, praying for guidance before feeling he had made the right decision. He strode over to Arthur's forge and waited until the older man finished what he was working on before he approached.

"Ewan!" Arthur drew off his gloves and apron, smiling in welcome. "What can I do for you?" He gestured for him to sit.

"You can give me permission to call on your daughter." Ewan figured Arthur was the sort of man who'd appreciate directness.

"I wondered when it would come to that." Arthur rested his heavy hands on his knees and closed his eyes. Even after a short acquaintance with him, Ewan knew him to be praying. He waited, respecting the man's need to seek God's will even as Ewan had before coming.

He's about to ask what my intentions are toward his daughter. Ewan straightened his shoulders and prepared to answer the question asked of would-be suitors by protective papas all the world over. He'd come with a ready answer to that.

"When you look at my Rosey," Arthur spoke slowly, drawing out the question to show its significance, "what do you see?"

Ewan paused to consider the unexpected question. He knew Arthur placed a great deal of importance on his reply, so he weighed his words carefully. There were as many ways to answer as there were things to appreciate about Rosalind herself.

"The first thing I saw was her beauty," he began honestly. " 'Twas why I spoke wi' you regarding her safety." At Arthur's nod of recollection, Ewan kept on. "Now, when I look upon her, I see a woman of warmth and integrity—a woman whose strength of character and generous heart I cannot help but admire. Her dedication to you and the rest of your family speaks well of her raising, and she carries herself as a God-fearing woman. She doesn't shirk from her duties, and I've yet to see her lose patience. In short," Ewan finished, admitting his hopes aloud for the first time, "when I look at your daughter, I see the woman I hope to share my life wi'."

He waited as Arthur thought over his response. *Did I say too little? Too much? Should I not hae mentioned her beauty? No, 'twould hae been dishonest and an obvious omission. Lord, when did feelings for Rosalind change my heart and priorities? Now everything seems to rest on this one conversation.*

"I'm well pleased wi' your answer, Ewan." Arthur gave an approving nod. "You see the beauty of her spirit and her worth beyond a pretty face and strong back. That's more than I can say for many a man hereabouts."

He paused a moment. "You may court my Rosey, provided you agree to a few conditions."

Ewan waited to hear the conditions before he agreed.

"Should she reject your suit, you'll respect her decision. Should she accept it, you'll be treating her wi' the propriety an unmarried lady deserves at all times." Arthur's gaze bore into Ewan fiercely as he laid down his edicts, immovable as a wall of stone. "Her reputation will not be shadowed in any way."

"Done." Ewan reached out to shake his hand, but Arthur stopped him, holding up a cautionary palm before speaking.

"And before you speak wi' my daughter, we'll pray together. 'Tis no small thing, and we'll seek God's blessing afore all else." Arthur's expression turned wistful. "Should you win her heart and hand, it may well be I'll not see my daughter often."

This last thought hit Ewan with the force of a fist to the stomach. *He thinks I'll take her far away. Is that what marriage to her would mean, Lord? Dividing a loving family? I hae sworn never to separate kin—and I will not change my mind on the matter. Guide me, Father, that I not inflict such pain, as I hae suffered, on the family of the woman I hope to make my bride. And what if it comes down to marriage or her family, Lord? I'll not place her in that situation. Your eyes see ways I've no way of finding on my own. Help me trust You to see things through as You will, for the benefit of us both.*

∽

"Look to your hair." Marlene's quick whisper caused Rosalind to glance over her shoulder.

"Why are Da and Ewan coming so soon?" She frowned in puzzlement. "Dinner is not near ready so early." Her breath caught in her throat as the icy hand of fear squeezed her heart in a suffocating grip. "Luke— he's unwell." Rosalind began to untie her apron strings as she hurried toward the approaching men, only to have Marlene snatch the strings and yank her backward.

"Calm yourself!" Marlene shook her head in exasperation. "Why would Mr. Gailbraith be coming with your father to tell you such a thing? And why would your father not be running to seek your aid? They're not coming here to discuss your little brother." She gave Rosalind a knowing look. "They want to talk about you. . .and Mr. Gailbraith."

"Me and. . ." The iciness subsided, replaced by a pooling warmth. Marlene had always known more about these things than she did. "You think he's asked Da to come courting me?"

"Yes. Now duck as though to check the fire, and smooth your hair and pinch your cheeks so you look your best." Marlene rolled her eyes. "You should have guessed it long ago—the way he looks at you as though he'll tear any man apart who so much as casts you a friendly smile. Why do you think his table is always so calm at lunch? He scowls with a possessive gleam. I'm only surprised he didn't speak with you before he sought your father's official approval. Johnny's already talked to me, and we're agreed he'll speak to Father after next meeting."

Rosalind stopped fussing with her hair to stare at her friend. "Johnny spoke wi' you first? 'Tisn't it proper to go to the girl's father afore making any type of declaration at all?"

"No, silly." Marlene shrugged. "The man speaks with the girl, if he has any consideration at all, and then speaks to her father as though it's the first time he dared say anything. It appeases a father's pride and paves the way for family approval."

"But Ewan never said a word to me." Rosalind frowned. *'Tis his fault I'm caught so unaware! He's made this awkward by speaking wi' Da afore giving me so much as an inkling. Hmph. Marlene knows how 'tis done, and obviously Johnny does as well. Why am I to be blindsided in this ridiculous fashion?*

"Marlene, may I borrow Rosalind for a moment?" Da's question sounded ominously formal as he pasted a smile on his face.

"Of course, Mr. MacLean." Marlene turned to the oven.

"Let us go walk to the shade of that tree." Da pointed with one hand as he offered her the crook of his arm.

Rosalind accepted it, trying to avoid Ewan's intense gaze as the three of them walked a distance from where Marlene stood. When they came to a halt, Da squeezed her hand tenderly.

"Rosey-mine, there comes a time when a father looks for his wee lassie and finds instead a lovely young lady. Perhaps she's a lovely young lady who has caught the eye of a bachelor." He gestured for Ewan to come closer. "Ewan hae properly sought my blessing afore coming to call, and I've gladly granted him permission to court you. Provided, that is, you are willing to receive his interest." His grip tightened, as though letting her know he'd enforce her decision either way.

"I see." Gratitude for Da's unconditional support welled within her. *He approves of Ewan, and that's reason enough to accept, even if he didn't hae a ready smile and a kind heart.*

She looked up to see the cautious hope flickering in his sea-green eyes and knew her answer. "I'm willing, Da."

The grin breaking out across Ewan's face urged a smile in return as Da put her hand in Ewan's.

"I'll be leaving you two to speak for a short while, then." He smiled and turned to walk back to where Marlene chopped potatoes. "Just a short while, mind!" he called over his shoulder, then left them in silence.

"Rosalind—" Ewan began. He didn't get far, as Rosalind checked to see if Da was watching, saw he wasn't, and lightly smacked Ewan's hand away. "What—"

"Listen to me, Ewan Gailbraith," she directed as she put her hands on her hips. "I'm willing to hae you pay me court and am flattered as well I should be, but 'tis a wee disgruntled I am, too, and that's a fact."

She shook a finger at his befuddled expression. "Don't look as though you don't ken what I mean. 'Twouldn't hae been overly difficult to give me some forewarning as to your intentions. I do not like to be caught unawares by anything, much less something of such importance." She finished speaking and waited for his reply. He had to understand straight from the start that he shouldn't be making such decisions without at least speaking to her first!

"I like hearing you say my name" was all he said.

"I—Did you not hear what else I said?" Rosalind demanded. " 'Tis vital you understand that I will not hae a husband who makes decisions first and speaks wi' me about them after the fact."

"Aye, Rosalind," he said, rumbling her name as though it were a blessing. "I should hae asked you first so as not to make things awkward for you." He took her hand in his once more, rubbing his thumb along her palm. "I value your thoughts and will seek them often. Does that put your mind at ease?"

No. If anything, my heart is beating fit to burst.

"Aye, that it does." She stepped slightly closer. "And 'tis honored I'll be to hae you come calling on me...Ewan."

Chapter 9

E wan stared at where the heaping mound of corn ears took up even more space than the apples had not too long ago. And folks were pulling up wagonloads outside to replenish the pile as it diminished throughout the night.

"Good evening," he greeted Rosalind as he moved to sit beside her.

"Good evening," she replied. "At least, 'twill be a good night for me, I'm thinking." Her smile held a hint of mischief.

"Because we'll spend it together?" That's what made it a good evening to him, after all—sitting close enough to catch the light, fresh scent of roses her hair always carried.

"No. Well, that, too," she amended when she saw his chagrin. "I aim to beat you in the shucking competition. My two crates will be the first filled, I promise you." Her blue eyes sparkled in lighthearted challenge, needling him to answer it.

"Wi' these wee little hands?" He made a show of holding one of her dainty hands between his two large, rough ones. " 'Twill take you twice as long to do half the work, though 'tis certain I am you'll put forth a grand effort."

Ewan didn't release her hand until she pulled slightly away. Then she surprised him by pressing her soft palm against his calloused one, stretching her fingers as far as they'd go. They both looked at the contrast silently for a moment. His sun-darkened skin and broad digits dwarfed her creamy delicacy.

"Well"—Rosalind's soft voice sounded slightly breathless as she turned her gaze to meet his—"there you hae it. 'Tis plain as the very nose on your face that I'll be the swifter betwixt us." Her hand exerted a slight, warm pressure against his as though to push him into agreement with her misguided boasting.

"Nay." His fingers curled over hers as he shook his head. "There is no arguing wi' what your eyes surely tell you, lass."

"Of course, which is why I'll win." She drew her hand away and lifted her chin. "My hands are small and light, so I'll be able to move more quickly than your large fingers can manage."

"We'll see." Ewan waited for Dustin Friemont to welcome everyone to the corn husking and ask God's blessing on the night's work. He tensed, ready to spring into action as the man officially began the competition.

Ewan dove into the work with determined zeal, scarcely sparing a glance at Rosalind's progress. That brief glance was enough to still his hands for a moment as he watched her swift, confident motions add another shucked ear to her already too-full crate. *How did she do that?*

He redoubled his efforts, loathe to let her best him after he'd bragged so certainly of his victory. Husks flew through the air and littered the floor in front of them as he increased his frantic pace. Ewan froze in disbelief as Rosalind stood up, signaling that her crates were completely filled. She'd not only defeated him in their private challenge, she'd bested absolutely everyone hard at work inside the walls of the barn!

She walked up to Dustin and claimed her prize—a finely sewn quilt decorated with colored scraps fashioned into an intricate pattern of interlocking rings. She exclaimed over it, causing an old woman in the far corner to beam with delight.

"How did you manage that?" he whispered after she sat at his side once more. "Will you share the trick you use?"

"Ewan Gailbraith!" Rosalind scowled at him in mock disappointment. "How could you think I've any sort of trick? 'Tis plain hard work and"—she grinned in victory as she flexed her fingers in a silent display—"skill."

"I see I've underestimated you, Rosalind." He leaned close and whispered so only she could hear his next words. "You can be sure that I'll not be making the same mistake next time."

Her pink blush was all the victory he needed as they set back to work. Ewan's grin only faded when a shadow fell across him and he looked up to find a familiar young man standing before Rosalind, legs splayed, jaw set belligerently. He remembered the slight young fellow as Marlene's older brother but had an inkling he'd be remembering him differently soon.

"Rose," the youth addressed her with maddening informality, and Ewan had to remind himself that they'd probably grown up together, and thus it was an appropriate address. "Why don't you come over and sit with Marlene and myself?" He extended his hand to her, overconfident that she'd take him up on the offer.

"Brent, I'm quite comfortable here." Rosalind spoke kindly but firmly enough that the lad should have accepted her words.

"Rose"—Brent leaned closer and spoke in a low tone that carried plain as day—"you needn't feel obligated to sit near strangers out of a misplaced sense of politeness. Come sit with me and mine, where you belong." *Now.* This last wasn't said aloud, but came across as strongly as if it had been trumpeted.

Ewan got to his feet, unwilling to let the stripling order his Rosalind about or attempt to stake a claim to her affection. He needn't have made the effort. Rosalind fixed Brent with an outraged stare and crossed her arms as a further barrier.

"Brent Friemont, 'tis not your place to decide where I belong. And 'tis angered I am to hear you label me as one of *yours*, as though I were a prize sow displayed at the fair."

Realizing his error too late, Brent stammered an apology.

"I appreciated your kind invitation, Brent"—Rosalind gentled her scowl but kept her tone disapproving—"but when I politely expressed disinterest, you should have behaved like a gentleman and respected my decision rather than try to force your way."

"Yes, Rose." The boy made a swift bow and retreated back to where the rest of his family sat, obviously watching them all with an avid curiosity—and a hint of apprehension as well.

Ewan returned his focus to where it belonged—Rosalind. She looked up at him, half chagrined over the scene, half defying him to question the way she'd handled the issue.

He sat beside her, moving as close as was decent, and gave voice to his opinion. "It seems as though I'm not the only one to underestimate you, Rosalind." He fingered the silken end of her braid to show support. "I'm only glad I'll have the chance to rectify that."

∽

Men. Rosalind viciously ripped off another corn husk and threw it down before reaching for the next one. *Bad enough that Ewan discomfits me so, but to hae Brent saunter up and try to stake a claim as though I hae no say in the matter. . . Ugh. Incredible!*

"Which do you prefer, the apple bee or the corn shucking?" Ewan's question broke through her thoughts as though he knew what she was thinking. He waited patiently for her answer.

"Neither." Rose gave in to the contrary mood. "My favorite gathering is the sugaring-off. 'Tis the most fun and tasty."

"Sugaring-off? I'd the notion 'twas only done in Vermont or such."

"No, we've sugar maples here as well." Rose took a shallow breath. "We don't harvest the sap until February. I suppose the railroad will hae moved on long before that." It was as close as she could come to asking what he planned for the future.

Will he continue to work for the rail lines, and take me wi' him to see all America? Excitement surged at the idea, even as her heart sank. *Could I leave Mam and Da and Luke behind if I knew 'twould be forever?*

Intent upon harvesting some clue from Ewan's answer, she peeked at his face from the corner of her eye. They both continued divesting ears of corn of their husks.

"Aye." The single syllable came out forced, and Rosalind saw a shadow pass over his countenance. He said no more, and she did not press the matter.

Lord, I've always wanted to travel the length and breadth of the nation. All the same, I yearned for that adventure with certain knowledge of everyone here waiting to welcome my return. I always thought to settle nearby when I finally wed. It never occurred to me that the man I marry might hae different ideas. Now 'tis far too soon to press Ewan about the matter, but 'twill have to be addressed sometime. Give me the wisdom to handle my doubts and find peace in the path You place before me.

"Rosalind?" Ewan rose to his feet. "Would you fancy a drink o' water?" He gestured toward the large bucket.

"Aye." She smiled her thanks, relieved to see no sign of the shadow from earlier. He behaved as an attentive suitor should and now 'twas the time to take note of such fine qualities. No sense borrowing trouble, as Da would say.

She reached for another ear and peeled back some of the crisp brown cover. A flash of deep red peeked out, and she covered it immediately.

Oh no! She could feel herself flushing a shade to rival the red corn. *I'll not kiss Ewan in front of the whole town! He'll be back in a moment!*

She looked about for Marlene. Rosalind had passed any red ears to her bolder best friend for years now. But Marlene sat next to Johnny—and Brent—across the way. *Oh bother.*

As Ewan shouldered his way back into view, Rosalind debated what to do. Would she dare slip the red ear into his pile? No. 'Twould still mean sharing their first kiss before everyone she ever knew. As Ewan stopped to say something to a man she didn't recognize, Rosalind dropped the ear and kicked it under the bench behind her skirts.

Ewan gave her an odd look as he handed her a tin of water, and she hastily gulped some to cover her unease. She smiled brightly and patted the bench beside her. Rosalind breathed a tiny sigh of relief as he settled onto the seat and began to share stories from his years working for the railroad.

"Now, I'll not be telling you all these are true, but men in the railroad camps hae been swapping stories for years. Some o' the tales sound reasonable enough to keep telling."

"Do you know any funny stories?" Rosalind asked. "I've heard about the wrecks, and those make me sad."

"Nay." Ewan shook his head. "Those are warnings, not tales to be shared when a man sits beside a pretty lass."

His smile made her flush once again.

"I'll tell you a legend about one spendthrift builder and the clever foreman who outwitted him."

"That sounds good." She straightened. "Let's hear it."

"There was a builder named Mr. Hill, who kept a tight fist around the finances." Ewan's own fist tightened around the hapless ear of corn he'd just finished shucking. "He disapproved mightily of anything that could be seen as at all wasteful. Well, one day he was walking along the tracks, inspecting the work, and he spotted something in the dirt. Sure enough, he'd found a new rail spike lying deserted in the roadbed. Outraged, he stomped off to take the section foreman to task for such carelessness. They didn't have spikes to throw away."

"What a horrible man." Rosalind shuddered. "I'd hate to be that poor foreman, having to answer to that. What happened to him?"

"The quick-thinking foreman saw him coming, spotted the spike, and rushed to meet the builder. He hurries up to the man, stands tall, and says, 'Thank goodness you found that spike, Mr. Hill. I've had three men looking for it for nearly a week!'"

Rosalind burst out laughing, only speaking when she finally caught her breath. "Oh, that's a good one. Should have taught that Mr. Hill a lesson. I'd like to think that really happened."

"Me, too." Ewan chuckled. "Can't you just picture the builder's expression? He probably gaped like a caught fish."

"Most likely," Rosalind agreed. "Tell another one, please! Out here we so rarely hear things like that. We just get news."

"Hmm." Ewan thought for a moment. "I could hae another story or so to coax a smile. 'Tis a grand reward for so little."

"Flatterer." Rosalind waggled a finger at him. "Fewer fulsome compliments and more humorous stories. I enjoy those more."

"All right." He took a moment, looking as though he enjoyed holding her interest. "Out in California, a railroad agent once got yelled at over doing things wi'out waiting for his orders to trickle down from faraway headquarters, as he should hae done. Then came a day, not long after, when the boss at headquarters received an urgent telegram from that selfsame agent: 'Grizzly bear on platform hugging conductor. Please wire instructions.'"

"No!" Rosalind's hands stilled as she looked up in shock. "Never tell me he waited afore helping that poor conductor!"

"I'm sure he took care of it before he ever sent the telegram," Ewan soothed. "The man was just trying to make a point. If he waited for official orders before doing everything, nothing would ever get done in time to do good."

"Well, in that case. . ." Rosalind relaxed. "If he kept his job, 'twas a rather clever way to argue his side of the matter."

"Aye, that's my thought, too." Ewan reached back for a mighty stretch and Rosalind, slightly more cautious since finding a red ear, peeled back a small section of husk as a safeguard.

Another gash of red blazed forth, and she hurriedly reached for another. As she grasped another ear, she let the red one roll off her lap. As before, she inconspicuously kicked it beneath the bench. Only this time, she kicked too hard. At the *thud* of the ear hitting the barn wall, Ewan looked back at her.

"What was that?" He looked around for the sound's source.

"Nothing." The word came out sounding as flustered as she felt. "You know, I'm starting to get a bit peckish." She hopped up. "Would you like me to fetch you an apple while I'm up?"

"Aye," he looked at her strangely. "A green one, please."

With a too-bright smile, she headed for the tables, selected two shiny apples, and went back. Before sitting on the bench, she looked down. It wouldn't do to slip on one of those pesky red ears she'd let drop. Wouldn't do at all.

There were no ears on the floor. Startled, she glanced up at a beaming Ewan. In each of his upraised hands lay one of the red ears.

⚭

"Oooh!" A swell of raucous calls filled Ewan's senses as people took note of the two ears he held up for all to see.

"Who's your lucky lady, Gailbraith?" one of the men called out. "Let her know now so she can run away!"

"I know who he'll choose!" Johnny bellowed. Beside him, Marlene was beaming and casting Rosalind knowing looks.

Rosalind, for her part, had turned as petal pink as her namesake flower and sat down as though her knees had given out. She couldn't have looked any more enticing had she tried.

Though he thought it impossible, Ewan's grin widened. *I knew I saw her hiding something behind her skirts.* Sure enough, when she'd gone to fetch the apples, he'd found two partly-unhusked ears of corn. Red ears. The thought of her squirreling away kisses charmed him. His Rosalind wouldn't hold up the red ear in triumph and boldly claim her forfeit. Instead, she clumsily hid the evidence.

Good thing I'm not shy. Ewan clasped Rosalind's hand and purposefully drew her to her feet. Her eyes, impossibly wide, shone with a beguiling mix of anxiety and anticipation.

"There's only one woman I've eyes"—Ewan waved one of the cobs of corn—"or ears for." Resisting the urge to hold her close, Ewan kept her hand in his and leaned forward to press a chaste kiss on her soft lips. After the barest moment—a moment far too short, to his way of thinking—he drew back.

Amid the stares and cheers of the crowd, Rosalind held his gaze and raised her hand to gently touch her lips. The gesture nearly made Ewan reach for her again, but he saw the moment when she remembered the whole town watched her reaction.

Ewan addressed the crowd, diverting their attention from Rosalind as best he could. " 'Tis the truth, no man could ask for more than that." He held up the second red ear and pretended to consider it. "Now then, since I've experienced perfection, 'twould be churlish of me to deny another the same opportunity."

At his words, it seemed as though every man in the barn stood and shouted to be chosen. Ewan made a show of considering whom he'd pass the second red ear to before tossing it to Johnny. Envious groans shook the barn clear to the rafters.

As though I'd give it to some other man who'd choose my Rosalind. And honestly, any other man would be daft to choose another girl. Johnny, enamored of Marlene as he is, was the only safe choice.

And Johnny made the most of his good fortune, bussing Marlene with more enthusiasm than grace. With everyone's attention turned to the other couple, Ewan and Rosalind sank back onto their bench. Their moment of excitement had ended.

"Thief." Rosalind whispered the indictment under her breath and out of the corner of her mouth. All the same, her eyes held no matching reproach to make him regret taking action.

"Sneak," Ewan muttered back, grinning at her resulting gasp.

Long seconds stretched between them before she answered. "Aye," she admitted, biting back an impish smile.

"Aye." Ewan shouldered a bit closer, beginning to regret his gift to Johnny. "You know what that makes the two of us?"

"What?" The question in her eyes seemed less lighthearted.

"It makes us"—Ewan spoke seriously, to let her know he meant what he said—"a likely pair."

Chapter 10

I s it true that the railroad will be moving on soon?" Marlene burst out with the question almost the instant Ewan and Johnny sat down for their pre-dinner-rush meal. "You've not even been here a month! Surely this type of haste isn't typical?"

Although Rosalind wouldn't have chosen to handle the issue in this manner, she shared Marlene's worries about whether the railroad would take their beaux away with it. She looked at Ewan, careful to school her features into a neutral expression. Whatever his decision—whether he stayed for winter or left now with plans of returning later—she planned on supporting it.

"Yes, sugar-pie." Johnny looked every bit as miserable as Marlene at the prospect of leaving. "We've lingered a bit long to enjoy the comforts of home-cooking and pretty smiles, so the foreman tells us we won't be able to delay any longer. Camp will be moved a good thirty miles away. We've no choice."

"Thirty miles!" Marlene sank down onto the nearest bench, tears dotting her pale eyelashes. "Can't they at least hold off until after Thanksgiving? That's only a few days away!"

"They say they won't risk losing our impressive pace." Ewan shook his head. "Though 'tis bound to slow. Tomorrow we head out."

"Why didn't they give us a warning?" Rosalind's firm resolve not to complain melted in the face of such an immediate separation. She bit her lip.

" 'Tis for the best." Ewan rolled his massive shoulders in a vain effort to relieve tension. "If they told the men ahead of time, they'd be prone to acting out. No man wants to go back to Hank's cooking in the midst of an empty wilderness—especially wi' winter coming. This late notice, 'tis a safeguard for all the town."

"But no safeguard against heartache." Marlene's whisper probably reached only Rosalind's ears, but she decided to take no chances Ewan would overhear such maudlin dramatics.

"Marlene, we've everything ready for the men. Why don't we leave off ringing the dinner bell just a wee little bit? The news has caught us all by surprise, and 'twould do us good to spend a few private moments together." She reached out to clasp Ewan's hand. "Why don't we walk a short distance afore dinner?"

"Aye," Ewan assented.

Marlene and Johnny didn't even follow, lost as they were in one another.

After walking only a short distance, Ewan began, "Rosalind, 'tis sorry I am this matter has come upon us so sudden. 'Tis said the men took such great cheer from your diner they laid track more quickly than was expected—too much of a good thing."

"'Tisn't as though we thought the railroad would hole up here forever," Rosalind said, "but we did think 'twould be a bit longer before you packed up and moved away from us."

"As did I." Ewan put his hands on her shoulders. "I'd not intended to hae you make any sort of decision this quickly."

Surely he wouldn't propose now. Ewan wouldn't expect me to marry and leave my family wi' such haste! I can't!

"Ewan"—Rosalind stared down at the toes of her shoes, unable to look at him—"I'm sorry, but I can't go wi' you."

"I know." The surprise in his voice caused her to look upward. He seemed almost offended. "I wouldn't ask that of you, Rosalind. To separate from family. . . 'Tis a horrible thing."

"Then"—her brow furrowed in confusion—"what decision would you hae me make?" *What else is there for me to decide?*

"Whether I go on wi' the railroad for now or make arrangements to stay the winter."

"Oh!" Rosalind threw her arms around him. "I'm so very glad!" She drew back after her initial burst of excitement and considered. "Won't the railroad need you? I'd not hae you leave them in the lurch when you've made a commitment. That you're a man of your word is one o' the things I admire so."

"Wi' winter coming on, the pace will slow. Johnny's capable of managing on his own by now. He's skilled enough." Ewan's gaze ran deep enough for her to drown in. "'Tis my commitment to you I wouldn't want questioned."

"Oh." Rosalind suddenly found it difficult to speak past the lump in her throat. *If he asked me to go wi' him right this minute, I'd say yes. 'Tis good he will do no such thing!*

"But we've only been courting a wee while. I do not want to put you off by making such a decision wi'out speaking wi' you first." His eyes twinkled with suppressed mirth. "A wonderful lass once warned me against such terrible folly."

"And right she was. 'Tis grateful I am that such a wise woman took pains to show you the error of your ways." She gave him a sidelong smile. " 'Twill make you a much better neighbor this winter." She watched the grin break out across his face and knew she'd not regret her choice.

"I've a sneaking suspicion that same lass will find many ways to make a better man of me." They started back.

"Do you know," Rosalind teased, "I think you might be right."

At the sight of Johnny seated next to Marlene with his arm around her shoulders, Rosalind stopped walking. "Ewan, have you discussed this wi' Johnny to make sure he won't resent it?"

"Aye." He stepped back to stand beside her. Her sudden stop had left him ahead. "Johnny all but insisted I stay behind. Says he needs to have someone he trusts watch o'er Marlene while he's away for the winter. He plans to return come springtime."

" 'Tis good." Rosalind began walking once more but gave a loud sigh. " 'Twould be perfect if Johnny could stay wi' you. I know Marlene will miss him something awful in the months ahead." *And 'twill only be the harder when she sees that I still hae you.* She left the last thought unspoken. She wouldn't say anything that could reflect poorly on her friend. Marlene was entitled to some sadness at the loss of her first true love.

"We'll be sure to include Marlene in fun outings so she won't have time enough to dwell on his absence." Ewan folded her hand in his and gave a reassuring squeeze. "Spring will be upon us before she knows it, and for now, she has you. Such a blessing as that cannot be o'erlooked for very long."

Rosalind gave a gentle squeeze in return but said nothing as they came to stand next to Marlene and Johnny.

Marlene's sobs wracked her petite frame, though Johnny spoke soothing words, promises he would return and they'd be strong for one another. "But I d–don't understand," Marlene gasped. "Why can't you stay if Ewan is going to? Why are you so set on leaving?"

"Now, sugar-pie," Johnny patted her back as one would an upset child's, bungling the earnest attempt to pacify her. "With Ewan gone, they'll need me all the more. We can't both abandon the crew all winter. They've no other blacksmith."

"Why doesn't Ewan go?" Marlene wailed, obviously only realizing the ugliness behind the words after she said them. "I don't mean that I don't want him to stay, too, but why are *you* going on with the railroad while *he* stays here in town?" There was no hiding the tinge of bitter accusation in the question.

Rosalind gaped at her in disbelief. Surely her best friend hadn't spoken such awful words? What would Ewan think?

"Marlene!" Johnny's stern disapproval startled her enough to stop the tears. "Ewan has every bit as much of a right to stay as I do. I counted on you easing his way while I went on ahead. Had someone told me to expect such an objection from my sweet sugar-pie, I wouldn't have believed it."

"I—I didn't mean it that way," Marlene sniffled apologetically. "Really, I do want Rose to be happy."

"That's my Marlene," Johnny encouraged. "Truth be told, Ewan is doing me a great favor by stepping down. I'll no longer be paid as only an apprentice. By sometime this spring, I'll be able to come back to you with enough to start a small home."

"Oh Johnny," she breathed, "do you mean it?"

"Of course I do!" He apparently couldn't refrain from adding, "It's only what I've been saying this whole time."

"Ewan, Rose, I'm so sorry for what I said." Marlene grasped their entwined hands in hers. "I wouldn't have you leave for my sake, Ewan. Really, truly I wouldn't."

Her earnest tone told Rosalind her best friend had earlier spoken out of frantic desperation. She forgave her on the spot. "I know that." Rosalind disengaged her hand to hug her friend. "This gives us that much more to look forward to come spring." She looked at Ewan and happiness bubbled inside her heart. *Though I hope there are things to look forward to now as well.*

⌒⌒

"Arthur?" Ewan made a beeline for the smithy as soon as he had a chance that afternoon. He waited for the older man's hammer to stop ringing before he went on. "I've a question to ask you."

"I assumed as much." Arthur's smile took the barb from the words.

"Though I should warn you that Marlene spilled the news at lunch. I know you've spoken wi' Rosey and decided to stay the winter. I'll not be standing in your way, Ewan."

" 'Tis glad I am to hear it," Ewan said. "Now that I've made the decision, I'll have to find a way to make it work. I was wondering whether you could tell me who used to live in the smaller house so close to your own? As near as I can tell, 'tisn't in use."

"Ah. That used to be Gilda's home. She lived there wi' Cade—they were Kaitlin's parents you ken—up until Cade passed on two years ago." He shrugged. " 'Twasn't safe to let her live alone at her age, and she said the place held too many memories of Cade while she was grieving. So you've the right o' it. Gilda stays wi' us, and the house has stood empty for a bit." He cast Ewan a sidelong glance. "I know Brent Friemont hoped to purchase it as a home not too far in the future."

"Brent Friemont?" Ewan recalled the youth's treatment of Rosalind at the corn husking and his menacing glare after Ewan claimed his kiss. "He'll be having no need of it," he stated flatly. "Do I have your approval?"

"Aye," Arthur agreed. "Rosey has never looked on Brent wi' the affection he bears for her. 'Twouldn't hae been a good match."

"Do I speak wi' you or Gilda about renting the house through winter?" Ewan smiled at Arthur's assessment of Brent.

"I'm all for it, but you'll have to speak wi' Gilda. Though she lives wi' us, 'tis still the home of her heart."

"And I'll treat it as such." He thought of Rosalind's grandmam, the roadmap of wrinkles around her loving gaze and the way she'd looked him over when they first met. "She's a good woman, and I'll not be showing disrespect to her memories. Should she decide not to let me have the place, 'twill be simple enough to build a small soddy." He thought of living half underground, shut in by snow and walled in by solid earth for months at a time. He'd bear with dirt and burrowing bugs to win Rosalind, but all the same. . . "I do hope Gilda will let me rent the house."

"She'll be at home now, if you're half so anxious to ask as I'm thinking you are." Arthur gave him a wry smile. "Gilda seems to have taken a liking to you, if that helps."

"I'll take all the advantages I can get when it comes t' courting your daughter." Ewan nodded his appreciation and began to leave the smithy.

"My thanks for your advice, Arthur."

He set off on the pleasant walk to the MacLean homestead. *Lord, if 'tisn't Your will that I stay in the house, I'll accept that. You know I hope to make Rosalind my bride, but I've yet to see how to do so wi'out either taking her from her family or taking part of her da's livelihood. I can't do either, nor can I ignore the feelings I bear for Rosalind herself. Before winter ends, I pray that You will show me how to proceed. I will not ask her to be my wife until I'm sure 'tis Your will, though I know 'twill be a temptation. Help me remember to seek You first, Father, so I don't lead Rosalind the wrong way.*

By the time he reached the house, Ewan felt the mantle of peace that was God's way of showing him he did the right thing. He raised his fist to knock on the door only to have it swing open before his hand met the wood even once. Gilda Banning stood on the other side of the threshold, eyes canny.

"So you've come to ask about the house, hae you?" Her assessment left him speechless for a moment, and she let out a gleeful chuckle. "Come in, come in, then. Kaitlin and Luke went to gather some vegetables from the garden. We'll have a nice chat, you and I."

"Thank you." Ewan stepped inside, still thrown off balance by her greeting. "How did you know why I came before I asked?"

"I've seen a good many years, lad." She sank into a carved rocker near the hearth. "I know you've come to talk about my home same as I know Brent Friemont had an eye on it as well."

He took a ladder-back chair and dragged it beside her. "I do not seek it as a wedding gift," Ewan spoke carefully.

"I should hope not!" Gilda snorted. "After knowing our Rose for less than a month, you know how special she is, but you'd be a fool t' propose a marriage so very soon."

"Aye," Ewan agreed, relieved that he wouldn't have to defend himself on that score. "I come to ask whether I might rent your lovely house for the duration of the winter, and perhaps a bit into the spring. I'll pay well, Mrs. Banning."

"And 'twill be well worth the price, to my way of thinking." The old woman rocked slowly, as though contemplating the matter. "I've not much inside, you see, but I did leave a table an' chairs and an empty trunk or so. It has a fireplace rather than a stove, but I'd suppose you know that from the size o' the chimney." She nodded and suddenly turned a gimlet eye on him. "What are your intentions toward my granddaughter, Mr.

Gailbraith, if you do not ask to buy the place after all?"

"I intend to court her honorably, Mrs. Banning."

"Psh. Call me Gilda." The old woman kept her gaze pinned on him. "And I knew you were honorable, else Arthur wouldn't let you court Rose, and my granddaughter wouldn't see you, and I wouldn't hae allowed you to rent my house." She leaned forward intently. "I mean, what are your plans after you win her, lad? Will you settle here or take her away wi' you?"

"That I cannot say at the moment," Ewan confessed. "I've more than enough money saved t' settle into a home, but Saddleback already has a fine blacksmith in Arthur. Just the same, I don't believe in separating families." He noted the spark of understanding in her eyes. "What answer would you hae wanted?"

"That, I cannot say, lad." She leaned back once more. "We, of course, want her to stay, but that is our desire, not necessarily hers. Our Rose thirsts for a bit o' adventure. She feels she missed her big chance, being just a babe when my Kaitlin brought her to the wilds of the Montana Territory. She can't recall the journey, after all, and wants to see a bit o' the world."

"And I'm no closer to an answer." Ewan shifted in the chair. "I appreciate your insight, Gilda, and your generosity."

"As I appreciate yours. Now"—she smiled—"let's talk about the terms of that rental."

Chapter 11

"arlene didn't take it very well when we packed up the supplies left at the diner." Rosalind frowned. "I wonder how long she'll be so blue. Surely this mood cannot last through the winter!"

"It won't." Mam stirred the hot tallow to keep it from lumping. "But the diner bore memories of her Johnny, and it brought her sadness to the surface. Give her a bit o' time."

"Aye." Grandmam dipped her too-thin candle in the wax again and drew it out, holding it aloft to harden. "She'll come 'round."

"I'm going to make the thickest candle ever." Luke eyed his already too-big contribution. "I'll make it thick enough that when I level the bottom, 'twill stand on its own."

"And if not," Grandmam noted, "we'll melt it down again. 'Twill not be a waste either way, and who knows? It may work."

Rosalind kept her doubts on the matter to herself, instead admiring the soft lavender-blue color of the candles. With each new layer of cooled wax, they took on a slightly darker shade.

" 'Twas so clever to soak the dried blueberries so they plumped and then juice them. It adds such a nice scent and lovely color." She dipped her candle once more and judged it to be thick enough. Rosalind hung it on the drying rack and began again. "The only drawback is they might make us hungry!"

"Mayhap next time we'll add a splash of oil of lilac instead of the blueberry juice." Mam surveyed the filling rack with satisfaction. "We'll be glad to have these come winter."

"Aye," Grandmam seconded. "If there's anything worse than being snowed in for months on end, 'tis being snowed in wi' only the hearth's light to see by. Makes it that much darker."

"Mam, may I give Marlene a candle or two for her nightstand?" Rosalind gave an appreciative sniff. "The treat might help to restore her good spirits. Coax a smile, even."

"I'm sure we can spare a few for such a good cause."

"You can give her mine, Rose." Luke generously held out the large, misshapen candle he'd been nursing the entire day.

"Oh, I'm not sure if 'twill fit in her candleholder, Luke." Rosalind gestured toward the monstrosity. "Best you keep it to read by. 'Twill be interesting to see how long 'twill last."

"Good idea, Rose." Luke headed back to dunk the thing yet again. "I don't think anyone's ever made one like this before."

"I believe you are the first, Luke." Mam ruffled his hair.

"Why don't you run o'er with these four?" Grandmam held them out to Rosalind. "You'll probably be glad to take a nice, quiet walk." Her eyes held a knowing glint as she looked at Rosalind.

"Aye." Rosalind took them thankfully. For the first time since the leaves had turned color, she'd have a moment to herself. With the railroad crew packed off, she could walk alone again.

She draped a light shawl about her shoulders to ward off the chill that warned of winter and set out down the well-worn path. The scents of fallen leaves and rich, dark earth freed by the harvest filled her senses as she moved along.

Father, I see the work of Your hands around me, and 'tis wondrous. Your imagination so far surpasses my own—all I seem to be able to think of is Ewan. How did he go from a man my parents warned me against to my possible future husband in such a short span of time? I remember praying not so long ago about trying to separate out my own impressions of the man wi' the caution Mam and Da exhorted me to use.

Now he has Da's approval, and while Mam had hoped for Brent as a son-in-law, she hasn't spoken against Ewan's courtship. Grandmam has even agreed to rent her house to him for the winter. Everything seems to point to an ideal match—can it be so easy? I know You guard o'er the seasons in our lives, but this time of beginnings seems almost too sweet. Why am I holding a fear that 'twon't last? Help me to trust in Your will, Father, as time ripens.

She knocked on the Friemonts' door, waiting until Delana Friemont opened it and ushered her inside with a welcoming smile.

"Rose! It is always good to see you." She took Rosalind's hands in hers and spoke more softly. "Perhaps you can cheer Marlene from her sullens. I will give her the rest of today to adjust to the idea of waiting for her young man, but that is enough."

"Aye." Rosalind nodded. " 'Twouldn't do to stay so for long. I'll hae a chat wi' her. She'll pull through this difficulty."

"Ja." Mrs. Friemont waved for her to go up into the loft where Marlene's bed reposed. Rosalind guessed that her friend had been up there since they'd come back from the diner.

"Marlene!" she called out in a hearty voice as she ascended the ladder. "I've come to see how you're doing this afternoon." She poked her head over the ladder to find Marlene sitting atop her bed, evidence of recent tears staining her white pillowcase.

Not a good sign, Rosalind inventoried, *though she's not crying now. That's more hopeful. Oh, unless she's cried so much she can't cry anymore. And I thought some blue candles would help?*

"Don't stand on the ladder all day," Marlene sniffed. "Come on up." She patted the mattress beside her and gave a ghost of a smile. "I promise I won't say anything awful."

"Hush." Rosalind stooped into the loft and sat beside Marlene. "I brought you a little something." She passed over the candles.

"They're purple! No, blue?" Marlene squinted in an attempt to determine. "Whatever did you put in the wax for color?"

"Mam added blueberry juice, and I thought they were a little more blue than purple, though I wouldn't argue wi' you on the matter." Rosalind took a deep breath. "Smell them."

"Mmm. . ." Marlene inhaled a few times before she put the candles down. "They make me want to eat some blueberries."

" 'Tis almost the same thing as what I said!" Rosalind laughed. "Still, I think 'twas a marvelous idea. Think of all the different things we could use! Raspberries for summer, apples for fall—and the berries at least would turn the whole batch pink."

"Custom candles," Marlene said. "Think of it—candles to match the color of your quilt or curtains, whichever you like."

"What would you use for green or yellow?" Rosalind tried to think of anything that would work. "I can only think of green beans or such, and I wouldn't want that scent all the time."

"Nor I." Marlene thought a moment. "We could stir pumpkin juice with a stick of cinnamon and see how that turns out."

"Maybe. That would give us something like yellow. But I don't like the smell of raw pumpkin o'ermuch—just baked."

"That's what the cinnamon is for, Rose." Marlene leaned back on her elbows and stared up at the ceiling rafters. "I can't believe he's already gone. Here yesterday, and today—"

"Working to save up for your wedding," Rosalind broke in. "And we both know your da would say you're too young to wed for a while yet. Johnny's doing what's best for your future, Marlene. He'll come back."

"Do you really think so?" Marlene plucked at a loose string on her quilt. "He won't meet some other girl before then?"

"Not one who could cast you from his memory. God made you special, and none can compare." Rosalind's heart ached at her friend's forlorn look. "He'll be back afore you know it."

"I'll know it the second my Johnny walks back into town," Marlene declared with her old confidence. "I know it will take a year or two before our home is ready—it takes so long to clear land, raise a house, and start a farm—but at least he'll be with me then. For now, I'll just have to think about something else." She looked at Rosalind with a speculative gaze. "So, how do you plan to get Ewan to propose?"

Chapter 12

N o, not like that." Grandmam shooed Rosalind away from the stuffed goose. "You keep it in the juices so it stays moist."

"I'd thought to add flour and such to make a bit o' gravy." Rosalind shrugged and slid a loaf of pumpkin spice bread from the old niche at the hearth. When Mam and Da first built the house, they'd not had a stove to call their own. Now, for Thanksgiving Day, every cooking contraption had been called into service.

"You make it right," Mam sided against Rosalind, "and there's no need for gravy."

"Da likes it for his potatoes and dressing," Rosalind pointed out. " 'Tis no insult to the bird."

"Aye." Grandmam's shoulders relaxed. "My Cade loved a dribble of thick gravy on his mashed potatoes, too. But you wait until the last possible moment—not until after the Thanksgiving meeting."

"Right." Rosalind pinned an errant curl behind her ear. "I should hae remembered that. When did I become such a muddled miss?"

"Oh"—Mam gave her a sideways look—"I'd say about the same time Ewan decided to stay through the lonely winter."

"Mam!" Rosalind shook her head but smiled at the truth in her mother's words. " 'Tis happy I am we've so much to be thankful for this Thanksgiving Day."

"And you want it to come off just right"—Grandmam shuffled back to her rocker—"and make sure you show Ewan he's made a sound decision, that's what 'tis."

"I hope I'm never so ungrateful as to o'erlook the others I'm blessed with." Rosalind walked over to give the old woman a hug. "Ewan's not the only one I thank God for."

"Aye." Mam came by to join the embrace. "Rose has the right o' it."

"All the same"—Grandmam settled back more comfortably after the moment passed—"I've the notion you ought to wear your best blue dress for the festivities today, Rose. It draws attention to your sparkling eyes."

"I'd already planned to," she admitted. "After all, Thanksgiving is a time when we thank the Lord by putting forth our best efforts!"

"Aye." Da stepped into the warmth of the house, trailed by Luke. " 'Tis glad I am to hear my women speak such humble thoughts."

Rosalind raised her eyebrows toward Mam and Grandmam—they had, after all, just been discussing a sort of vanity. Neither gave the slightest hint of amusement but carried on as though Da had the right of it.

It brought to mind Grandmam's old lesson: A still tongue gathers praise when a busy one catches naught but air.

"Luke!" Rosalind gently slapped his hand away from one of the carefully arranged platters of food. "You know that's for the community dinner!"

"But picnic eggs are my favorite!" His brown eyes pled for a wee taste.

"Just one." Rosalind handed him one of the boiled eggs, hollowed and refilled with a mashed mix of yolk, lard, pickle brine, and salt. They happened to be a favorite of hers, too. She popped one into her own mouth as she rearranged the platter to cover the empty spaces they'd made.

"We'll change into our Sunday best and make our way to the Friemonts' for the special Thanksgiving service." Da's declaration was the cue for everyone to fly into action, readying themselves to leave.

Rosalind helped prepare the dishes she, Mam, and Grandmam had worked on since the day before for carrying to Delana's kitchen. This Thanksgiving would bring a feast the likes of which Saddleback had never seen before!

With the work done, Rosalind slipped into her blue cotton dress, straightening the crisp white collar that framed her face with starched purity. She smoothed her hair one last time and pulled on her cloak and gloves.

"Is everyone ready?" Da turned to check, and Ma plunked the platter bearing the stuffed goose into his open arms.

Everyone else took up a dish or two before stepping outside, and Rosalind found Ewan about to knock on their door. She favored him with a smile as he took the basket of biscuits from her and offered her his arm.

"Thank you." She slipped her hand into the warm crook of his elbow and set off.

"My pleasure." He took care to shorten his stride, going slowly so she wouldn't have to rush to keep alongside him.

Such a thoughtful man. She peeked up at him. *And such a handsome one.* The Lord had outdone Himself the day He fashioned Ewan Gailbraith, and she meant to give thanks for it. After all, it wasn't every day a girl walked before the town in her best dress, on the arm of a kind, handsome suitor as they prepared to praise God for another wonderful year. No, days just didn't get any better than this.

The wide Montana sky stretched before them, clear as could be. The air crisped with the nip of winter's cold, but the sunshine chased thoughts of snow away. They reached the Friemonts' home in a few moments—far too soon, to Rosalind's way of thinking. She reluctantly slipped her hand from Ewan's arm, taking back the biscuits and following the women into Delana's kitchen.

The warm fragrance of baked apples wrapped itself around her like a welcome as she set the basket on one of two already-too-full tables. Pies, loaves of flavored breads, biscuits, muffins, corn cake, and maple sweeties vied for space between roasted chicken, turkey, and goose. Dishes of mashed potatoes, sweet potatoes, dressing, coleslaw, and Rosalind's deviled eggs crowded in alongside. She'd never seen such a feast—the women of the town had really outdone themselves this year. But though the kitchen seemed full of busy women, several of them were missing.

Rosalind took a swift tally. Jakob and Isaac Albright's mail-order brides bustled back and forth importantly as Delana and Marlene worked furiously over the red-hot stove. Mam, having made sure all the dishes were deposited in the warmth of the kitchen, was bundling Grandmam into a chair in the corner. A glance out the window showed the Twadley girls, along with the Hornton and Preston women, hovering close by, fingering each others' woolen capes and laughing in the spirit of the day. The men plunked benches into neat rows, preparing for the Thanksgiving service.

Rosalind gave a deep sigh of satisfaction. *All present and accounted for.* By God's grace, everyone in the entire community had gathered to give thanks.

Rosalind's gaze drifted past the chatting women to where Ewan held a serious conversation with the Friemont men. The earnestness of his gaze grabbed her heart, and his sudden smile brought a matching one to her own face.

This Thanksgiving, no one has more to be grateful for than I do. Thank You, Jesus, for bringing Ewan into my life. 'Tis more than I'd dared hope for.

Ewan looked up from his discussion with Dustin Friemont and spied Rosalind peeking at him through the window. At his quick wave, she grinned and ducked out of sight.

Ah, Lord, thank You for my precious Rosalind. Has it really only been a matter of mere weeks since You brought her into my life? He paused for a moment, considering the fact that he'd arrived in her hometown. *Or rather, You led me to her? Either way, the result is the same—we're together. For that, I'll be forever grateful, Father. Though the winter ahead may seem long and at times lonely when we're snowed in, apart from one another, the knowledge that she's nearby and safe will be a treasure I cherish. The only thing that could make this day—nay, this entire season—better would be if Johnny were here to share his joy wi' Marlene as I am able to share my happiness wi' my Rosalind. Father, keep an eye on the lad as he works through this winter. I've the notion You'll see him work harder than ever before. You've given him a new motivation in little Marlene. Thank You, Father.*

At that final word, a cloud passed over Ewan's bright day, and he frowned in sudden sorrow. *And Lord, please watch o'er my own da, wherever he may be this day.*

Ewan looked up to see the townspeople taking their seats upon the rough benches that served as pews. He scanned the crowd to find Rosalind's family before wending his way toward them and settling himself beside her. As the light fragrance of rosewater reached his senses, he smiled once more.

Dustin Friemont stood before the congregation in lieu of the circuit riding preacher. The man cleared his throat, a last minute call for the attention of those still shifting about. When all were watching, he spoke. "We all know that today is the day of Thanksgiving, where we show our gratitude to the Lord above for the blessings He's given us, and we remind our loved ones how we appreciate them." He stopped to shoot a glance at the pretty, older blond woman Ewan recalled as Dustin's wife, Delana. "I'd like to start the day with a hymn. I believe we all know 'For the Beauty of the Earth.'"

Ewan sat back and let the song wash over him, joining in as the half-forgotten melody grew full with the voices of many.

> *"For the beauty of the earth,*
> *for the glory of the skies,*
> *for the love which from our birth*
> *over and around us lies;*
> *Lord of all, to Thee we raise*
> *this our hymn of grateful praise."*

How fitting, Lord. Wi' the beauty of the glorious skies above us and the rich earth beneath our feet, we are truly surrounded by Your love.

> *"For the joy of human love,*
> *brother, sister, parent, child;*
> *friends on earth and friends above;*
> *for all gentle thoughts and mild:*
> *Lord of all, to Thee we raise*
> *this our hymn of grateful praise."*

And this. When for the first time in years I am wi' people I love as I would family. And wi' Rosalind, who I bear husbandly affection for although we are not yet wed. This is fitting, for 'tis the people of Saddleback who are its greatest lure, and their souls Your greatest treasure.

The hymn came to an end all too quickly, but Ewan listened closely as Dustin began to speak once again, his Bible open to the passage he and Ewan had been discussing scant moments before. "Ewan Gailbraith, a newcomer to Saddleback, saw me rifling through the pages of my Bible in search of Psalm 65 this morning. And, while it is a wonderful passage advocating that we thank the Lord for His bounty, I seem to recall reading the same chapter and verse last year. But the Word of Christ"—he held up the Bible—"is full of wisdom, and Mr. Gailbraith directed my attention to the book of Deuteronomy. I'll be reading from chapter 8 this morning." With a nod to Ewan, he took a breath as though to begin. But no words came for a moment.

"Actually"—Mr. Friemont pinned him with a very intense gaze before continuing—"I, for one, would be glad to have you do the honors."

Ewan blinked as the other man gestured for him to come up. Several others were nodding, and Rosalind went so far as to give him an encouraging nudge. He got to his feet and made his way before the congregation before accepting Mr. Friemont's Bible.

"This is irregular," Dustin Friemont admitted. "But it seems to me that the verse is fitting, and it's equally fitting to have the man who chose it be the one to speak on it." With this, he went to sit beside his wife, leaving Ewan alone before the population of Saddleback.

"Well,"—Ewan cleared his throat—"I can't say I've ever filled in for a preacher before, so I apologize in advance for my inexperience. That being said, this is a verse I keep dear to my heart, and I hope you'll do the same.

"Deuteronomy, chapter 8, verses 7 through 10: 'For the Lord thy God bringeth thee into a good land, a land of brooks of water, of fountains and depths that spring out of valleys and hills; a land of wheat, and barley, and vines, and fig trees, and pomegranates; a land of oil olive, and honey; a land wherein thou shalt eat bread without scarceness, thou shalt not lack any thing in it; a land whose stones are iron, and out of whose hills thou mayest dig brass. When thou hast eaten and art full, then thou shalt bless the Lord thy God for the good land which he hath given thee.'"

Ewan paused to let the words sink in. "Now, I hadn't thought to speak on this passage, but a few things do come to my mind. First is that the Lord our God has brought us all into a good land, a land of brooks of water, valleys and hills, and wheat. . . . Those words weren't written about the Montana Territory, but they certainly do an excellent job of describing nature's bounty in this area." Several people were nodding, and he warmed to his speech.

"And when I see the good folk who've settled here, sensing that God has been welcomed into this community—and smell the food in the kitchen—it seems to me that we don't lack any good thing. And how appropriate 'tis that verse 10 speaks of eating and being physically full of the things God has given us in His care for our souls, that we may bless Him for all He's given us." He looked around, giving just one more comment. "So it seems to me, we should get to that eating so we can bless Him with full hearts and bellies!"

The men chortled their approval and everyone clapped, nodding their agreement with Ewan's assessment.

"Before we sit down to enjoy the fruits of our labors and the skills of our women's hands, I'd like to lead us in a simple praise—an old favorite." Ewan tilted back his head and sang the verse, singing it again as the townspeople joined in:

> *"Praise God from whom all blessings flow;*
> *Praise Him, all creatures here below;*
> *Praise Him above, ye heavenly host;*
> *Praise Father, Son and Holy Ghost. Amen."*

As they all sat down to the best spread Ewan had ever seen in his life, he looked over at Rosalind, and the words of praise echoed in his mind once again.

Your blessings hae flowed upon me, Jesus. I praise You above all others, and thank You for Your loving grace. Amen.

Chapter 13

*A*fter being uninhabited for so long, this place needs a bit o' upkeep, Ewan mused after a night spent trying to bundle up against chill drafts. *I'll see if I can get some pitch to fill in those gaps.*

He gulped his too-hot coffee in an attempt to warm up and ate his fried eggs straight from the pan. *No sense making extra dishes to wash when no one's around to quibble about niceties.*

Then he went to the firmly shut curtains and thrust them aside, eager to see the glow of the sun—and the warmth it promised. After working a forge for so many years, heat was more natural to him than cold would ever be.

He blinked at the view before him. *Snow!* A blanket of white covered the ground, coated tree branches, and dusted his windowpane. *No wonder 'twas so cold—a snowstorm blew in o'ernight.* Ewan pulled on an extra pair of socks, then struggled to jam his boots over them. He took his coat from the peg by the door and slid it over his shoulders before plunking on his seldom-used hat and mittens. Blacksmiths rarely had use for the things.

Girding himself for a cold wind, he opened the door and stepped outside. Before he so much as drew a breath of fresh air, something whizzed over to plunk on his jacket.

"I got him!" Luke pointed at him. "Did you see that throw? I just aimed and *thwunk*, he didn't know until 'twas too late!"

While the lad all but danced with pride, Ewan crouched down and scooped up some snow of his own. Packing it into a round ball, he waited for the right moment before he let it fly. *Whooosh-umph*, his snowball soared toward the boy, only to be intercepted by another expertly thrown one. He scowled as both burst into harmless pieces and fell softly to the ground. Then he looked to see who'd interfered with the lad's just desserts.

"Rosalind?" He looked in disbelief to where his lass, bundled in a woolen cloak, calmly packed her next volley. "You're firing at me?" Ewan put the shock of betrayal in his tone.

"Now, Ewan, I did no such thing." She neatly placed yet another snowball in the line before her. "I fired at your snowball. That's an entirely different matter, you know." The laughter in her voice made it hard not to smile in return.

"Two against one is clear as day," he growled. "This means war." He began packing snow as quickly as he could scoop it up, his jacket bearing the wet stains attesting to his opponents' ruthlessness. "Who fires on an unarmed man?" he roared, letting fly a few of his own shots. "Take that, and that, and—mmph!" A snowball hit him smack in the mouth before he'd truly begun.

"Nice one, Rose!" Luke shrieked with merriment, laughing so hard he began to cough.

"That's enough, now," Rosalind kicked apart her snowballs in a show of truce before walking over to her brother. "Let's go in for a sip o' cider, shall we?" She tugged his hat down.

"Will you cry craven the moment your opponent is ready to do battle?" Ewan protested the abrupt ending. "Stand and fight, or"—he lobbed a set of snowballs, each finding one of the siblings across the way—"surrender!"

"I said that's enough." The tightness in Rosalind's tone took him by surprise. "If you want some cider, come inside wi' us." She shooed young Luke into the warmth of the house and marched in behind him, leaving Ewan standing alone.

What? I've never thought o' Rosalind as fickle, but she abandoned the challenge quickly enough. Something hae set her back up, and 'tis best I find out what afore I make another misstep. Surely a reason lies behind her change of heart.

He resolutely made his way to the still-open door of the house. *There's a good sign, at least.* Ewan stomped the snow from his boots before venturing into the MacLean home.

Arthur raised a hand in greeting, Mrs. MacLean poured cider into mugs, and Luke, seated beside the roaring fire, coughed after sending some of his drink down the wrong way. Ewan noticed that Rosalind hadn't taken off her warm cloak.

"Ewan, would you walk me to the barn?" She laid a small, gloved hand on his arm. "I've yet to check on the livestock."

"O' course." Ewan led her out the door, walking with her in silence on the short trek to the barn. He waited.

"I wanted to apologize for being so curt." She stood before him, her hands worrying the fabric of her skirts. " 'Twas rude and uncalled for. 'Twill not happen again, Ewan, I promise."

"I thought that last snowball must have hit harder than I intended. Don't worry that I took offense at it, Rosalind."

"Aye. But in the future"—she looked up at him, big blue eyes earnest and pleading—"when I say 'tis time to go inside, I will ask that you not question it. The cold weather makes it all too easy to catch chill, and we've no doctor hereabouts."

" 'Tis wise of you to take care, Rosalind. I hadn't thought of the lack of doctors out here, and the last thing I would want is for you to catch ill." He could scarcely stand to speak of the possibility. "As soon as you say the word, I'll take you back inside. You've my word on it, and that's all you need."

"Thank you." She looked as though she wanted to say more but paused before adding, "Trust is a foundation to build on."

"Aye, Rosalind." He covered her shoulder with his hand. "And I'm aiming to build something to last a lifetime."

∽

"Hae we enough snow to build a man?" Luke peered through the frost-covered window after the second snowstorm days later.

"There will be," Rosalind judged. "For now, we wait for the storm to end and the sun to come out and soften it for us." *And warm the frigid air enough so you can play awhile wi'out gasping for breath and coughing. Even then, 'twill be a small snowman. All too soon you'll be spending your days and nights near the warmth of the fire. Best to enjoy the outdoors for now.*

"This time I want to make a great big one." Luke stretched a hand above his head. "With Ewan to help, we can do it this year. Last time 'twas a sad and puny man we made, to be sure."

"Last year's snowman was my favorite," Grandmam spoke up as she rocked back and forth. "Reminded me of you when you were that small. 'Twould be better to build two of those than one great big man. Every-one tries t' build the same old thing."

"Oh." Luke frowned as he thought it over. "Maybe we'll try to make a small one and a big one, so they're friends."

"As long as the small one comes first, for Grandmam." Rosalind gave her a conspiratorial smile. They both knew Luke would only be able to make a small one, and should he start after his larger goal, would protest leaving it unfinished.

"Aye," Luke agreed generously, "for our grandmam." He hopped up and went over to press a kiss on her wrinkled cheek.

Rosalind smiled and continued knitting the scarf she planned for Ewan. *He doesn't hae one, and though he says nothing, I see that the cold bothers him just as it does Da. Fire is their element, and ice doesna agree wi' blacksmiths.*

In my worry o'er Luke, I was harsh wi' Ewan. He doesn't know of Luke's weakness, though he'll find out afore too long. For now, Luke lights up at the way Ewan treats him—like any regular lad. So long as it poses no risk, we'll let it be.

Her fingers stiff, Rosalind put away her knitting and went over to the trunk where the family Bible was kept. Kneeling, she drew it out, feeling cracks in the worn leather cover. She opened it to the first pages, full of family records.

Tears pricked her eyes at the names of Cade Banning and James MacLean. Her grandda and her baby brother were the most recent in a chain of loss stretching back over decades. She ran her fingers over the ink.

Gone but not forgotten. How long will it be until Grandmam's name joins that of her husband's? And how many harsh winters will Luke weather? Ten? Twenty? Will he marry and have wee ones of his own? I pray 'tis so.

Her gaze came to rest on the marriage register. It was Da's Bible, and so did not bear the date of Rosalind's grandparents' wedding. She traced the names of her parents—Arthur MacLean and Kaitlin Banning. *Will mine and Ewan be the next names written and kept here for our children to read someday?*

She turned the fine, brittle pages to the chapter she sought—Ecclesiastes 3—and read to herself. *"To every thing there is a season, and a time to every purpose under the heaven: A time to be born, and a time to die; a time to plant, and a time to pluck up that which is planted."*

Life and death, side by side in the family records, and placed together in scripture, as well. Joy tempered with sorrow; a balance struck between the two.

Lord, all things are to come in Your time. As the seasons change, so, too, do we. This winter seems the most important season I've ever faced. Please help me grow into the woman You'd hae me be and, if 'tis Your plan, the woman Ewan will love. Come spring, a new beginning will bloom all around—I'll say honestly that I hope for a piece of that wellspring in my own life.

Rosalind carefully closed the Bible and placed it in the trunk once more. She looked up to see Da watching her, a question in his gaze. Ma unfolded extra quilts to place on the beds—the hearth wouldn't stave off cold when darkness fell.

I've not seen Ewan in two days. Only two days into a storm, and it seems as though he's been gone from me for weeks. He's snowed in, same as we are. Only Da goes outside, using the guideline to the barn.

Grandmam's house—and Ewan—sat much too far away to string a guideline. It was part of the reason she'd moved. With no way of knowing when the storm would end, Rosalind couldn't even look forward to a day she'd see him again. Marlene endured a distance much greater but with certain knowledge to help her bide her time.

It seems almost a worse torture to know Ewan is so close, but that I can't reach him. Rosalind took up her knitting once more. *Does he regret the decision we made? Is he wishing he had gone on wi' the railroad—wi' Johnny for companionship and work to hasten the long hours? My Ewan works hard day in and day out—how can he stand being cooped up in four walls, all alone, wi' so little to keep him occupied?*

Rosalind looked to the blocked window and couldn't help but wonder, *Is he thinking of me while I think of him?*

Chapter 14

E wan shoved back the curtain without much hope of seeing anything but the wall of white that had stood between him and Rosalind for days on end. Was it wishful thinking or could he see the faint yellow glow of sunlight through the thinning snow?

Yes. . .yes. The blizzard has passed, and the sun is beginning its work. Soon I'll see my Rosalind again.

Ewan stoked the fire and put on some coffee before starting the porridge.

Lord, 'tis by Your grace I had the time to prepare for the winter ahead. Weeks ago, I'd worried 'twas too soon to ask Rosalind whether I should stay through the winter. Now I see 'twas Your timing, ensuring I could chop enough wood to last the cold of the winter.

I'd wondered whether 'twould drive me half mad, being trapped within four walls wi' no work to do and no one wi' whom to speak or pass the time. I was wrong to doubt the wisdom of Your will.

For too long I've worked, focusing on what needed to be done, falling onto my pallet at night wi' only the time to thank You for seeing me through the day and giving me a livelihood. I traveled across this new world, at first in search of my father, then in search of solace from my failure. Yet in all that searching, I lost my true focus.

Now I've taken time to seek You as I hae not in too many years. I don't de-serve the grace of Your love nor the joy I find in Rosalind, but I treasure both. In the barren sleep of winter, a new beginning stirs to life. I aim to not lose sight of that, Lord.

Whistling, Ewan added a pinch of brown sugar to his porridge. He poured a mug full of the strong, steaming coffee, leaving it black. When he pushed away from the table, his glance fell on the just-finished project in the corner.

"More evidence of Your timing, Lord. Those snowshoes will come in handy soon," Ewan determined aloud. He opened the door of the house to a blockage of thick snow, scooped some into the pot he'd used to make the oatmeal, and cleaned it. He filled it with icy white once more before shutting the door and returning to the hearth.

While the water heated, Ewan dug out his razor and strop. With sharpened blade, small mirror, and warmed water, he set to. The raspy scrape of the razor, punctuated by an occasional *swish* in the water, filled the still house. Ewan ran a hand over his now-smooth jaw and nodded at his reflection. *Now I'm ready to see Rosalind.*

The strong, bitter scent of his coffee had him reaching for the mug again. He drained it in one long swallow. He looked around the cabin, checking off items. *Morning devotions done, bed made, breakfast eaten, pot cleaned, face shaven, snowshoes finished.*

He drummed his fingers on the tabletop. *I wonder. . .* He peered through the curtains again. *Maybe.* He grabbed the poker from the hearth and swung the door open again, giving the wall of ice an experimental prod. Since the door wasn't on the same side of the house as the window, the wall of snow here might be thicker. *Hmm.* No snow rumbled forward to fill the gap. He cautiously worked the poker farther and farther until his arm was thrust into the snow at the top of the door. Finally, there was no resistance. The snow, already thawing, piled only a few feet outside the door!

Ewan withdrew and shut the door, warming his half-frozen arm by the fire before donning his jacket, hat, and worn mittens. With the aid of the poker, he broke a sizeable opening through the snowbank and watched as the top portion collapsed down. Ewan kicked through it, smiling at the sight of the snowy hill nearby that must be Rosalind's home.

With the fire banked and his snowshoes tightly strapped to his boots, Ewan made his way. It was slow going, putting one foot before the other, cautiously testing the firm pack of snow before transferring his weight. Finally, he stood before the mound, seeing a corner of the roof poking out of the snowy whiteness.

Will it seem odd that I didn't wait a wee while longer for the snow to clear on its lonesome? Ewan's gloved hands clenched. *No matter. Everyone will be as eager as I am to taste some fresh air.* He dug into the snow, pushing it aside until he reached the wall. *It fell more deeply here—'tis far thicker.* Ewan tapped on the unearthed windowpane, waited, and tapped again before the curtains drew back.

Luke pressed his nose to the windowpane and squinted through the frost. Ewan rubbed the pane clear of ice as Luke disappeared.

Rosalind's eyes widened when she saw him, and Ewan grinned. She pressed one small, bare hand against the glass, and he swiftly pressed his thickly gloved one over it on his side.

"I'll hae you out in a minute!" he yelled, knowing she understood him when she nodded and drew her hand back. He pushed the snow aside feverishly, packing it down in front of the door before giving a mighty knock.

"Ewan!" Rosalind swung the door open, the heated blast of air from within matching the warmth of her gaze. "You're soaking!" She pulled him inside.

∽

Rosalind curled her fingers into the sopping fabric of his coat sleeve, pulling him close.

"'Twould hae melted soon enough," she chided, tugging the coat from his broad shoulders. She laid it out by the fire and held out her hand for his dripping gloves. She twisted them as dry as she could before turning back. Rosalind found his green eyes watching her with a love that brought a warmth to her heart. He'd not said a word, just let her cluck over him like a fussy hen.

He raised a brow and held out one large hand in a silent invitation. She put her hand in his and stood close, reaching up to cup his clean-shaven cheek. *He shaved for me, just as he broke through the snow for me.*

"I couldn't wait another day." Ewan's deep rumble washed over her as he smoothed his free hand over her hair, his fingertips playing with the end of her braid.

"I'm glad you didn't." She returned his gaze until something new—chagrin?—flickered on his face. For the first time since she'd seen him at the window, Rosalind realized her entire family, from Grandmam all the way down to young Luke, was watching. She glanced at Da. She drew back the hand that cupped Ewan's strong jaw, missing the contact immediately.

"Don't just stand there." Grandmam shook her head, but all could see the smile on her face. "Sit down so Luke can help you with those snowshoes."

"I'll warm some mulled cider." Mam busied herself at the hearth as everyone sprang into motion.

"Good to see you, Ewan." Da spoke solemnly, but Rosalind heard the humor behind it. He put out his pipe.

"Ewan?" Luke flopped down at his feet, untying the snowshoes. "Will you help me make a snowman? A grand big one?" He held his hand high over his head.

Rosalind cleared her throat.

"Oh." Luke seemed properly chastened. "Two, then. A bitty one for Grandmam first, and then the grand big one?" His voice rose with anxious hope.

"Luke!" Rosalind intervened. "Ewan broke through the snow o'er his place and ours and only just sat before the fire!"

"Indeed," Mam added. "His things are wet with melted ice."

"I know." Luke seemed to shrink into himself, his thin voice tugging at Rosalind's heart. "I thought that so long as he was already snowy, 'twould be a good time, you see." He stacked the snowshoes carefully by the hearth. " 'Twasn't my intent to be rude."

"Nor were you, lad." Ewan's smile robbed the room of any chill of discomfort. "Sound planning, to my way o' thinking. Now, if you can convince your bonny sister to lend a hand, I'd say this is as good a time as any." He shot Rosalind a quick wink.

"Rose?" Luke's shining eyes pled for her assent, and she couldn't withhold it.

"Aye, then. Let's both pile on our winter clothes." Rosalind frowned at Ewan's sodden coat and gloves.

"I've an old coat o' your da's in a trunk hereabouts." Mam moved some embroidered pillowcases off the top of the chest. "Should do a sight better than that mess. Ah, there." She shook out the old garment. "We don't want you catching a chill, Mr. Gailbraith."

"Thank you, Mrs. MacLean." Ewan accepted the coat and turned to Grandmam. "Now, Mrs. Banning, what's all this about a tiny snowman?"

"I'm of the opinion that snowmen should come in different sizes"— Grandmam eyed Ewan as he held Rosalind's winter cloak for her—"just as folks do. The small ones are most often more loveable."

"Aye." Ewan put his hands on Rosalind's shoulders, emphasizing the disparity between their heights. " 'Tis right you are."

"I disagree." Rosalind turned, tilting her head back to look up at him. "Da is a big bear o' a man—same as you."

"And a more loveable fellow I've yet to meet." Mam walked over to Da and smiled up at him.

"Ready!" Luke's proclamation broke the tender moment as he led Rosalind and Ewan outdoors.

"Ooh." The chill wind made Rosalind shiver before she joined her brother. Together, they packed a base for the smaller snowman while Ewan began work on the larger.

Da and Mam came out to join them. "We thought we'd lend a hand."

"Ah." Mam took a deep breath of the clean, crisp air. "So nice to be outside again. And we have you to thank for that, Mr. Gailbraith."

"What use is the wide open when you've no one to share it wi'?" Ewan's smile sent a thrill through Rosalind.

"We're more than happy to share this beautiful day wi' you." Rosalind tried to imbue the words with the depth of her joy but feared she fell far short.

"I think this is done." Luke frowned in concentration as he gauged the base for the tiny snowman. "She wants it small."

"Here." Da plunked a large handful of hardened snow atop Luke's finished portion. "Let's start on the middle."

"I'll go see what branches and such I can find." Mam headed for a copse of trees, leaving Rosalind standing alone.

Since Da helped Luke, she began packing snow to help Ewan. She tacked it onto the already massive chunk he worked to make round.

"How's that?" He stepped back to examine the misshapen lump.

"Well. . ." Rosalind gave the matter due consideration as she stepped around the beginnings of the sculpture. This one level reached her hip! "Seems to me. . ." She crouched down and made a show of inspecting it. "Yes. . .I know what will set it right."

"What?"

"If you look here"—Rosalind gestured him closer and bit back her grin as Ewan moved toward her—"it needs. . ."

"It needs what?" He looked down at the huge snow lump, then back up at her.

"Leveling off," she told him solemnly before shoving a goodly amount of the excess all over him.

"Hey!" Ewan straightened up, brushing snow from his face and shaking it from his coat.

Rosalind laughed as he gave a little dance to free his collar of the icy deluge. He stopped moving. Her breath caught. Bits of the ice clung to Ewan's coal black hair, catching the winter sunshine as it melted. Standing tall and proud, he was magnificent.

"Rosalind." His voice lingered over her name as though relishing every syllable.

"Oh!" She spluttered as he took advantage of her gawking to exact revenge. He threw a spray of snow so it coated her. The icy specks melted on her tongue, stung her nose, and trickled into her hair where her cloak fell back. "You'll pay for that, Ewan Gailbraith!" She packed a snowball and advanced on him.

"I hope so." He snagged the snow from her hand and slipped a strong arm around her waist before she could react. His grin had a devilish charm. "I hope I get exactly what I deserve." The warmth in his gaze left no doubt what he meant.

Rosalind opened her mouth to tell him she felt the same. . .then shrieked as she felt her own snowball trickling down her back.

Chapter 15

"The pond is frozen over!" Luke barreled into the house a week later, his breath coming in hard gasps of excitement.

Ewan slapped his knee. "Well then. Sounds like we're going ice skating." He stood up. "I'll go get my skates and be right back."

"We'll be ready," Rosalind promised. "Though I'd like to go fetch Marlene, if you don't mind."

"You get your friend, I'll get my skates, and you"—Ewan mussed Luke's hair—"get ready." He set out, his long stride quickly covering the distance between the MacLean household and Gilda's house. He opened the trunk where he'd stowed most of his own possessions and withdrew the metal skates.

Holding them by the laces, Ewan walked back to Rosalind's home. Luke met him at the door, flushed and eager.

"Rose isn't back yet." The boy's voice lowered to a confiding whisper. "Marlene always takes a long time to do anything."

Ewan crouched down to look at the lad eye to eye. "Someday you'll see that pretty girls are worth the wait."

"But. . ." Luke frowned. "Rose doesn't make anybody wait if she can help it."

"I know." Ewan gave the lad a wink. "That makes her worth even more." He straightened up and saw the girls approaching. . .with a man escorting Rosalind—Brent Friemont.

"Luke," he stooped once more and spoke with urgency, "who is that young man walking wi' your sister?"

"Oh. That's Brent Friemont, Marlene's brother."

"Yes, I know his name." Ewan tried again. "Has he been courting Rosalind for long?"

"Courting? He makes big eyes at her and sits next to her whenever he can." Luke scoffed. "Brent burnt down the outhouse a few months ago."

"He burnt—" Ewan stopped himself. There was more important information he needed right away. "And your sister?"

"No." Luke gave him a strange look. "He didn't burn Rose. 'Twas an accident wi' the privy."

"I meant," Ewan clarified, torn between exasperation and amusement, "did Rose encourage his attentions?" *The lad made a nuisance o' himself at the husking bee, but from the way Rose dismissed him, I thought he was no serious rival.*

"Hardly." Luke snorted. "Everyone hereabouts thought she'd marry Brent, but she looks on him as a brother, same as me. Almost." He thought for a moment. "She likes me better."

"As do I." Ewan patted the boy on the shoulder and stood to his full height as the three companions joined them. His jaw tightened as he saw Brent's hand laid possessively over Rosalind's, which lay nestled in the crook of his arm.

"Thank you, Brent." Rosalind looked anything but pleased as she tried to disentangle.

Ewan's sudden good cheer vanished as Brent tightened his grasp, saying, "Of course, Rose. I'll escort you all the way to the pond. We wouldn't want you to stumble again."

"As I've already told you, Brent, 'twas naught but a bit of snow I was shaking from the top of my boot." Rosalind tugged free at last. "I did not stumble at all." She gave Ewan a beseeching glance.

As Brent reached for her hand once more, Ewan stepped between them. "I'd be pleased to carry your skates, Rosalind."

"Thank you." The heartfelt appreciation in her tone spurred Brent into action.

"I'll do that." He yanked the laces from her hand.

The lad fell for it! "Well, since your hands are full, I'll be happy to escort the lady." Ewan smoothly offered Rosalind his arm. "Miss Friemont"—he gave a slight bow to Marlene—"good to see you."

"And you, Mr. Gailbraith." The amusement in her smile let him know she hadn't missed how he stressed the last word. "You've met my brother, Brent Friemont, haven't you?"

"Oh, we've met." Ewan looked at the lad in disgust before smiling at his sister. "Shall we go on to the pond?"

With that, he and Rosalind led the way, leaving Brent to trail behind. Ewan set a quick pace, deliberately putting more distance between

Rosalind and him and the others.

"He needs time to come to terms wi' it, that's all." Rosalind spoke only when they were out of earshot. "Brent has nurtured certain. . .hopes, for a long while now."

"Hopes?" Ewan raised a brow. "Or expectations, Rosalind?"

"Expectations." Her whisper made him uneasy. "Expectations encouraged by his parents and my mother—but not by me." Her blue eyes transfixed him. "Though I never told him plainly. I should hae, long ago."

"He's not the sort to understand the subtle approach," Ewan agreed. "Though it should be clear as day by now."

"'Tis clear to him now," Rosalind assured him. "He just hasn't accepted it yet."

"Accepted what?" He knew what she meant but had an itch to hear her say the words aloud.

"That *you*"—her smile plainly told him she knew what he was up to and didn't mind humoring his whim—"are the only man I'm interested in courting."

�◌

"He's your brother," Rosalind grumbled to Marlene as Brent skated in circles around Ewan, edging closer in a blatant bid to make him uncomfortable. "Can't you do something?"

"They're competing over you," Marlene shot back. "And since when has my brother ever listened to a word I say—unless it's 'dinner'?" She watched as Ewan changed directions, leisurely skimming backwards while Brent continued his annoying tactics. "Nice footwork, there. If you ask me, I'd say Ewan can handle Brent without any assistance from either of us."

"Of course he can." Rosalind beamed with pride. "Ewan's handled far more than whatever ice tricks Brent can throw at him. I just wish. . ." her voice trailed off.

"You wish what?" Marlene did a neat turn and stop, narrowly avoiding Luke as he zoomed around the perimeter of the pond.

"That Brent hadn't invited himself along." Rosalind sighed. "Not that he doesn't have every right to come to the pond, but. . .this was supposed to be a fun outing. And now. . .well, you see." She gestured to where the two men had evidently decided to stage an impromptu race across the pond. "They're being. . ." She searched for a word other than *competitive* and came up short.

"Men?" Marlene zigzagged. "And you don't think it's even a tiny bit fun to have two men competing for your affection?"

"No!" Rosalind slid to a halt. "I'm not a prize at some country fair to be won by the man who can skate the fastest or eat the most pies in a single sitting. 'Tis pure foolishness, Marlene."

"Love makes fools out of us all, sooner or later." Marlene moved gently, leaving wavelike tracks in her wake as she circled Rosalind. "If a race or pie could bring Johnny back right now, I'd do it without thinking twice. But it's not so simple."

"No, it isn't." Rosalind reached out to clasp one of her friend's hands, and they skated side by side. "Here I am, going on about myself when my Ewan is scant paces away. Do you miss Johnny terribly, Marlene?" She gave a soft squeeze in sympathy.

"Part of me does," she admitted. "But I'm more worried about the part of me that's glad he went on with the railroad. I keep thinking that since he's gone now—when we'll be snowed in most of the time anyway—he'll be here in the spring. That's when we'll be able to see each other more. That's when he can start working the land he'll buy and building our house. If he stayed now, he'd be gone then. This way is best."

"Exactly!" Rosalind stared at her friend. "This is the way I knew you'd be once you'd thought it o'er."

"I did behave like the worst brat." Marlene flushed. "I'm blessed that you understood, Ewan forgave me, and Johnny wasn't scared away forever by my terrible temper!"

"You'll have to do far worse to frighten any of us away." Rosalind let go of Marlene's hand to do a quick spin. "We know what a wonderful woman lies beneath a passing mood. And in just a few short weeks, you've already unearthed her! Johnny will find an even better catch than he remembers when he comes back."

"I hope so—oof!" Marlene fell into Rosalind as Brent whizzed by too closely, throwing her off balance. Both girls crashed to the ice in an ungainly heap of arms and skirts and skates.

"Ooh," Rosalind moaned, rubbing the back of her head where it had met the ice so suddenly. "Are you all right, Marlene?" She disentangled her skates from her friend's and knelt beside her.

"Yes. I—I think so." She gingerly sat up, rubbing her elbow. "Just caught me off guard. Where is. . .Brent!" She glowered at her brother. "See what your showing off has done?"

As Ewan helped Rosalind, Brent yanked on Marlene's arms to pull her to her feet.

"I'll help!" Luke came speeding toward them, only to hit a slippery patch and come crashing down himself.

"Luke!" Rosalind pushed away from Ewan and raced to her brother's side. "Are you all right? Say something." Her brother's labored breathing chilled her in a way the hard ice and winter wind had not. "Let's get you back to the house."

"Knocked the wind out of you, did it?" Ewan lifted the small boy to his feet. "Well, I'd say we've done enough damage for one afternoon. Let's see if we can talk your mam into giving us some more of that wonderful mulled cider of hers." He led Luke to solid ground, and everyone unlaced their metal blades for the trek home.

Rosalind took care to walk slowly, leaving Ewan's side to hover around Luke. His flushed cheeks and continued coughing made her throat clench shut. *I was so busy worrying about myself and talking wi' Marlene, I didn't watch him closely enough. We should hae left before any o' this happened. 'Tis my fault he struggles so.*

Lord, please be wi' my brother. Put Your healing hand o'er him and help him to breathe. I'll sit him by the hearth and get him something warm to drink. Please don't let this episode worsen from my negligence, Father. His breath rasps and his chest heaves—please ease his breathing, Lord. Please.

Before they got to the house, her fervent prayers had been answered. While he still rasped, Luke's coughing had abated. She bundled him by the fire and gave him the first cup of hot cider, relaxing only when his faint wheeze was barely audible.

"Rosalind," Ewan spoke from behind her. "Why don't we walk Marlene and Brent home?"

"Of course." Rosalind shot him an apologetic smile. For a short time, she'd all but forgotten about everyone else!

The walk passed pleasantly enough, with Marlene and Brent soon ensconced in the Friemont house. Rosalind found herself suddenly alone with Ewan as they made their way back home.

Ewan waited until they were midway on the return to stop. "Rosalind, what's wrong?"

"Wrong?" Rosalind frowned. "Nothing. Marlene's seen the wisdom of Johnny's decision, neither of us suffered more than a bruise from the fall, and Luke's fine. What could be wrong?"

"Go back to the part about Luke being fine. 'Tisn't usual for a sister to fuss so o'er a twelve-year-old boy." Ewan peered at Rosalind. "He's nearing manhood, by then."

At about that same age, I was taking care of Mam wi' my father gone on to America. I worked hard and checked for Da's letters every day, trying to fill his shoes and hold everything together.

"He fell, too," Rosalind reminded him, but the answer didn't satisfy. Her gaze wouldn't meet his completely.

"I know." Ewan tilted her chin toward him. "I can see for myself that Luke's small for his age—small enough not t' spend all his time at the forge. But I've never seen him there. And today, when a small tumble knocked the wind out o' him, he gasped for breath all the way back home. So I'll ask you again, Rosalind. . ." He paused meaningfully. "What is wrong?"

"Will you start to treat him differently if something is?" she hedged, her eyes searching his face intently. "Or will you continue to see him as a normal boy and not coddle him?"

"You coddle him enough for both of us, t' my way of thinking." He said it gently, but firmly enough to reassure her.

"Luke's never been strong." She pulled her chin from his grasp to hold his hand in hers. "He was born wi' weak lungs. The doctors say 'tis nothing short o' a miracle he survived past infancy. He can't abide the smoke o' the forge—that's why he doesn't work wi' Da. We don't speak on it, as it pains them both."

"I see." Ewan nodded. "And the cold? 'Tis the reason he coughed and you stopped the snowball fight?"

"Aye," she admitted. "He had an episode then. . .and again today. I keep close watch o'er him so they don't worsen, but today I wasn't careful enough. It could hae been much worse."

" 'Twasn't your fault that he fell, Rosalind."

"No, but he'd probably begun rasping afore that even." She looked down at the toes of her boots. "I should hae checked on him sooner. He will not admit when he's done too much."

"What happens when it worsens?" He pulled her closer, putting his arm about her waist.

"He coughs so hard his body is wracked wi' it. His chest heaves and he fights for breath until his face goes pale and his mouth turns blue.

There's not a winter as goes by but he gets terribly ill. A simple cold sets him coughing, and it settles in his chest, and then"—the tears in her eyes when she looked up at him flooded his heart—"we all fight so he'll see the spring."

"Why didn't you tell me?" He cupped her cheek and used the pad of his thumb to wipe away her tears. "Let me help you."

"I didn't want you to treat him as though he were too fragile to do anything. He's a boy like any other and needs to laugh and play and feel useful. Luke brightens whenever you're around because you don't molly-coddle him." She bit her lip. "Da loves him and tries so hard to give him freedom tempered wi' safeguards, but Luke sees through it. I didn't want that for you or Luke."

"I understand." He took a deep breath. "And I'll treat him no differ-ently. We'll leave it to you to shoo us back into the warmth of the house when you feel 'tis the right time."

"Thank you, Ewan." She rose on tiptoe to plant a soft kiss on his cheek.

He fought the urge to turn his head, knowing it wasn't the right time. Ewan settled for keeping his arm around her waist as they walked back to the house.

I may not be able to protect Rosalind from Luke's weakness, he reasoned, *but I can make it easier for her to look after him. A nice group we'll be. . . Rosalind watches o'er Luke, I'll watch o'er Rosalind, and God will watch o'er us all. May Christmas come to find us all hearty and full of joy.*

Chapter 16

"A nd the angel said unto them, Fear not: for, behold, I bring you good tidings of great joy, which shall be to all people.' " Da's voice rang with conviction as he read the Christmas story. " 'For unto you is born this day in the city of David a Saviour, which is Christ the Lord. And this shall be a sign unto you; Ye shall find the babe wrapped in swaddling clothes, lying in a manger. And suddenly there was with the angel a multitude of heavenly host praising God, and saying, Glory to God in the highest, and on earth peace, good will toward men.' Luke, chapter 2, verses 10 to 14." He reverently shut the family Bible.

Rosalind blinked, trying to clear the tears from her eyes. The wonder of that scene—the majesty of a newborn King come to save all men.

Jesus, You are so good to us. You sacrificed Your splendor to be born a man, and we did not appreciate it. The Prince of Heaven offered a manger. Each time I hear the words, I marvel at Your greatness—the most powerful of all brought to us as a helpless babe. I struggle with pride, yet Your example shows the meaning of true humility. Thank You for Your loving grace, which brings us such undeserved joy.

Her tears stopped, and she found Ewan watching her, his own face shining with the light of love.

"We've so many blessings to be thankful for this Christmas," he said. "Christ's own love is mirrored at this hearth. 'Tis been many a year since I took part in such a celebration."

"We're glad to have you, Ewan." Rosalind stood and walked over to place a hand on his shoulder. His joy had been mixed with such wistfulness, she wanted to brush away the sorrow. "Shall we sing a few Christmas carols?"

" 'Tis been too long since I heard the Irish Christmas Carol." Ewan looked around hopefully. "Do you all know it?"

"Of course!" Luke hummed the tune. " 'Tis Grandmam's favorite."

"Aye, 'tis." Grandmam rocked back, smiling in remembrance and anticipation. "Why don't you start it for us, Mr. Gailbraith?"

"I'd be honored." Ewan cleared his throat and broke into the melody, his rich baritone flowing over the words as everyone joined in.

"Christmas day is come; let's all prepare for mirth,
Which fills the heav'ns and earth at this amazing birth.
Through both the joyous angels in strife and hurry fly,
with glory and hosannas, 'All Holy' do they cry. . ."

Rosalind closed her eyes and let the song wash over her. *My family is well, Ewan is wi' us, and we're celebrating the Lord's birth. What could be better?*

When the final note quavered in the air, she opened her eyes. "Any other favorites?"

And so they praised the night away, singing beloved hymns such as "O Come, All Ye Faithful," "Angels, from the Realms of Glory," and "Joy to the World."

When the candles guttered, eyelids drooped, and stomachs groaned with satisfaction, Ewan rose from the settle. "Will you walk wi' me a wee while?"

Rosalind looked to Da for permission. At his short nod, she swirled her thick cloak over her shoulders and stepped into the thick night with Ewan. Only a single candle and the light from the heavens illuminated their path. Rosalind could see her breaths coming in little white puffs of the frigid night air as he pulled her close.

"Ewan, why are we stopping?" Rosalind stamped her feet to warm them as he set the candle on a sturdy log and took both her hands in his own. A curious warmth suddenly took away the chill.

"Rosalind," he began, "there is an old Irish marriage blessing. Do you know it?"

"Nay." Rosalind fixed her gaze upon him, understanding his purpose in bringing her outside. They were alone, under the stars, and he spoke of marriage!

She didn't dare breathe as he recited the blessing:

"May God be wi' you and bless you.
May you see your children's children.

May you be poor in misfortunes
and rich in blessings.
May you know nothing but happiness
from this day forward."

He paused, giving her time to savor the sweetness of the words. "Rosalind, God has blessed me simply by letting me know you." He sank to his knees, still clasping her hands. "I love you. Will you make me rich in His blessings and bring me even more happiness by saying you'll wed me?"

Tears streaked down her face as Rosalind let out the breath she'd been holding to kneel in front of him. "Yes, Ewan. Oh yes!" She threw her arms around him and sank into his warm embrace as his lips sought her own.

He pulled away a short while later and fumbled in his coat pocket. "Here." He held up a small, carved box, dwarfed by his palm.

Rosalind took it and opened the lid to find a simple gold band inside. She gasped as he drew it out and slid it onto her left ring finger.

" 'Twas my mother's." His hoarse whisper made her realize his eyes shone with unshed tears. " 'Tis all I hae left o' her, and I know she'd smile to see the beautiful bride I've given it to."

"And I'm proud to wear it," she whispered. "I love you, Ewan Gailbraith."

Chapter 17

"Still no word as to when the circuit rider will pass through?" Ewan worked to clear underbrush and rotten logs from around the bases of the sugar maples.

"None. 'Twas a harsh winter, so 'tisn't surprising." Arthur grinned. "Probably settled in somewhere to wait it out. Don't worry. Now that 'tis warm enough for the sap to run, he'll turn up."

"Good." Ewan carried a load of dead brush over to where they'd have the boiling place.

Lord, winter begins to change to spring, and still Rosalind is naught but my intended! Close to three months now, I've waited as patiently as I can. I'm anxious to make her my bride in truth, though I see the wisdom in Your timing. I've yet to determine where I'll set up household wi' my Rosalind. If I stay, I'll take Arthur's livelihood. Should I go, I separate her from the family I've come to love as well.

"Hold a moment, son." Arthur put a hand on Ewan's forearm, halting him. "I wanted a word wi' you. I know you want to be wed, and we've both been praying o'er where you'll settle. But I was wondering whether you're any closer to a decision?"

"I don't want to take Rosalind away from Saddleback," Ewan stated flatly before softening. "To tell the truth, I don't want to leave, myself. And yet, should I stay. . ." He let the thought hang, unable to speak of the harsh reality to the man who'd been so kind.

"You're worried you'll take away my customers." Arthur nodded. "I surmised as much when you asked my blessing. Hae you any solution to the problem?"

Ewan straightened his shoulders. "I've thought I might turn my hand to farming. I've a solid bit of money tucked away, more than I'd need for a good while. 'Twould do to seed a new spread, and I'm used to working wi' my hands."

"You're a blacksmith, son." Arthur clapped a hand on his shoulder, frowning. "'Twouldn't do to try to change who you are."

For the first time, Ewan noted how the fine lines about the older man's mouth and eyes had deepened. Was it merely the strain of winter, or something else?

"I'm not a young man anymore." Arthur rubbed the back of his neck. "And I'm starting to feel my age. The cold brings a stiffness to my fingers and a tightness to my chest."

"I see." And Ewan could see what it cost the great man to admit it. "Wi' spring coming, that 'twill ease."

"Aye, for a while. But each year the stiffness hae lingered a bit longer, and the twinges hae turned to steady aches." Arthur looked ruefully at his strong hands. "I've seen forty-five years, Ewan. At this age, I'd thought to have a son beside me at the forge, taking on the lion's share o' the work."

Ewan glanced back to where Luke snapped dead branches a ways off. He looked back to Arthur. They both knew Luke wouldn't be the help to his father's business that Arthur had hoped for.

"Aye, you see what I'm saying. Kaitlin and I lost two babes between Rose and Luke—one too soon to tell whether the child was a lad or lassie, and one boy. Our James didna live to see his second year." Arthur's eyes burned with a fierce light. "And we both know Luke isna fit for smithing, and I won't hae him risking his life to try. I'll not lose my son to pride."

Not knowing what to say, Ewan simply nodded. He waited and listened, fighting not to compare Arthur with his own father. He'd begun to see where Arthur was heading with this conversation.

"Now the Lord hae seen fit to bring a fine man to my doorstep, who's won my Rosey's heart and hae proven himself a man of his word." Arthur paused. "And he's a blacksmith wi' no forge to call his own and loathe to take my daughter far from our family. 'Tis no stretch to see God's hand in this.

"I make a good living here, and wi' the railroad tracks laid, more business will be passing through than a lone old man can handle. Ewan, I'd be honored if you'd work by my side at the forge."

For a moment, Ewan couldn't speak, choked by an avalanche of thoughts. *I knew 'twas my lot to ever bear the burden of my poor decision. My da turned his back on me when I'd not yet reached the age o' sixteen. In all the years since he went to America, I've not laid eyes on the man, though I've tried to track him down.*

Now here's a man not bound to me by blood, calling me "son" and asking me to stand alongside him.

"I'm the one who's honored, Arthur." Ewan embraced his father-in-law-to-be with a hearty slap on the back. "Though you're no old man yet. You've a need for grandchildren before you claim that title."

"And that's another joy you'll be bringing me." Arthur stepped back. "I've high expectations," he warned.

Ewan grinned. "I plan to meet every one."

☙

"Do you know what you'll do when the circuit riding preacher finally does arrive?" Marlene drove a spike into one of the sugar maples. "Or has Ewan still said nothing about whether you'll stay in Saddleback or not? I pray you'll stay!"

"He's mentioned trying his hand at farming," Rosalind answered. "I think he fears taking away Da's business if he opens his smithy here, but neither of us wants to move very far."

"What happened to all your great dreams of travel?" Marlene stepped back as Rosalind pushed a trough into place beneath the hollow tube. "You've always said you want to see the world beyond our small corner of it. Not that I'm complaining if you're choosing to stay here with us, mind."

"I still do." Rosalind moved to the next tree with a cleared base. "Wi' the railroad tracks already laid, trains will start passing through. Ewan and I will hae the freedom to hop aboard whenever—and to wherever—we please and be back more quickly than I ever dreamed. Besides"—she gave a small smile—"I'm thinking marriage might be enough of an adventure to last a short while, at least. My own house will offer quite a change."

"Most likely," Marlene agreed. "I know I can't wait for mine! With spring upon us, my Johnny should be coming back any day." She peered about as though half expecting to see him pop out from behind the tree she just finished tapping.

"Or it could be a month," Rosalind gently reminded. Seeing the shadow creeping over her friend's face, she quickly changed the subject. "And what of Johnny? Will Da have to expect competition from your beau?" She said it lightly but couldn't hide the tinge of concern she felt.

Da, Ewan, and Johnny? 'Tis two too many blacksmiths for a single town, even wi' the railroad trade.

"Oh no." Marlene brushed her concerns aside and tripped over to the next tree. "Johnny doesn't actually like smithing. Says it's hot, dirty, and loud. He'd prefer to be a wainwright, just working on wheels. I'm glad I won't be washing soot from his shirts every week! Does that put your mind at ease?"

"Yes." Rosalind didn't pretend not to know what Marlene meant. "Mayhap Da will be the blacksmith, Ewan the farrier, and Johnny the wainwright as Saddleback grows larger. The railroad will bring people. Our skilled menfolk will keep them nearby."

"That's a thought." Marlene handed the auger to Rosalind. "Of course, Johnny needs to come back and the preacher needs to show up before any of those plans will bear fruit!"

"Parson Burchill always had a fondness for maple sweeties." Rosalind moved on to the final tree in the immediate area. "Wi' the lure of those along wi' the welcome of warmer days, he'll turn up soon." She stepped back to survey her work. "I hope."

Talk turned to their hope chests as the girls made their way back to the sugaring-off shelter. They found everyone congregated there, waiting for the wooden troughs to fill.

The Twadleys, Horntons, and Prestons would be tapping trees nearer to home, so only a few households were represented out here. The MacLeans; Ewan; Marlene's parents; Brent, of course; and Marlene's uncles, Jakob and Isaac Albright, with their mail-order brides; made up the work crew. Grandmam sat bundled by the boiling fire, overseeing everything to her heart's content. Fourteen neighbors welcoming spring and greeting each other after a long winter of snowy solitude—the sugar they'd make this day only sweetened the cheerful meeting.

They snacked on cold biscuits and cheese, chatting about anything and everything until it was time to get to work. The sap ran from the trunks in thick, gooey streams. As the hollowed troughs filled, everyone took care to replace them with empty ones and pour the bounty into buckets. The first troughs filled always made the very best sugar, so they boiled separately.

"Amazing how the ants always appear, isn't it?" Marlene brushed a few of the insects away, saving them from drowning in the sap. "And they never learn that the sap will kill them."

"Don't worry. You know the milk foam will bring all the bugs and bits o' bark to the top, and we'll skim it out," Rosalind teased. She knew that was Marlene's least favorite part of the sugaring.

"I remember," her friend spoke flatly. "Better out with the foam than floating in my syrup though." She gave a shudder.

They hauled full buckets back to the boiling fire, handing them off to their mothers and Luke, who watched the sap boil with eagle eyes as it separated into syrup and sugar. A smaller pot hung with the other large ones, promising a special treat.

Everyone took turns emptying troughs, filling buckets, watching the boiling sap, and shooing away greedy squirrels and dogs that crept close enough to pose a threat. Humans weren't the only ones who had a taste for something sweet every now and again.

" 'Tis hard work," Ewan commented. "Though the rewards will be sweet enough to merit it. I'd not thought the animals would cause problems. Shouldn't the fire and noise scare them away?"

"You'd think." Rosalind walked with him to the farthest sugar maples to check the troughs. "But there're actually stories about livestock trying to steal a taste." She caught his disbelieving look. "Really! There's an old tale about a prize bull named Prince who popped his head into one of his owner's tins of hot sugar. The heat shocked him so that he ran off wi' the best of the batch stuck all around his muzzle, and the cows followed!"

"There's a yarn, to be sure." Ewan shook his head. "Though I don't doubt you believe 'tis the truth, Rosalind."

"What?" She stopped dead in her tracks. "You think that I'm easily taken in by false stories, do you now, Ewan Gailbraith?"

"No." He held up his hands in mute apology. "I just meant that you wouldn't knowingly pass on an untruth. You've too strong a character for something like that. 'Twas a compliment!"

"From the man who tells stories of conductors wi' bears and three-man-hunts for a solitary lost railroad spike." She shook her head. "They're naught but tales told to teach us."

"And what is the story of the bull and the maple sugar supposed to teach us?" Ewan folded his arms across his chest.

"To keep close watch o'er the things we value," Rosalind explained, "lest someone more daring come and take it away."

"In that case"—laughing, he swept her into his arms—"I suppose I should just keep a tight hold on you. Even though it seems Brent has accepted our engagement, I'd rather be careful."

"Ewan!" She reluctantly pushed away. "We've work to be doing. Now isn't the time to be stealing kisses—wi' half the town only paces away!" She moved to pick up the dropped bucket.

"Seems like the perfect time." He stepped close once more. He lowered his head and whispered in her ear, "After all, we're harvesting sweets today." With that, he pressed his lips to hers in a fleeting caress before swiping the bucket from her.

"You're incorrigible," she said, the sting of the reprimand stolen by her flushed cheeks and gentle smile.

"I'm in love," he corrected, sweeping her hand into his. "And in the mood to celebrate. Your da has asked me to work alongside him at the smithy. I'll not need to forsake my trade to turn my hands to a plow nor move us from Saddleback."

"Oh Ewan!" This time she threw her arms around him. "Why didn't you say so sooner? This is wonderful news—just perfect!"

"And so"—he planted a swift peck on her nose—"are you."

"I hate to disappoint," she warned, "but no one's perfect."

Chapter 18

I hate to say it, Rosalind, but you were right." Ewan sat heavily on a log placed by the fire for that purpose. "You're not quite perfect, after all." He shook his head.

"I know," she responded, looking puzzled. "But what, in particular, has made you change your mind so very quickly?"

"How can you like this better than the corn husking?" He winked. "I happen to have some very fond memories of that day." His roundabout mention of their first kiss made her blush that delightful pink shade he'd come to be so fond of.

" 'Tis harder work than the corn husking," she admitted, not taking the bait. "And 'tis far colder, too, but my favorite part of the day is coming up now. You'll change your mind back soon."

"I look forward to it." He gave a mighty stretch.

"You'll need this." She handed him a small wooden spoon with a rather long handle. "And you'll want to follow me." He watched as she took the last pot left on the fire—the smaller one that's sap had boiled down to a sludge-like syrup—and walked around the shanty and out of sight.

He hurried to his feet and followed, finding everyone eagerly crowding around Rosalind and her still-hot pot—each of them brandishing one of the curious wooden spoons like his. He watched as she set the pot on a sturdy old tree stump and backed away until she stood beside him.

Together, they watched as first Luke, then everyone else, dipped a spoonful of the thick syrup and hurried away, dropping the contents on a patch of hard snow a little ways off. Luke picked up his newly hardened piece almost right away and bit into it, his eyes closed with obvious enjoyment as he swallowed.

"This is the sugaring-off." Rosalind nudged him forward. "Go ahead—they'll all keep coming back for more until there's none left at all. Believe me, you'll want to try some for yourself."

Shrugging, Ewan stepped forward, waited for Luke to scurry away with his third helping, and loaded his own spoon with the hot, gloppy brown mixture. He went back to where Rosalind waited with her own portion and mimicked her as she flipped the syrup onto the hard-packed snow.

Almost immediately, the syrup froze into a hardened disk. Ewan picked it up and bit into the crunchy sweet that's cold flavor melted on his tongue. He started walking back to the pot before he finished the last bite of his first taste of the treat. He ignored Rosalind's laughter as he returned to her side with a heaping spoonful of the goop and eagerly flipped it onto the snow. He couldn't ignore her when she snatched his sweet from right under his nose.

"Thank you, sweetheart." She bit into it with relish. "So thoughtful of you to fetch more for me. Very gentlemanly!" she called as he tromped off once again to scrape the last spoonful from the very bottom of the pot as everyone watched.

Everyone but Arthur and his wife. Ewan noticed that Arthur began coughing as the day wore on and kept putting his hand to his head, as though in pain. He'd seen Mrs. MacLean rubbing her husband's temples to comfort him, but he grew pale.

"Mam and Da are going home." Rosalind pinched the folds of her skirts. "Da has a headache he says is worsening. I heard him coughing. . . . I hope he isn't taking ill. Perhaps some extra rest will do the trick, and that's why Mam is taking him home for now. I'll need to keep a close eye on Luke. The days are warmer, but the nights bring a harsh chill as the sun sets."

"You're good to care so." He led her toward the fire. "And we're finishing up the boiling. 'Twill be done soon."

After the work ended, they all gathered around the fire in the waning light to share stories and laughter. Rosalind prevailed upon Ewan to tell more of his railroad legends, and he had to search his memory to find one worthy of the occasion.

"Ah. I'll tell about Mr. Villard's special train."

"Mr. Villard? The railroad owner who ran the Last Spike ceremony?" Jakob Albright frowned.

"The same one. And funny enough, this story—which has been sworn to me as true—takes place on the ride up to Independence Creek for that very ceremony." Ewan paused for effect, watching to see that he had everyone's attention before he began.

"Well, Mr. Villard brought his wife, their babe, and the babe's nurse along to be a part of his triumph. After a stop in St. Paul, Mrs. Villard made the appalling discovery that all the babe's linens were soiled—there were none clean in the hamper. Obviously, this just would not do. She notified her husband of the problem."

"Seems to me," Marlene's father, Dustin, commented, "that they should have packed enough of the linens to begin with."

"Or been responsible enough to do a wash," harrumphed Delana Friemont. "You'd think between the mother and the nurse, one of the two would have taken care of the matter long before."

"Aye," Ewan agreed. "But the fact of the matter was that they were stopped in St. Paul wi' naught but a hamper full o' soiled linen. Mr. Villard ordered the hamper be rushed to the Pullman laundry service, where it would be washed and returned before the train even pulled out of St. Paul."

" 'Tis good to own a railroad, I see," Gilda cackled. "To have your high and mighty wife send her laundry to the workers!"

"Now, I never met Mrs. Villard personally, mind," Ewan continued, "so I can't speak as to how hoity-toity a miss she may or may not hae been. But whichever the case, as the train made its way toward Helena, the distraught nurse came before her mistress and whispered that the hamper was nowhere on board. The whole thing had been left behind in St. Paul after all."

Ewan noted that Luke slipped away from the fire, and, after a short while, Rosalind followed after him. Unwilling to draw attention to their absence, he finished the railroad legend.

"So Mr. Villard ordered that an engine and car should be found immediately and made to follow their train at all speed to bring his wife the hamper of linens. And so the special train, not weighted by a heavy load, sped o'er the tracks and managed to overtake the Villard family before they reached Helena.

"Flushed wi' the triumph of his idea, Villard watched the gleeful nurse open the hamper. . .and find naught but the same soiled linens."

Gasps and laughter sounded around the fire as everyone speculated on who Mr. Villard blamed for the entire affair and what they ever did about the baby. Who could imagine a special train sent to fetch a baby's laundry—and that laundry not done?

Ewan, for his part, searched the darkness beyond the perimeter of the fire, trying to find Rosalind and Luke. As they still did not appear, a frisson of tension shot down his spine. *After such a fine day, surely nothing is wrong?*

⚯

Something was very wrong. Rosalind could feel the unease as a palpable thing while she searched for her younger brother.

"Luke!" She whispered, at first, loathe to make a scene and embarrass him. Holding her lantern aloft to better see her way, she kept on. Darkness pressed in around the modest light, throwing shadows wherever she turned. "Luke!" she called more loudly after he still had not answered.

He knew better than to wander off into the woods alone—especially in the dark. He could fall or find himself in a much worse predicament. After a harsh winter, predators would be more aggressive. Luke should still be within earshot, but Rosalind heard no answering call to soothe her frayed nerves.

Lord, there are dangers out in the wild, but Luke faces even more. 'Tis growing colder by the moment. I've not checked in on him since before the sugaring-off. Please, do not let him be in trouble. For the first time in my memory, Luke's made it through the winter wi'out a severe illness. Now that spring is upon us, 'twould be cruel for his weakness to sicken him. Guide my footsteps and help me find my brother. Let him be safe.

"Luke!" Praying fervently between calls, she stopped and listened. There it was—the shallow rasp of Luke's breathing. She turned toward the sound, her lantern's light showing her brother sitting on the cold ground, his back against a tree.

"Rose." He gave a game smile. "I'm all right." But the words came out hard and fast—forced.

"No, you're not." She knelt beside him and threw her cloak around them both. *I've heard him speak like this afore—when he's holding his breath, trying to push back the coughing.* "Don't fight it, Luke. 'Twill go easier if you don't try to hold it back." She stood, pulling him to his feet.

Guided by the lantern light, she kept a slow pace, careful not to overexert him. He coughed and rasped and coughed in spite of her best efforts. Luke needed to be where the air was warm and where she could get a hot drink down him to ease his throat and breathing.

"When did the tightness begin?" She kept her voice steady, not accusing or angry or frightened. "How long?"

"The sugaring-off." His words ended in a horrible hacking that shook his entire frame.

Of course. Breathing in the cold air, then hurrying to eat frozen sweets would bring this on. And I was too wrapped up in Ewan to think of it. I didn't watch Luke as closely as I should.

"Why did you not say so?" Rosalind couldn't bite back the question. *Did it seem I would not care if he needed my help?*

"I didn't—" Coughs interrupted his answer, and they stopped mere yards away from the boiling fire. Finally, they subsided. "I didn't want to miss any of the fun. And"—he glanced sideways at her—"I didn't want you to miss any of it either."

"There will always be opportunities for fun!" She hugged him tight around the shoulders as they kept walking. "Don't you know that you're more important than any combination of sweets and stories? You're my brother and you always come first."

"Sorry." The piteous mumble wrung her heartstrings as they stepped into the flickering light of the big fire.

"Rosalind! Luke!" Ewan hurried over to greet them. "We were beginning to worry about you." He hunkered down to peer at Luke. One look obviously told him her brother wasn't well, because he scooped the boy into his arms before addressing everyone.

"'Tis been a long day, and I'm as tuckered as Luke, here." He spoke loudly enough to hide the sound of the boy's ragged breathing. "So I'll be taking Rosalind home now. We wish you all a pleasant night. I hope t' see you again soon."

With Rosalind's nod, he started out. She carried the lantern; he carried the more precious cargo. Even nestled against Ewan's warmth, Luke's coughing grew steadily worse before they reached the house.

"Mam!" Rosalind pushed open the door and rushed inside, dragging a chair as close to the roaring hearth fire as she dared. She hurried to put on a kettle of water while Ewan deposited Luke in the chair.

Mam took one look at her son's pale face, heard the labored breathing, and pulled out a warm quilt to wrap around him. She pulled off his gloves, chafing his hands as she knelt at his side. "How long has he been this way?" Her question sent another pang of guilt through Rosalind as she brewed the tea.

"He says his chest started feeling tight after the sugaring-off."

Rosalind spoke for Luke, as he fought for breath. She scooped out some of the eucalyptus leaves and peppermint that had always helped to ease his coughing before and prayerfully would again.

"Why didn't he come wi' us when his da felt poorly?" Mam's face fell. "I should hae checked on him afore I took your father off." She smoothed back Luke's hair. "I'm sorry, son."

"No." Rosalind choked on the words as she finally handed over a mug of steaming tea. " 'Tis my fault. You left him in my care, but I didn't realize aught was amiss until he left the fire and did not immediately return to join us." She bowed her head. "I went after him and found him trying to stop the coughing."

"You weren't holding it in, were you?" Mam turned a harsh gaze on Luke as he breathed in the warm steam from his mug. At his sheepish nod, she sighed. "That always makes it worse."

"Aye." Rosalind sat wearily on the settle, beside Ewan. "As I brought him back to the fire, and then on to home, he worsened."

" 'Tis true." Ewan frowned. "I carried the lad and could feel it as he found it harder and harder to draw breath."

"You did what you could." Mam sat back on her heels. "Thank you, Ewan, for helping Rose bring him home. Now we keep him warm and propped up, and hope that 'twill pass quickly."

Please, Father, Rosalind prayed as Ewan took his leave. *Please let this be a short episode. Do not let him worsen but instead feel better. Let Luke be well again come morning. Amen.*

Chapter 19

Four mornings later, Ewan knocked on the MacLean door, carrying a brace of freshly caught rabbits. *Wi' Arthur and Luke on the mend, nothing will go down half so good as hot rabbit stew—best thing to bring a man back to his feet.* When Rosalind, eyes heavy with dark circles, opened the door, his smile vanished.

"What's happened?" He shouldered past her, dropping the skinned game atop the wooden table. An unnatural stillness filled the house for a brief moment before both Arthur and Luke broke into coughing spasms, the sound shattering the silence.

"They were doing better." Rosalind's voice came in an exhausted whisper. "It seemed as though they were on their way to recovery just yesterday. But come nightfall. . ."

"Fever came upon them both." Gilda, rocking more erratically than Ewan had ever seen, spoke up. "Their breathing labored. . .the coughing wracks their bodies. Nothing helps."

Ewan sat heavily on the settle, running a hand over his face. For two days after he'd carried Luke home, Rosalind and Kaitlin had tended to Arthur and Luke night and day. Only yesterday it had seemed they'd turned the corner and the worst of it had passed. But now. . . He stared helplessly to where Rosalind stooped by Luke, propping him up on cushions to ease his breathing.

"When they're more upright, they take in more air," she explained as she noticed him watching. "That and the heat and the tea are all we can do for them. Mam's asleep now after staying up all night. They were improving—" She broke off in a stifled sob that wrung Ewan's heart.

He walked over to where she slumped by the hearth and fell to his knees. With his arms wrapped around her, her weary head nestled against his shoulders, she wept. Ewan prayed.

Lord, put Your hand on this home and Your children wi'in it. Bring healing to Arthur, ease to Luke's lungs, and rest to the women who've worn themselves weak with worry. This illness is more than we alone can handle, Father. We turn to Your wisdom and mercy, and seek Your blessings upon those we hold dear.

He stroked the soft strands of Rosalind's hair that had come free from her braid over the long night. He listened as her sobs quieted, until her breathing came long and deep in the even cadence of sleep. He shifted slowly, so as not to wake her. He swept her into his arms in one smooth motion and looked up at the loft ladder, where her bed must be.

I dare not climb it wi' her in my arms. Even were there no danger of bumping her head or worse, I'd not risk waking her.

"When she wakes, she'll take pains not to close her eyes for a scant moment, lest she sleep again," Gilda warned. "Lay her on the settle, so she can catch whatever rest she's able. Poor lass hae worn herself to a frazzle, helping her mam tend everyone these past days. The false hopes o' yesterday stole what strength she had left." The old woman kept rocking, her gaze flitting from one family member to the next in an unceasing vigil.

Ewan nodded, easing Rosalind down onto the furniture so gently she scarcely stirred. He pulled a crocheted afghan over her to keep her as comfortable as possible. That done, he stood, trying to think of ways he could help her—help them all.

Heavenly Father, when I was a wee lad, I caught ill in such a way. Mam did all the things Kaitlin and Rosalind have already seen to, but something tickles the edges of my memory—a warmth pressed to my chest, the strong smell making my eyes water. What kind of poultice did she use when all else failed to make me well? What made me feel better, though I disliked it? I remember thinking I'd never get rid of the smell. . .of what? What was that scent?

He looked at the shelves full of baking supplies, spices, teas, and herbal remedies. Nothing fit the memory. Ewan paced back and forth—from the hearth, to the table, and back again—keeping his distance from Rosalind for fear he'd wake her with his heavy tread. He passed the kettle, the pot, the skinned rabbits, and the door to the root cellar more times than he could count, vainly trying to recall Mam's treatment.

Hearth. . .rocker. . .table. . .root cellar door. Luke beside the hearth, stirring with fever. The rhythmic rocking of Gilda's concern. The scrubbed wooden surface of the table. The metal ring of the root cellar door—*the root cellar!*

He grasped the metal ring and heaved upward, descending into the cool darkness beneath without stopping to grab a candle. Without a light, he groped around, searching for the answer that had plagued him all morning.

There. Ewan's hands closed around the burlap sack and he followed the light back into the warmth of the house. He cautiously shut the cellar door, mindful not only of Rosalind's sleep but of Gilda's avidly curious gaze.

"Onions?" She peered in disbelief as he shook some onto the table. "You had a sudden hankering for onions, of all things?"

"I remembered an old remedy my mother used when I was young an' fought to breathe." He grabbed a knife and began chopping the pungent bulbs. "I could only recall the strength of the scent—how much I disliked it—but that it worked. She chopped onions, boiled them down, and wrapped the mash in flannel. Than she placed the hot poultice on my chest, changing it out for new whenever the old one cooled." Ewan kept his voice low even as he chopped. " 'Twas the only thing that finally worked. I thought it might do the same for Arthur and Luke. They'll reek of the stuff for what seems like ages, but 'tis more than worth it."

"Aye." Gilda's rocker gave a final, protesting creak as she got to her feet. "I'll put some water on to boil and then help you. If they must be replaced when they cool, we'll need a great many of those onions." She worked as she whispered, and Ewan slid the first batch of chopped pieces into the heating water.

The two of them worked quietly, the only sounds the soft bubbling of the onions, the *snick* of their knives, and under it all, the horrible rattling gasps as Luke tried to breathe.

⌒

Rosalind lifted her head from the settle, blinking to find herself there. *How did I. . . Oh no, I must have fallen asleep!* Yet another instance of her failing to take proper care of Luke, and now her da. She swung her feet to the floor, tossing the afghan over the back of the settle.

"I didn't mean to fall asleep." She bustled over to where Luke lay, half propped up on a mound of pillows. "You should hae woken me." She looked pointedly at Ewan. "You know that."

"Aye." He plopped a steaming poultice on Luke's heat-pinkened chest. "I knew you'd want me to hae woken you. 'Tis why I didn't." With maddening calmness, he took another poultice to where Da lay on the great bed and changed it out.

"What are those?" Rosalind wrinkled her nose as she processed the pungent odor rising from the flannel packs. "Onions?"

"Aye." Grandmam stirred a pot. "Your Ewan remembered a remedy his mam used when he was but a lad."

"To a certain point." Ewan gave a wry grin. "I knew she made a smelly poultice, which eased the ache in my chest, but try as I might, I couldn't recall what she put in it."

"Lad near wore out the floorboards, pacing around while he tried to recollect what the mystery ingredient was. Finally, he looked at the root cellar door and remembered 'twas onions."

"I'd never hae thought to boil onions to ease a cough." Rosalind felt Luke's forehead with the back of her hand. "He's still o'er-warm." She cast a concerned glance over at Da, wondering whether the onions had wrought any effect on his symptoms.

"Arthur's taken well to it," Grandmam answered Rosalind's unspoken question. "He's stopped coughing, at least."

"Praise the Lord for that," Rosalind whispered, relieved that at least one of them was improving. Perhaps the onion treatment would eventually aid Luke as well. She looked to where he lay, half reclining, his breaths shallow and raspy. . . . No. She bent closer, listening intently.

No. Please, let me be wrong, she prayed, even as the ominous rattle came again. Luke fought not only tightness—there was fluid gathering in his lungs. With each breath, the rattling gurgle gave hideous warning. Rosalind dropped down, putting her arms about her brother and holding him close. *Come on, Luke. Fight it. Just keep breathing. Let the poultice do its work.*

Jesus, please, help him. This is as bad as he's ever been. His chest and ribs ache from the coughing. His head pounds wi' it. Only in this uneasy sleep does he find any respite. 'Tis grateful I am that Da begins to recover, but what of my brother? He's never been hardy—he can't take a prolonged illness. The tears she thought long shed came slipping to the surface once more as she battled for her brother the only way she knew how—on her knees. Prayer was the most powerful tool she could wield, if it served the Lord's purpose to grant her request. *If 'twasn't the Lord's will. . .* That didn't even bear thinking on.

Father, 'tis my negligence that is to blame. I should hae checked on him, watched him more closely. I should hae made him sip more broth and tea to ease his throat. I should never hae allowed myself to fall asleep when he needed me. Lord, don't let Luke suffer for my failings. Please, make him well. Let Ewan's treatment work for Luke as it has for Da. Please, Lord. Please. . .

The shrill of a steam whistle broke through her thoughts. Startled, she looked up to see Ewan bolt out the door, leaving his coat and hat behind as he raced off into the distance. He was heading for the train tracks.

∽

Please, Lord. Don't let me be too late. Let the train stop. 'Tis the answer we've all been praying for—the train can bring Luke to the doctor at Fort Benton where a wagon through the cold could not. Let me be on time.

He ran faster than he'd ever imagined—not for his life, but for Luke's. Ewan pictured Rosalind's tired face, the bruised-looking circles around her eyes, and pushed himself even harder. He rounded the smithy and found the train—already stopped.

Thank You, Father.

Ewan rushed aboard to have a short conversation with the engineer, a man by the name of Brody whom he'd worked with before.

"Brody, I've a sick little boy not far off who needs the care o' a real doctor. Will you wait a very short while so I can fetch him? 'Tis a matter o' life and death." Ewan didn't take a breath until he'd gotten through all of his request.

"We'll wait." Brody shook Ewan's hand. "I'm glad to see the railroad put to such worthy use. We've only stopped now to let off Johnny Mathers. Go on, now. Get the boy."

God's timing. Ewan didn't even stay to look for Johnny, instead rushing back to the MacLean household. When he stormed through the door, Rosalind stared in cautious hope.

"They're holding the train for Luke." Ewan began grabbing the boy's coat off the peg by the door. "The railroad will get him to Fort Benton—and the doctor—when he wouldn't make it on the long wagon ride. Arthur, Kaitlin?" He strode over to the bed, waking them both. "The train is waiting to take Luke to Fort Benton. He needs a doctor's care. Will you trust me to look after your son?"

"Aye." Arthur nodded weakly. "Though one of us should go."

"Rose will go." Gilda stood up. "I'm too old to start a new journey, and Kaitlin should stay to help keep you on the mend."

"Aye, Rosalind should go," Kaitlin said, though Ewan could tell she was torn between staying with her husband and going with her son—any mother's greatest dilemma.

"I'm ready." Rosalind held a valise in one arm and her cloak in the other. "I've packed tea and blankets and socks. . .everything I can think of to keep him comfortable on the journey. If 'tis settled, we need to go before the engineer changes his mind and sticks to his schedule."

"That's my girl." Ewan scooped Luke into his arms and strode toward her. "We'll be back before you know it. I give you my word."

"Godspeed!" Kaitlin called with a break in her voice. "We'll be in constant prayer."

With that, Ewan and Rosalind hurried out the door and toward the waiting train—their last chance to help Luke. Ewan didn't relax until they were on the train, steaming toward Benton at full speed.

They spoke little during the journey. Rosalind kept anxious eyes on her brother, propping him up and giving him sips of water as he slipped in and out of consciousness.

Ewan repeated a litany of prayer. *Thank You, Jesus, for sending the train. Let it not be too late. Work through the doctor in Benton to heal our Luke. . . .*

If asked, Ewan wouldn't have been able to say how long they spent on the train, only that it seemed much longer than it probably actually was. When they arrived, he tipped a porter to go fetch the doctor.

"He'll be all right now." Rosalind spoke words of hope, but her face was drawn with concern as she mopped Luke's brow. "He has to be."

"Hello?" A man clambered into the car with them, lugging a physician's bag. "I'm Dr. Carmichael. This must be the boy." Wasting no time, he knelt beside Luke.

Ewan and Rosalind watched with bated breath as he checked for fever and listened to Luke's breathing and heartbeat. The doctor's ruddy face grew long, his eyes dulling behind the round spectacles perched on his nose.

"I'm afraid it's not good news." Dr. Carmichael sat back, shoving his spectacles higher. "His fever is quite high and, I'd guess, has been for some time." He waited for Rosalind's despairing nod before continuing to share his assessment. "The cough has settled in his chest—pneumonia."

"What can we do?" Ewan strove to remain calm and find how best to serve Luke. "How do we help him now?"

"Make him as comfortable as possible. Keep him propped up, give him hot fluids, and make sure he's warm." Dr. Carmichael looked defeated as he spoke the words.

"We've done all that." Rosalind spoke in desperation. "We've been doing it since he first fell ill. Is there nothing else?"

"The only other thing I'm sure you've already been doing." The doctor looked from one face to another. "Pray."

Chapter 20

I s there no hope?" Rosalind turned to Ewan as the doctor left.

"Only if 'tis the Lord's will." His bleak stare offered little of the comfort she sought, though he reached out to take her hand in his. "Though I'll not pretend to understand it."

"No." A dry sob escaped her. "God won't take him away from us. We need him. God won't give us more sorrow than we can bear. Surely not. Luke!" She shook him, alarmed at how light he felt in her arms. "Luke!" Rosalind called louder, trying to rouse him where the doctor had failed. "Come on. Open your eyes."

His pale face seemed even more drawn, the dreaded tinge of blue creeping into his lips to steal him further away from her.

"Lucas Mathias MacLean," she ordered, ignoring the way her voice shook, "wake up this instant. Do you hear me, Luke? Open your eyes." She jostled him slightly.

"Rosalind," Ewan began, but her fierce glare silenced him.

"No. He'll listen. He'll wake up." She cupped Luke's face in her hands. "He's not so warm anymore. Maybe the fever is breaking." The blue tinge deepened, and his breathing grew shallow. "No. Wake up, Luke. You have to wake up." The whispered plea did no good.

"You have to!" This last came in a shriek as his chest rose and fell one last time and was still. His skin grew cold beneath her hands.

"No, Luke. Luke." She clutched him, leaning as close as possible. "Don't leave! Please, Luke. Don't go. It's my fault," she babbled, tears streaming down her face. "I know 'tis. I should hae taken better care o' you. I love you. I'll do better. I promise I'll do better, if you'll only just wake up. Smile at me one more time, little brother. Luke? Luke!"

But it was too late. She knew it by his unnatural stillness, the cold clamminess of his skin, the blue that was deeper than ever before in his lips and fingernails.

"Rosalind." She felt Ewan's warm hand on her shoulder, heard his deep, melancholy tones. "'Tis over. He's gone."

"No!" The heartbroken whisper was all she managed before the swirling darkness claimed her thoughts.

⌒

At the parson's house, Ewan covered Rosalind with his own coat and sat by the fire to wait. She'd revived fairly quickly, though not before his own heart had skipped a beat in mortal dread. They'd made it through the short burial before she cried herself into unconsciousness once again. The train had moved on and wouldn't be taking them home to Saddleback. Arthur and Kaitlin wouldn't have even the cold comfort of burying their son.

"I brought you some tea to warm your bones." The parson's wife whisked in and set down the tray. "Though I'm afraid it won't help with the sorrow. Only God's grace and His time will lessen that burden." She glanced around before leaving them alone in the small parlor.

With Rosalind sleeping, Ewan had no company but his own grief, which came rushing forward in the silence. Tears welled in his eyes as he thought of lively little Luke, so welcoming, such a blessing to his family. He remembered how the boy had welcomed him to the table, threw snowballs with reckless abandon, skated as though he hoped to fly off the ice, and bolted down frozen maple syrup with more enthusiasm than sense.

Gone. Lost to us forever. Why, God? He buried his head in his hands, trying to swallow the tears and the pain. *Why now? Why Luke? I understand Your wanting him by Your side, but could You not hae spared him to us for a while longer, knowing he was Yours for all time?* He struggled to understand, to accept, but failed. It seemed like years he sat in the chair, trying to fathom the reasons why Luke should be robbed of his life and his family stripped of their joy. No understanding came.

"Luke." Rosalind stirred, her eyes opening. For an all-too-brief moment, she seemed fine. Then remembrance clouded the bright blue, and she hugged her knees to her chest. "He's gone."

"Yes." Ewan walked over to sit beside her, drawing her close to offer what little solace he could. "He's gone to be with our heavenly Father now. We'll see him again someday."

"I know," she whispered. "But it doesn't make it easier today." She drew a shaky breath. "At least—at least he's where each breath he draws doesn't pain him. He's beyond the reach of that now. 'Tis all I can think of to be glad about."

" 'Tis no small thing," he soothed. "We always want what's best for the ones we love. Luke has that, and we should rejoice that he's found peace and joy with our Savior."

"Yes." She straightened her shoulders a little. "He's happy. I should be happy for him. And I am." She looked up at him, her eyes shining with tears once more. " 'Tis myself, and Mam and Da and Grandmam, that I grieve for. 'Tis our loss."

"Aye." Ewan rubbed his hand over her back. " 'Tis certainly our loss. But, Rosalind"—he tipped her chin to keep her gaze fixed on him—" 'tisn't your fault."

"Ewan"—she tried to pull away from him—"you don't understand...."

"I understand better than you think." He moved to cup her cheek with his palm. "You watched o'er him as best you could, and he cherished your love. There was nothing you could do about his weak lungs, or the illness, save stay by his side and offer what comfort and aid you could. You did all of that."

"No." She shook her head so vehemently that she freed herself from his grasp. "I could hae done more. I should hae watched him more closely. I shouldna hae fallen asleep. I should hae—" She gasped back a sob. "I should hae shown him every moment how much he meant to me—how I loved him."

"You did, Rosalind." He took her fidgeting hands in his. "It may not feel that way now, but you did. Wi' every smile, every snowball, every mug of hot cider...you loved him each day he was wi' us. I saw it, and I know he did, too."

"Do you think so?" She met his gaze, seeking reassurance.

"I'm certain." He shifted a tiny bit. "His life was never ours to keep, Rosalind." His eyes stung. "No one's is."

"Ewan?" Her gaze was searching. "What—what made you say that last part? Are you feeling poorly?" Her voice rose as she pressed the back of her hand to his forehead. "We'll call Dr. Carmichael again...."

"No." He captured her hand and held it. "I wasn't referring to myself. I thought of my mother." He saw that she waited for him to share more. *Maybe my experience will help her through the grief,* he reasoned. *Besides, there's nothing I want hidden betwixt us.*

"When I was about Luke's age"—he winced at her hiss of indrawn breath but continued—"my da left Ireland to seek his fortune in America. He charged me to look after Mam and look after things while he was away. He planned to send money back to us so we could book passage to join him."

"Go on."

"It seems that Da was one of many, many men who had the same idea. Work was harder to find than he'd anticipated, and it took longer to gather the money. Months passed, then years. I worked at odd jobs—smithing, shoeing, whatever I could be paid to turn a hand to—and managed to keep food on the table and a roof o'er our heads. Every scrap o' money Da sent, we saved to buy our fare. But every day, the light in Mam's eyes dimmed just a wee bit more. She missed Da so."

"It must hae been hard for you both." She squeezed his hand.

"Aye, 'twas." He took a deep breath. "Finally, I could no longer bear watching her fade away before my eyes from missing him. As the man of the house, I made the decision to use our money for a single ticket. I sent her ahead, alone. The plan was for me to follow later. She gave me her wedding band, the only thing she owned of any value. If I needed to, she instructed me to sell it."

"How wonderful of you." She nestled close. "So selfless of you—to send your mam back to your da and ask to be left all alone. Such love. Your parents must hae been proud."

"No." The words thickened in his throat, but he managed to grind them out. "Mam never stepped foot on the American shore. Alone on a miserable ship, she caught an illness on board. Wi' no one to look after her, she died during the voyage."

"Oh Ewan." Her grip tightened. "That wasn't your fault." She spoke with fierce conviction. "You have to know that."

"I didn't know"—his voice became hoarse—"I didn't know about her death until Da wrote me. The letter reprimanded me for sending Mam alone when he'd left her in my care. 'Twas the last I ever heard from him." He ignored her shocked gasp and plowed ahead. "I saved money on my own, refusing to sell Mam's ring. When I made it to America, I spent years searching for him, but it didn't work." He paused and choked out the final words. "I don't even know whether or not he's still alive."

"Ewan." She held his head to her shoulder and rocked back and forth. "You can't blame yourself for your mother's death. You did the best you could by her. 'Twasn't fair o' your father to lash out at you. I'm sure 'twas done only in grief."

"Perhaps." He straightened up. "I've never told anyone about this." He traced the band of gold adorning her finger. "But you wear her ring, and you are to bear my name. We should hae no secrets betwixt us. And just as I had to come to terms wi' my mam's death, so, too, do you hae to stop blaming yourself for Luke's."

"Luke. . ." Her face fell at the mention of her brother.

"You did the best you could by him," Ewan softly echoed her own words. " 'Tisn't fair to blame yourself in your grief."

Silence stretched between them for a long while.

Finally, Rosalind spoke. "You're right." They sat for a while longer. "Ewan?"

"Yes, Rosalind?"

"Not too long ago, I was reading Da's Bible. I looked at the death records—and the marriage lines—and wondered what our future held."

"Oh?"

"And I turned to one o' my favorite chapters—Ecclesiastes 3."

" 'To every thing there is a season,' " he recited along with her, " 'and a time to every purpose under the heaven: A time to be born, and a time to die.'" They both stopped.

"And I thought how strange it was that, in the family records, birth and death are placed side by side and that it is the same in the scriptures." She bit her lip. "Ewan? When we have a son—"

"We'll name him Luke," he finished firmly. She nodded, a ghost of a smile breaking through her grief. "Rosalind, that chapter continues until it comes to another portion I think applies here."

" 'A time to laugh; a time to mourn'?" she asked. "For now is certainly the time to mourn."

"Aye, 'tis." He threaded his fingers through her hair. "Though I was thinking of the part that says, 'a time to lose; a time to keep.'"

"Oh." Rosalind thought for a moment. "We've lost Luke. What is there to keep? Our grief?" She seemed despondent at the very thought.

"No, though Luke will always be in our hearts." Ewan waited until her gaze met his. "You and I, Rosalind. Our love. The beginning of our life together. That is what we are to keep—hope for the future and trust that the Lord will see us through."

"Oh Ewan." She kissed his cheek. "How right you are. And that is the way Luke would hae wanted it—that we allow for grief but look forward to the promise of tomorrow."

"And when we wed, my Rosalind," Ewan vowed, "'twill be a time to keep."

Epilogue

Montana, 1889

C an you believe it?" Marlene squealed, all but dancing for joy. "After two years of waiting, I'm finally married!"

"Wi' a home already built and a farm already in operation. Johnny's worked hard to make ready for his beautiful bride." Rosalind smiled. "I'm thinking 'twon't be long before you join your mam and me." She patted her rounded tummy with affection and looked at Delana, who was two months farther along. "Isn't that right, Mrs. Friemont?"

"Ja." Delana laughed. "Though I hadn't thought to bear a babe near the time when my daughter would!"

"It's a wonderful surprise." Marlene leaned over her mother's swollen stomach. "She's going to be a sister, I think."

"Not mine." Rosalind cupped her hands over her own swollen midriff. "I bear a son. Ewan and I—we've decided to name him Isaac." Her eyes sparkled more with joy than sorrow, a sign of God's healing and the passage of time.

"What a wonderful idea!" Mam drew her into a tight clasp, her own eyes looking suspiciously moist. "Luke would hae liked that."

"Yes, he would." Marlene reached out to grasp both of their hands. "It's a lovely gesture, and I'm so happy for you!"

"We'll speak of it more when the babes are born." Delana smiled. "For now, we've much to celebrate. My daughter, a bride, and Montana declared an official state!"

"Yes. It's a grand day for a wedding—a day to be remembered." Johnny came up behind the women to steal a kiss from his blushing bride. "We're going to blow the anvils now."

They all hurried to the clearing, where Ewan and Johnny carefully overturned one anvil, pouring black gunpowder into the base's hollow before positioning the second anvil directly atop it. A thin trail of the gunpowder spilled over the side, waiting to be lit.

"And here we go! Everybody step far back, out of the way!" Johnny lit the trail of powder and rushed to Marlene's side. At that moment, the anvils began to dance, emitting a loud series of sparks until the pressure built up sufficiently to overturn the top anvil with a spectacular *boom*!

When the gunpowder supply was exhausted—and everyone's ears rang with the sound of the merry tradition—Ewan stepped forward. Rosalind watched with pride as her husband waited for everyone's attention and began his speech.

"When I married my beautiful Rosalind o'er a year ago, 'twas a day of great joy. And also one tempered wi' sorrow wi' young Luke"—he paused for a moment as several people drew shaky breaths—"gone to heaven. But we know he would hae wanted us to celebrate."

He broke into a grin. "Now, after a long, patient wait, Johnny and Marlene hae wed on this joyous day. I'm both pleased and honored to speak an old Irish blessing upon their marriage and on all who are gathered here today. If my wife would join me. . ." He held out his hand, beckoning Rosalind to come to his side.

Surprised, she did so. Suddenly, she knew he'd planned the blessing to be a celebration of their own marriage, as much as Johnny and Marlene's. Looking into the deep green of his gaze, she spoke the ancient words with him:

> *"May love and laughter light your days,*
> *and warm your heart and home.*
> *May good and faithful friends be yours,*
> *wherever you may roam.*
> *May peace and plenty bless your world*
> *with joy that long endures.*
> *May all life's passing seasons bring*
> *the best to you and yours."*

A Time to Laugh

Dedication

This is dedicated to Julia Rich, my reader and support system as I wrote this book. And, as always, thanks to the wonderful team at Barbour and to our Lord who oversees the work.

Chapter 1

Saddleback, Montana, 1916

Y*ou can't catch me!" Isaac Friemont stuck his thumbs in his ears, waggling his fingers at Nessa Gailbraith as she flew toward him from across the meadow. When she got too close for comfort, he took off again.*

"That does it, Isaac!" Nessa puffed the words as she shot after him. "Those were my best stockings, and you've ruined them!" She picked up a burst of speed and grabbed the tail of his shirt as it flapped behind him.

"Okay, okay." Caught, he put his hands up in mock surrender. "I promise I'll never again use your stockings to catch tadpoles."

His earnest blue eyes made Nessa grudgingly relinquish her grip on his shirt.

"Unless you take them off to dip your feet in the pond and leave them under my nose!" With that, he sprung away like a hare eluding a wolf.

"Isaac Friemont, you come back here!" Nessa hollered as she took up the chase once more, glorying in the feel of the soft spring grass between her toes. Nothing could be better than playing with her best friend in the warm sunshine. "You know I'll get you sooner or later!"

Vanessa Gailbraith's fond smile at the memory wavered as she considered that last line, uttered with all the brash confidence of youth. How disappointed her nine-year-old self would have been to know that it would be later rather than sooner. A full decade later, and she still chased after Isaac Friemont in a thrilling mixture of excitement and frustration.

And Isaac still runs like the wind. Nessa grimaced ruefully. No matter how much she felt ready for marriage, Isaac's stubbornness outstripped hers. She'd sent more prayers to heaven than she could count, but it seemed the Lord's will aligned with Isaac's so far. But Nessa's prayers brought a new sense of peace of late. Soon things would change. . . .

"Nessa"—Julia's voice nabbed her attention—"you've got that look again."

"What look?" Nessa widened her eyes at her best friend.

"The one that means you've hatched another scheme to make Isaac notice you." Julia shook her head. "The one that means you'll try to elicit my help. The look," she finished triumphantly, "that always comes before a lot of trouble."

"I've no idea what you mean." Nessa shrugged off Julia's concerns. "Though I was thinking that a new hairstyle might be in order, as it's becoming so hot."

"That's true enough," Julia agreed as she gazed at the expanse of blue overhead. "Not a cloud in sight nor whisper of a breeze. Wait." Her eyes narrowed in suspicion. "What kind of hairstyle were you thinking of, Nessa?"

"It's so thick and heavy it's always escaping my pins." Nessa reached up to finger a burnished mahogany strand. "And then it frizzes something awful around my face. I despair of looking like a proper lady whenever I catch a glimpse of myself in the mirror over the washstand." She heaved a woeful sigh.

"And there's nothing more to it than that?" Julia quirked an eyebrow. "Because every single other time you've altered your appearance—or tried to, at least—it's been in hopes of attracting Isaac's notice. To my recollection, none of those endeavors ended well at all. *Disastrous* is more the word."

"I'm sure I don't know what you mean." Nessa tilted her chin toward the sky. "Every young lady tries to look her best, with some efforts making better progress than others."

"Then I suppose you're about due for something to work," Julia teased. "Seeing as how everything else failed so badly!"

"Now that's not true, and you know it!"

"Oh, I know it *is* true. I remember the time you ordered that special face scrub and walked around looking as though you'd been boiled." Julia bit her lip to keep from laughing.

"Pumice was supposed to reveal a natural glow," Nessa defended indignantly before giving in to a small smile of her own. "Though I did shine like a lantern until Dr. Bunting's Sunburn Remedy arrived. At any rate, this is nothing like that. I just want you to give my hair a little trim."

"Me?" Her best friend leaned back. "I've never cut your hair before. Why on earth would you put the shears in my hand?"

"You cut your little brothers' hair, and they always look nice. Hair is hair, so I would think you'd be able to manage."

"I don't know. Kyle's and Leon's hair are a lot straighter than yours." Julia eyed Nessa's thick, curly locks with obvious trepidation. "And it's harder to mess up when it's supposed to be short. A woman's hair is her crowning glory, Nessa!"

"No, your hair is your crowning glory." Nessa gestured at her friend's sleek blond bun. "Mine resembles a dandelion. . .all fluffed and scattered." She smoothed the springy tendrils creeping away from her pins. "Since these curls won't stay down, I thought we could try trimming them so they twist around my face instead of whipping in the wind. It's the newest fashion—how hard can it be? I have a copy of *McCall's* magazine at home to show you what I mean. Will you help me?"

"I'll do my best," Julia agreed. "But I can't promise it will turn out the way you want it."

"That's fine." Nessa cast a glance toward the direction of the Friemont homestead. *I'm used to things not turning out the way I'd hoped.*

◌

"Hopes aren't promises." Isaac Friemont mixed the oats, linseed, and old milk to slop the hogs. The thick mixture oozed into the trough as he waited for his father's response.

"And the best laid plans are not guaranteed to be followed," Pa rejoined. "Arthur, Jakob, and I were to have an entire extra year before the womenfolk arrived. We'd hoped to have a home built and a farm running by that time."

"But Ma came early and brought with her everything from windows to trees." Isaac grinned as he finished the familiar story. His parents had a difficult start in the Montana wilderness, but they'd prospered through hard work and love.

"Your ma brought a sight more than wagonloads of goods, son."

"I know. . . . She brought along the Bannings and Grandma Albright and her little brother, Isaac. When he left to go be a miner, she named me after him."

"She certainly did. There's family history in your name, and we both thought it fit, seeing as how you surprised us coming so many years after your sister. But I wasn't talking about that. When your ma made the journey to Montana, she carried determination, love, and faith that through God we could build a home—and a family—together." Dustin Friemont straightened from where he'd been reinforcing the pigpen. "I pray that someday you'll have a helpmeet who brings you such joy.

We've long thought your friendship with Nessa would turn to something deeper, but you know your own mind."

"I do care for Nessa." Isaac put down the slop bucket. "She's been one of my closest friends since we were toddlers."

"Sure surprised your ma and me when we discovered your ma was pregnant with you eighteen years after Marlene. Your ma and Rosalind Galbraith never expected to bear children within scant years of one another." Pa headed for the barn. "Seemed like a God-given blessing that you and Nessa had each other before the railroad brought new folks and children of their own."

"We've gained steady friends in the Horntons," Isaac agreed. "But it can't be forgotten that our family and the MacLeans founded Saddleback. This land is precious as blood to me, Julia, Nessa. . .all of us."

"Still another thing you and Nessa share." Pa spoke lightly, but Isaac knew that the conversation had been steered back to its original purpose.

"Yes." He bit back a heavy sigh as he grabbed a currycomb and began to brush Goliath—the biggest horse in town. Possibly the biggest horse in all Montana, for that matter. "You, Ma, and practically everyone else in Saddleback have been dropping hints that it's time I spoke for Nessa."

"You understand we're not trying to pressure you?" Pa gave a wry grin. "Well, most of us aren't. We want to know your intentions. Nessa is a beautiful girl who will make some man a wonderful wife. But so long as there's the conception that you two have an understanding, the other men in town maintain more of a distance. It's come to the point where you need to prove up on your claim or move on, son."

At the not-so-subtle reminder that Isaac was of an age to be establishing his own spread and acquiring a wife to work alongside him, Isaac's jaw clenched. Why were land and women used to take the measure of a man?

"It's not fair to Nessa to string her along if you don't believe she's the woman for you." Pa prodded him to respond after a stretch of silence. "That doesn't mean you can't let her loose and pursue the gal who's caught your eye."

"Subtle, Pa." Isaac shook his head. "No one's caught my eye, as you put it. Nessa's the best girl I'll ever meet."

"Then why do you hesitate?"

How could a man tell his father he chafed at having his entire life decided for him? That Isaac Friemont often wished he could follow his uncle Isaac Albright's example and make his own way? Instead, everyone took for granted that he'd stay in town—a dutiful son—and marry Nessa as they expected.

"When a path has been laid before you," Isaac struggled to explain, "everyone assumes you'll take it. Saddleback will always be my home, and Nessa has always been the girl by my side. It seems the path heads straight down the aisle." He swallowed hard. "But you understand that a man has to make his own way. If I marry Nessa, when have I stood on my own?"

Chapter 2

Alone in front of the looking glass, her eyes closed, Nessa wondered if she'd made the right choice. Cracking open a single eyelid, she spied the curls strewn about the floor and squeezed her eyes shut again in a hurry.

"I'm back." Julia's voice sounded from the doorway. "I snagged Da's shaving brush so I can sweep the bits off your neck." With that, a ticklish stroke caught Nessa behind the ear.

"Oh," she gasped, eyes flying open as she giggled at the sensation. The mirth faded as she stared at her reflection. Biting her lip, Nessa turned her head from one side to the other, silently appraising her new hairstyle from every angle.

"Well?" Julia stood behind her, hands clasped tightly.

"I love it!" Her reddish brown locks retained most of their original length but boasted fashionable curls framing her face and resting gently at the nape of her neck. "Even better than I'd hoped! But"—she sobered as she considered—"I've liked things and have been proven wrong before. What do *you* think?"

"Well, not that I'm completely impartial, but I'd say it's charming. Those little curls add softness to your face and make your eyes seem brighter." Her friend couldn't resist teasing her. "How does it feel to have one of your plans actually work?"

"Ha, ha." Nessa deadpanned but couldn't keep her smile at bay for long. The springy tendrils made her eyes seem bigger, drawing attention away from a jaw a hint too strong for beauty and a mouth too wide for ladylike poise. "It's. . .nice."

"I should say so." Julia whisked the hair on the floor into a dustpan. "Hmm. . .I'd say there's just enough for a dolly for Meagan." She transferred the wisps to her palm and held it up for Nessa's inspection. "Though you'd have to sew on the hair. I've no skill for such detailed work."

"You always think of others." Nessa gave her friend a hug. "And I'd be glad to make your little sister a dolly." When she drew back from the hug, she cocked her head to one side.

"Nessa Gailbraith, are you trying to see your reflection even now?" Julia shook her head. "Vanity is a sin, you know."

"How could I know such a thing when I've never before looked half as good as I do now?" Nessa batted her lashes playfully. "But, no, I wasn't looking into the mirror. I was thinking how odd it is that the one thing I'm more skilled at than you is the last thing anyone would ever suspect."

"Your sewing, you mean?" Julia tucked the hair into a small box. "Mine is serviceable and solid, but you have a way with a needle fit to make thread dance into place. And others know it well. Why would you think your talent an unlikely one?"

"Simply because it requires long periods of sitting still and paying attention to exacting detail." Nessa shrugged. "I surprise even myself that I've the patience for such work. You must admit, I've precious little patience in other matters."

"True. And yet you've waited long years for Isaac to declare his love." Julia tweaked one curl. "With time and happiness, you'll settle well into the role of wife and mother."

"How is it you always say exactly the right thing. . .and somehow sound like a wise old woman when you're scarcely a month older than I am? At times I'm sure God intended our friendship since I so lack your wisdom and discernment."

"And your joy and enthusiasm make life more exciting." Julia gave her a swift hug. "Now that your hair is done, when will you contrive to show Isaac your new glamour?"

"You make it sound as though I went out to California and visited Max Factor's studio. Glamour," Nessa scoffed. "Oh, wait. Did I tell you I'd ordered pressed face powder?"

"You didn't!" Julia's pretty blue eyes grew round. "I know it's in fashion, but what place is there for such airs in Montana? Besides, if Nancy Rutgers were to ever catch on to it, she'd denounce you as a loose woman!"

"Oh, Nancy is a stiff-necked matron, to be sure." Nessa set her jaw. "But there is no shame in powder, Julia. I'm not rouging my lips or painting my nails, after all. Powder bears no scandal—especially if no one knows of it."

"How do you always make your plans sound perfectly reasonable even when I know there's something amiss?" Julia frowned and gave Nessa a critical glance. "Besides, your complexion is fine on its own. Why use artifice?"

"I overheard Isaac say he thought freckles to be a sure sign of wildness in a girl." Nessa bowed her head. "And I can never seem to resist tearing off my bonnet when there's no one about to see. So here I have these little spots on my nose."

"Your freckles are just as charming as your new hairstyle," Julia declared. "And Isaac is foolish to say aught against freckles when there are girls like Marcy Adams who were born with them and it doesn't mean she goes without her bonnet."

"Marcy Adams *is* beautiful," Nessa conceded. "But everyone knows the cause of my freckles. A swipe of powder will serve to lessen them, that's all. No one need know."

"I'll never speak enough sense to make you heed me." Julia smiled fondly. "You were always one to defy expectation."

CO

"Expectation." Isaac ground the word through gritted teeth as he stabbed his pitchfork into the hayloft. "The force standing against the free will God saw fit to grant us. Bane of a man's life."

"What is?" Michael's voice had Isaac peering over the edge of the hayloft before he swung a pitchfork load of hay onto his friend's head.

"Hello, Michael." Isaac waited until the other man started up the ladder before he continued feeding the horses. "Good thing I didn't pitch hay all over before I knew you were here."

"Why do you think I asked the question?" Michael's head popped over the top of the ladder. "I figured you didn't know I'd shown up, or you wouldn't waste time talking to yourself."

"And why wouldn't I?" Isaac tossed a pitchfork, and Michael easily caught it. "I'll have you know I'm good company."

"Poor fellow." Michael shrugged. "You know somethin' is weighin' heavy on a man's mind when he talks to himself and claims to enjoy the conversation. Now what was it you were calling the 'bane of a man's life'?"

"What do you think?" Isaac raised his brows.

"On a rough guess, I'd have to say. . .women?"

"Close enough," Isaac snorted. "The expectations of women are stifling our God-given free wills to the point where some men can't even see it happening anymore."

"Knowin' you as well as I do"—Michael leaned on his pitchfork and speculated—"I'd think this had something to do with Nessa."

"Pa cornered me earlier today to have a discussion," Isaac grimly acknowledged. "Said time's come when I need to claim her or cut her loose so someone else can speak up."

"Ah." Michael tilted his head. "Can't say you didn't see this comin'. Have you made your decision yet, or is that what all the grumbling was about when I walked in?"

"What do you think?" Isaac flung another forkful of hay over the side of the loft. "If I'd made my decision, there'd be no need to talk about it—even with myself."

"Have you talked to God about it?" Michael's simple question pulled Isaac up short. "And I don't mean in the past either."

"I've prayed about it for a long time," Isaac admitted, "but didn't seek the Lord's wisdom after my talk with Pa. Don't know what I was thinking." *No wonder I've got no peace!*

"I'm going to go grab a drink of water. Maybe you ought to rectify your oversight while I'm gone, and we can talk about what decision you come to." With that, he hightailed it.

Lord, You know it rubs me the wrong way to have my bride chosen for me, but I'm ready to set up my own household. Pa's right that I need a helpmeet to do so, and wiser heads than my own have pointed me in Nessa's direction. Is that the answer?

"Well?" Michael, already back, had waited until Isaac opened his eyes again. "Any new insight?"

"Yeah." Isaac's grip tightened. "It's not Nessa who's the problem. It's me."

"Already knew that." His friend softened the words with a grin. "You don't like havin' the choice made for you—I understand that. Any man would. All the same, I think you're askin' yourself the wrong questions."

"How so?"

"You've been wondering whether or not you would feel right about marryin' Nessa—that's the way of it, yes?"

"Basically."

"That's as valid a question as any." Michael nodded. "But have you thought about the other side of the matter?"

"You mean wondering if Nessa wants to marry me?" Isaac's disbelief all but echoed in the rafters. "That's a given."

"Nothing about a woman is a sure bet," Michael shook a finger at his friend in warning. "And that's not what I meant. What I was wondering is if you thought about how you'd like it if you saw her marryin' some other guy when you moved on?"

"I'd be fi—" Something stopped Isaac from finishing his response. Nessa married to someone else? He threw down the pitchfork, causing little bits of hay to rise and tickle his nose. "She wouldn't," he evaded flatly.

"That didn't answer the question. You can't expect to not take her as your wife and have her pine away the rest of her life. We both know Nessa's got too much spirit for that."

"She's. . ." *Mine.* Isaac shook the thought from his head. He didn't own Nessa. "Free to do as she pleases of course." The words caught in his craw, forcing him to retract them. "But I wouldn't like it." The thought of Nessa belonging to another man hadn't really hit him until that moment. "Not one bit."

"Now"—Michael rested his pitchfork against the wall—"*that's* an answer."

∞

Nessa clutched the handle of her bucket and hurried to the shady nook where she'd found an early batch of raspberries. Her family would enjoy them this evening with sweetened cream, and perhaps there would be enough left over to bake tarts the next morning. She might even save one for—

"Isaac!" She gasped and stepped backward as he burst from the trees to her left. "Oh, you gave me such a start! What are you doing here?"

"Hoped to find you." His response took her breath away.

"Well, here we are." Nessa raised a hand to straighten her bonnet, only to realize she'd forgotten it yet again. Of all the times to be running about like a hoyden. . .

"Nessa," he stepped closer as he spoke, her name rumbling from deep in his chest, "there are things we need to speak of."

"Yes?" She didn't even try to hide the hopeful note of her voice as she gazed into his blue eyes. His hair shone golden in the sun's late rays. Hard to believe the scraggly friend of her childhood had grown into such a handsome man.

"Here." He cupped her elbow and led her to a flat rock shaded by a large tree. After he saw her comfortably seated, he straightened up to eye her thoughtfully. "You're looking well, Nessa."

"Thank you," she murmured, her fingers toying with one of her curls. This was it, the moment she'd prayed for, dreamed of—Isaac was going to go down on one knee and propose! He'd finally admit his deep love for her and beg her to be the wife at his side through the coming years. She gave a soft sigh.

"Now, Nessa," he stepped back a pace as he addressed her, "you know as well as I that all of Saddleback has been expecting us to wed for years now. We've a certain duty, if you will, to come through. Our families hope to be joined through our union."

"Certainly," she breathed. Here he was, speaking words of duty and responsibility. No wonder he'd distanced himself, so that when his proclamations of love came, he'd move close and take her in his arms. . . *Thank You, Lord!*

"Vanessa Gailbraith"—he stiffly knelt and took her hand in his— "will you stand before the town as my wife?"

"Oh—" The joyous "yes" died on her lips, a frown creasing her brow. Where was the declaration of love? The romantic vow that he could consider no other woman when she'd stood beside him for so long? The promise that he would cherish her as they joined their lives forever? He proposed as the suns rays set, but the beauty of the approaching night was lost to him.

"This must no longer be delayed." He'd obviously sensed her hesitation. "We cannot avoid the path laid before us, Nessa." His eyes pierced her with their intensity. "Let us bow to the inevitable and make the best of the bounty we've been given."

"The inevitable," she echoed faintly, clutching his hand so she wouldn't sway in her seat as his words hammered into the hopes of her heart. *Does he not love me, Lord?*

"Indeed." He nodded gravely. "We're of the same age, have known each other for all our lives. Our long-standing friendship shows we'll deal well enough together as man and wife."

"Well enough!" This time her echo bore more strength. How dare he ruin the moment she'd dreamed of for years with such rubbish as he now spoke. Her jaw clenched shut against the small part of her that whispered to accept his proposal and be content with whatever he offered.

"The timing is right for us to wed." He let go of her hand and rose to his feet.

"Oh?" She watched in fascination as her beloved began to pace before her, his hands tightening into fists as he moved back and forth.

Numbly, she wondered whether he was stalking reasons why they should marry, trying to capture them and convince himself it was the logical choice.

"The planting season is over with the harvest yet to begin. The weather is well enough, and the entire town will be able to attend the ceremony. It is an opportunity to engender the goodwill of all Saddleback—very important as we set about carving our place here."

"I see." She stared up at him, willing him to see what she saw—that this travesty of a proposal didn't take into account all that they could build in their lifetime. To see their home, their children, their love as the treasure it could be. But no, he plowed on ahead with his speech.

"I knew you would. We're alike in that we understand the foundation of marriage really is—" He paused to give her a searching glance.

Her heart resumed its beat at the force of his gaze. Had he finally come to his senses? Would he cite the benefits of romance and tenderness?

"Hard work." His emphatic declaration doused her flicker of hope. "Raising a house, taming the land, and eking out a living all require backbreaking labor and determination. And I know better than anyone how hard you'll work alongside me, Nessa. What say we begin building that life now?"

"Isaac—" She choked on the words as he stood before her, proud of his reasons, certain in her response. Oblivious to her needs. "I—"

"Don't cry, Nessa." Isaac squatted beside her, running a work-roughened thumb over her cheek. "All you must do is say yes."

As she looked into the eyes of the man she'd loved so long, Nessa almost convinced herself to do it. He could recognize their love after their marriage, couldn't he? Isaac spoke of children, after all. And God had answered her prayers to be Isaac's wife. She took a gulp of air and prepared to agree.

"See, there's no need to be emotional."

His indulgent smile made her stomach lurch. "I—" Nessa stood, brushing away his hand. "I'm sorry, Isaac. I can't." Her tears made everything blend in a swirl of evening's darkness and her own despair. She pushed past him and ran as fast as her legs could carry her.

Chapter 3

"What?" Isaac watched as the woman he'd just proposed to ran away as if she chased after something precious.

He'd seen the eyes whose sparkle teased him his entire life awash with tears of joy. Everyone knew Nessa wanted to be his wife—Nessa herself had made sure of it. So why did she flee what she claimed to have wanted so badly?

"Nothing is sure when it comes to women." Michael's words from earlier that day rose to his thoughts.

Fair enough, Isaac allowed. But it wasn't unreasonable to assume that the woman who had been all but a man's betrothed since the cradle should accept his proposal. Really, asking the question itself was more a formality than anything else.

To think he'd wasted so much thought and time in preparing his proposal! He kicked the stone upon which she'd sat, dislodging smaller pieces to rain on the grass beneath. How dare she refuse him? Nessa had led him on for years only to reject him when he came to the sticking point? Unbelievable!

He strode through the woods, breaths coming fast and shallow as he stomped away from the site of his humiliation. Nessa was *his* by rights. Her willingness to be his bride was owed him. How could she turn her back on him as though his offer was hardly worth the breath it took her to refuse?

Lord, I pushed aside my own desires to shoulder my responsibility to Nessa and our families. I longed to choose my own wife, lay the path I'd follow, but knew it wasn't my place to flout the plan You had for me. I bowed to what I believed to be Your will. How could I make such a mistake? How can it be that my denying the desires of my heart in obedience to You have been an error? What did I misinterpret? Why am I struck so deeply by Nessa's rejection, when I scarcely wanted her acceptance at all? What went wrong?

Isaac slowed, turning the matter over in his mind. He breathed deeply, shaking his head to clear it. *What went wrong?* The points he'd made ticked through his mind, each as sound as the last until their combined weight should have felled any opposition. Had he not given in to expectation? What more could he offer than his home, his name, and his children?

Had Nessa, like an infant demanding some shiny bauble, tired of the prize as soon as it was within reach? Could a woman be so contrary? It wasn't like the girl he knew—always smiling, laughing even when she shouldn't, thinking of others, trying new things. That adventuresome Nessa wouldn't shy away from anything.

Isaac snorted. Even now Nessa hadn't shied away—she'd run. And how, exactly, was he to explain that to Pa? *I'm sorry, but the proposal was. . .*

⚭

"Unforgivable, that's what it was!" Nessa's chest heaved as she drew Julia outside. "You'll never in a hundred years guess what Isaac Friemont's done now." She swiped at the tears trickling down her cheeks, angry at the sign of her own weakness.

"Don't tell me he made fun of your haircut!" Julia's horrified gasp brought Nessa up short.

Was it only scant hours ago that her troubles were so small? "No. He liked that." She waved the issue of her hairstyle away with an agitated flourish. "It's even worse!" She dropped down to the hay-strewn floor and drew her knees to her chest.

"Even worse?" Her friend's hushed tones spoke of a woman who now understood how dire the situation must be. "What?"

"The lout. . . Unthinkable—" Nessa blew her nose into her hanky and tried to form a coherent explanation. "Brute. He talked. . .duty, and—and w–work." The last word ended in a wail.

"I'm not following, dear." Julia gracefully sank next to her, offering a clean handkerchief. "What is it Isaac has done?"

"Oh Julia." Closing her eyes, Nessa took a steadying breath before blurting out the terrible truth. "He proposed!" A fresh flood of tears welled before she could say another word.

"You wanted him to propose." Julia's reminder prodded Nessa's heart. "So why are you so upset now?"

"He doesn't love me." The grim revelation dried her tears.

"Surely you're mistaken!" Her friend put a consoling arm about her shoulders. "If Isaac's proposed, it means he *wants* to marry you, after all. This should be a celebration!"

"No." Nessa wrenched from her friend's awkward hug. "Listen to me, Julia. He spoke of duty and responsibility, expectation of the town, obligation to our families. Not a tender word of love in the whole bunch. Do you see?"

"He probably thought you knew that part already," Julia soothed. "Men don't often speak of such things. The fact he proposed must have seemed to him a declaration of his feelings."

"Perhaps." Nessa glowered. "Perhaps I could believe that if he hadn't gone on to speak of how it was a good time for a wedding, between planting and harvesting. If he hadn't said we could no longer delay or avoid the *inevitable. . .*"

"Ooh." Julia's quick intake of air gave Nessa a savage satisfaction. "That was an unfortunate phrase, but Isaac's never been the poetic sort, you know. He must have meant. . .um. . .anticipated. Yes, he must have meant he didn't want to wait any longer before claiming you as his own."

"It gets worse," Nessa interrupted. "Isaac explained that we knew we'd get on well enough, since we've been friends for so long, and that we both knew what the true foundation for marriage was."

"Love." Her friend's voice rang with certainty.

"According to Isaac"—Nessa paused for dramatic emphasis—"the basis for marriage is a partnership to undertake hard work."

"No!"

"Yes!"

"No wonder you're all to pieces!" Julia blinked, astonishment painting her features. "Of all the things to say!"

"And even so, since I'd prayed so long and God granted me my greatest desire, I almost accepted him."

"You did not," Julia groaned. "Tell me you didn't!"

"I didn't." Nessa rose to her feet. "He saw my tears, you understand, and he told me not to be emotional."

"He must have been struck in the head." Julia hurried after her. "Isaac's wits have gone a-begging, for sure."

"Of course he's out of his mind," Nessa agreed. Tears pooled at her collar as she choked out her final word on the subject. "He couldn't possibly be his normal self if, after so many years, he asked me to marry him."

Isaac snuck a glance at Nessa where she sat in a pew across the aisle. She sat straight and tall, her fancy hairstyle wisping around her face like a burnished halo. She nodded to friends, but Isaac saw the telltale signs that all wasn't well.

A tightness at the corners of her mouth reined in her usually generous smile. Dark circles smudged beneath Nessa's brown eyes, showing her strain. Most telling of all, she hadn't so much as glanced at him a single time all morning. Clearly, the disastrous episode two days before plagued her spirits much the same way it did his own.

Good. She should suffer in equal measure for her senseless actions. He'd gone to the Gailbraith home, the blacksmith shop, and even Nessa's favorite shady nook by the stream—all to no avail. How was he to straighten things out if she continued to avoid him? This would end today if Isaac had anything to say about it.

After church everyone exited the same doors. Isaac planned to hasten to the back and wait for Nessa to pass through. Then he'd snag her elbow and lead her around the building. With everyone about, she wouldn't make a scene of refusing to speak to him.

As far as Isaac knew, Nessa had been as close-mouthed about the whole thing as he had been. He tilted his head to the side, stretching his neck, and caught Julia Mathers glaring at him. *All right. Nessa told Julia. Women can't help themselves when it comes to talking.* At least he was still reasonably sure she hadn't told her family. *They* were perfectly pleasant.

"Good people of Saddleback," Rev. Matthews intoned, calling the congregation to attention, "let us raise our voices in praise to the Lord. Alma?"

Alma took her place on the piano bench and began to play a familiar hymn.

"'God moves in a mysterious way, His wonders to perform.'" Isaac raised his voice with the rest of the congregation. *Mysterious seems about right.*

"'He plants His footsteps in the sea, and rides upon the storm.'" The words mimicked the turbulence Isaac felt. Was Nessa's strange behavior a squall to be waited out? If so, what would be left of their friendship by the end of it all?

Isaac pondered the whirl of questions made all the more urgent by the words of praise. When the music ended, he'd found no answers. He listened as Alma began the next hymn.

"All the way my Savior leads me;
What have I to ask beside?
Can I doubt His tender mercy,
Who through life has been my Guide?"

Lord, it's not that I doubt Your wisdom. I question my understanding of
Your will and Nessa's reaction to my proposal. Aside from Your leadership, I
would seek understanding. Isaac prayed as the music swelled around him,
coming to its close: " 'This my song through endless ages: Jesus led me
all the way.' "

And He will lead me through what is to come. Some of the restless en-
ergy eased from Isaac's shoulders as he took his seat in the family pew.

"Thank you, Alma." Rev. Matthews inclined his head in recognition
before he began the sermon. "Our praise this morning focused around
man's inability to fathom the perfection of God's plans for us. This is
widely acknowledged among believers. It is the next part that becomes
difficult."

Without understanding, what can follow?

"It is trusting God's plans, following His path obediently, that is
the downfall of many men." The reverend's words hit Isaac with almost
palpable force. "When we do not understand why, it becomes a struggle.
But it is not for us to know the ways of the Lord. We don't need to, for
He knows our hearts. First Chronicles 28:9 says, 'For the Lord searcheth
all hearts, and understandeth all the imaginations of the thoughts.' Our
Father knows our needs and understands our desires, and He has plans
for each one of us. We need no further reassurance than this."

All along I've prayed for Your guidance but not Your will. Show me Your
path, Lord. Let this conversation with Nessa today make clear Your purpose,
whether it be that we wed or not.

Swept away in the power of the morning's message, Isaac was surprised to see people rising from their seats. As politely as possible, he
shouldered his way up the aisle until he reached the double mahogany
doors of the church. There he waited for Nessa.

"Isaac!" Julia stopped in front of him and put her hand on his arm,
trying to guide him outside. "Can you spare a moment? There's something we need to discuss."

"Right now?" He tried to keep his displeasure out of his expression. There was really no polite way to refuse a lady, but he had to catch Nessa before she slipped away. "I was hoping to speak with Nessa." He watched his quarry make her way toward the door.

"Ah," Julia sidestepped to block his view. Considering her impressive height and wide bonnet, she managed quite well. "To tell you the truth, Isaac," she said leaning in, all trace of good humor having fled from her voice, "I don't think that's a good idea."

"You're a good friend to Nessa." Isaac placed his hands on Julia's shoulders to keep her in place as he moved to the side. *Where is she?* "I appreciate that. But this is a private matter."

"All the more reason"—she spoke through gritted teeth, though her polite smile didn't waver—"*not* to force the issue in front of the entire community after church."

"She's been eluding me all week." Isaac pasted a smile on his own lips. "I've no choice."

"Of course you do." Julia pinned him with a glare. "And so does Nessa. I suggest you remember that, Isaac Friemont." With that, she swept down the steps.

Isaac scanned the crowd for any sign of Nessa but found none. A muscle at the side of his jaw began to work furiously as he was forced to admit that Julia's ploy had worked—Nessa was gone.

Chapter 4

All her life Nessa had seen the Friemont household as an extension of her own family. She loved the large home, brightened by plentiful windows, kept clean and welcoming by Isaac's mother. Delana Friemont stood as godmother and adopted aunt to her, and typically there was nothing Nessa loved better than to visit her.

Today she'd give her eyeteeth to be anywhere else. Nessa closed her eyes and drew a deep breath, capturing her doubts along with the yeasty warmth of fresh-baked bread. It would be all right—the women would prepare a midday feast and work in a quilting circle while the men went hunting.

After a long winter and late spring, there was not much left in their smokehouse. The men wisely put off hunting until after most animals bore young, so the thought of readily available fresh meat was almost tantalizing enough to make Nessa push aside her worries that Isaac had told his mother about his failed proposal. If she had to answer to Delana, so be it. *But it would be wonderful if it wasn't in front of all the women I hold dear.* Nessa cast a glance at her family as they approached the door. Rosalind Gailbraith and Kaitlin MacLean were strong, brave women Nessa wanted to emulate. Unfortunately, her mother and grandmother were also shrewdly discerning, and she'd been dodging their gentle questions for a week now.

"Come in, come in!" Delana ushered them all inside.

Amid a flurry of greetings, Nessa placed her basket of bread on a table already laden with baked goods. Aside from her own family and Michael Hornton's mother, all the women bore direct relation to the Friemonts.

Isaac's older brother, Brent, had a soft-spoken wife named Diane. His younger sister, Marlene, was Julia's mother and Ma's best friend. Their surname was Mathers, but that was through marriage. As far as everyone in Saddleback was concerned, they were part of the Friemont family. It struck Nessa as astounding how young Isaac was when compared to the rest of his family. An eighteen-year gap between Marlene and Isaac made him the youngest by a long stretch. In fact, his nephews and nieces were closer to him in age.

"Nessa?" Julia's hug captured her attention. "I wasn't sure you'd come!"

"Of course I came. It's Saddleback tradition, after all. Besides," she lowered her voice, "I couldn't come up with an honest excuse not to come. At least, none Ma would accept."

"It'll be all right." Julia linked arms with Nessa, gesturing to the window. "The men are already gathered and ready to go, the younger girls are watching the children in the yard, and we'll be left to our own devices as soon as we've cooked enough food to feed everybody thrice over."

"Seems to me," Nessa judged, casting an eye over the tables loaded with biscuits, johnnycake, fresh bread, cinnamon rolls, and pies, "there's not much more cooking to be done."

"And Grandmam has rabbit stew already bubbling away." Julia surveyed the spread with approval. "Mrs. Hornton brought two of her own baked chickens, and Pa got down our last ham. Uncle Brent and Diane showed up with a wheel of their cheese, too. Looks like we'll be able to quilt and chat all morning!"

"Yes." Out of the corner of her eye, Nessa saw Ma and Delana and Mrs. Mathers whispering together in the corner, heads bent. "That's what I was afraid of."

∽

"Brent, Johnny, would you go ahead and check the rabbit snares?" Dad took the lead, as he had since he founded Saddleback. "Ewan, Michael, Isaac, Robert, and I will head for the clearing and start watching for deer."

"Right." Johnny answered for himself and Brent as they shouldered their muskets and started off. The sooner the snares were emptied, the sooner they'd catch more rabbits.

Isaac gathered his things and set off toward the meadow. Keeping the hunting party small was, to his way of thinking, the wisest course. So long as only a small portion of Saddleback men came, there would be little noise to startle their prey. Even better, they'd not need to spend days trying to shoot and butcher enough for a dozen families.

Not to mention the fact that many newcomers, newly alighted from the railroad, still hadn't quite grasped the idea of selective hunting. More often than not, the greenhorns would shoot young bucks or mothers who would repopulate the area.

"You ever gonna tell me just what happened with Nessa?" Michael fell into stride beside Isaac.

"I already told you," Isaac said, glancing around to ensure none of the other men was close enough to overhear, "she said no. The rest isn't important—or at least not until I can talk to Nessa about what went wrong."

"That's what you said a week ago." Michael pointed out. "The fact that she's darted away from the sight of you presents an obstacle. Are you going to try to catch her today?"

"After the hunt, when everyone's finished working and full of good food. It'll attract less notice."

"Wasn't that the plan after church?"

"Julia interfered." Isaac's field of vision narrowed as he scowled. "She might stand between me and Nessa again."

"I'll take care of that." A change in his best friend's tone jolted Isaac from his own plans.

"Sounds like you've got something up your sleeve, Michael." He spoke lightly, testing the waters.

"I've had my eye on Julia Mathers for a bit," his friend admitted easily. "Always planned on asking to court her after you and Nessa were settled. Nothing like a wedding in the town to make a woman feel romantic, you know."

"Romance," Isaac scoffed. "You know her, she knows you—what do you need fancy words and flowers for? Just settle it."

"Hmm." Michael's noncommittal murmur didn't bother Isaac half as much as his friend's speculative look.

"What?"

"Nothing much." Michael shook his head. "But after that comment, I have an inkling why things went wrong with Nessa."

⚭

"I must say," Grandmam declared as she ran a hand over the fabric before her, "that the wedding ring pattern is my favorite."

"Must be because you're such a romantic, Kaitlin," Delana chimed in. "And it's stood you in good stead—you shared so many happy years with

Arthur before he passed on."

"Grandpap was a special man," Nessa agreed.

"Aye." Grandmam nodded. "And though I miss him still, I wouldna choose any different. 'Tis happy I am my own Rosalind found such a love in Ewan. Every mother wishes a happy marriage for her daughter."

Nessa closed her eyes at the talk of marriage, the hard lump of regret at Isaac's proposal choking her words. The women were circling around the topic of her and Isaac, preparing to draw out the truth. When she looked up, she knew it wasn't her imagination—Grandmam gave Ma a meaningful glance before Ma turned to her.

"Indeed." Ma never missed a stitch, even as she fixed her gaze on Nessa. "It is my fondest hope that our Nessa will have a happy home and loving family." She paused, and Nessa prayed she'd leave it at that. But Ma continued, "Your Da and I want grandchildren to dandle on our knees before too long."

An expectant silence fell over the sewing circle as every pair of eyes focused on Nessa. Not that she saw it happen, but she could feel the intensity as she focused on her quilting. The moment she looked up, she'd have to speak.

"With Brent and Marlene happily wed to their true loves," Delana ventured when the silence drew taut and uncomfortable for everyone, "I've grandchildren aplenty. All that's left to complete our family is a bride for Isaac." She heaved a deep sigh, which was followed by absolute stillness.

Without looking up, Nessa knew the others were not only staring at her, but they'd *stopped quilting*. Biting her lip, Nessa picked up the pace of her own stitches, plunging the needle in and out of the fabric with such intensity she couldn't possibly engage in conversation.

I am not going to give in, she promised herself. *I am going to sit here and sew until they start talking about something else, or—* She pulled her thread so taut, it snapped. In the stillness of the circle, Nessa fancied she actually heard a faint snap as it happened.

"That's all right." Marlene spoke from across the circle. "You're so far ahead of all of us it would do the circle good to have you stop for a minute. While you're rethreading your needle, we can chat about Isaac. It's hard to believe my little brother has grown into such a strong man. Mom's right—he's ready for a wife now. Don't you think so, Nessa?"

Nessa looked at the broken edges of her thread and knew she'd have to say something. She cleared her throat and made one last effort to avoid the conversation everyone else seemed determined to have.

"I know how you feel, Marlene." She looked up to find her suspicions confirmed. Not only were all the women staring at her, but they leaned forward to catch every word. "Why, Robbie has grown so fast I can scarce credit it. Thirteen already."

"Oh yes." Julia pounced on Nessa's gambit. "Just the other day we were talking about how swiftly time passes. He is growing by leaps and bounds. We're all so proud of him, aren't we?" She addressed the question to her own mother.

"Absolutely." Marlene didn't so much as blink at the shift in topic. "All of the boys are growing so rapidly, but none more so than Isaac. I daresay Timothy and even Robbie look up to him as a role model. Am I right, Rosalind?"

"To an extent." Ma smiled at her best friend before fixing on Nessa once again. "But it is time Isaac set up his home and raised a family. Though we've not openly discussed the matter, I'd hope it won't be long before that happens. Is there any news you'd like to share with us, Nessa?"

She bit back a groan as she surveyed all the hopeful faces around her. There was no escape from answering the question. Nessa would have to tell them the truth.

"Well," she hedged, "I don't think Isaac will be marrying all that soon." Nessa pushed through the disappointed gasps to add, "At least, he won't be marrying me."

"Why ever not?" Grandmam abandoned all pretense of polite conversation. "Everyone knows the two of you are close, and something's changed in the past week. What happened?"

"He proposed," Nessa's words came in a whisper, "and I turned him down." She'd expected solemn silence to greet this announcement, a quiet even more oppressive and stifling than before she spoke. She'd been wrong.

"What?"

"No!"

"Surely not!"

All these exclamations, joined by squeals, shrieks, gasps, groans, snorts, and even a single inelegant "Huh?" would have made Nessa smile at any other time. It wasn't often that someone stumped the women of Saddleback, Montana. Finally, the outburst calmed, leaving her

Grandmam's soft question hovering between them.

"Why, dearie?" Those two words held a wealth of loving support and concern, bolstering Nessa so she could answer.

"I love him, Grandmam. I want to marry him." She saw the confusion in Ma's eyes. "But more than I want to marry him, I want him to love me."

"He cares deeply for you, Nessa," Delana assured her.

"As a friend, Delana." Her eyes filled with tears. "His proposal made it clear that he doesn't love me in the manner Dustin loves you, Da loves Ma, and Johnny loves Marlene."

"Surely you misunderstood," Marlene protested.

"No, she didn't." Julia said. "She told me precisely what Isaac said, and Nessa was right to refuse him."

"Such a thing is hard to mistake," Grandmam agreed.

"Love can grow in a marriage," Delana mused. "And you've your friendship as a solid foundation for that."

"No." Nessa rubbed her aching temples. "I want a husband who loves me, not as a friend, but as a man loves a woman. Just as much, I want Isaac to have a wife he loves that much." Tears slipped down her cheeks. "I'm not that woman."

Chapter 5

"W*hat* went wrong with Nessa?" Her brother's voice cracked, causing thirteen-year-old Robbie to flush a dull red.

"Quiet, Robbie!" Michael tried to nip the problem in the bud. "You know we keep our voices down when we're hunting."

"We're not at the clearing just yet," the youth stood firm.

"And time's wasting," Isaac agreed. "We'd better get going if we want to bag anything today."

"Wait!" Robbie stepped in front of him. "Nessa's been quiet all week, so I know something's wrong. Nessa's *never* quiet."

Isaac bit back a grin at the truth of that statement. "That's between your sister and me, Robbie."

"I should have known you'd said something mean." Robbie thrust out his chin. "The last time she acted so strange was when you laughed at her bonnet."

"That's different," Isaac protested. "I thought she was wearing that thing as a joke! Who puts a bird's nest on a hat?"

"Listen, I never said the hat wasn't ugly." Robbie crossed his arms over his chest. "What I want to know is what happened *this* time? What did you say to Nessa?"

"It's not so much what I said, as what she did." Isaac revealed as much as he intended to. This conversation was over.

"Oh?" Ewan Gailbraith put a hand on Robbie's shoulder. "And what did my daughter say, Isaac? I wouldn't intrude, but Nessa has been glum lately, and if she's been rude, it's my responsibility to see she rectifies her mistake."

She made a mistake, all right, Isaac reflected, *but you can't force her to become my fiancée.* Aloud, he said, "It's not a matter of manners, Mr. Gailbraith."

"It is if she insulted you, Isaac." Pa had obviously realized nobody followed him and doubled back. "You've been out of sorts yourself. If either of you has been rude to the other, it's past time you should have worked it out. We won't have this tension between our families. Did she offend you?"

I'd say she offended me—how much more insulting can a woman be than to tell a man she doesn't want to marry him?

"It's more a matter of pride," Michael explained.

"There's no room for pride in Saddleback," Pa said. "It puts distance between friends and strain between neighbors."

"Aye," Ewan agreed. "Proverbs says, 'A man's pride shall bring him low: but honour shall uphold the humble in spirit.'" He, Pa, and Robbie all looked at Isaac expectantly.

"I decided it was time Nessa and I got married, and she felt differently." He spit the words out in a rush.

"*That's* the problem?" Robbie hooted. "You're climbing the wrong fence there. Nessa does so want to marry you."

"That's what I thought, too." Isaac's jaw clenched. "We're both wrong. Now that everyone knows, we can leave it be and go hunting like we planned." *I know I feel like shooting something.*

"Wait a moment, lad." Ewan put out his paw of a hand. "You mean to say you proposed—proper—and Nessa turned you down?"

"I got down on one knee and everything," Isaac muttered.

"Then where did it go wrong?" Pa took off his hat to scratch his head. "Must be something I'm missing."

Isaac turned to Michael with raised brows.

"How should I know?" Michael shrugged. "You haven't told me anything more than that. I had wondered if you'd given her a proper proposal, is all, and you say you have."

"I did. Down on one knee, asked her to marry me... What more does a woman want than that? I mentioned children even!"

"What else did you say, exactly?" Ewan's brows knit together in concentration. "And what did Nessa say to you?"

"She mostly listened. Until she said she couldn't marry me and ran off." His hand closed into a fist.

"All right, then it must have been something you said." Michael sounded reasonable enough, but Isaac glowered at the implication that he'd botched his own proposal.

"I did everything right—held her hand, cupped her cheek, wiped her tears—"

"Tears?" Ewan's angry rumble interrupted him. "She cried? What did you say that made my little girl cry?"

"I spoke of joining our families, asked her to stand before the town as my wife." Isaac's fist knocked against a nearby tree with every point he made. "When she hesitated, I reminded her of our long-standing friendship and told her how certain I was that we could work alongside one another to build a life. What could possibly have been wrong with that?"

"Sounds good to me," Robbie put in. "And you said you mentioned kids, right? 'Cause Nessa wants lots of babies."

"Yes, I said that." Isaac rubbed his chin with his hand and noticed blood oozing from scrapes in his knuckles. "I thought she was crying because she was happy."

"She should have been happy," Pa agreed. "Sounds like a well thought out, sincere proposal. You took her wants and feelings into account and assured her you'd work hard for your family. What more could a girl want?"

∽

"More, please." Nessa drank deeply of the sun-warmed water, scarcely registering the tinny flavor as she handed the cup back to a young boy. "Thank you." Most of the water they'd drawn was boiling over one of the many fires they'd lit to keep flies at bay. Baskets of tansy and bitter herbs were scattered about for the same reason.

Everyone had eaten a light repast of bread and cheese as soon as the men returned, as no one wanted an over-full stomach for the work to come. The men had come back with a bighorn sheep and a sizable elk, both older males.

They bled both at the same time, putting the blood aside to make sausage later. Nessa and the other women tried to keep things as clean as possible, rinsing and hanging the hides as the men skinned both animals, taking the organs while they dressed the kills.

Nessa threw herself into the work, glad to have a task that occupied her hands and her mind. She took the length of elk intestine, flushing water through it time and time again until the water ran clear. Then she rinsed it a few more times just to be safe before she placed it in a bucket. She repeated the process with the sheep entrails while the other women cleaned the other organs.

A great deal of blood, dirt, water, and hard work later, the men finished butchering the meat and hanging it in the near-bursting smokehouse. Delana put the fragile livers in her icebox, declaring she'd make liverwurst the next day. Nessa bit back a grimace as she helped ready the feast for that evening. Everyone had brought a change of clothes, and the garments soiled with blood were already soaking in cold water to avoid stains.

When everyone was worn out and washed up, they sank onto the benches with sighs of pleasure. Nessa couldn't tell which made the men happier—to be at rest or to have so much good food in front of them. Oh, who was she fooling? The meaty musk of smoked ham mingled with the pungent aromas of succulent roast chicken and rabbit stew layered over yeasty bread. The wholesome scent of creamy mashed potatoes begging to be drowned in thick, hearty gravy. Her mouth watered as Dustin Friemont blessed the meal.

"Dear Lord, we thank You for the bounty we're about to receive. We're glad to share it with our good neighbors and even better friends after a hard day's work. The success of our hunt belongs to You. Thank You for Your provision and love. Amen."

There was very little speaking for the next twenty minutes as all filled their plates and emptied them almost as rapidly. It wasn't until the women had cleared the table and brought out dessert that conversation and laughter joined the heady fragrances of cinnamon, buttery pastry, and strong coffee filling the air.

Still, Nessa didn't join in. She placed a forkful of apple pie in her mouth, savoring the sweet cinnamon and flaky crust, drawing out her enjoyment so she wouldn't have to speak. That wasn't nearly as difficult as pretending she didn't notice the concerned glances the women shot her way, and—more disheartening still—the puzzled expressions from the men.

Isaac, in sharp contrast to everyone else, didn't so much as look at her. Obviously, he'd told the men about her rejection. Still more apparent, he no longer wished to speak with her. Gone was the man who'd shadowed her footsteps for the past week, seeking to set things right. Something had changed with him. Perhaps he'd realized what she'd been mourning for days—he didn't really want to marry her. Maybe he wasn't looking at her because he wanted to spare her the gleam of relief in his eyes.

Nessa put down her fork, leaving half her pie untouched as she murmured an excuse and left the table. She walked toward the outhouse but veered off toward the far corner of the yard once she was out of sight. Wrapping her arms around her waist, she hunched against the cold of the night, the chill claiming her heart.

"Irish wishes are prayers indeed,
And this especially true,
When the wishes are made and sent
On any day to You."

Nessa recited the old rhyme her da had taught her, looking up to the sky as she spoke. "Lord, I'm speeding my prayers to You tonight. Before, when I asked You for my dearest wish—that Isaac and I would wed—I meant it in earnest. But now I see that my prayers were self-serving.

"All along I should have asked for the guidance to do Your will—not my own. Now Isaac has proposed, and the distance between us is growing greater than ever before. I blame my own childish wishing. If it is Your gracious plan that Isaac come to love me as I do him, I'll rejoice in it. But if that is not to be, Father, let my heart make room for the man of Your choosing."

The chill left her as she prayed, and she unwrapped her arms from about herself when she finished. Not quite ready to return to the others, she moved toward a whispering aspen. Fingering a fragile leaf, engrossed in the way it captured the silvery gild of moonlight, she didn't notice her father's approach until she heard his voice.

"Nessa?" He stood beside her. "Are you all right? Isaac mentioned his. . .er. . .the difficulty between you."

"I'd thought as much." She released the paper-thin leaf to pat her father's arm and strove to inject a lighthearted note in her voice. "Believe it or not, I've been the recipient of a great many odd glances this evening."

"Are we so transparent, then?" Da shook his head.

"To those who love you," Nessa answered. "The women cornered me in the sewing circle, you know."

"What a polite battle that must have been."

"Indeed. And all through dinner I sat silent, with hardly a word spoken to me after the great revelation of Isaac's proposal."

" 'Twasn't the proposal that stunned us, sweetheart." He placed an arm around her shoulders. "And none of us meant to make you feel awkward or left out."

"Oh no. Quite the contrary." Her first real grin of the day made her cheeks ache. "The men were trying to avoid the topic altogether, and the women were trying to refrain from smothering me with advice. I don't know which group had the more difficult challenge."

"I'd say the women were trying to keep their opinions to themselves," Da chuckled. "It won't last long, you know."

"Yes." Nessa sighed. "I fully expect to be cornered again in the near future. Probably when we get home. Ma's fit to burst at the seams, trying to hold it all in."

"Isn't it surprising that I got to you first?"

"Mmm," Nessa murmured noncommittally. "And what words of wisdom have you, the representative for the men of North Saddleback?" She softened the words with a smile. In all honesty, Nessa hoped her father was privy to knowledge beyond her understanding. Perhaps he could set everything to rights, the way he did whenever she was hurt as a child.

"So solemn you make it sound, and yet I take my position as your father more seriously than any friendship I hold dear. I cherish you, Vanessa Gilda Gailbraith." He gave her a squeeze before releasing her and shifting to face her. "And any man who wouldn't do the same doesn't deserve your hand."

She couldn't hold back her gasp. "How does Isaac know why I refused him?" She'd thought he'd never unravel her reasoning without someone to tug him into place.

"He doesn't." Da gave a deep sigh. "But when he related his proposal, there was only one thing missing as could make you deny the very man you've wanted so long."

"I don't know that there was only one thing wrong with it," Nessa frowned. "But that was the main problem, yes. Did you tell him?"

"No. Some things a man has to figure out for himself."

"What am I to do, Da?" She rested her head against his shoulder, just as she had when she was a little girl and he'd gathered her in his arms to chase away the hurt of a burnt finger or twisted ankle. "I can't bear to explain to him that he doesn't love me. It was already too hard admitting it to myself."

"You pray and you wait and you see how God will move Isaac's heart." Da put his hands on her shoulders and stepped back, forcing her to meet his gaze. "He may not realize the depth of his feelings for you, Nessa, but a man doesn't propose lightly. Your refusal will make him search his soul for the reason, and I think you were wise to tell him no. In time Isaac should come to see that he loves you."

"You think so?" She gulped back the tears that rose once more from the small part of herself that still hoped Isaac would come for her.

" 'Boast not thyself of to morrow; for thou knowest not what a day may bring forth,' " her father quoted. "Proverbs reminds us that we can't know what the future holds, but we can have faith in the Lord, who will see us through it."

Chapter 6

"Mr. Hepplewhite." Isaac tipped his hat. Rumor had it that Saddleback's newest widower had tired of a life of luxury and wanted the adventure of the West. If that was so, the man would need good sense and better neighbors to make a go of it.

"Mr. Friemont," the older man acknowledged, a glint of amusement in his gray eyes. "I can see I was right in my initial estimation of the town population."

"Oh?" Pa raised a brow.

"If I forget a man's name, the best thing I can do is try Mr. Friemont."

"Hardly," Isaac grinned. "There are only three of us—Pa, Brent, and myself. Unless you're including my nephews." His brow furrowed at the thought, since two of his nephews were scarce years younger than himself.

"That's what I thought," Hepplewhite chortled. "One of the perks of founding the town, I'd say. Ah." He motioned to a well-dressed man about Isaac's age, and the fellow immediately headed toward them. "Here's the other Mr. Hepplewhite, my son, Lawrence." His father beamed with pride. "Lawrence, Misters Dustin and Isaac Friemont."

"Pleased to meet you." Lawrence shook hands with a solid grip and friendly smile. "We're grateful for all the help the community is pitching in, especially since Dad arrived while I was fetching my sister."

"He'd already commissioned the house," Pa pointed out. "This barn raising is the first chance Saddleback has to really come together and welcome your family. We'll all get to know each other pretty well while the men swing hammers and the women make a meal you've never seen the likes of."

"Sounds good to me," Lawrence agreed. "It looks like the whole town has already showed up—more people than we expected."

"Since the railroad came through, Saddleback's been growing by leaps and bounds," Isaac pointed out. "And we're glad for the company."

"I'd introduce you to my daughter, but I'm not quite sure where she is." Mr. Hepplewhite scanned the crowd once again before shrugging.

"The women are probably flocked around her already," Pa reassured the man. "There will be time aplenty to socialize once the barn's built."

"Right."

"Hello, folks!" Mr. Hepplewhite climbed atop a pile of lumber to gather everyone's attention. "Now, I've heard that sometimes we perk up all this hard work with the spirit of competition. Sounds like a good motivator to me. What say the men split up into four groups of five or six. The first to raise a wall wins this bicycle!" He motioned toward a quilt-covered object.

Isaac blinked twice as a girl floated forward and pulled the covering away with a single, graceful flourish. He didn't spare so much as a glance for the bicycle; all of his attention was captured by the vision of loveliness beside it.

White-blond hair in perfect order, creamy skin kissed by roses, dainty features, and a full-skirted dress of pale yellow—Clementine Hepplewhite was the postcard for femininity. He'd never seen such fragile beauty in the hardworking world of Montana, where men worked hard and their women matched them.

Clementine—and he knew that was her name, for he'd met everyone else and would never have forgotten such delicacy—was not built for work. No, such a girl would be protected, cossetted. She was the type of woman who needed a man to care for her. He stood straighter at the very thought, only tearing his gaze away when Michael stepped in his line of vision.

"Seems like you have one too many Friemonts," he joked. "With your dad, Brent, and Johnny, and their sons, they've already topped six. What say you and I team up with the Gailbraiths and the Hepplewhites?"

"Absolutely." Here was a chance to show the Hepplewhites what he was made of, perhaps earn the father's approval and Clementine's admiration.

"I saw Nessa eying that bike," Michael continued. "Would be a nice gesture to win it for her—reestablish the friendship and so forth."

"Nessa wants it?" Isaac searched for her, finding her in her faded blue calico dress with her burnished locks escaping their pins with an ease born of practice.

Sure enough, she was keeping her gaze fixed on the bicycle. Isaac knew she would be stewing that she couldn't join her family's team to help win. Nessa had never been one just to sit back and let the men handle things.

"Yes, let's win it for Nessa," he said aloud to his team. *And for Clementine*, he added silently.

∞

"Don't look now"—Julia nudged Nessa—"but I think Isaac noticed your fascination with that contraption. He's joining your father and brother."

"Do you think Da may be right? That Isaac does care for me but doesn't realize it yet?" Nessa kept her voice low.

"I'd say it's a distinct possibility." Julia beamed. "They're taking their places now—Isaac, your father and Robbie, and the Hepplewhite men."

"And Michael Hornton," Nessa teased as her friend's gaze never left the one man whose name she hadn't spoken. "Surely you wouldn't want to leave him out."

"Of course not." Julia gave Nessa a warning glance. "Don't read too much into a simple oversight."

"Never." Nessa bit her lip. "Though I did notice your line of sight goes directly over to where Michael is standing. You must be struggling to decide which team to cheer on!"

"I've already made my choice," Julia murmured. Nessa's knowing look made her add hastily, "If it weren't for Isaac trying to get that bicycle for you, I would have rooted for my father and brother."

"Only proper," Nessa agreed. "But you've the soul of a romantic."

"Leave off and wave to Isaac in encouragement." Julia smiled toward Michael. "The whole team is looking this way."

Nessa grinned and waved, meeting Isaac's gaze before nodding at Michael, Da, Robbie, Mr. Hepplewhite, and his son. She felt her eyes widen in surprise as she found the stranger's gazed fixed on her, his hand raised to return her salute.

"What was Mr. Hepplewhite's name?" Nessa asked. "I didn't quite catch it."

"Malvern, I believe. Hard to forget, a name like that. Why do you want to know? You'll probably never need it." Julia squinted at the stocky, white-haired man as he gestured for the building to start. "Nice enough man though."

"I meant his son," Nessa chuckled. "You know, the young, fairly handsome one working beside him? The man who waved back at us?"

"Ooh." Julia blushed. "I hardly even noticed him."

"That does it. You are going to stop pretending you aren't interested in Michael Hornton. If you don't even notice a handsome, eligible new man, you're practically smitten."

"Not smitten," she protested. "Just. . .interested."

"Finally!" Nessa elbowed her best friend. "I can't believe it took you so long to admit it, after all the years I've pined for Isaac. Well, at least now I can tell you I think he's noticed you, too."

"How's that?" Julia turned her full attention on Nessa. "What makes you think so?"

"There's a way he sneaks glances at you when he thinks nobody's watching. And he's mentioned several times how he wishes more women were of your height."

"Oh bother. If he wanted me, he'd say so. Not that he wants another woman who's as tall as I am." She demurred, but Nessa noticed how her friend instinctively smoothed her skirts.

"A compliment's a compliment. Besides, now you know he's no-ticed you. . .and liked what he saw." Nessa knew that if her friend wasn't wearing her bonnet, everyone would see that Julia's ears were turning bright red.

"Amazing how quickly they work, isn't it?"

"Mmhmm." Nessa was surprised to see just how much the men had accomplished while they'd been chatting. She tore her gaze from where Isaac and Mr. Hepplewhite—Jr.—were hammering nails into a support beam.

Both had removed their jackets, unbuttoned the top of their shirts, and rolled up their sleeves. She couldn't help but notice that Isaac was much broader and more muscular than the new arrival, his skin turned golden by his hours of work in the sunshine. Still, the young Mr. Hepplewhite had a kind of determined concentration she admired, especially since he was rather obviously unused to this type of work.

"We should go see what we can do to help out." Julia reminded Nessa that they shouldn't have been lingering in the shade to watch the men—even though the other three unmarried girls in Saddleback were doing the same thing.

"At the very least, we should introduce ourselves to Miss Hepplewhite." Nessa looked around for the girl, searching for her pale yellow dress. In all honesty, she'd been looking at the bicycle earlier and didn't have too much to go on.

"There she is."

Nessa followed Julia to a space farther back in the shade, to the right of where they'd been standing. She couldn't help but notice the new girl's porcelain prettiness. Nessa looked at her hairstyle and dress with appreciation. *Wonder how long she'll manage to keep that perfect coiffure and fancy dress from wilting in the heat. She'll probably manage far longer than I ever could.*

"Hello, Miss Hepplewhite." Nessa noticed she clasped a small hand gloved in white lace, of all things. "I'm Vanessa Gailbraith, and this is Julia Mathers. We're so pleased to welcome you to Saddleback."

"A pleasure to meet you." Miss Hepplewhite drew her hand back and nodded pleasantly to Julia. "It's good to see that there are a few young, unattached women other than myself. Why, when we stopped over in Virginia City, it was positively embarrassing the way men shouted proposals the moment they clapped eyes on me! So good to see this place is far more civilized."

"We like to think so." Nessa glanced at Julia for her reaction to this pronouncement. She gave a faint shrug and tried to keep the conversation. "It must be difficult to be the only woman of a household."

"Well, we do have Darla, but she's just the housekeeper." Miss Hepplewhite gave a small sigh. "It has been rather trying without another lady to converse with—so different from all my friends at finishing school."

"Such a lovely dress you're wearing." The ever-diplomatic Julia was quick to change to another topic so as not to defend the maligned Darla. "You must keep up on the latest fashions."

"But of course. I love to read *Godey's Lady's Book* and *McCall's Magazine*—that's how I learned about these gloves. Clever little things, aren't they? And so much cooler than leather." Miss Hepplewhite warmed to her topic. "I had these boots made specifically to wear with them." She lifted her skirts a scant inch and poked out a creamy white leather half boot. "Some say having mother-of-pearl buttons are the height of extravagance, but it matches the gloves, you see."

"Indeed," Nessa acknowledged, for the girl had turned her wrist to show two small mother-of-pearl buttons fastening her gloves. "I've never seen the like." *And never thought to. Those lovely things will be ruined and useless in less than a fortnight!*

"I do wonder how you keep your skin so fashionably light when you don't wear a bonnet." Julia must have heard the disbelief in Nessa's tone, for she shot her a warning look.

"Normally I do, but I have the most cunning little parasol—came with the gloves, you see." She reached beside the tree shading her delicate features and produced the parasol with a flourish. "White lace over satin, and the handle is mother-of-pearl, too. I simply couldn't resist it!"

"It completes the ensemble perfectly," Nessa praised. She hoped her smile didn't show how hard she was struggling not to laugh. Miss Hepplewhite was pretty as a picture, a walking work of art. It wouldn't be long before she became more practical in her attire. At least the woman was friendly, and Nessa put down her thoughtless comments to nervous excitement over meeting the town.

"I almost hate to ask, since we've only just met, but I've really no other avenues to seek such information." Miss Hepplewhite hesitated for a brief moment before making her request. "Could either of you tell me if that handsome man is engaged? He's quite appealing, in a rugged sort of way."

Nessa's gaze followed the new woman's gesture, straight to. . .

Chapter 7

"Isaac!" Michael bellowed and gestured for his friend to drop the hammer, indicating that they'd finished erecting their wall before any other team had managed.

"Done!" Isaac gave the last nail one more solid whack, feeling the force of the blow travel pleasantly up his arm before he put down the hammer and raised his hands above his head. There was nothing like healthy competition and good, hard work to distract a man from women. On that thought, he started looking around for Nessa...and Miss Hepplewhite. Luckily enough, they stood together, heading right for him. Isaac straightened his shoulders as they approached, taking the moment to appreciate the contrast between the two women.

"Miss Clementine Hepplewhite, meet Mr. Isaac Friemont." Nessa's introduction came with an overly bright smile, her voice sounding forced as she spoke directly to him for the first time since the "incident."

"A pleasure," Isaac responded as he gave a slight bow. He would've tipped his hat, but he'd taken it off to cool down.

"Such a gentleman!" The gesture obviously pleased Miss Hepplewhite. "When I discovered dear Vanessa knew you, I simply had to come congratulate you. You worked so quickly." She finished this with a glance of admiration. "Obviously, Mr. Friemont, you're quite accustomed to manly labor. Your expertise made up for my father's and brother's lack of it."

"I wouldn't say that." *But it's nice to hear you say it.* "It takes the efforts of the whole team." He tore his gaze away from Miss Hepplewhite to see a sour expression hastily erased from Nessa's face. Thinking she might have interpreted the new girl's compliment as a disparagement to her father and brother, Isaac added, "And the Gailbraiths and my friend Michael are old hands at this sort of thing."

"They're more used to working over iron than lumber," Nessa

allowed. The barest glimmer of a smile let him know she appreciated his comment.

"Would that be your friend Michael with Miss Mathers?" Miss Hepplewhite reclaimed his attention as she glanced toward Julia.

"Yes. I'd be happy to introduce you." He watched carefully for her reaction. Could the new arrival have fixed her interest on his best friend? Isaac caught himself frowning at the thought.

"If you like." She gave a dainty shrug but placed the delicate lace of her gloved palm on his forearm.

Isaac took a minute to note the frilly gloves, which were almost practical next to the ridiculous fluff of an umbrella she held in her other hand. *They must be dressing like this in all the big cities. Pretty little furbelows, but won't hold up out here.* He shifted his gaze to find Nessa already leading the way over to Michael and Julia. Seemed as though she didn't care a twit if he escorted another woman around. His jaw clenched as he started forward, only to have to slow to a shuffle to accommodate Miss Hepplewhite's tiny steps.

"Congratulations on your win, Isaac!" Julia addressed him after the obligatory introductions were made. "I was just asking Michael what you planned to do with your new bicycle." She cast a pointed glance toward Nessa, who was studiously avoiding his gaze.

"Why, didn't they tell you?" Lawrence Hepplewhite strode to join their group. "Isaac, in particular, was quite intent about claiming victory. I understood his reasons—and agreed completely—when the other members of our team revealed a unanimous desire to give the prize to such a lovely young lady." Lawrence stared at Nessa until his sister offered a formal introduction.

Isaac's lip curled in distaste as Lawrence bowed low over Nessa's hand. If the upstart had taken the liberty of pressing a kiss on her soft skin, Isaac would have stepped forward. *How did I ever think he was a good fellow? I should have seen right through his fancy manners and known he'd cause trouble.*

"Me?" Nessa's hopeful query diverted Isaac's scowl from Lawrence.

"Of course." His expression softened at her delight. "I know you've always secretly wanted one."

"I had no business wasting wishes on a bicycle when Da bought that incredible automobile. The Model T is a marvel. There's no need for any other source of transportation!"

"Ah, but there is a need to earn one of your lovely smiles," the upstart oozed. "There can be no greater purpose than to bring a lady joy."

"Oh." Nessa blinked at the man's fulsome compliment, obviously at a loss. "I would say that the greatest purpose is to serve Christ by loving our fellow man."

"But some of us know that a gift can be an expression of such love." Lawrence Hepplewhite recovered swiftly and showed no sign of registering Isaac's glower.

"Indeed." Miss Hepplewhite exerted a slight pressure to gain Isaac's attention, as he hadn't realized her hand still lay on his arm. "Especially if the gift is pretty. Don't you agree, Mr. Friemont?" She raised and lowered her lashes in a becoming show of modesty.

"Beauty is welcome wherever she walks." He smiled at her even as he wondered what possessed him to speak like a popinjay.

"Oh Mr. Friemont!" She peeked up at him through her lashes. "Who would believe that such a strong man could be so gallant?"

"Certainly not I." Nessa's mutter was probably not intended for anyone's ears, but Isaac caught the words.

Since when did Nessa care about pretty phrases? He wondered. *And why didn't I know about it?*

He never paid attention to me. Nessa all but rolled her eyes as Clementine flirted with Isaac and—*Good grief!*—he flirted back.

"Bicycles are monstrous contraptions," Clementine declared. "I can't imagine why anyone would want to try and balance on a spindly seat and two thin wheels. It scarcely seems safe!"

"Challenges are invigorating." Nessa bit off the words as her rival pressed up against Isaac's side as though afraid of the very idea of bicycling. "Good for improving character."

"Besides, it looks like fun to me." Isaac's support brought a warm tingling to her fingertips, a sort of itch to get on that bicycle and show him that he should be noticing *her*.

"Riding a bicycle can be very entertaining," Lawrence Hepplewhite broke in. "Though I've tried it only a few times, what little expertise I boast is at your service, Miss Gailbraith." His gray eyes, alight with interest, darkened when he turned to his sister. "Don't let Clementine's misgivings dissuade you from enjoying new things."

"After the barn is finished, I'd appreciate whatever advice you could give me, Mr. Hepplewhite." Her stomach gave an odd flutter at his admiring gaze.

"Please, call me Lawrence." He stepped a little closer.

"That's hardly proper on such short acquaintance." Isaac's protest should have irked her, but he'd shaken off Clementine's hand as he stepped forward.

"We don't stand much on such formalities in Saddleback," she reminded him, trying to control her grin as Isaac gave Lawrence a measuring look. "Particularly as his father makes a second Mr. Hepplewhite. Why, that's the reason we all call you and Brent by your first names. Your pa is Mr. Friemont. Same case here."

"Not by a long shot, Nessa." Isaac all but growled her name. "We've known each other for years." His emphasis on the "we" did not go unnoticed. "That gives us the right to address each other as friends."

Clementine sidled up once more. "Oh, but it's so fun to make new friends. And with Lawrence and myself so new to town, it would certainly put me at ease to have you address me by my Christian name...Isaac." As Clementine gave him a melting glance, Nessa abruptly began to reconsider her position on allowing such forward behavior.

"Perhaps—" She started to retract her earlier insistence, only to be silenced by Isaac.

"Clementine," his voice lingered on her name, "makes a good argument. We all want you and your brother to feel at home."

"I'm glad that's settled," Nessa tried not to sound disgruntled as Isaac gave her a cocky grin. *"Lawrence."* A burst of satisfaction streaked through her as Isaac's grin faded and Lawrence's widened in pleasure.

"I trust that this will be the beginning of a close"—Lawrence paused meaningfully—"friendship, Nessa."

"Va-nessa," Isaac snapped. "Her given name is Vanessa. Family and close friends use her pet name. You've yet to earn the privilege, Hepplewhite." His words didn't make Lawrence so much as shift his stance, much less back away, which raised the newcomer in Nessa's estimation.

"Most of the town calls me Nessa," she pointed out, an angry heat suffusing her face. "It is our hope that the Hepplewhites will become close friends, so I've no objection to Lawrence's use of it." She didn't even look at Isaac, determined to flout his possessive posturing. How dare he try to make decisions for her...while another woman hung on his arm, no less!

"I have no pet name," Clementine sniffed. "They're rather common, you know. What reason to corrupt a perfectly good name with a pithy diminutive?" She gave a small smile, "Though 'Nessa' does have a sort of rural charm. I can see why you like it." The slight emphasis on "you" had to have been inadvertent.

"I do like it," Nessa agreed, "but can see why you'd rather not attempt a moniker. 'Clemmy' doesn't have the dignity of 'Clementine.'" She watched as the girl's pale complexion grew mottled. *Lord, forgive me for not regretting that.*

"I don't usually let people call me 'Mike.'" Michael attempted to salvage the conversation with a rueful grimace. "Puts me in mind of a mischievous lad."

"Which you were, if memory serves." Julia's tongue-in-cheek comment took Nessa by surprise, as her best friend usually subscribed to the role of peacemaker. But here she was, gently teasing Michael in an attempt to elicit his attention.

"The truth is no reason for saying so, Julia!" Michael's fond grin brought forth an appreciative chuckle from everyone.

"Perhaps I've more mischief than you realized," she countered, eyes sparkling with triumph.

"Sounds like I'll have to pay closer attention." Michael shifted toward her, and Julia gave a soft smile.

"The women of Saddleback deserve every consideration," Lawrence agreed, his gaze fixed on Nessa. "When Dad decided to move to Montana, I'd no idea we'd discover such lovely ladies. If I'd only known, I would have hastened our arrival."

"We're gratified your family is here now," Nessa murmured. Out of the corner of her eye, she saw Clementine give Isaac a coy look. *At least, I'm glad you and your father are.*

Chapter 8

I don't like that Hepplewhite boy," Isaac announced as he shoved a wheelbarrow full of ash over to a bare patch. He, his pa, and his brother, Brent, were liming the soil that would lie fallow this year. Turning up the loamy earth and spreading ash, pulverized limestone, or shards of seashells made the fields far better able to sustain crops.

"He's two years older than you are." Brent swiped a shovelful and shook it out, spreading it thickly on the overturned soil. "Seems wrong for you to call him a boy."

"Years don't make a man." Isaac dropped the handles with an audible *thud*. "It's experience. And Hepplewhite hasn't done enough hard labor and man's work to qualify just yet. I have."

"God has a different purpose for each one of us, son." Pa grunted as he lifted his own full shovel, and Isaac was struck once again by how quickly his father had aged over the past five years. "Lawrence Hepplewhite has a fine education and was a respected accountant back in South Carolina. He may not have swung a hammer much, but he's a quick study. I doubt you'll find anyone to say he's not as much a man as you are."

"He's going to have to earn my respect." Isaac blinked as a piece of ash landed in his eye. "I, for one, am not going to take for granted that he's a good man, or a welcome one."

"Isaac Bartholomew Friemont." Pa stopped shoveling, his tone ominous. He never used Isaac's full name unless it preceded a stern lecture— at the very least. "There is no good reason not to welcome a Christian brother to our town. What can that boy have done to rile you so quickly? Seemed like you and Nessa were getting along with Lawrence and Clementine the other day."

"That's the problem, Pa." Brent had planted his shovel in the ground and was leaning on the handle to watch Isaac's dressing-down. "I'd guess

Nessa and Lawrence got along a little too well for my brother's taste. Am I right, Isaac?"

"He's overfamiliar with her," Isaac defended. "Not even an hour after meeting her he was already calling her 'Nessa.'"

"No man should disrespect a lady by using her given name without her permission." Pa frowned. "I'll have a word with Ewan about Lawrence's behavior. It doesn't bode well."

"Hepplewhite wrangled permission," Isaac admitted.

"Then it's Nessa's choice," Brent reminded him. "And if she's happy, you don't have the right to challenge it."

I should. He didn't speak the words out loud. If Nessa hadn't rejected his proposal, she'd be his intended. Then he could keep Lawrence Hepplewhite from sniffing around her. Isaac jabbed his shovel into the wheelbarrow, hearing the dull scrape of metal on metal. They'd need more ash soon.

"I still don't know why she turned me down." He muttered the bitter words, hating the taste of them but recognizing that he needed to understand her reasoning if he was to change it. If he wanted to change it, at all.

"Did you talk to her about it?" Brent nabbed the last bit of ash. "I hate to see you make the same mistake I did."

"Mistake?" Isaac straightened up. "What mistake?"

"I wouldn't call it a real mistake—it's what made me free to marry Diane, after all." His brother's defensive tone told Isaac it was a story worth listening to—closely.

"She's a fine wife to you," Pa affirmed.

"Who did you lose before you met Diane?" Isaac slapped his hat against his knee, raising a flurry of ash motes.

"Rosalind MacLean," Brent grumbled. "Once Ewan came to town, she didn't spare so much as a glance for me."

"Nessa's *mother*?" He shook off the strangeness of that concept. After all, Brent was twenty years his senior. But the very idea that his brother might have. . . *No.* Best not to consider that idea too closely. Isaac shuddered.

"She didn't even have two years on me, remember." Brent shrugged. "Like you and Nessa, I always assumed the two of us were going to be married. Our families were close, there weren't many young women, she was an attractive girl. . . Seemed like a foregone conclusion to me."

"Makes sense. I take it she didn't agree?"

"Not so much. She and our sister were best friends, and Rosalind didn't see me as a suitor. When the railroad came through, it brought a lot of men. Our brother-in-law, Johnny, for one. Ewan Gailbraith for another. Anyone with two eyes could see the way he looked at her, and I determined to set him straight."

My problem exactly. "What'd you do?"

"Tried to claim Rosalind at an apple bee." Brent inspected the toes of his boots rather than look Isaac in the eye. "Told her to sit next to me, where she belonged."

Isaac sucked in a quick breath as he imagined how Nessa would react to an order like that. He then coughed on the ashes he'd inhaled, making Brent thump his back before continuing.

"I can see you get the idea. She told me she didn't belong to anyone then spent the day with Ewan. That day stretched into a lifetime." Brent shook his head. "Now that I have Diane, it's easy to see God's hand in my foolishness. But if you can learn from my error, I don't see any reason why you shouldn't."

"Any advice on what would work?"

"Wouldn't presume to guess. Not even if you promised to manure this entire field alone." Brent grinned. "You should know by now that there's no predicting what a woman will do."

Nessa brushed the last of the dirt from around the sharp edges of the glass, then carefully lifted and set it aside. Beneath, the early potatoes—planted on April 10 as *The Farmer's Almanac* advised—were frost-free and thriving. She tilted her watering can and heard the gentle lapping of water flowing over thirsty ground.

"How do they look?" Ma called from where she was thinning the tomatoes. A basketful of the red vegetables sat beside her.

"Very good," Nessa answered as she headed for the pump and refilled the watering can. It was best to have the soil around the potatoes as soft as possible so she could remove them easily and move the plants to richer soil. If all went well, they'd have a small crop of early potatoes by Independence Day. "I'll be over to help you with the watermelon before you know it, Julia!"

Today Julia and Marlene helped with the Gailbraith garden. Tomorrow Ma and Nessa would go to their place. It wasn't a necessary arrangement—if the women decided to tend their own gardens, it would work well enough—but sharing the work made the time go by more quickly.

Nessa gently tugged one of the plants from its wet cocoon, carrying it over to the southern slope where it would grow best. She planted it next to the others she'd already moved, humming while she worked. With no one close enough to notice, she pulled off her gloves and tucked them in her apron pocket, reveling in the moist earth she shaped and patted into place. She'd put them back on when she needed to put away the plate of glass or cart the wheelbarrow around.

After she finished transplanting the potatoes, Nessa looked at her hands. Small and a bit too tan, with long fingers tapering to nails cut short, her hands held no pretensions. No milky-white softness here. No jewels to prove her importance. Callouses—not overly thick—protected her palms. Dirt lined her nail beds, no matter that she'd washed at the pump. She'd need soap to fully remove it.

Nessa liked her hands, liked that they showed how hard she worked for the people and land she loved. All the same, she couldn't quell a surge of disappointment at the sight of her bare left ring finger. A wedding band may not be a flashy adornment, but what it symbolized was more valuable than any precious metal or stone.

A lump pressed against the back of her throat as she realized, once again, that she might have thrown away her only chance to be Isaac's wife. Da thought Isaac would come to realize he loved her, but that was before Clementine Hepplewhite arrived in town with her delicate white lace and fragile beauty.

"Ready to work with the sweet corn?" Julia walked up to her and gestured to the hills she'd packed around the watermelon. Every five feet or so stood a little heap of dirt to nourish the crisp, juicy fruit as it grew into a summertime treat. "I finished about the same time you were done with those potatoes."

"All right." Nessa fell into step as her friend passed the rows of poles lashed together and covered with peas and beans.

"After we're finished with those, we can weed around the lettuce," Julia suggested. At Nessa's silent nod, she added, "Then we can pick up all the slugs and keep them as pets."

"What?" She halted. "Since when have you developed a fondness for squishy, sticky, oozing, slimy garden pests?"

"I haven't, but there was no other way I could make sure you were listening." Julia nudged her with an elbow. "Since when do you quietly agree to everything I say?"

"Since I stopped trusting myself to make sound decisions." Nessa sighed. "Especially since you never put a foot wrong."

"What are talking about?" Her best friend gaped at her over stalks of sweet corn. "If I had half your courage, I'd speak my mind often enough to find a little trouble."

"And if I had half your sense," Nessa retorted, "I'd know when to shut my mouth and avoid it!"

"You're thinking of Isaac, aren't you?" She sobered. "However difficult it is to believe, you made the right decision when you refused him. Where there is no love, there can be no marriage. On that account we're both right."

"That's just it." Nessa closed her eyes against a sour taste in the back of her throat. "I love him. Maybe I could have loved enough for both of us. Maybe he would have come to love me back. Perhaps it would have been better to live half my dream and not refuse it out of greed for the other part."

"Oh yes. I see what you mean." Julia's blithe agreement made Nessa abandon her hunched posture. "That verse in Ecclesiastes does say, 'Live joyfully with the wife whom thou...' What was that last bit again? 'The wife whom thou' *likest* a great deal? No. That wasn't it. Maybe it was 'the wife who lovest' *thou*? Nope. That's not right either. Help me out here, Nessa, with the exact phrasing of God's words. He tells a man that he should 'Live joyfully with...' " She trailed off expectantly.

" '...the wife whom thou lovest.' " Nessa finished the verse, torn between crying over the fact Isaac didn't love her and laughing at the way her friend had proven her point.

That pretty much sums up the extremes of life—tears and laughter. My time to cry is over, she decided. *No more pining over Isaac.*

Chapter 9

Oh yes, it was time. Isaac waved to Rosalind Gailbraith as he stalked silently to where Nessa and Julia worked, hunkered down among the corn. This time she wouldn't escape him. This time he'd wrangle an answer and hear her reason for refusing his proposal.

Julia spotted him first, eyes widening as he edged into view. To his surprise, she didn't warn Nessa or move to block his approach. Instead, she gave him a searching glance, followed by a wary nod.

She must believe Nessa is prepared for this conversation, he realized. His shadow fell over Nessa, making her look over her shoulder.

As Nessa rose to her feet, Julia tilted her head in silent question. If Julia left, it would be the first time the two of them had been alone since he proposed. What she saw in Nessa's expression must have reassured her, because Julia gave a small smile before brushing past him. She looked back once, a warning glint in her eyes, before she left them to the rustle of the corn and the heavy silence between them.

"Isaac?" Nessa spoke more softly than he'd ever heard her, the question in her voice belying her usual confidence.

"Nessa." Now that he stood before her, all the words he planned flew from his mind. He'd never seen her look this way—not happy, teasing, hopeful, peaceful, excited, angry, or even sad. Something more complex flickered in the depths of her brown eyes. With a flash of understanding, he recognized it as vulnerability. *But how can I hurt her when she rejected me?*

"What is it?" She prompted gently after he still hadn't said a word beyond her name. "Is there something you need?"

"I need you to tell me why you refused me." He gave up trying to sound detached. "You. . .seemed to care for me."

"I still do." She spoke more steadily now, sounding like the strong woman he'd watched her become.

"But you don't want me for your husband." If realizations could land physical blows, he'd be flat on the ground.

"No!" She sounded surprised by the very thought. "I've always hoped. . ." She gestured toward him then herself.

"Then why don't we?" He caught her hand in his. "What's holding you back?"

"You honestly don't know, do you?" Nessa tugged her hand away, straightening her shoulders in resignation.

"Is it that I didn't officially seek your father's blessing before I proposed? You see, I thought I already had it. I thought everyone wanted us to wed."

"Everyone but you." Her whisper tickled his ears, a plaintive murmur that made no sense.

"What gave you that idea?" He shoved his hand through his hair. "I proposed, I've sought you out since you refused, and I'm asking you to accept me as your husband. What other way can I show you I want you as my wife? You're the one who's putting a stop to this marriage."

"In a way, that's true. But my hesitation isn't the root of our problem." She must have read his frustration as she continued. "If you wanted me for your bride, really and truly, would you have paid such attention to Clementine Hepplewhite?"

"That was after you turned me down!" A dull pounding sounded in his temples. "She was new to town, sought me out while you were getting cozy with Lawrence! It has nothing to do with what lies between us, Nessa."

"It has everything to do with what lies between us, Isaac." She swallowed visibly. "And if you can't see that, then there's not much hope for us."

"You're being nonsensical," he growled.

"No, Isaac," she choked out the words as she turned from him, "for the first time, I'm being the sensible one." With that, she left him standing in the garden alone with a slug oozing over the tip of his boot.

He kicked it away, striding away from the Gailbraith home. Moving away from Nessa and away from the unshakable notion that he'd missed something important.

∽

Nessa didn't look back to see if Isaac would follow. She knew he wouldn't. It had been enough of a blow to his pride that she'd refused to marry him then come as close as she could to telling him it was all his fault.

Which it is. She harrumphed as she kept placing one foot before the other. Ma would know she needed some time to herself after her conversation with Isaac. Julia would tell her, giving Nessa the freedom to sort through the muddle of her thoughts.

First things first. Once she'd gone a reasonable distance—to the wooden bridge over their stream—she snatched up a smooth stone and flung it into the sparkling water. The initial splash faded into a series of soft plops as droplets caught the sun and dropped back. The stream, still full from winter's snow, moved too quickly for there to be rings upsetting the surface.

Instead, she spotted an alarmed frog hopping for safety, a thirsty dragonfly abandoning its drink, and a hungry fish streaking after its thwarted dinner. Her emotions taking their toll on those around her once again, Nessa couldn't help but see her love for Isaac as close kin to that stone. Both upset the balance of daily life, brought no joy, and left a sinking feeling behind.

I will not cry. Not for Isaac, not again. She sniffed as she made the resolution, stepping over the bridge to keep walking. *Never mind that not only does he not love me; it doesn't even occur to him that he should!*

She dried her tears with angry swipes, unable to stop them from falling. She trudged onward.

Oh Lord, I've made a mess of it. But why do I still have this love for Isaac if it is not shared? You know me down to the number of hairs on my head, and I won't pretend I am without various flaws of character. But You love me despite those faults. Am I so unappealing that a man—lacking perfection in his own right—can't do the same? Is there something I am supposed to do to win Isaac's love, or am I to transfer my feelings to another man? I pledged to follow Your will, Lord, but I'm more bewildered than ever about how.

Nessa realized she'd wandered all the way to her Da's smithy when the scent of smoke wafted past her. She hastened to the door then waited a moment to allow her eyes to adjust to the darkness of the smithy.

The forge in the center of the room burned bright and hot, the smoke pushed up the chimney by rigged bellows. The thick stones encircling its heat held a clatter of tools readily at hand. Da, a bandana over his face, heavy leather apron and gloves catching sparks, beat a piece of red-hot iron over his anvil.

Robbie poured fresh water into the tempering bath, spotting her before their father did.

"Nessa! Did you bring us tarts?" He rushed forward, clearly hoping for one of the sweet treats his sister sometimes surprised them with. When he moved closer, the smile dropped from his face. "You've been crying."

Belatedly, Nessa realized that some of the smithy's ash would have clung to the tracks of her tears. She pulled a handkerchief from her sleeve and scrubbed her cheeks.

"Robbie!" Da roared over the noise of the forge. "Come finish this for me!" When his son clearly had control over the piece, he pulled down his bandana and took Nessa's elbow.

The bandana was unique to her father and Robbie, made by Nessa's mother. Made of leather, save a small portion over the nose and mouth that was filled with regular fabric, Rosalind Gailbraith insisted the bandana be worn at the smithy. She feared that the weakness of the lungs that had claimed both her father and brother would seize hold of her family now. Nessa understood the precaution, as more than a few moments of breathing the thick air of the smithy set her throat to scratching.

"So he still hasn't reasoned it out, eh?" Da led her to a bench outside.

"No." Nessa offered a small smile. "You were right, Da. I wanted to tell him what the problem was, but he needs to know it from his heart."

"Aye. Is he any closer to understanding your side of things?"

"Hard to say." She twisted her handkerchief in her lap. "He wants to understand, made it clear that he wants to marry me, and believes that should be the end of the matter. Isaac's only question was why, if I cared for him, did I refuse his proposal?"

"And what did you tell him, Nessa?" Her father pulled off his great leather gloves and draped them over his knee.

"That if he couldn't see the answer, there was little hope for us."

"I don't suppose he took that too kindly, did he?" Da heaved a sigh. "But remember, Nessa, mighty works aren't accomplished by hope."

"If Isaac loving me constitutes a mighty work, things are even worse than I thought," she muttered.

"Ach, Nessa. Loving you is no hardship." He put an arm about her in reassurance. "Isaac knows he's blessed to have you in his life. The mighty work is where God makes Isaac into the husband you deserve."

Chapter 10

"The new tire arrived," Lawrence Hepplewhite told Isaac after church service two weeks later. "Mr. Gailbraith invited us over for Sunday dinner, so we'll bring it by then. He said you and Michael are welcome to join us. A little late to celebrate our victory, but better now than never."

"Unfortunate that you rolled over a nail when you tried to ride it over to Nessa's." Isaac bit back a grin at the memory.

"I like to think I recovered well," Lawrence defended. "Most men would have ended up with their backsides meeting the earth. You'll see when you have a crack at it this afternoon."

"So I will." He eyed the fellow with grudging respect. Lawrence Hepplewhite wasn't one to stand on false pride. Pa had been right, too, about how the new man was a quick study.

"There was something I wanted to discuss with you." Lawrence steered the conversation toward his real purpose. "Man-to-man, as it were. Can you spare a moment?"

"Certainly."

"Excellent." The other man rolled his shoulders as though to ease tension. "You seem close to everyone in the town, but I wondered at your relationship with Miss Gailbraith. Is there an. . .understanding between you?"

"I'd say there's anything but understanding," Isaac muttered. "Though—"

"Good to hear." Lawrence couldn't contain his satisfaction. "The way you and Clementine get along, I had hoped Nessa was free to receive other attention. Didn't want to step on your toes, you know. Wouldn't be honorable to interfere if there was already an arrangement made there."

"Right." Isaac gritted his teeth. "To tell the truth—" He didn't get out another word before Lawrence steamed ahead.

"Not that I'm going to question my good fortune, but it seems odd.

For the life of me, I can't comprehend why such a fine woman hasn't been snapped up already."

"It hasn't been for lack of trying," he divulged.

"Well, faint heart ne'er won fair maiden, and all that." Hepplewhite straightened his hat brim. "Something you might want to remember yourself, Friemont."

"What are you implying?" His comment stopped Isaac from clarifying that he still might be interested in courting Nessa. For the man to hint that Isaac hadn't been brave enough to pursue what he wanted was ludicrous. It hadn't been lack of courage on Isaac's part that caused Nessa to balk. That much was certain.

"Wasn't implying anything in particular." Hepplewhite grinned. "Just so happens I know Clementine will be very pleased to hear you'll be joining us for dinner."

"A lovely woman, your sister," Isaac praised. "It will be a pleasure to share her company this afternoon."

"I'll mention you said so. Until then."

"Yes." Isaac watched the other man walk away, acutely aware that Hepplewhite had been unwilling to hear Isaac express interest in Nessa. *If she'd accepted my proposal, I wouldn't have to make a claim,* he fumed. *But since she didn't, I don't have the grounds to tell Lawrence to back off.*

Almost a month had passed since she'd rebuffed his proposal, and she still wouldn't explain her reasons. The way things stood, if Nessa returned the interest of Saddleback's newest bachelor, Isaac couldn't do much about it.

"Isaac," a feminine purr shook him from his thoughts. "I'm so glad to hear we'll be spending the afternoon together."

"Clementine,"—he tipped his hat in acknowledgment—"you're looking well today."

"Oh, this old thing?" She ran a gloved hand over pale purple satin skirts. "So kind of you to say so."

"I wouldn't say it if it weren't true." Isaac smiled at the look of consternation on her face. "It's one of the reasons I'm not known for my fancy compliments."

"Then shame on the women who've neglected to give you cause to use them, I'd say." She dimpled up at him.

"It wasn't my intention to give you the idea that our ladies aren't lovely in their own right." Isaac frowned.

"Of course they are!" Clementine patted his arm. "Why, take Nessa, for example. Her natural charm shines through despite her worn clothing and browned skin. Quite a departure from the fashion, I know, but Lawrence seems quite taken with her."

"Fashion doesn't concern Nessa overmuch," Isaac admitted. Her simple dress and uncomplicated hairstyle weren't as intricate or elegant as Clementine's. That was obvious at a glance. All the same, she looked as pretty as she ever had.

"Indeed," she replied as her brother spoke to Nessa. "Sometimes we all need to reevaluate our priorities."

"Clementine," Isaac said as Nessa laughed at something Lawrence said, leaning close to him, "I couldn't agree more."

∽

"Of course you can!" Nessa dished out a second helping of rhubarb pie, handing the plate to Lawrence.

"Thank you." He slid his fork into the creamy filling with a murmur of approval. "Haven't tasted anything this good since the barn raising. Darla has a way with roasts and stews and such, but pie...that's another matter entirely."

"I'd rather not have a house full of sweets," Clementine announced. "Besides, our housekeeper does the best she can. If she falls short of the mark from time to time, that's to be expected." She raised her cup to her lips for a small sip.

"It was my intent to praise our hostess, not disparage Darla." Lawrence set his fork down. "Nor should you."

"We all fall short of the mark now and again," Isaac interjected. "I'm certain that's all Clementine meant."

"Precisely," she nodded virtuously. "Though there's little enough to do around here, I wonder her cooking doesn't improve."

"We always find something to occupy us," Nessa puzzled. "And while you're setting up your home, I can scarcely imagine you don't find your hands full long into the evening."

"Oh, Darla takes care of all that." Clementine waved her hand dismissively. "It's what a housekeeper is for."

"Right." Mr. Hepplewhite nodded enthusiastically. "Exactly why I offered her a substantial raise to come to Montana with us. Good help is hard to find, and industrious as Darla is, she has mentioned that there are scarcely enough hours in a day."

"Perhaps if you are dissatisfied with her baking, as she works so hard on other projects, you could step in." Ma addressed the suggestion to Clementine, whose eyes widened.

"Why would I do her work for her?" She set her cup down.

"You've time to fill, and helping another person is always worthwhile." Grandmam fixed Clementine with a gimlet eye. "Besides, if you think Darla's cooking isn't good enough, why would you sit back and let your father and brother make do?"

"Because she can't cook." Lawrence's dry tone would have had Nessa chuckling if she weren't so taken aback.

"Surely you exaggerate, Lawrence." Isaac swiftly came to Clementine's defense.

"No, he doesn't." Mr. Hepplewhite clapped one hand to his well-fed stomach. "Clementine could charm the birds from the trees, but she wouldn't be able to make a meal of them."

By this point, the girl flushed rosy pink, with even Isaac taken aback by this unwelcome revelation.

Nessa couldn't help but feel responsible for having inadvertently caused this conversation. "We've all had our share of mishaps in the kitchen," she heard herself saying. "The next time you find yourself lacking a pastime, I'd be glad to give you some suggestions. Cooking is much more enjoyable when you've others around."

"Whenever you like," Grandmam seconded.

"You'll be able to whip up a home-cooked meal after a few sessions," Ma assured her, not noticing that Clementine's becoming blush bled from her face with each comment.

If the girl became any paler, Nessa feared she'd faint. For the first time, she wondered whether Clementine's impressive curves and teensy waist were enhanced by a corset. Most women had eschewed the rigid confines in favor of comfort, but it did seem that Miss Hepplewhite's preoccupation with appearance hid a surprise or two.

"Oh, I—I c–couldn't," she stammered.

"Of course you could." Isaac remained oblivious to his dinner partner's distress. "The Gailbraith's are great cooks, and they don't give invitations they don't mean."

"Unless you'd like to practice in your own home, with Darla," Nessa intervened. "The more comfortable you are, the better the results will be, I'm sure."

"Perhaps." Clementine's color began to return. "Once things settle down and Darla's not so busy, I'll ask her."

"Where is Darla this afternoon?" Nessa remembered seeing the thin woman with mouse-brown hair at church. "Enjoying her afternoon off, I suppose? Next time we'll have to be sure she knows she's welcome to join us."

"The housekeeper?" Clementine all but squeaked.

"Why not?" Da rumbled. "She sounds like a good, hardworking woman. You'll find we value those traits in Saddleback."

"My mother was housekeeper and cook to Delana's family years ago." Grandmam's chin jutted out. "And my father was stable master. The Albrights treated us all like family, asked us to come to Montana with them. If they hadn't been such wonderful people, my Arthur would never have left me to come settle this place with Dustin Friemont."

"There's no reason why Darla should be left alone on a Sunday afternoon simply because she works hard for her living," Isaac added.

"No," said Lawrence, "there really isn't." He looked, Nessa decided, as though the thought hadn't crossed his mind and, more important, the realization bothered him.

He's far different from his sister. Nessa nodded. Lawrence was new to town, but she could see he had a kind heart and generous spirit. *Yes, Lawrence Hepplewhite has the makings of a fine man.*

Chapter 11

L egs pumping, chin jutted forward as his coat billowed about him, Lawrence eagerly demonstrated how to ride the bicycle. He looked, Isaac decided, about as foolish as a man could. Riding a horse never made a fellow look so ungainly. He slid his glance over to take in Nessa's reaction.

"Wonderful!" Her brown eyes wide, specks of gold dancing in delight, she clasped her hands together in anticipation. Nessa's gaze never left Lawrence as he made a neat stop just before her and hopped off in a fluid motion. "You balance so easily!"

"Takes some practice," Lawrence admitted. "You have to learn to find your center so the whole thing doesn't topple when you lift your feet off the ground. I fell off the first time I attempted it." His self-effacing grin elicited a smile from Nessa.

Lawrence would have fallen off, Isaac speculated. A man who tried so hard to please others couldn't possibly be steady of his own accord. *Listen to the man trumpet his failure to gain sympathy. Didn't he know mistakes were to be learned from privately?*

"If you'd like to try, Isaac, I'll walk you through it." Lawrence issued the challenge airily enough, but Isaac wondered whether the other man had read the distaste in his expression.

To refuse would be churlish, particularly as Isaac wrestled with a stab of remorse over his unworthy attitude. He nodded with what little enthusiasm he could muster and straddled the bike. He kept his feet planted on the ground as he eased onto the narrow, but surprisingly well-padded seat and gripped the handles.

Isaac leaned to the left, then the right, experimenting with how best to keep the contraption upright. *Shouldn't be too difficult,* he decided.

"I find it best to lean forward a bit and sit further back on the seat." Lawrence's helpful advice made Isaac glower.

"I like to think I can manage just fine and remain upright." He stiffened his spine and placed one booted foot on a pedal. Immediately, the whole thing leaned, and he had to shift to compensate. "Then again, no sense ignoring good advice." He leaned forward slightly.

"Got a feel for it now?" Lawrence gestured. "When you're ready, push off with your support leg and then pedal before you lose momentum. If you slow too much, it'll topple over."

"Mmmhh," Isaac grunted as he shoved off, the bicycle suddenly seeming far too narrow and light to hold him. He plunked his foot on the other pedal and started to pump his legs as Lawrence had done. For a moment, the wind rushed past his face and through his hair, and it seemed almost as though he'd left the earth.

Thunk! He hit an embedded rock, the bicycle bouncing. Isaac steered the handles to compensate but miscalculated. With a ringing crash, he and the machine hit the earth.

He lay there, stunned momentarily, before the dust settled and he saw Nessa, Clementine, Michael, Julia, and Lawrence all rushing toward him. Isaac began disentangling his legs, lunging to his feet just before they reached him. He righted the bicycle instead of rubbing his bruised backside, making a show of inspecting it.

"Are you all right?" Nessa entwined her arm with his, trying to give him support. She looked him over. "Nothing sprained or broken?" The anxiety in her eyes went a long way toward soothing his battered pride.

"It'll take more than a tumble to put me out of commission." He couldn't help glancing at Lawrence as he spoke.

"Oh, I was so frightened for you!" Clementine took hold of his other arm, clinging to him with grasping fingers.

"No need, Clementine." He desperately hoped those weren't tears sparkling in her eyes. "All's well that ends well. I should have leaned forward like your brother suggested. No damage done save a knock to my hard head."

Nessa chuckled at the admission, but Clementine ran her small hand through his hair. "You hit your head?"

"Er. . ." He was so distracted by the soft pressure of her touch and the cool breeze touching his scalp as she lifted his hair, he found it hard to speak. "No, I meant it figuratively, that's all."

"Thank goodness you're unharmed!" She stopped stroking his hair, her hand coming to rest on his shoulder.

It was only then that Isaac realized Nessa had stepped away from him and now held the bicycle. Lawrence stood beside her, the two of them so wrapped up in each other they didn't notice the sudden silence.

All at once, Isaac's stomach lurched. Perhaps more had been damaged in the fall than he'd realized.

When Clementine had started threading her fingers through Isaac's hair, a muscle in Nessa's cheek had begun to twitch. So she'd let go of his arm, unclenched her jaw, and allowed Lawrence to draw her into conversation.

"Happens to most people their first times out," he was saying. "Unless you start slow, with someone walking beside you to steady things. I would have offered to spot Isaac, but he seemed the sort to stand on his own."

"So true," Nessa murmured. Isaac was the sort to stand—or fall—on his own terms. Until he realized he needed the loving support others offered, Nessa would have to watch him fall. "It seems your sister is doing a thorough job of looking after him now."

"Yes." Lawrence gave her a searching glance. "I wouldn't blame you if you decided to hold off."

Nessa realized how sharp she must have sounded. "Oh no!" Her fingers tightened on the handlebars and she moved to stand beside the bike rather than in front of it. "With your assistance, I'm sure it's perfectly safe."

"You've a healthy measure of pluck, Nessa." He grinned in approval. "It's rare a man is fortunate enough to behold such a melding of bravery and beauty. I'd be honored to guide you."

"You flatter me, Lawrence," she chided, her smile taking the sting from her admonishment. "But you do it so well, I can't complain overmuch."

"Flattery is a term for empty words." He placed his hand over hers, his expression earnest. "My compliment is sincere, Nessa." The warmth of his palm seeped through the thin stretch of her glove.

"Then I thank you." She watched with some regret as he removed his hand.

"If I may?" At her nod, he placed his arm around her, his hand bracing her waist. "Step over the center bar. It's difficult with skirts, so I'll brace you."

Awareness of his proximity thrilled through her. Isaac had never looked at her so intensely. Nessa dutifully raised one foot until she stood astride the bicycle. She looked questioningly at Lawrence.

"Now, take your seat, sitting as far back as you can while still reaching the pedals." He stepped behind her, bracing her waist with both hands as she stretched her feet toward the pedals.

Her breath hissed at the familiarity of the contact, absorbing the warmth of his nearness. Had he not supported her, she would have tipped over. Nessa hastily set her feet back on the ground.

"All right, Nessa?" Julia watched them with an odd look on her face, as though she, like Nessa, wasn't entirely certain it was a good idea to be so near Lawrence.

"Yes. It's a bit more difficult to balance than I thought it would be."

"I'll second that." Isaac reached out to grasp one of the handlebars. "There, I've got you steady if you'd like to slide off."

"She's doing splendidly," Lawrence objected. "I've things well in hand."

"I noticed." The dark look Isaac shot at Lawrence, who still hadn't removed his supportive clasp, sent a tingle through Nessa.

She tamped it down. Isaac didn't love her, had been absorbed in Clementine all day, and now tried to put a stop to her bicycle lesson? No. He could play dog in the manger with someone else.

"Thank you, Isaac," she brushed his hand off the bike as she spoke, "but thanks to Lawrence I feel quite secure."

"Then we'll proceed with the lesson," Julia seconded. "I'd like to see it step by step and then decide if I've the courage to attempt a ride."

"I'll brace you." Michael's hasty offer was accompanied by a narrow glance at Lawrence.

Nessa wondered whether her friend noticed. Either way, Julia fairly glowed with happiness at Michael's words. Isaac could learn a few things from his best friend, Nessa decided.

"To get on with it, place your feet on the pedals again, leaning forward this time," Lawrence directed. "Concentrate on balancing, and when you feel you've got it right, I'll loosen my grip."

Nessa followed his instructions, wobbling from side to side but never falling with Lawrence supporting her. After a while, she felt steady enough to try it on her own. As Lawrence lifted his hands, Nessa wanted them back. Nevertheless, she gamely pushed off at a slow pace, pedaling immediately.

"That's it!" Lawrence jogged beside her, hands outstretched and ready should she falter.

Reassured, Nessa pedaled faster, tightening her grip on the handlebars and relying on her own sense of balance to keep her upright.

"There you go!" Lawrence fell behind, shouting instructions to slow down before she turned back and not to stop until she'd reached them once more.

The wind kissed her cheeks, cooling the hot rush of excitement as she skimmed over the road, instinctively leaning to one side or the other as she steered past the spring ruts. The sound of her heart thrummed in her ears, her breath caught at the glorious suspension of weight. It felt as though everything, all her worries, all her disappointments, dropped from her shoulders as she whizzed forward.

This, Nessa decided, *is freedom.*

Chapter 12

T*his,* Isaac fumed, *is a disaster.*

One week had passed since they'd ridden the bicycle, since Isaac had fallen in front of everyone and Lawrence had put his hands around Nessa's trim waist. The time hadn't done much to temper his frustration.

As Isaac stewed, Lawrence remained glued to Nessa's side at the church social. Worse still, Nessa encouraged the attention, her eyes sparkling, pert nose tilted to display those beguiling freckles of hers, and a smile on her lips. She'd never looked better, and it was all for Lawrence Hepplewhite.

"Isaac!" Clementine emerged from a crowd of admirers to place one small hand trustingly in the crook of his arm. "I've had the most delicious notion."

"And what would that be?" He patted her hand, drinking in the sight of her smile as she peeped up at him from beneath the brim of her bonnet.

"I've heard of this place called Columbia Gardens—do you know about it?"

"In Butte?" Isaac searched his memory. "Didn't the Copper King make a sort of amusement park out there?"

"Yes, but it's much more than that." She spoke more quickly in her excitement, "There's a fine hotel, a ballroom, even a swimming pool. Not to mention the carousel and roller coaster."

"I've always thought a roller coaster sounded like a great adventure." Isaac shared some of her enthusiasm. "Up, down, and around, whizzing through the air. . .thrilling."

"I could never bring myself to try such a thing." She gave a small shudder. "But it sounds as though there's something for everyone. I've spoken with Lawrence about making a trip there in the next week or so.

We'd love to have you join us."

"I'd enjoy that." He rubbed the back of his neck. "The thing is...some of us were hoping to go to Yellowstone, now that it's open to private automobiles."

"Can't you do both?" She gave a tiny pout.

"I doubt I could leave the farm that long." He searched for Michael. "We haven't mentioned the trip to Yellowstone in a while. I'd have to check and see if everyone's still aboard. If I can't come to Butte with you"—he stooped to catch her gaze—"would you consider joining our Yellowstone expedition?"

"I'd so hoped we could spend some time together"—she caught her lower lip between pearly teeth—"without all the...distractions here in Saddleback."

Isaac noted her gaze flick to Nessa, who was now drinking some punch with Lawrence. *If Clementine comes to Yellowstone, there will be no way to exclude her brother.* "Ah, there's Michael. Let's see if we're still set on Yellowstone." He waved his friend over, noticing that Julia clasped Michael's arm.

"What's running through your mind, Isaac?" He sounded happy.

"Wondering whether we're still set to go to Yellowstone this July," he probed. "Nobody's mentioned it in a while."

"I was looking forward to it," Julia answered. "Nessa is, too."

"Then we can't disappoint." Michael patted her hand. "Next week would be perfect timing, too."

"Nessa's grandmother will come as chaperone." Julia waved to Nessa, who made her way toward their group immediately.

"Yes?" Nessa hurried forward, Lawrence stuck to her side like a shadow.

"We were thinking of making that trip to Yellowstone next week," Michael began. "Are you and your grandmother still interested in joining us?"

"Absolutely!" Nessa tugged on Lawrence's sleeve. "We've plenty of room if you'd like to see the sights with us."

"Clementine and I had considered Columbia Gardens." Lawrence glanced at his sister. "But I, for one, would rather enjoy the company of the Yellowstone expedition. What do you say, Clementine?"

"I won't be the lone naysayer," Clementine demurred. "Aside from Mrs. MacLean, will the six of us make up the entire group?"

"I should like to keep us down to the two touring cars," Isaac planned aloud. "No sense in making it a caravan."

"Small and simple," Michael agreed, his smile all for Julia. "Just close friends."

⚭

"So tell me again what the arrangements are?" Grandmam asked as Nessa started to pack.

"Six days to tour the park, plus the traveling time there and back," Nessa reminded. "When we're in hotels, we can order our meals. On the road we'll have to fend for ourselves." She tucked oats, cornmeal, sugar, and flour into a large pot before replacing the lid. Packing space was limited, with seven people traveling in two cars.

Grandmam peered at what Nessa had already set aside. "You've got rashers of bacon, salt pork, and jerked beef in this sack. And this crate is full of eggs, I'd guess?" She gestured to the straw-packed wooden box.

"Yes, though I don't expect they'll hold up as well." Nessa frowned.

"We brought eggs in wagons," Grandmam chuckled. "If the straw worked for that, it'll do fine now."

"I hope so. Julia's packing a crate of apples, two rounds of cheese, and some canned preserves and such."

"Sounds like you've got the food portion all figured out." Grandmam began filling her own trunk. "Best be sure you have your own things packed."

"Yes, I already started but was trying to decide what clothes I'll need," Nessa mused aloud as she considered her own traveling trunk.

"Don't forget a light cloak and a heavy one," Grandmam cautioned. "There're parts of Yellowstone as get right cold even in the midst of summer."

"Right." Nessa folded her winter cape and laid it atop her stockings, chemises, and petticoats. These were placed over a spare pair of half boots and her toiletry case. She tossed in an apron to conceal the worst of the dirt she'd gather on the trip.

"How much room do you have left?" Grandmam peered in Nessa's trunk. "Good. You can put two dresses in there and have three altogether."

"I was going to wear the blue calico and pack the green merino wool. That leaves the yellow cotton or the dusky rose dress."

"Take the rose," Grandmam instructed. "Looks lovely on you."

"And the yellow will show dust far more quickly." Nessa neatly folded the two chosen garments and smoothed them in. "Good thinking."

"I wasn't thinking of the dust, Nessa." Grandmam chuckled. "More along the lines of how that Clementine wears pale colors all the time."

"And I wouldn't want to set myself up for comparison to her ensembles," Nessa concluded with a grimace.

"Pastel is for girls," Grandmam corrected. "More vibrant tones are for women. Darker hues hint at the depth of your character, Nessa. Besides, they look good with your hair and eyes."

"Thank you, Grandmam." Nessa kissed her wrinkled cheek. "Having you on the trip may well be my favorite part of it."

"I hope not!" She smiled. "Not with Isaac and Lawrence taking the lead."

"To tell the truth, I've been praying about that." Nessa added her travel diary and a sun hat to her trunk and closed it tightly. "Isaac has been the one I've loved since childhood, but despite my prayers, he's not shown the same for me. It took his proposal for me to realize I've been asking God for what I want, rather than seeking His will."

"So this trip will give you time to see if Lawrence is the man God plans to be your husband?" Grandmam peered over the top of her spectacles. "And let you see how serious things are between Isaac and Clementine, while you're at it?"

"Yes." Nessa gave her grandmam a hug. "Sometimes I wonder if there's anything in my head you don't already know."

" 'Tis no special talent on my part." Kaitlin MacLean stroked her granddaughter's hair. "You've an open mind, clear soul, and honest heart. They speak for themselves."

"Even so, Isaac doesn't hear me. The longer he refuses to listen, the more I feel God nudging me in another direction."

"Don't be too hasty, dearie," Grandmam warned as she shut her own trunk. "Your grandda used to say, 'Slow and steady as you go, and you won't run into a gopher hole.' "

"I remember him saying that." Nessa focused on the memory. "Didn't he come up with that after you twisted your ankle?"

"Aye. Delana brought me to Arthur when she took herself to Dustin. Added along with her younger brothers, Mama Albright, and your great-grandparents, we were a sizable party. But when we arrived, we found surprised men, a single barn, dozens of gopher holes, and not much else."

"And you taking care of Ma, just newly born." Nessa shook her head. "Looking at Saddleback today, it's almost impossible to imagine."

"Time has a way of changing things." Grandmam sank into her rocker with a happy sigh.

Nessa thought of Isaac. "I hope so, Grandmam. I really do."

Chapter 13

"Everybody ready to go?" Isaac asked as they stood beside the freshly refueled cars. "We'll reach Mammoth Hot Springs before dark."

"Wonderful," Clementine cooed. "I can't wait to freshen up. I feel so. . .disheveled." She gave a moue of distaste.

"You look pretty as a picture," Isaac disagreed. He told the truth, as she'd smoothed her hair and shaken the wrinkles from her cream linen dress. She'd donned her bonnet before stepping foot outside the closed automobile, her skin milky white.

"It's so exciting!" Nessa's grin stretched from ear to ear. A breeze teased the soft tendrils of her hair, lifting them into a sort of blurry frame about her face. Her simple blue calico dress looked distinctly rumpled, and her hat hung askew from the ribbon about her neck. The sun had lingered on her face, leaving its ruddy kiss on the tip of her nose and the apples of her cheeks. Much more, and she'd burn.

"Nessa, it seems you've caught some sun." He cast a glance at Lawrence's open-air Model T. "Perhaps you'd like to ride in my closed-top for the rest of the day?"

"No, thank you." Nessa remarked coolly. "I like riding alongside Lawrence, with the wind in our hair and the road before us."

"We've had a good time of it," Lawrence agreed. "A man can't ask for more than enjoying a drive with two lovely ladies." His smile included Mrs. MacLean, who smiled back.

"And we've plenty of those to go around." Isaac looked down at Clementine. For the first time, he realized how short she was. The tip of her hat all but brushed his nose.

"We should get on our way." Julia got him back on track. She and Michael climbed into the back of Isaac's car, where they'd ridden for the entire trip.

Isaac gave Clementine an arm up, noticing Lawrence do the same for Nessa and Mrs. MacLean. He moved to the front of the automobile, grasped the lever, and began cranking it until he judged it long enough.

Isaac slid into the seat, turned the key, and listened with satisfaction as the car spluttered to life. *Whhhrrr, whhrrrr* gave way to a loud growl as it started, the force of the engine making the car vibrate. With a low rumble, the car was ready to go.

Isaac made sure Lawrence was prepared, released the brake lever, and then eased his Ford back onto the road. For a while, he lost himself in the pleasure of driving, the power and speed he controlled.

Clementine fanned herself, so Isaac reached forward and opened the windshield. The inch-thick panes of glass tilted outward, allowing a welcome rush of summer air.

They passed lodgepole pines, catching a glimpse of the occasional coyote, as they approached their destination. When they passed Fort Yellowstone on their left, Isaac knew the impressive structure ahead must be the Mammoth Hot Springs Hotel.

"I hear it's built right where the National Hotel used to be," Michael observed.

"Supposedly it's been remodeled entirely in the past few years," Clementine added. "I wonder what type of improvements they've made."

"Electricity and plumbing," Isaac speculated. "There've been quite a few advancements made." They drove past a houselike building with a sign proclaiming HAMILTON STORE and pulled up in front of the hotel.

"So many automobiles!" Clementine peeped through the window. "I'd have thought this would be more of an isolated retreat."

"I hear the number of visitors began to grow by leaps and bounds when they started allowing private cars." Isaac took his foot off the gas pedal, pressing down on the far right pedal to slow the car. The transmission slowed to a stop as they coasted into an open space. He set the brake before hopping out.

Lawrence pulled in beside them, giving a cheery *oouuugggaaa* on his horn.

After ensuring Clementine was safely on the ground—the car was high for such a tiny woman to climb down—Isaac beat Lawrence to Nessa's door. "We've made it." He clung to her hand until she pulled it away.

"Yes." Her smile broadened. "The start of a great adventure."

⚭

"There"—Nessa gestured to her small trunk and the one next to it—"those are mine and Grandmam's."

"Got them." Lawrence stacked one atop the other and hefted both, taking a step backward at the weight but recovering swiftly.

"This?" Isaac's disbelieving tone had Nessa turning around to see Clementine claiming what looked to be a massive steamer trunk.

I knew it! Nessa pursed her lips against a smile as Isaac unstrapped the monstrosity. *It had to be hers!*

"Yes." Clementine lowered her lashes. "I didn't realize the other ladies would be bringing so little."

"Good thing they did." Lawrence sounded muffled from behind the two pieces of luggage he carried. "Or we would have needed another Ford to carry it all."

"That's not fair, Larry!" Clementine's cry had the strange effect of Lawrence setting down the trunks with a thud.

Larry? Nessa wrinkled her nose.

"You know better than to call me that." Lawrence glowered at his sister. "Old nickname," he explained to the rest of them.

"We already established that we'd only use monikers if the person approved," Nessa reminded. "And so far, I'm the only one. Besides, it's obvious you've far outstripped your childhood name."

"Yes." Lawrence grabbed the trunks once again. "Let's get settled, then."

He led the way, with Isaac and Michael each grasping one end of Clementine's portmanteau. Julia's large valise slid around atop it alongside the smaller three satchels the men had packed.

"I don't understand why everyone is carrying on so," claimed a peevish Clementine. "They may not be bringing them inside, but I know the other women brought extra bags and crates." She kicked a pebble, sending it skittering in the dirt.

"They," Isaac grunted as he shifted his grip, "packed the food and supplies we'll need when we're not at a hotel."

"What?" Clementine stopped in the middle of the dusty walkway, forcing Isaac and Michael to halt or run into her. "I was led to believe we have accommodations arranged each night."

Lawrence emerged from the hotel, having set his burden inside. "We do. We've rented tents for the nights we won't be in a hotel."

"Tents?" Clementine pronounced the word in the tone Nessa reserved for plague-ridden rats.

"Yes." Isaac mopped his brow with a bandana, having dropped the luggage when Clementine blocked the road.

"Girls in one, guys in another," Michael rolled his shoulders. "We'll be staying in hotels mostly."

"Such an exciting plan!" Nessa plucked one of the satchels to lighten the load.

"Let's get to it." Lawrence took it from her, every inch the gentleman. He grabbed Julia's valise as well.

When he turned his back, Nessa snatched another satchel, with Julia grasping the other. Isaac gave them both appreciative grins before frowning at Clementine, who stood in the middle of the road, mouth agape, as though impersonating a statue.

"Once we get inside, we can rest and freshen up." Nessa's comment got through, and Clementine started moving again.

Everyone pretended not to hear Clementine's dark mutters as they entered the hotel. Within a quarter hour, they'd found their rooms and deposited their things. The men went out to hang their food supply in nearby trees to avoid attracting bears, leaving the women in their room.

"Satisfactory," Clementine pronounced as she sank onto one of the beds. "Though it's not a very large room, is it?"

"It doesn't need to be." Grandmam splashed her face with water from the washbasin. "And they said there's a real bathroom down the hall, with full plumbing."

"Magnificent," Nessa breathed as she pulled the curtains aside and beheld the vista before her. A whole nation of pines stretched from the perimeter of the hotel to the hills beyond. Billows of steam puffed into the air from the one sparsely foliaged area. "Have a look!" She stepped aside so Julia could take in the panorama.

"Incredible!" Julia craned her neck to see the pillows of steam rising. "Those must be the hot springs. And over there is the executive house. The president of the park lives there."

"I can see why." Grandmam replaced Julia at the window.

"Haven't you seen enough trees for one day?" Clementine peered at her fingernails. "That's practically all we've seen the entire day! Tomorrow we'll see some interesting sights."

"If you ask me, the mountains, pines, good earth, and endless sky are interesting sights." Nessa began to unbutton one of her shoes. "God's imagination is boundless." She slid it off then turned it upside down to see the source of her irritation bounce onto the floorboards.

"I suppose you'd think rocks are fascinating, too." Clementine watched Nessa pick up the pebble.

"To tell the truth"—she made a point of depositing the stone in the wastebasket—"I was thinking about how some of God's creations can be surprisingly irritating."

Chapter 14

T hat's what she's called," Isaac insisted, addressing Clementine's question about the tall, peaked rock formation before them.

"Liberty Cap?" She scrunched her nose as she surveyed the rocky outgrowth before her. "I've never seen a hat that ugly. Who would wear such a thing?"

"The French." Lawrence studied the tall cone of the old hot spring. "During the Revolution, they wore peaked caps that looked something like this. Must be where the name came from."

"It looks almost as though a giant put his hand on it and smushed the whole thing down," Nessa observed. "But maybe it grew up in stages so it looks like there are different levels of it."

"That sounds like as good a guess as any." Isaac locked his tripod into place and mounted his Sereco view camera, adjusting the rack and pinion until he had the vantage he wanted. He tightened the milled-head screw and racked the bellows closer to the front for a wider angle, switching out the extra rapid portrait lens for the rapid rectilinear lens, which was better for landscape work. He checked his adjustments one last time before taking the picture. "Got it!" He carefully packed his equipment back into its carrying case.

"I hope it turns out well." Nessa tilted her head back for one last look at the towering stone.

"It will." Isaac snapped the case shut. "Miracle of technology—that's the wonder of photography. Quickest way to capture a memory and keep it perfectly forever."

"I don't know about that." Michael rested a hand on Julia's shoulder. "In the time it took you to set all that up, Julia sketched the Liberty Cap from two different angles."

"Fair enough," Isaac acknowledged. "What I should have said is that it's the best way for those of us without an innate talent for traditional art."

"Don't be so modest." Clementine linked her arm through his. "Just watching you set up all that complex equipment was more than impressive."

"Thank you." He soaked in her smile. "I also snapped a panoramic shot of the Devil's Thumb."

"That other great big rocky tower?" She peered as though it were far, far away. "I wonder why they call it the Devil's Thumb." She gave a little shiver.

"According to this printed guide, over thirty of the sites have names related to the devil." Mrs. MacLean read aloud. "Seems as though when they were discovered, the men thought them a good example of the type of fire and brimstone sinners might expect after death."

"I thought we were going to see pretty things"—Clementine nibbled her lower lip—"not what some people think is a representation of hell."

"No need to be afraid." Lawrence tucked Nessa by his side, and Isaac reflexively tightened his hold on Clementine.

"Not if your heart is right before the Lord," Kaitlin MacLean added.

They looked at the large formation thrusting up from the earth and unanimously agreed that it did resemble a thumb. Everyone relaxed a bit as they piled back into the cars and made their way to Mammoth Hot Springs.

That site, Isaac wasn't pleased to see, was far more crowded. Getting a picture without people standing in the way or steam filming over his lens made him move back and be content with whatever came of it.

"Would you look at all the people who brought their bathing costumes." Nessa's eyes were wide as they watched people climb into the enormous hot springs, looking for all the world as though they were soaking in large tubs.

"It's supposed to be good for the health," Lawrence explained. "Would you like to try it?"

"No, thank you." Nessa's blush surprised Isaac. Apparently she didn't approve of the fashionable bath suits women wore, exposing their lower limbs to a daring degree.

"One of the hotels has geyser water pumped directly into real bathtubs." Isaac spoke up before he started to wonder how Nessa would look in one of those bath costumes. "So we'll have a chance to try it out later."

By the time they reached Camp Sheridan, a recently abandoned army headquarters that had been turned into lodgings for tourists, Isaac's stomach began to growl. He drove until he found a nice open space where they could set up a fire and make dinner.

"What's that?" Clementine squinted at what looked to be a cemetery.

Not for the first time, Isaac wondered whether Clementine's vision was poor. "The army's burial ground for the soldiers who guarded the park up until this past year."

Nessa, with Lawrence at her side, joined them.

"Why were there soldiers?" Clementine's eyes widened in fright, her hand grasping Isaac's sleeve. "Is this place so very dangerous?"

"No." Mrs. MacLean swept past them. "More like people are dangerous to this place. The army was here to guard the land, protect it against poachers and vandals. That type of thing. Started some twenty years ago, and they just left the post last year."

"So it's safe." Clementine leaned against Isaac in relief.

"Don't worry." He put his arm around her waist so she wouldn't sag all the way to the ground. "I've got you."

∽

"Here you are." Clementine thrust a handful of bedraggled weeds toward Nessa. "Dandelions." Clumps of dirt fell from the roots, wispy seeds scattering in the wind.

"Thank you." Nessa took them and shook the rest of the dirt free. "It's a good start."

"Start?" Clementine ran a gloved hand across her forehead as though she'd been swinging a pickax all day. "How much more do you need?"

"We need about four quarts worth of the greens, rinsed." She laid them atop a flat area on a log bleached almost white by the sun and weather. "And it's best to pick the leaves of plants that haven't bloomed already. Otherwise, they tend to be bitter."

"How can you tell they're dandelions without the poufy ball on the end?"

"The leaves." Julia picked one from the torn stalks. "Low to the ground, light green, with lots of elongated round edges."

Clementine squinted before giving a hesitant nod. "Is there a basket or something I can use since we need a lot more?"

"Put them in the pockets of an apron." Nessa shook out her spare. "Use this if you like."

"All right." Clementine took the apron strings and wrapped them about her waist. "If you're certain this is all I can do to help."

"You can finish peeling the potatoes." Grandmam held one up.

"I'm not very good with sharp things." Clementine took one look at the brown lumpy vegetable and paring knife before wandering off. She didn't head toward the open areas where the most vegetation could be found.

No, Clementine made her way toward the cars, where the men were repositioning supplies, checking the tires, and making sure the engines didn't overheat. Nessa didn't quite know the whole of it, but it was obvious that they were engrossed in the automobiles.

"Valiant attempt to have her be useful," Julia commented. "She just snatched a handful of grass though. Do you think she's foolish, lazy, or vain?"

"Given the option, I'd say she doesn't see this as important," Nessa said. "Though I'm not sure why you listed vanity among the options."

"Seems to me Clementine displays all the hallmarks of someone with poor vision." Julia rapidly plucked a patch of dandelion greens while she spoke. "All the same, she doesn't wear glasses. I wondered whether it was because she didn't consider them fashionable."

"Perhaps." Nessa recalled the way Clementine clung to Isaac's arm, giving prettily concerned glances whenever she surveyed things at a distance. *Can it be she's not acting frail but genuinely relies on others to navigate her way through life?* As Nessa filled her pockets with greens, she promised herself she would keep a closer eye on Clementine.

She busied herself with rinsing the dandelions, tearing the leaves before she added them to the boiling water. Clementine stood next to Isaac, as though she hadn't a care in the world.

"I'm ready to add the salt pork." Grandmam peered into the saucepan before dropping the small cuts of meat inside.

Nessa popped the cover over the entire mixture before cutting the potatoes into manageable chunks. It'd be a while before Grandmam added them to the pan.

"I've set up the Dutch oven." Julia motioned to the cast iron contraption nestled in the ashes of the fire. "What say we use the milk we bought at Hamilton's this morning and bake some corn bread?"

"Sure." Grandmam began to pour cornmeal, flour, and salt into a bowl while Nessa went to fetch a few eggs.

"Nessa!" Lawrence straightened up as she approached, wiping his hands on a bandana. "I hope you've come to tell us dinner's ready. Smells good."

"I'm afraid I just came for a few eggs." She pushed aside the packing straw and carefully gathered a few. "The greens and pork need to simmer before we add the potatoes. It'll be about another hour or so."

"What're the eggs for?" Clementine fingered the leaves in her apron pocket.

"Corn bread." Nessa wasn't sure what to say to the other woman. *I've never met someone who abandons their work to others.*

"If I wasn't so sure you'd send me away again, I'd offer to help." Clementine had a righteous look on her features. "But I know better now."

"You sent her away?" Lawrence's tone was incredulous. For the first time, his gaze held no familiar spark of admiration.

"We asked her to help gather greens." Nessa gaped at the other woman. How dare she imply that they'd excluded her!

"A fool's errand." Clementine reached into her apron pocket and produced a handful of grass. "No one would actually cook this!"

"Those aren't dandelion greens," Nessa all but snapped. "And we do use those."

"Dandelions are good for lots of things." Isaac stepped forward, away from Clementine. "Fried blossoms, salads. . . Nessa wouldn't send you on a wild goose chase."

"How was I to know?" The woman put her hands on her hips. "It sounded ridiculous."

"I've never heard of eating dandelions," her brother mused. "But if Nessa asked you to pick a few, you should have trusted her judgment."

"Thank you." Nessa chose not to point out that Lawrence hadn't trusted her a moment ago. Isaac had. As she walked back to the cook fire, Nessa wondered whether or not that was significant.

Lord, I came here in hopes that You'd reveal Your plan to me. So how is it that I constantly feel as though I'm walking in circles?

Chapter 15

"You could've knocked me over with a feather when I tasted that dinner," Clementine trilled as they got under way once more. "Who would've imagined dandelion leaves with pork and potatoes would be such a tasty dish?"

"Nessa, Mrs. MacLean, and I did." Julia's dry tone made Isaac grin. "It's why we asked you to help gather the greens."

"You'll have to forgive me for thinking you were having a little joke at my expense."

"In all the years I've known them, Julia, Nessa, and Mrs. MacLean have never ill-used anyone." Michael sounded loud in the closed car. "It's an insult to all three that you would imagine otherwise."

"A simple misunderstanding, that's all it was." Clementine toyed with the fingers of her kid leather gloves.

"Admitting you were wrong is a step in the right direction." Isaac slowed to take a curve. "Apologizing for misjudging the other women is another."

"Apologize!" Clementine sniffed. "When I've done nothing wrong? Believe me, no one saw fit to inform me that I'd be expected to pick weeds and cook on this vacation. As far as I'm concerned, I offered to help. That's all there is to it."

"No." Michael's harsh tone belied his even words. "Helping is a way of life out here, not deserving of any particular credit."

"Well, I never!"

"Perhaps you should." Isaac frowned but resisted the urge to shift his gaze from the road. "We men do the driving, look after the cars, carry the luggage, and oversee the arrangements. Nessa, Julia, and Mrs. MacLean packed provisions for the trip and are quick to lend a hand or prepare a meal. We all do our parts."

"Isaac," she placed a beseeching hand on his shoulder as she entreated, "surely you see that I only wanted to help. I never meant to give offense."

"I know." Some of his ire dissipated. "But by implying that the others were treating you poorly, you did insult them. I know a soft heart like yours wouldn't want to leave it like that."

"You're right." She shifted in her seat. "Julia, I'm sorry. And I'll tell the others at our next stop."

"Thank you." Julia sounded more relaxed. "We'll all appreciate that."

The rest of the drive passed amicably, but Isaac stayed silent. Clementine's behavior bothered him, but he couldn't pin down the reason why. It wasn't fair to compare her to Nessa, who'd grown up working alongside her mother and her grandmother. Clementine was gently reared, housed at a finishing school where she learned to manage a household—not the day-to-day upkeep. He'd thought she would learn what was needed to survive and run a family. For the first time, he wondered if she was willing to put in that kind of work.

He shook the doubts from his mind as they pulled up to the Main Terrace, which featured incredible plateaus of deposited limestone. While Isaac set up his camera, he was pleased to see Clementine talking to Nessa and Mrs. MacLean, obviously apologizing for her unintended rude remarks. He was thrilled as he snapped what should be a wonderful shot of the Bethesda Geyser.

"I'm surprised there aren't bathers here as well." Lawrence flipped through the guide as Nessa joined them. "Says here that it's particularly known for its healing waters. Someone commented, 'The Angel of Health is continually stirring the waters.'"

"Must be why this particular part is called Angel Terrace." Nessa scooted close to Lawrence, looking at the pamphlet. "Whatever the reason, you must be glad of the chance to photograph the geyser without jostling other tourists."

"True." Isaac relished that small smile, one of the precious few he'd enjoyed for the past five weeks.

Isaac was still smiling when he secured his photography case and they passed through Yellowstone's Golden Gate. According to the blurb Michael read, the gold-colored lichens on the walls of the short canyons were the cause for the park's name.

"So unusual," Julia marveled.

They appreciated the view in silence until they came to a place where the shoulder of the road was widened and they could pull off. The muted roar of a waterfall lured them out of the automobiles.

"I can't see it." Clementine rose to her tiptoes as she spoke for the first time since her apology.

"Let's follow the path." Lawrence offered Nessa his arm. They led the way, everyone falling into place behind them.

Isaac sought out Clementine, regretting that she was so hard struck by his earlier disapproval. Her bright smile went a long way toward easing his doubts.

Clementine Hepplewhite might have been a sheltered young girl, but she was growing into an intriguing—not to mention beautiful—woman.

⚭

"There!" Nessa leaned forward to get a better view through the slatted windshield. "That's got to be Electric Peak! I'm almost sorry we decided not to try traversing it."

"The roads only go so far," Lawrence reminded her. "And though it doesn't look so imposing from here, it's almost eleven thousand feet high."

"That's why she said 'almost,'" Grandmam pointed out. "If Nessa had her heart set on making it to the top of that mountain, not even rain could stop her."

"She's an intrepid woman." Lawrence's indulgent smile made Nessa feel more like a wayward child than a courageous explorer.

"Rain is the one thing that would certainly stop me from attempting Electric Peak, Grandmam." Nessa read aloud, " 'It was named by Hayden Survey topographers from their "hair-raising" experience involving electricity on top of the mountain.' "

"Sounds dangerous." Lawrence bore down on the gas pedal as though eager to make a quick escape.

"It was. One Henry Gannett ascended the mountain in 1872, only to be struck by lightning. Happened to his follower, too." Nessa shivered. "I'm glad to say that they both survived. Escaped with tingles, singed hair, and ruined clothing."

Grandmam added, "I'm sorry to say it, but they had no business going to high ground during a thunderstorm."

"Agreed." Lawrence cleared his throat. "Does that guide say anything about other areas where unsuspecting explorers might be electrocuted?"

"Not that I see." Nessa turned the pamphlet over. "Though it does

mention that the incident happened in July. They probably never anticipated a thunderstorm."

"Looks like we've made it to the campsite." Lawrence made a shallow turn westward, following Isaac's lead. "The trees are thinning out."

"Look at all those blue-striped tents." Grandmam scooted to the side
for a better look. "Wait. Why is Isaac turning away from them?" Sure
enough, he was following a small side road.

"The blue-striped tents belong to the Wylie Camping Company,"
Lawrence explained. "We've made arrangements with Shaw and Powell."

In a few moments, they pulled up near a rustic wooden structure
bustling with activity. A large sign proclaimed DINING HALL.

Before too long they were led to their tents—on foot. The automobiles couldn't come any closer, the man explained, on account of no roads
and problems with spooking their horses. Shaw and Powell ran a tour
with horse-drawn Studebaker coaches.

"Remember that your group needs to leave a goodly ways before we
do," the man cautioned as he stopped before two tents. "That way we'll
be far enough apart so the horses don't spook and we won't have any
nasty problems."

"I take it you've already had some problems since the park began admitting automobiles?" Isaac thrust his hands in his pockets at the man's
emphatic nod. "We'll be on our way directly after breakfast, then."

"I appreciate that." He shook Isaac's hand then disappeared into the
village of tents blanketing the ground.

"We'll go get the luggage." Lawrence undid the top button of his
coat.

"Thank you." Clementine opened the flap of the first tent and
ducked inside. After a scant moment, she emerged and headed for the
second.

Nessa and Julia shared a disbelieving glance as Clementine poked
her head through the opening.

"They're exactly the same!" Distress rang in her pronouncement. She
marched outside carrying a stack of blankets. "We'll all freeze tonight."

"What are you doing?" Grandmam gave voice to the question on
everyone's mind.

"While the men fetch our luggage, they'll have to see about getting more blankets." She hugged the bundle close to her chest. "Obviously someone needs to take things in hand. The management of

this. . .place. . .leaves much to be desired."

"It's a campground." Julia stated what was obvious to the rest of them. "It's not a resort."

"That doesn't mean we should lower our standards," Clementine insisted.

"Nor do we demand special treatment from a facility that has already made special arrangements for us." Isaac's furrowed brow made Clementine's lip tremble.

"I brought my winter cloak, so if you're cold, you can use one of my blankets." Nessa gently took the pile from Clementine and returned it to the second tent.

"But. . .we'll be cold. And in tents." Clementine looked at the ground as she whispered, "What if bears come?"

An unexpected wave of sympathy coursed through Nessa. Clementine's demands were all false bravado. Deep down, she was just afraid of the unfamiliar.

"We'll be fine." Isaac tucked her in the crook of his arm, and Nessa's sympathy ebbed. "The campfires will keep the wildlife away, and the tents are only for one night. Besides, we'll be in the tent right next to you if you need us."

"Exactly." Lawrence drew Nessa close as though she, too, needed comforting.

Watching Isaac with Clementine, Nessa began to think she just might.

Chapter 16

W hat's that?" Clementine screeched as something moved in the trees beside the road.

Isaac eased off the gas and hit the brake pedal, causing the car to chuff to a halt. Behind him, Lawrence did the same. Both Fords came to a stop a ways from where the heavy shadow lumbered in the woods.

"It could be a bear!" Clementine hastily rolled up her window. "Why would you stop?"

"The creature had antlers," Julia soothed. "It wasn't a bear. Probably an elk or a moose. Don't you want to see it?" Not waiting for an answer, she stepped out of the car, Michael on her heels.

"Come with us." Isaac had already exited the vehicle and stood beside Clementine's door.

"Why do you want to see it?" She reluctantly took his hand. "Don't you usually shoot deer and things with antlers? Why marvel at one now?"

"Sometimes it's good to look at something from a new perspective." Nessa came around the back of the touring car. "It's a moose!"

"Huge one, too." Lawrence came up beside Nessa.

I should have known he'd pop up wherever Nessa went. Isaac grimaced.

"Is it safe?" Clementine clung to his arm but looked at Lawrence.

"If Mrs. MacLean isn't afraid to get an up-close look, I'd say so." Her brother grinned. "Though she's one woman in a million."

"We like to think so." Nessa beamed up at him.

"You missed it!" The rest of their group hurried back.

"Oh well, I'll just have to catch the next one." Clementine hopped back into the car and swung the door shut.

"I've never seen one so big," Michael described. "The antlers were as long as my arm."

"What about it's nose?" Julia rubbed her own.

"Sounds like a moose all right." Isaac finished winding the crank, and the rest of them climbed inside the vehicles. "They're supposed to like willows, and there are a lot of those in this area."

They kept going at a leisurely pace, taking in the sights around them. A small creek alongside the road displayed on odd greenish-yellow tinge to the water, causing Julia to consult the pamphlet.

"This must be Lemonade Creek," she decided. "Called that because of its yellow color. Some guides claim to carry sacks of sugar to add to the water so they can serve some to the tourists."

"I love lemonade!" Clementine peeped out the window. "But I don't see how there can be a creek full of lemon juice."

"It's not." Isaac grinned. "You'll notice the pamphlet didn't actually advise drinking the water. Must be caused by minerals or such from all the hot springs."

"Oh." Disappointed, she sank back onto the padded seat.

He kept driving, passing a rock face full of smooth black shards of what the guide said was volcanic glass. The area was called Obsidian Cliff. The creek running through went by the same name. The black glass caught the sunlight, reflecting patches of yellow light so that the water seemed to dance.

Isaac decided to bypass Clearwater Springs, which was labeled as dangerous. Apparently, visitors regularly didn't heed the warning signs, moving too far on the thin crust of earth covering the heat below. None of them fancied getting burned when they'd already seen Mammoth and Bethesda springs, so they admired the pockmarked landscape from within the safety of the Fords.

They didn't get out to stretch their legs until reaching Frying Pan Spring. The large spring spread out on both sides of the road—the most unusual body of water Isaac had ever seen.

"Is it boiling?" Mrs. MacLean reached a hand high over the bubbling water. "Why is there no steam?"

"I don't know." Nessa stared at the surface of the water. "It looks like hot grease sputtering on a griddle, but it should be giving off a lot of heat if that were the case."

"The man from Shaw and Powell said you could boil an egg in under a minute." Lawrence pried open the crate and pulled one out. "Anyone care to test the theory?"

"Use this." Julia passed him a ladle so he wouldn't touch the surface of the water. "Just in case."

Everyone watched in silence as Lawrence placed the egg in the bowl of the ladle and cautiously lowered it until the entire egg was submerged in the bubbling water. The minute seemed to stretch out as they waited for the results.

"If the handle of that ladle isn't getting warm," Kaitlin MacLean advised, "then the water's not hot."

"Not heated at all." Lawrence drew the ladle and egg out of the water. He put out a cautious finger to give the shell a single, swift tap. "It's cold!" The affront in his voice made it hard for Isaac to hide his amusement.

"Guess you were taken in," he observed.

"I don't blame you." Nessa took the ladle, replacing it and the egg as she spoke. "What Isaac doesn't understand is that sometimes you hope for success in spite of evidence to the contrary."

∽

"I like what you said back there." Lawrence snuck a quick glance at her before returning his attention to the road. "Made me wonder though. What is it you hope for, Nessa?"

"A lot of different things. I'm not sure I could pin them all down to describe them." She gazed out the window at lush thickets of bristling evergreens.

"It'll be a little while until we stop again." He didn't push any further, just left Nessa feeling as though it might help her sort out her thoughts to have him listen.

"A loving marriage, a happy family, staying close to the people I love…" She shrugged. "The same as any other girl, I'd suppose." *Except that I wanted to share all of that with Isaac. Now that's looking less and less likely.*

"Sounds like the same things everyone wants." He darted another glance at Nessa. "Women and men alike."

"I hope so," Grandmam chimed in. "It takes one of each to make a marriage!"

"So it does." Lawrence adjusted the windshields. "Looks like we're coming to a stop."

Sure enough, Isaac's car was slowing toward an offshoot. The sign proclaimed HAZLE LAKE.

"They misspelled Hazel, unless it was intentional." Nessa puzzled over this until Grandmam explained that an early park tour guide had named the lake, and the misspelling stuck.

Nessa looked out over the water, which displayed an unusual color combination of amber and green. The sunlight danced on the water's movement, making the peaks of lazy waves glint gold.

"What an ugly lake." Clementine's pronouncement robbed Nessa of her smile. "All brown and brackish."

"It does seem very muddy," Lawrence agreed. "As though a lot of silt and dirt swirls around inside. Not the most pleasant view we've seen."

"I disagree." Isaac's firm declaration distracted Nessa from Lawrence's inadvertent insult. "One moment it looks green, another warm brown. And see how the sun plays on the surface, sending sparkles scattering across the water?" He stared into Nessa's eyes as he spoke, letting her know he wasn't only speaking of the lake. "Hazle, however they spelled it, is the perfect description for its unique splendor."

"It just looks dirty to me." Clementine's comment couldn't dampen the glow Nessa felt spreading across her face.

Isaac's opinion was the only one that mattered. She didn't say anything as they went back to the cars and drove on to the next wonder Yellowstone protected.

"Beryl Spring." Lawrence shouldered his way through another group of tourists. "Now this is worth stopping for!"

Nessa waited until a space opened then stepped forward to view the hot spring. The blue-green water gave off a hazy steam, showing why it had been named for an aqua gemstone.

"A man could get lost in those depths." Michael's ardent tone caused Nessa to turn to her right. He stood with his arm looped casually about her best friend's waist, looking deeply into Julia's eyes. "Pure color layered over deep mystery."

Julia blushed but never looked away from the man speaking such sweet words. Her friend, Nessa realized, had progressed from an unspoken crush to being completely enamored. *Which is well and good, because the man she admires looks back at her with the same soft gaze.*

Against her most stringent determination not to, Nessa found herself looking at Isaac. *Here's to hoping. . .*

Chapter 17

The day seemed to fly by; none of the tensions from the previous day seemed to be dampening anyone's spirits. Aside from Clementine's fear of moose and Lawrence's dunder-headed comment about not appreciating Hazle Lake, Isaac would say that today was going very well.

They stopped for a lunch of beans 'n' bacon, which Clementine crumbled the bacon for.

As everyone finished the meal, Isaac brought up the prospect of taking a side loop road. "It's a one-way scenic trip, less than two miles," he explained. "Follows the Firehole River to Firehole Falls then rejoins the main road at the Cascades. Anybody interested?"

"Yes, please!" Nessa swiftly began cleaning up. "I don't know what it is about waterfalls, but I've never seen one I didn't fall completely in love with."

"That decides it then." Lawrence rose to his feet to help. "We can't stand in the path of love."

His comment made Nessa duck her head, depriving Isaac of seeing her reaction. *Just how serious are they becoming?* A heavy weight settled in his chest, the anticipation of taking the detour evaporating.

"Is there any chance we might get blocked with someone coming up such a small road from the other direction?" Michael was giving the automobiles a measuring look. "The Fords will probably take up all the space if it's not much more than a horse trail."

"The road only goes one way." Isaac clapped his friend on the shoulder, surreptitiously glancing over to where Lawrence was helping Nessa into his car. "So nobody will get in our way."

"We won't get wet, will we?" Clementine joined them. "I didn't think to pack a slicker. I wonder what else I forgot."

"Not much, from the size of your portmanteau." Isaac smiled to soften the words. "I suspect you came prepared for just about everything."

"You might be right," she simpered. "Though I know we ladies wouldn't make it far without your help."

"And the trip wouldn't be half as rewarding without your company." Isaac took hold of her elbow and helped her into the car. Her fancy beaded reticule snagged on the door handle, causing him to have to disentangle the delicate strap.

Clementine inspected the small purse. "No damage done. You were so quick to save it!"

If there was one thing at which she excelled, Isaac decided, it was making a man feel that his efforts were appreciated. *Clementine wouldn't refuse a proposal and not explain why.* The thought caught him off guard, and he almost missed the turn off.

The side road hadn't been paved yet, so Isaac was careful to avoid the worst ruts. He was gratified to see Lawrence follow him around the pitfalls—Nessa and Mrs. MacLean were safe enough. He drove alongside the river, its water much clearer than any of the creeks they'd seen up until now.

"It's so peaceful," Julia murmured.

Everyone stayed fairly quiet, ostensibly just drinking in the still, undisturbed beauty. When the roaring of the falls pulsed loudly in his ears, Isaac decided to stop. If he kept driving, he wouldn't get the chance to truly appreciate the view. Neither, he realized, would Lawrence.

"Wonderful idea to walk toward the falls," Michael commended.

"Something about drawing closer, hearing the power of the water churning more and more loudly—it's like we're closing in on a hidden treasure." Nessa couldn't contain her enthusiasm, and Isaac felt as though she shared it with everybody else.

When they first viewed the falls, it was through a framework of pine branches. Falling from a height of forty feet, the water rushed over a rock ledge and stretched to reach the churning pool below.

Isaac immediately turned around and went back for his camera case. During the time it took him to set everything up, Michael had gone back for Julia's art case, and she settled on a flat stone, busily filling her sketchbook with black strokes. Somehow those lines captured the elegance and sense of motion evoked by the waterfall. Isaac couldn't wait to develop his photograph and see what the film had captured.

"Doesn't it make you want to pick your way to the pool at its base, throw off your shoes, and dip your toes in the water?" Nessa breathed a sigh of appreciation.

"Never." Clementine's shocked gasp leeched some of the color from Nessa's cheeks. "Such a trek would absolutely ruin my skirts. And who knows what poisonous plants lay there!"

"It's not for everyone," Isaac placated. He shared a glance with Nessa. "But I know I would be tempted to try it."

"Not today!" Lawrence brushed a fly from his shoulder. "We'd best get back on the road so we make it to the Fountain Hotel before dark. There are still the Cascades to see today."

Isaac flipped the clasps on his photography case shut. He couldn't resist one last glimpse of the falls before he left. When he turned around, he saw that Nessa had done the same. She must have felt his gaze upon her, because she looked right at him. The same wistful admiration she'd bestowed on the falls stayed in her eyes as their eyes locked. She looked as though she was saying farewell to their long friendship, just as she had the water behind him.

Oh no, Nessa, he tried to convey in silence. *Don't think you're abandoning me in your past the way you're leaving this waterfall behind. We're not through yet.*

∞

The intensity in Isaac's gaze haunted Nessa long into the day. The tumbling fury of the Cascades pounding out a fierce rhythm seemed to seep into her skull as she tried to decipher the message he'd given her. But just like the dancing, foam-flecked water, she kept running up against the stones of confusion.

Her progress slowed, her purpose uncertain, she walked through the rest of the day like a shadow. Lawrence, seeming to sense that Nessa was grappling with something and wasn't her usual self, stayed close and supported her. He made conversation that didn't require more than the occasional nod or polite smile.

She'd seen that glint in Isaac's deep blue eyes often enough to recognize it as determination. All the same, she couldn't begin to guess what he was determined to do. What did it have to do with her?

He'd made it more than clear he was pursuing Clementine now. The petite blond perched next to him every moment of the drive to and through Yellowstone, with Isaac not making a single mention of how that relegated Nessa to Lawrence's vehicle.

God, I'm baffled by his behavior. If he has feelings for me, why didn't he show them before? Why in such a cryptic way now? Lawrence is clear about his intentions—he's kind, attentive, and admiring. So why do my thoughts come back to Isaac again and again when he is so clearly taken with Clementine? I pray that by the end of this trip, You'll have given my heart the wisdom to make sense of it all.

Finally, Nessa drove the conundrum from her mind. If that one look had shown that God was working in Isaac's heart, so be it. If the Lord guided her to Lawrence, she'd follow. She'd made too many mistakes when she relied on her own emotions to trust them now. When they rolled to a stop, Nessa breathed a little easier. Everything was in God's hands.

CHRISTMAS TREE ROCK, the plaque read. She shaded her eyes and peered into the middle of Firehole River. There a large rock sprawled across the center of the softly rushing water. A single lodgepole pine stood straight and true, growing right out of the rock.

"I've never seen a tree grow through solid rock like that." Lawrence stared at it. "Incredible!"

"Must be an unusually strong tree," Nessa speculated, "to thrive despite the challenges it faces." *I wish I were strong enough to do the same.*

"Look at how the roots thrust right into the rock, taking what they need to keep the tree alive." Isaac was once again setting up his camera. "Now that's determination!"

"Is that all any of you sees when you look at this miracle?" Grandmam's eyes shone.

"The tree stands alone," Isaac replied. He glanced back at the unwavering center in the middle as though to be sure.

"No." Nessa suddenly understood what Grandmam was seeing. "The tree stands on the rock. The rock supports and gives life to the tree, even though the plant should be too weak."

"Exactly." Two tears rolled down Grandmam's face, causing Nessa to fold her arms around her. "It's just like us," she said. "The Lord is our Rock and our salvation. Even though we're weak on our own, He sustains us."

"It's beautiful." Nessa felt as though it was an entirely new sight that lay before her, bathed in the beauty of love.

"Since my Arthur died," Grandmam sniffed, "I've struggled with feeling alone. That tree reminds me that God is always with me. That's what I see."

Isaac came out from behind his camera. "That's what everyone should see." He replaced Nessa, hugging Grandmam in the all-enveloping way only a man can hold a beloved old woman. "Thank you for showing us."

Chapter 18

I wanted to catch a word with you." Michael found Isaac wiping dust off the windshields of his car. "Without anyone to overhear us."

"Sounds serious," Isaac teased. One look at his friend's face sobered him up. "Where is everyone else?"

"Looking for Clementine's lost earring." Michael gave a fleeting grin. "So there are five people in that hotel room, crawling around the floor in hopes of finding a lonely garnet."

"I don't see how that's funny." Isaac's brow knit. "It might be an heirloom or a treasured gift from her father."

"Julia swiped it." Michael gave a wink. "To give us some time to talk. She'll 'find' it in a little while."

"So what do you need to say?" Isaac leaned against the Ford, swiping at his boots with the dust cloth.

"Since we're stuck in the backseat with you and Clementine this whole trip," Michael began, "we can't help but notice you and she seem to be hitting it off, so speak."

"Stuck?" Isaac raised his brows in mock affront.

"You know what I mean." Michael looked at the Ford.

"All right, all right. Yeah, we've been spending a lot of time together." He shrugged. "Nessa and Mrs. MacLean have been more than content to ride with Lawrence in the open-air runabout."

"True, but even when we're out of the car, it seems Clementine's vying with your sleeve just about every time we turn around. She hangs on your arm that much."

"The ground's less than steady, and her shoes weren't the best choice for exploring." Isaac wouldn't mention his suspicion that Clementine's vision wasn't as good as it seemed.

"Julia thinks Clementine might need spectacles," Michael commented. "So we were wondering if you'd noticed the same thing and were being a good Christian brother. . .or if it went deeper than that."

"I noticed," Isaac admitted. He wasn't betraying any secrets now that Michael had brought it up. "She needs support on the uneven paths. I also can't help but notice what a lovely young woman she is and how she appreciates the courtesy I show her. There's something appealing about being needed."

"And you think Nessa doesn't need you?" His friend tilted his head as though working out a kink. "Is that the problem?"

"The problem," Isaac spoke as clearly as possible, "is that Nessa rejected my proposal. She doesn't want to marry me."

"I wouldn't be so sure about that." Michael gave him a slanted look, as though he were privy to secret information.

"What did Julia tell you?" In spite of himself, Isaac stopped leaning on the car, standing at attention.

"Nothing I'm able to repeat. But I will say that neither Julia nor I nor Nessa feels that Clementine is a good match for you."

"Nessa doesn't have the right to judge who is or isn't a good match for me." Isaac slapped his hat on his head. "Not when she turned me down and still hasn't explained why."

"Is it that she hasn't explained"—Michael crossed his arms over his chest and glowered as he finished—"or that you weren't really listening to what she had to say about what she needs?"

"She hasn't explained." He bit off the sour words.

"Leave off thinking about Nessa for a moment." Michael shoved aside the topic and plowed ahead. "Do you see Clementine as a potential wife? Are you courting her in earnest?"

"To an extent. A man could do far worse than to have a woman like Clementine on his arm." Isaac straightened his hat. "She's pretty, God-fearing, appreciative, honest to a fault. . ."

"To a fault." Michael latched onto that last phrase. "Have you noticed that she speaks without realizing the impact of her words? Like two days ago when she intimated that the other women were excluding her, making fun of her?"

"It's what she perceived to be the truth." Isaac remembered how woebegone she'd looked as she'd apologized. "Admitting a mistake and apologizing for it will stick in anyone's craw, but she did it anyway. She's even started helping where she can."

"That's another thing, Isaac. How can Clementine help you build a home and a family? She dresses well and moves gracefully, but can you honestly see her doing a lick of hard work?"

"She hasn't had to," he defended. "Clementine might have come into things later than Julia or Nessa, but she'll learn."

"If she wants to." Michael spoke in a low tone as everyone poured out the doors of the Fountain Hotel. "Are you even sure about that? Just think about it, Isaac."

"I will." He jerked the doors open. "And I expect you to support whatever decision I come to."

∞

"We saw geysers erupting from our bedroom window," Nessa mentioned. "Did you see the same thing?"

"Can't say we saw geysers erupting from your window." Lawrence shook his head in a fair imitation of regret. "The hotel didn't see fit to equip our rooms so. From our vantage point it looked like they were coming from the Lower Geyser Basin."

"You knew what I meant!" Nessa laughed at his mischievous smile. "Good to hear you spotted a few geysers yourself, though I would have been thrilled if the Excelsior had gone off. It's supposed to blast to a height of three hundred feet!"

"You know it hasn't had a documented eruption for over fifteen years." Grandmam clicked her tongue. "Don't you think we've already seen more than enough wonders to have justified this entire trip? I've already made many memories."

"As have I." Lawrence tightened his grip on the steering wheel. "You're in every last one, Nessa."

"You do have a way around a compliment, boy," Grandmam said approvingly from the backseat. "One would think the two of you have been alone instead of part of a large group."

Lawrence lowered his voice so the wind carried his words only to Nessa's ears. "Maybe sometimes it just feels that way."

"It's easy to lose oneself in awe of the sights we've seen." She deflected the compliment and steered the conversation to safer ground. "Which has been your favorite so far?"

"Which has been yours?" He glanced at her out of the corner of his eyes.

"Each is so unique, I'd be hard-pressed to choose just one." Nessa propped her arm on the windowsill. "That would be like choosing a favorite dish or a favorite person!"

"Sometimes we come across something so special, the choice is easy." Lawrence tried to catch her eye, but Nessa looked away and busied herself with looking out the window.

"Mine was the Christmas Tree Rock." Grandmam eased the silence. "Such a powerful reminder of God's love will always be precious to me. I'll hold it close for years to come."

"I think I would choose the same," Nessa agreed. "Not only because of that reminder, which would be enough on its own, but for the joy it brought you." She reached across the back of the seat to clasp her grandmother's hand.

"The tree is an example to us all." This time Lawrence caught her eye as she turned back around. "With enough determination, we can conquer even the most difficult circumstances and achieve our goals."

"Is Isaac slowing down?" Nessa strove to keep her tone casual, ignoring the flush of heat she knew made her cheeks glow. It would be far too easy to lose her head over Lawrence's kind attentions and fulsome words. She'd only known the man for a few weeks, and he'd given her more compliments than Isaac had managed in an entire lifetime!

Slightly uneasy at the thought of further encouraging Lawrence when she wasn't certain of her feelings for Isaac, she climbed out of the car without waiting for him to get the door. His puzzled expression as he passed her to help Grandmam made Nessa wince. She hadn't meant to make it so obvious that she wanted to distance herself.

She gave him a bright smile to compensate for her rudeness, exclaiming, "I can't wait to see this. The Grand Prismatic Spring—doesn't it just sound mysterious and lovely all at the same time?" Nessa allowed him to place her hand in the crook of one arm, as he already escorted Grandmam with the other.

"Mysterious and lovely," Lawrence echoed, his gaze resting on her face. "An intriguing combination, to be sure."

Nessa's discomfort fled as she caught a glimpse of the spring. Steam rolled off the surface of the water in a filmy vapor. It seemed mystical, as though this spring had existed since the dawn of time, softly warming the air through ages until humans finally discovered its enchanting beauty.

"There!" An unfamiliar woman pointed high above the spring, where the misty steam thinned and spread.

Nessa looked up and caught her breath at the shimmering light of an almost translucent rainbow. It quivered, suspended in the air by light and water, ebbing and flowing like a living thing. She stared at the phenomenon until it, much like the steam itself, evaporated into the air above.

"So that's why it's named after a prism." Lawrence shifted so that his hands rested on her shoulders. "It captures and reflects light in the same way as fine-cut crystal."

"The rainbow is a promise," Nessa said, remembering the story of Noah's flood. "A covenant between the Lord and Noah that He'd never again send a flood to destroy mankind. I've always thought how fitting a symbol it was."

"Because it uses water and light?" Lawrence sounded puzzled.

"No." She turned, gently shaking his hands from her shoulders. "It's symbolic of a promise because it's delicate, temporary, and meaningful only so long as those who see it honor God's will. It can't be captured or destroyed. It has to be believed in completely."

"That's beautiful." He reached down and took her hands in his, not meeting her gaze as he added, "It sounds a lot like love."

Chapter 19

B iscuit Basin—they got the name right, that's for sure." Isaac
scanned the area, noting the rock formations that looked a lot like,
well, biscuits.

"Just like a man to notice something that resembles food." Clementine tapped his arm with the ivory fan she'd pulled out of her reticule.
Then she snapped it open and languidly waved it before her face for a
little while.

"So I take it your attention was caught by the Sapphire Pool?" Isaac
raised his brows in silent challenge.

"Absolutely. The color is incredible!" She busied herself with tucking
the fan into the small beaded bag. Though Isaac wouldn't have thought it
possible, the thing fit.

"How like a woman to notice something named after a jewel." He
closed the trap with a satisfied smile. His grin grew as everyone save
Clementine burst into laughter.

"He's got you there, sis," Lawrence all but hooted.

"Now, wait a minute, Isaac Friemont!" Nessa shook her forefinger at
him. "I noticed the biscuit-shaped rocks before admiring the sapphire
pool. What do you make of that?"

"You're the exception." The retort softened into a compliment as he
spoke it aloud. "A rarity among women."

"My thoughts exactly." Lawrence brushed a soft tendril behind Nessa's ear in a purely possessive motion.

"Thank you." Nessa fingered the errant strand. "Both of you." It
gratified Isaac to no end to see that saucy little curl spring right back to
caress her temple.

"We should be getting on," Lawrence said, clearing his throat and
tossing Isaac a dark glower, "since we want to see the Hillside Springs
before stopping for dinner."

"Fair enough." Isaac looked down as Clementine's cool hand snaked around his elbow. "Let's return to the automobiles."

As the day wore on, Clementine's idle chatter began to grate on Isaac's patience. She talked about her clothes, her jewelry, the parties she'd been to, the lovely vacations she'd had, the classes she'd taken at finishing school, and on and on until Isaac felt his temples throbbing. When did Clementine become so garrulous?

He resolved to find an open area for lunch close to Hillside Springs, if for no other reason than to escape her recitation for a few moments. From the amount of shifting Michael was doing behind him—Isaac could feel it every time his friend's knees hit the back of his seat—Isaac wasn't the only one who looked forward to some peace.

At Hillside Springs, it was with great reluctance that he helped Clementine out of the Ford. The little hands whose clasp he'd found sweet suddenly seemed like small, cold vises. As she gave a cry of distress over a tiny mud puddle, he wondered how he'd ever admired her fancy getups.

What sane woman traipsed around a forest in high-heeled boots, lace gloves, and satin gowns, carrying delicate purses? Isaac shut his eyes when she whipped out her fan once more. He hadn't even thought of the expensive earrings she'd left lying on a table in her hotel room. Was all this because she hadn't had enough time to order suitable clothing or because she didn't want to?

Michael's concern has me chewing over some things I wouldn't look at too closely before. Am I mirroring his doubts, or am I taking off my blinders? Give me wisdom, Lord.

Lawrence, Nessa, and Mrs. MacLean somehow beat them to the springs, and Isaac couldn't help but notice Nessa looked mighty pretty in her light, rose-colored cotton and sensible half boots. She'd forgotten her hat—again—and the sun practically danced on the opportunity to glisten in the deep red strands of her riotous curls. He drank in the view until Lawrence spotted him looking and placed his arm around Nessa's trim waist.

That man is getting too close for comfort.

"How strange!" Clementine's exclamation had him looking at the sight they'd stopped to appreciate.

"It's red." He couldn't quite keep the astonishment from his voice as he looked at the shocking color of the springs before him. Thankfully, the red had none of the purplish black undertones of blood.

"Tomato Soup Springs," Julia read from her ever-present pamphlet. She wasn't one to ever leave literature behind. "I'd say the reason for the nickname is pretty obvious."

"Biscuit Basin and Tomato Soup Springs." Isaac pulled his arm away from Clementine and rubbed his stomach. "Sounds like lunch to me! Is anybody else ready to stop and eat?"

"Yes!" Michael and Julia spoke as one, looked at each other in surprise, and shared a delighted smile. Obviously, Isaac wasn't the only one who wanted a reprieve from Clementine.

More than all the words she'd spewed, that simple fact spoke volumes.

"Let's see if it works!" Nessa edged closer to Handkerchief Pool.

"Wait." Lawrence caught her by the arm. "The ground could be thin, or you might get burned. I'll make sure it's safe." With that, he nudged ahead of Nessa to block her way.

"It would have been fine," she muttered under her breath. Why Lawrence decided to treat her like a child was beyond understanding. She could make her own decisions, and it was on the tip of her tongue to tell him so when he whipped out a large white handkerchief, reached above the opening of the pool, and let go.

"Oh!" Everyone let loose excited gasps as the anomaly sucked in the clean linen, only to spit it back out freshly steamed. The handkerchief was tossed high in the air, allowing Lawrence to catch it neatly.

"Would you look at that," he marveled. "Something in that guide was actually true!"

"It's not fair to blame the guide because Frying Pan Lake didn't boil your egg," Grandmam chided. "It only said that it was a story the guides sometimes told."

"Well, it didn't mention that the story was false," Lawrence grumbled. "But this Handkerchief Pool is real enough!"

"I'd like to try it!" Clementine's excitement caused Isaac to lead her up to the spring—ahead of Nessa, who bit her lip so she didn't childishly demand that it was her turn.

In the end everyone enjoyed the sport, leaving with smiles on their faces and damp hankies in their pockets as another group took their place. By then the sun was sinking low in the sky, so they drove straight on to the Old Faithful Inn.

Nessa couldn't contain her smile at the "World's Largest Log Cabin," another Yellowstone claim to be taken with a grain of salt. All the same, it was a towering structure, about four stories tall, made almost entirely out of cut logs. The great doors were painted bright red, held in place with huge iron hinges, beckoning travelers to come inside.

"This is incredible!" Julia exclaimed as they entered the threshold. As with the basic structure, every bit of the interior was crafted from native logs, many of which hadn't been straightened but rather cunningly placed so that the angles or curves of the wood became decorative as well as functional.

They'd stepped into a large open space, filled with hardwood floors, wooden benches, and a massive stone fireplace stretching all the way to the ceiling. That drew Nessa's gaze upward, displaying the walkways guarded by rails that ringed around the open-area fireplace for two more stories.

"What's that?" Nessa tilted her head back to spy a room, set at the tallest point of the ceiling, the peak of the roof making the high room look like a small house.

"The crow's nest." Lawrence stood so close she could feel his breath tickling her escaped curls. "They keep it as an orchestra house; the music plays every night for the guests."

"Fascinating." She stepped away from him, using the pretext of inspecting the fireplace more closely. One side was open, but the other three housed great niches cut into the face of the stones, storage places for massive amounts of firewood.

"We're on the third floor." Isaac called. "Up those stairs." He gestured toward steps made of logs hewn lengthwise and stacked in the staggered pattern of a stairwell.

"Before we go up, do you think we can see Old Faithful spout off?" Clementine, as usual, clung to Isaac's arm. "It's supposed to be fairly regular."

"The hotel worker mentioned that, as best they could calculate, it would be due for another eruption in about ten minutes." Michael turned to Julia. "Would you like to see it in the glow of the sunset?"

Julia's cheeks glowed in a fair approximation as she nodded. By now it was obvious that Michael returned her interest...and was stealthily moving their courtship forward. The pair trooped outside, leaving everyone else to follow them out the door and up the gravel path that led to the famous geyser.

"Shall we?" Lawrence offered his arm with his customary flourish.

The gesture had charmed Nessa the first few times but was beginning to seem superfluous and overly formal. "Yes."

They walked the short distance, their group assembling as the little curls of steam rising from the ground began to grow larger, the transparent wisps darkening to white billows until the escalating rumble was drowned out by the *whoooosh* of water.

The first time the water pushed into the air, it didn't reach very high. Clementine was just voicing her disappointment when the action repeated, the eruption climbing taller. A rapid succession followed, each burst scaling greater heights, until a great *hiss* sounded and the water seemed to fly as high as the mountains in the background.

Nessa caught her breath, engrossed in the beauty before her. Water and steam danced high in the air, capturing the golden rose glow of the setting sun for a few playful moments. Then the eruptions slowed, grew smaller, and retreated back into the earth below.

Chapter 20

D o you think you got good pictures of the Kepler Cascades?"
Clementine didn't stop talking long enough for Isaac to answer.
"I thought they were amazing—a series of waterfalls. Who would
have thought up something like that? Over a hundred feet!"

"God thought it up." Julia somehow managed to stay polite beneath
the onslaught of Clementine's declarations. "Same as He created all the
incredible things we've seen on this trip."

"Oh yes, of course!" And Clementine was off again.

Isaac focused on the road, trying to block out some of the noise by
concocting outrageous schemes to make her ride in her brother's car for
the duration of the trip. Aside from mutilating the Ford itself, which he
refused to even contemplate despite the dire circumstances, he considered a range of options.

So far, the best of the lot was asking Julia to feign car sickness, the
threat of which should have Clementine scrambling away as fast as she
possibly could. The only hitch was the dishonesty of it, which ruined
everything. Isaac entertained a few fleeting thoughts about whether Julia
had ever had motion sickness in the past so a casual mention could be
made. . . .

As they rounded a corner around Shoshone Lake, Michael cut
through Clementine's litany. His friend manfully ignored the peevish
glance she sent his way, instead gesturing to the pamphlet in his hand. "I
thought you might like to know that this was the site of the last stage-
coach holdup in Yellowstone." He politely inquired, "Is anyone interested
in hearing the details?"

"To tell the truth, I've never enjoyed stories about—"

"Yes!" Julia and Isaac drowned out what would surely have been another of Clementine's rambling stories.

"Seems one Edwin B. Trafton decided to emulate the Turtle Rock robbery of 1908." Michael spoke slowly, and Isaac knew his friend was trying to draw the story out.

God bless Michael, he prayed quickly before interrupting. "I don't remember everything about that incident. Could you remind me of the details?"

"Sure. In 1908 a robber—identity still unknown—held up a train of thirty stagecoaches at Turtle Rock. Accounts vary, saying he made off with one thousand to three thousand dollars he took from tourists. He was never caught."

"Gracious," Clementine breathed. Her gaze darted around the rocks bordering the road as she locked the door.

"So in 1914 a fellow by the name of Edwin Trafton decided that holding up tourists was a grand idea. He waited at Shoshone Point, held up fifteen coaches, and stole over nine hundred dollars—a good bit less than his predecessor."

"How was he caught?" Julia sounded puzzled.

"Seems he didn't realize the tourists thought it was all a part of the tour itself." Laughter tinged Michael's voice as he continued on. They snapped pictures of him to remember the incident, and the police used those to identify and capture him."

"What a foolish man!" Clementine cackled next to Isaac. "Some folks just don't know when to leave good enough alone." With that, she was off and running about the time when one of her friends did something similar.

As she prattled on, Isaac decided they'd need to stop for an even earlier lunch that day.

⌒

"Who thinks we should send Clementine for the ham and have her cut slices of it while we bake the biscuits?" Nessa all but whispered the words, though she needn't have bothered. Clementine seemed as affixed to Isaac's side as ever, so she wouldn't overhear Nessa's scheming.

"She'll make them uneven," Grandmam fretted.

"But she'll be over there, using that great big stump," Julia pointed out. She gave a happy little sigh. "All the way over there."

"Let's ask Lawrence to help her," Nessa hurriedly added as she spotted him sauntering toward her. "So she won't cut herself or anything horrible like that."

"I'll make the arrangements." With a knowing glance, Grandmam bustled off. She did a fine job of catching Lawrence's arm and turning him toward Clementine, hands waving in the air as she described exactly what she needed him to do.

"The reasons why I want Clementine off in the distance is obvious," Julia remarked. "What has Lawrence done to earn exile?"

"I can't so much as scratch my nose without him offering me his handkerchief." Nessa knew she was grumbling, but she couldn't stem the tide. "Every time I turn around, he's opening a door or carrying my luggage or holding my elbow as though I can't walk without his support. He's driving me half mad."

"You wanted an attentive suitor," her friend observed. "Seems like Lawrence fits the bill quite nicely."

"He does not fit the bill." Nessa poured flour into the mixing bowl she'd set atop the egg crate. "He weaseled his way into the bill then stretched it all out of proportion. Oh, listen to me. Lawrence hasn't done a single thing wrong, and here I am, sniping over all his kindness." A wave of guilt swamped her. "He's been a perfect gentleman."

"Maybe that's the problem." Julia handed her the salt. "Lawrence might just be a little too perfect. You've never been one to follow the rules as strictly as he seems to."

"You're a genius, you know that?" Nessa gave her friend a quick hug as Grandmam came back toward them. "I couldn't figure out what was bothering me, and you hit on it without even trying. Lawrence does need his feathers ruffled a little, and I might be just the woman to do it!"

"You've got that look again." Julia's smile disappeared, replaced by a look of caution. "Think about it carefully."

"How could it go wrong?" Nessa thought for a moment as she mixed the biscuit dough. "It's not as though I'd do something scandalous—just shake him out of his staid routine a little."

"If there's one thing I've learned after all the years of our friendship, it's that something can always go wrong."

"In what way could a little fun backfire?"

"What if Lawrence decides he needs to keep a closer watch on you to protect you from your impulsive shenanigans?" Julia helped shape the dough into biscuits then popped the first batch into the Dutch oven. "Could make him even more starchy."

"Oh no." Nessa wiped her hands on her apron. "He might react poorly and start to hover even more!"

"Lawrence?" Grandmam guessed. "He has been following you about like a babe in leading strings. You don't enjoy all the attention he gives you?"

"Some of it." Nessa blew a few wisps of hair from her forehead, venting her exasperation. "In the beginning, he made me feel special. The attention was flattering, not to mention a refreshing change from Isaac's obtuseness."

"So what changed?" Julia used the tongs to put more hot ashes atop the oven. "Or rather, who?"

"Who?" Nessa frowned. "You mean, did he become smothering or did I come to realize I didn't want to be smothered?" She waited for Julia's nod. "Both. He's latched on more tightly, and it's made me want to break free."

"You aren't bound to him, Nessa." Grandmam patted her arm.

"Exactly!" Nessa nodded eagerly. "Maybe that's why I chafe at the way he acts as though I am. He's starting to seem possessive, but I'm not a possession for him to claim."

"Your ma had the same problem with Isaac's brother, you know." Grandmam pulled the pan of fluffy biscuits from the Dutch oven. "Men claim women as their own as a way of showing they care."

"Here I thought it was to warn off other men," Nessa griped. She hadn't missed the way Isaac glowered at Lawrence.

"That, too." Grandmam laughed. "To men it's all part of the same thing. You, my dear, have to decide whom you'll allow to claim your heart."

Chapter 21

L *ord, how can it take no more than a couple of days and a few words from a well-meaning friend to reveal Clementine's shortcomings, when I've spent so much time hoping she'd make the perfect bride? I concentrated on bemoaning my responsibilities, reluctant to fulfill them. No more. Show me Your way, and I will take it.*

"Looks like it's been a rough day for you." Michael flopped down on his bed. "Hope that's not because of our talk the other day." He spoke freely because Lawrence was out trying to find shoe polish, of all things, for his sister.

"Part of it is." Isaac pulled off his boots. "It made me take a long hard look at Clementine—past her pretty smiles."

"What did you see?"

"She's everything I ever thought I truly wanted in a wife."

"Is that so?" Michael tried to sound casual, but Isaac knew his friend had grave misgivings.

"Clementine is sweet, pretty, always has a ready smile, and makes a man want to protect her." Isaac smiled at the pained look on Michael's face. "Funny thing is. . .I was wrong."

"You had me worried for a minute there."

"Couldn't resist." He leaned back. "Clementine isn't a woman I'll ever be able to really talk to, spend my life with day in and day out. She can't keep a house or raise children, and she'd be miserable as a farmer's wife. It'll never work."

"So glad you realized that." Michael slapped his knee, a sly look crossing over his face. "Figure anything else out, while you were at it?"

"That's not so clear." Isaac rolled over, propping his head on his hand. "I realize now that Nessa isn't just the wife everyone expected me to take—she's the wife I should have always wanted." He thought he heard footsteps outside, but then a door opened and he put it from his mind.

"So what are you prepared to do about it?"

"I can't say. She rejected my proposal, and I'm still not certain why. That's a huge barrier, so I wonder if Nessa isn't the one for me but someone a lot more like her than Clementine ever will be. Could be I need to travel around, meet more women than Saddleback has to offer."

"You've come a long way for one day." Michael dropped his head onto the pillow. "So I'm going to leave it at being glad you're no longer considering Clementine."

"Exactly." Isaac shut his eyes. "Tomorrow I'll need to take Clementine aside and gently tell her the proposal she may be hoping for won't be coming."

"Wonderful to hear you've that much worked out."

"It's a start." Isaac unbent his knees, lying flat. "The rest will be clear sooner or later."

"So long as it's not too late," his friend muttered.

"What's that supposed to mean?" Isaac sat up as another floorboard creaked in the hall outside.

"How do you feel when Lawrence puts his arm around Nessa's waist? Or sticks to her side like a shadow?"

"Like I want to pry him off with a crowbar." Isaac tensed at the very thought. "He hovers around too close."

"Why should that bother you if it doesn't bother Nessa?"

"It shouldn't, but it does anyway." Isaac heaved a sigh. "Nessa may not have accepted my proposal, but that doesn't mean I'll quietly let her chain herself to Lawrence Hepplewhite."

The doorknob rattled as Lawrence let himself in. There was no way to know how much he'd overheard, but from the forced cheerfulness in his face, Isaac suspected it had been everything since that first floorboard squeaked.

Sneakiness got added to the growing list of things Isaac didn't like about that man. Now what was he going to do about it?

∞

"Where are those two going?" Nessa watched as Isaac led Clementine under the relative privacy of a shady tree.

"Not far." Grandmam eyed the couple. "I'd be more concerned about what they were saying."

"Nessa?" Lawrence came up so quietly he made her give a little jump. "Can I have a word with you?"

"What is it?" She untied her apron strings.

"I meant in private." He offered her his arm, leaving her with no choice but to take it. Lawrence took her to a tree on the opposite side of the field, letting her sit on a flat rock eerily similar to the one she'd sat on while Isaac gave her that travesty of a proposal.

"Nessa, you know Isaac and I share a room with Michael. An interesting conversation took place last night, and I wanted to talk with you about it." He looked distinctly uncomfortable, his gaze shifting around as though he were reluctant to look at her.

"What is it, Lawrence?"

"I've noticed the looks that pass between you and Isaac sometimes but had hoped you might come to feel an abiding affection for me." He dropped to one knee. "Nessa, I want you to be my wife. I'll treasure you through the years to come, delight in our children, and strive to give you everything you've ever wanted. Wait." He put a finger to her lips, silencing her when she would have interrupted.

Since Nessa wasn't positive what she would have said, she let him continue. The idea of refusing another proposal turned her stomach.

"But after last night, I'm more aware of your history with Isaac. I know he proposed to you, and I know you refused him."

How much did Isaac tell him? And why?

"I can see you have questions. Let me say that I don't know why you refused him, but it doesn't matter to me. All that matters is that you refused him and you're free to marry me."

"Lawrence, Isaac and I—" She paused, searching for words to explain what even she didn't fully understand.

"It's in the past." He gave a small, rueful smile. "I know you aren't in love with me yet, but I hope one day you'll look at me with the same admiration I feel for you."

"You're a really wonderful guy, but I don't think—"

"If you're worried about Isaac, I can assure you that he's moved on. He's done a lot of thinking these past few days, and he says Clementine is all he's ever truly wanted in a wife." He gave a slight nod in response to her surprise. "I know that he planned to have an important conversation with her today—something about a proposal."

"Now?" Nessa craned her neck, trying to look past Lawrence to where Clementine and Isaac were still alone together.

"I think so." He gave her a look of sympathy. "It's why I took you aside now, so you could be prepared. They probably won't announce anything today—it's only proper for a man to seek the blessing of the woman's father before saying anything. But I wanted you to know that you're. . .free."

"Free," she echoed, numb from the tightness in her chest.

"To marry me," he encouraged. "Don't answer now. Just think about it."

"Thank you for telling me." Nessa struggled to stand up. "It's a lot to think about."

Chapter 22

I can't believe it, Lord! It's only been weeks since he proposed to me, and now he wants to marry someone else? I know I asked for You to make things clear, but I never imagined it would hurt so much.

Nessa all but ran through the forest until she couldn't see Lawrence anymore. Then she abandoned all pretense, leaned her back against a tree, wrapped her arms around her stomach, and sobbed. She took in great, shuddering gasps of air, but they all caught in her throat.

I knew he didn't love me, she tried to reason with herself, but the thought only made her cry harder. *But I hoped that maybe, somewhere deep inside, he did. Then he'd come to realize it, and we'd both be so happy. . . .*

Her knees buckled as she sank to the ground, feeling the rough bark catch at the back of her dress as she scraped down, and not caring if it was ruined. She rested her head on her knees, holding her breath in a failed effort to stop the sobs.

What am I to do? The thoughts poured forth in tears. *Pretend I know nothing? Does Isaac really love her, Jesus? If so, am I to accept Lawrence's proposal, though I don't love him?*

Maybe. Her sobs faded into sniffles and hiccoughs. *Maybe I am supposed to marry Lawrence. I've chased love all my life, and look what it's brought me to. Lawrence won't be tricked—he knows I don't care for him as he cares for me. How do I know, Lord?*

And suddenly, she knew. She had to talk to Isaac. Nessa shakily rose to her feet, swiping the last tears from her face, breathing slowly until there was no sign of her sorrow. She brushed leaves from her dress, tidied her hair as best she could, straightened her shoulders, and walked back to find Isaac.

Her resolve wavered a moment when she saw he was still alone with Clementine, who was nodding and waving her arms in grand motions.

Probably planning the wedding ceremony. Nessa choked on the bitter thought but pressed forward. She didn't even look at anyone else, keeping her gaze fixed firmly ahead.

By the time she drew near, Clementine was leaving Isaac. Joy glinted in the other woman's pale blue eyes and smiling features, but Clementine didn't say a word—just gave a friendly little wave and veered off toward the cook fire. So they weren't announcing it yet, just as Lawrence predicted.

Nessa's step faltered for a moment, her fists clenching against the realization. Somehow, she kept going, though the look of surprise that flitted across his face didn't bode well. "How was your talk with Clementine?" She forced herself to sound casual but suspected she'd failed abysmally.

"Far better than I'd hoped." Satisfaction underwrote every word as he rocked back on his heels. "I did see you went off with Lawrence for a while." He stopped rocking. "Anything interesting happen?" His brow furrowed anxiously.

He knows. Just like he told Lawrence about his intentions toward Clementine, Lawrence admitted his own plans. Nessa tried to swallow the lump in her throat. *He hopes it went well so nothing will mar the success of his romance with Clementine.*

"He proposed to me." The words tumbled from her mouth before she could stop them.

"So soon?" Isaac blurted out, as though he had any room to judge. He'd known Clementine for precisely the same amount of time Lawrence had known her, after all!

"Yes." She looked away momentarily, closing her eyes against a fresh wave of grief.

"What did you say?" He stepped closer, obviously eager to hear that the woman he'd proposed to first wouldn't present a threat to his new engagement.

"I didn't answer him. Yet." She met his gaze defiantly, but her bravado sheered away as she saw the muscle in his jaw clench. "First I had to talk with you, Isaac."

"You think I'd stand in your way?"

I hoped so, her heart cried. "No. But I had to find out if you, that is, whether. . ." She couldn't seem to force the words out. Nessa took a deep breath and tried again "Whether the proposal was real. That you meant what you said to Clementine."

"A man doesn't propose lightly." Isaac's voice sounded tight, as though forced from his chest. "I meant everything I said, Nessa. You should know that."

"Are you absolutely sure?" She couldn't hold the words back, giving him one last chance to take her in his arms and prove that he loved her, not Clementine.

"When have you known me to make a decision in haste?" Isaac had a point, considering she'd waited for him for years before he came to the sticking point. And then they both got stuck there—until now.

"That's it, then." She tried to act as though his revelation hadn't been a fatal blow. "I'm sorry to have ruined your plans, but it turns out to be for the best. You know I wish you every happiness." *Even at the cost of my own.*

"As I do for you." His breath came fast and shallow. "Good-bye, Nessa." With that, Isaac turned and stalked off, leaving her more alone than she'd ever been.

"AAAGGGHHH." Isaac unleashed an angry bellow and smashed his fist into a nearby tree, scarcely noticing the scrape of the bark against his knuckles. The rage seeped from his chest to pulse in his aching hand, allowing him to breathe again.

"Did you know," Michael's voice reached Isaac before he saw his friend approach, "that an impressive number of birds took flight from just about the spot where you're standing?"

"No." Isaac growled the syllable, a short warning that should have his friend backing off.

"It's true." Michael moved closer, his gaze scanning the broken bark of the tree and flitting to Isaac's hand. "And I'm going to take a wild guess and say you're the cause for it."

"Mmh." Isaac grunted and looked at his hand. His knuckles had swollen, the scrapes on the back of his hand sluggishly oozing blood.

"It's enough to make a friend worry about how your conversation with Clementine went."

"Fine." He still wasn't sure he wanted to talk.

"How about you walk me through that, then?" Michael cheerfully settled himself on a low branch.

"Go away," Isaac ground the words out. Now wasn't the time to discuss Clementine. Now was the time he needed to sort out his thoughts about Lawrence's proposal.

"No such luck." His friend shifted into a more comfortable position. "The last thing you need right now is to be left on your own." He gestured from Isaac's injured hand to the newly scarred tree. "Think of the damage you could do to our beloved national park with no one around to make you behave."

"Michael," Isaac gave up trying to intimidate his old friend, feeling the beginnings of a reluctant smile, "you should consider a career in politics."

"Nah. I'm too busy considering how to propose to Julia, then getting her to the altar and never letting her go. Love can do that to a man." Michael leaned forward. "But I think you already know that."

Isaac changed the subject. "Clementine took it well when I let her down. I told her she needed to consider what would really make her happy. . .and whether or not she'd find it in Saddleback. It didn't take long before her eyes lit up and she started nattering on about this fellow back in Charleston who'd proposed when he heard she was leaving."

"A fickle woman," his friend noted.

"She's not the only one." Isaac gave a short bark of laughter. "Nessa came to tell me Lawrence has proposed."

"No." Michael just about fell off his branch.

"Yes. But she hasn't answered him. . .yet." Isaac considered for a moment whether he'd do irreparable damage to his hand if he hit another tree. Or a rock.

"What?" was the most coherent thought his best friend managed.

"That sums it up." Isaac snorted. "Looks like that's God's answer— Nessa is going to marry Lawrence."

"You said she hadn't answered him."

"Yet." Isaac lowered himself to the ground but sprang up again to start pacing. "Nessa asked me if I'd really meant my proposal. Like she wanted me to tell her I wasn't serious so she could be free to run off with Lawrence and not feel guilty about it."

"That can't be right." Michael frowned. "We're missing something here."

"I told her I meant every word, and she apologized for ruining my plans. Said it all worked out for the best." Isaac cracked his knuckles and winced as pain shot up his arm.

"Maybe she thinks she's clearing the way for you and Clementine." Hope tinged the suggestion.

"Nope. She knew what I'd talked to Clementine about—asked how it went. When I told her it'd gone really well, that's when she started looking all hangdog and asked if I'd really meant the proposal." Isaac spared his hand and kicked a small rock, making it ricochet off a larger one with a loud *clunk*. "Nessa knew I still wanted her, and she felt bad because she's all set to marry Lawrence Hepplewhite."

"Isaac," his friend said slowly, as though turning his thoughts over to inspect the underside, "how would she know about what you said to Clementine?"

"I'm pretty sure Lawrence overheard us last night." Isaac kicked the larger rock, which didn't do more than scuffle a few inches. "Rotten sneak. Probably made me out to be some pitiful, lovesick boy when he talked to Nessa."

"I'm telling you," Michael protested, "I think something's not right here."

"That's true." Isaac shook his foot to alleviate the sting. "Nothing's turning out right."

Chapter 23

T he day wore on, hour after interminable hour. Nessa scarcely managed to scrape up enthusiasm for the Dragon's Mouth Spring,
which normally would have made her delighted. The underground
spring rushed up through a small hillside, emitting steam, and made
rumbling, rasping sounds as though one of the mythical creatures
crouched just inside the rocky overhang.

Since even this imagination-inspiring sight failed to chase away
her doldrums, Nessa knew her heartsickness wouldn't be ebbing anytime soon. She kept her face turned during the drive, hoping that
Lawrence would think she was enraptured by the majestic mountains
and massive bison dotting the landscape. No sense making him feel as
though his proposal depressed her.

They stopped at Rainy Lake, where the surface of the water rippled
and ringed in little circles everywhere. Supposedly tiny springs beneath
the surface disturbed the water, making it seem as though a perpetual
rain fell above the lake. Nessa couldn't help but think that rain wasn't the
only option—it would look the same if she stood in the middle and allowed herself to cry all the tears she held within.

The next few miles, they passed by Calcite Springs, and all pressed
handkerchiefs or bandanas over their noses to ward away the offensive
stench the land belched into the air. It smelled of rotten eggs and bitter
medicine, strong enough to make everyone swallow back gags.

When they reached the hotel and the women were left in their
room, Clementine hummed and slipped into a fresh dress, looking the
very picture of a woman in love. Nessa couldn't remain silent for another
moment. She had to be sure that if she was to bear the agony of a broken
heart, Isaac's wife would love him as well as she.

"Do you love him?" The question came out more like a demand, but
Nessa didn't bat an eyelash.

"What?" Clementine looked taken aback. In fact, she took a step away from Nessa. "I'm sure I don't know what you mean."

"It's simple." Nessa advanced a step as she spoke. "Isaac told me about your conversation today and the decision you reached. So I'm going to ask again, do you love him?" Her voice cracked. "You shouldn't marry him if you don't."

"Isaac told you?" Clementine's eyes narrowed; then she shrugged. "Well, to be honest, I hadn't thought so. I didn't realize it until today, as a matter of fact. How I could have taken him for granted for so long is beyond my understanding, but when I'm away from him—like now—I feel as though the best part of me has been ripped away. That must be love, right?"

"I suppose you'll have to wait to make it official." Nessa felt as though her entire body had gone numb.

"Yes, Daddy must be convinced that it's the right thing to do." Clementine shook the pins from her hair and picked up a silver-backed brush from her dresser set.

"That shouldn't be too hard." Nessa turned away, falling into a chair when she felt her legs would no longer support her weight.

"Maybe." She stroked her blond hair. "Maybe not, since I already told Daddy I didn't want to marry him."

"Why would you do a thing like that?" Nessa scarcely noticed that Grandmam and Julia were hanging on their words, eyes wide as they drank in the conversation.

"Because he stutters and wheezes and is a little on the scrawny side. I never thought I could love someone who wasn't handsome, but there you have it."

"Isaac is handsome." Nessa sprang to her feet. "And he doesn't stutter at all!"

"I meant Charlie!" Clementine set her brush down with a thud. "He has breathing problems, that's all."

"Charlie?" Julia couldn't keep silent anymore. "Who's Charlie?"

"The man I want to marry." Clementine rolled her eyes. "At what point in this little talk did we start talking about Isaac?"

"You want to marry someone named Charlie?" Nessa echoed the words, wondering for a brief moment whether a good shaking would make Clementine speak sensibly.

"Yes. Charlie Peterson, from back home." Clementine's frown

disappeared. "You thought Isaac and I were engaged? Whatever gave you that idea? He was very clear that he'd decided we wouldn't make a good couple when he spoke to me."

Nessa sat down again, abruptly. If Julia hadn't slid the chair behind her, she would have fallen to the ground in shock as she mentally relived what Isaac had told her that afternoon.

"I had to find out if you, that is, whether. . .the proposal was real. That you meant what you said to Clementine?" That was what she'd asked. She knew she'd specifically mentioned the proposal Lawrence assured her was coming. Isaac's response made no sense if he hadn't proposed.

"A man doesn't propose lightly. I meant everything I said, Nessa. You should know that."

Unless. . .unless he'd thought she'd known he had broken it off with Clementine and was telling her he'd meant what he'd said when he proposed to her!

Can it be that Isaac still wants to marry me?

☙

Isaac put down the washcloth and tossed on his shirt as a loud knock sounded at the door. He moved quicker than Michael or Lawrence and opened it to find four women—and every one of them hopping mad.

"Isaac!" Nessa's scowl disappeared for a fleeting second before it returned with a vengeance. "Excuse me," she pushed past him and headed straight for Lawrence.

"What's going on?" Michael directed the question to Julia, but she shook her head and put a finger to her lips, obviously cautioning them not to interrupt.

"Hello, my love." Lawrence gave a ghost of a smile.

"Don't," Nessa spat out, jabbing him in the chest with her index finger with each word, "call me that, Lawrence Hepplewhite. You"—she gave an extra hard jab, judging by the wince it provoked, before she continued— "are a sneaking, rotten, no-good, dirty, rotten liar. How dare you!" She'd stopped jabbing with each word as she spoke more quickly, poking indiscriminately until Lawrence had backed up all the way to the wall.

"You said rotten twice." Isaac leaned back to enjoy the show. He didn't know what Lawrence had done to get Nessa all het up, but it must've been a humdinger. She'd never been this angry in all the years he'd know her.

"I know." Nessa didn't even turn around. "That's because he's really"—she started jabbing again at this point—"really rotten!"

"What is it, Nessa?" Lawrence tried to capture her hand and hold it close, but she yanked it away.

"No. You no longer have the right to call me Nessa." She paused for a moment. "Or even Vanessa. It's Miss Gailbraith to you. If I decide to let you speak to me in the future."

"Why don't you tell me what this is all about?" Lawrence, Isaac noted while smothering a laugh, was wise enough not to use any name at all in that question.

"I'm not entirely sure, but the gist of what I can figure out is that you lied to me to make me think Isaac and Clementine were engaged. And you did it so I'd say yes to your proposal."

"What?" Isaac couldn't prevent a strangled yelp.

"Shh." Julia and Mrs. MacLean hushed him immediately, but Isaac was through standing back.

"You did, didn't you?" Clementine, her hair rippling down her back, looking more rumpled than Isaac had ever seen her, was practically quivering in indignation. "How could you use me like that, Larry? I'm your sister!" She ended on a shriek.

"I knew something wasn't right." Michael crowed in triumph until Julia nudged him with her elbow.

"Is this true?" Isaac kept his voice low and calm as he came to stand beside Nessa, placing his hand at the small of her back. "I figured I didn't like you because you had your eye on Nessa, but there's more to it than that, isn't there? You have no honor."

"Don't you insult me, Isaac Friemont." Lawrence's chest puffed out in agitation. "You can't blame me for being the smarter man and seeing what a treasure Nessa—" He broke off when Nessa raised her finger. "Er, Miss Gailbraith is. I knew the moment I saw her, and she's been under your nose for your whole life. I was just man enough to step forward."

"Real men don't lie," Nessa growled. "You knew I had feelings for Isaac, and you used them to hurt me!"

"You have feelings for me?" Isaac stopped glaring at Lawrence to look down at Nessa. "What type of feelings?"

"Don't distract me." She swatted his arm. "I'm busy telling Mr. Hepplewhite that I wouldn't marry him now if he were the last man in Montana."

"He's not," Isaac swiftly pointed out. "I'm still there."

"Why did I think we were in Wyoming right now?" Clementine sounded genuinely worried.

"We are," Mrs. MacLean assured her. "Don't worry."

"You can't blame a man for trying." Lawrence gave Nessa a look of longing that made Isaac's temper boil.

"Yes, I can." His fist clenched, Isaac stepped forward.

"Don't!" Nessa stopped him. "All I want is for him to admit what he did—own up to it."

"Yes, I tricked you." Lawrence began to look petulant. "But not for long enough." That statement had Isaac taking another step toward him, and the smaller man hastily added, "It was wrong of me. But when I overheard Isaac tell Michael he was going to break things off with Clementine, I knew I'd have to act fast. Can you forgive me for an act of desperation?"

"No." Isaac shook his head so hard he saw spots.

"Not yet," Nessa amended. "That will take time, at the very least. We don't know how much of the damage you caused can be fixed."

"Fixed?" Isaac put his hands around Nessa's waist. "So you figured out that I was talking about the time I proposed to you?"

"Yes." She gave a small smile. "That's what I meant."

"So you'll be my wife?" He grinned.

"I didn't say that. We still have some things to work out."

Chapter 24

Like what?" he demanded.

The disgruntled expression on his face made Nessa want to laugh and kiss him at the same time. "You never courted me, for one." She twinkled up at him. "The rest should fall into place after that."

"I didn't think I had to court you," he grumbled. "You were already supposed to love me."

"I do."

"Then what's the hold up? You want poems? Fancy words? Freshly picked flowers? That's all courting is."

"No, it's not." She sighed. "Courting isn't just about making the woman fall in love with you, you know."

"What else is it for?" He looked around the room, obviously hoping someone would take pity on him.

"To show the woman you love her," Julia burst out. She may even have mumbled "blockhead" under her breath, but Isaac either didn't hear it or disregarded it.

"You mean you don't already know that I love you?" He looked genuinely confused, but that didn't stop her from pushing away.

"How would I know it when you didn't even know it?" Nessa demanded. "You didn't say a word about love when you proposed!" If her finger hadn't been all achy from jabbing Lawrence, Isaac would've felt her displeasure.

"You're right." His astonished admission eased some of her temper. "I didn't know it then. I should have, but I didn't." He spoke as though the whole thing were an incredible revelation.

"Men!" Nessa harrumphed, including both Lawrence and Isaac in that miserable category. She noticed all the women nodding and felt marginally better. "Even when I told you I cared for you, you didn't say you cared for me. That's important." She tilted her head back to scowl at him.

His smile was deeply offensive until he cupped her face in his hands, lowered his head, and touched his lips to hers. For a moment, she forgot why she'd been so riled, but then she had no choice but to wrap her arms around his neck. Otherwise, she would surely have melted into a puddle on the floor.

"Nessa?" He spoke her name softly after he drew back.

"Hmm?" She still hadn't quite recovered from his kiss.

"I love you." He whispered it in her ear, but from the whoops and hollers coming from everyone but Lawrence, nobody missed it.

"Well," Nessa told him, "it's about time."

"Who's riding with Lawrence and Clementine?" Isaac glanced over to where the siblings stood by their vehicle.

"I want to stay with you." Nessa gave him a look that made Isaac want to tuck her in the car, hop in beside her, and leave everyone else behind. Not that this was possible.

"Whichever car Julia rides in, I'll be beside her." Michael took her hand in his with a questioning glance."

"I'll stay with Lawrence," Mrs. MacLean volunteered.

"Are you sure?" Julia looked vaguely guilty. "Clementine can talk a blue streak."

"Oh, so can I." The older woman laughed. "And I'd say Lawrence needs a good, long lecture after what he tried to pull. I'll enjoy giving it to him."

"I almost feel sorry for him," Nessa giggled. "Almost."

With that, they all took their places and were off. About four miles after the Roosevelt Lodge, they arrived at Crescent Hill, which stood west of the road. It didn't look much more impressive than any of the other hills, so Isaac asked Nessa why it was marked as an attraction.

"Hold on, let me read it." She squinted at the paper as they drove past, giving an outraged gasp as she read. "You'll never believe what this horrible man named Truman Everts did."

"What?" Julia perked up at the promise of a good tale.

"In 1885 he was part of the Washburn expedition—you know, the one that found the black mud hole they named the Devil's Inkpot?" She waited for their agreement before she continued. "He was fifty-seven years old, and most of the area was frozen, but he decided to head off on his own."

"That can't be good," Isaac commented. He reflected that Nessa's way of telling a story was far more interesting than Clementine's had ever been.

"No, it wasn't. He never came back. The expedition searched high and low for him but eventually was forced to move on or risk running out of supplies. Everyone figured Everts had to be dead by that time and informed his family of the tragedy."

"I don't see how that makes him a horrible man," Michael protested. "A foolish one, certainly, but not a horrible one."

"What a sad thing to have happen." Julia sounded upset.

"Oh, I'm not done yet." Nessa kept on, using a very dramatic tone. "The family was heartbroken and hired an explorer to go back to the dangerous, isolated area to find Everts's body. He was supposed to bring it back for burial, at which point he would receive a substantial reward."

"So he should, for taking on a job like that." Isaac slowed the car as they came near Hellroaring Creek.

"Well, the man found Everts, who'd been lost for thirty-seven days. And, to everybody's surprise, he'd survived. He'd lost an incredible amount of weight and was practically at death's door, crawling on the ground without any idea of where he was."

"How horrible," Julia remarked, quickly adding, "but wonderful he was rescued."

"When he got home, he refused to give the man the reward, saying that the job had been to bring home his dead body, which his rescuer certainly hadn't done." Nessa's voice rang with disgust. "Can you believe it? That's the thanks the man got for rescuing Truman Everts."

"He was horrible." Michael pounded his fist on the back of Isaac's seat. "It might have been better for everyone involved if he'd just been found dead."

"Michael!" Julia's remonstrance had the desired effect.

"Sorry, that is too harsh. Every life is precious to God," Michael amended. "It's not for me to judge."

"All the same, that was a terrible thing to do," Isaac couldn't help but say. "Maybe he's distantly related to Lawrence."

"Isaac!" Nessa gave him a light shove. "Lawrence did an awful thing, but he didn't succeed. Isn't that what really matters?"

"Yes, to us, anyway." Isaac took his eyes off the road just long enough to smile at Nessa. "That's the most important thing in the world."

Chapter 25

H e proposed! Michael proposed!" Julia barely waited for Nessa to put
down the bucket she'd been using to slop the pigs before grabbing
her in a tight hug. They hopped and hugged and squealed together
until the pigs joined in with the loud squeals of their own.

"Tell me all about it." Nessa dragged her friend away from the pigs
and into the flower garden. "Every detail."

"You know he'd already asked my father for his blessing," Julia began.
"So he came in the evening and asked me to go for a walk. He held my
hand and took me to that little old wooden bridge over the stream by the
meadow."

"In the moonlight?" Nessa sighed. "That's so romantic."

"Isn't it?" Julia couldn't stop beaming. "And under the stars, he looked
into my eyes and told me he'd composed a poem. And then he looked
away and said it had been so horrible he burned it. Claimed it was a
stroke of mercy for us both that he couldn't even remember it."

"He's probably right." Nessa couldn't resist saying it.

"I still would have liked to hear it." Julia shrugged. "No matter how
bad it was."

"Get back to the proposal itself, won't you?"

"So he sank down to one knee, never letting go of my hand, and
he asked me to be his wife. 'Julia,' he said, 'by now you must know how
deeply I respect you, and that the trip to Yellowstone would never have
been half as enjoyable without you by my side. I've wanted to marry you
for a while now, but until recently I wasn't sure if you returned the love I
felt for you. Now I can only hope that you'll do me the honor of becoming my wife.'"

"And you accepted him, right?" Nessa waggled her brows. "Did he
kiss you?"

"Yes, and yes." Julia laughed. "That's all the detail you're going to get though. I just couldn't wait until I could tell you this morning. Besides, I wanted to ask you something."

"I hope you're thinking about a double wedding." Nessa knew by her friend's smile that she was right. "That'll be perfect! Isaac and me pledging to love each other forever at the same ceremony where you and Michael do the same—what could be better?"

"Nothing I can imagine," her friend said with a laugh. "Can you believe that two months ago you were the one running to my house to tell me about Isaac's proposal?"

"What a difference two months make." Nessa shook her head. "If you'd asked me then, I'd have said Isaac and I would never marry. Not if that's what he wanted from a wife."

"But things have changed. Now we're planning a double wedding!" Julia gave her another hug. "It'll be in the church of course. Michael and I will go after you and Isaac, since your engagement came first. Mama wants me to wear her wedding dress, but I'll have to let out the hem first. I'm a good four inches taller than she is."

"I'll probably wear my ma's gown, too," Nessa confessed. "Though I'll need to modify it a little bit, because I don't wear corsets."

"With your tiny waist, you won't need to do much. Saturday, let's get together and work on our dresses." Julia grabbed Nessa's hands. "The wedding could take place the week after, unless you think folks would be scandalized."

"I doubt it. Everyone's been expecting this since we returned from Yellowstone and the Hepplewhites packed up," her friend assured her. "No one's ever left Saddleback so quickly, but the new family that bought their land seems nice."

"After my last error in judgment, I think I'll wait until they've been around for a while before I agree with you." Nessa smoothed her skirts. "For now, we both have a lot of things to do. We can't leave our families with a lot of work piled up."

"All right. I'll see you later—to plan for our wedding!"

∽

"So you did it, then?" Isaac didn't really even need to ask. His friend's face told him everything he needed to know.

"She said yes." Michael flopped down onto the soft but scratchy hay. "Didn't even have to think twice, just promised to join her life with mine as though she couldn't imagine saying no. I'm the luckiest man in the world, Isaac. Couldn't ask for a better woman than my Julia."

"That's right." Isaac gave him a friendly punch to the shoulder. "But only because Nessa's taken."

"I should have known you'd try to claim something like that." Michael shook his head. "I suppose the wisest thing would be to let you continue on in your way of thinking."

"When have you ever done the wisest thing?"

"A good bit more often than you, my friend." Michael lobbed a fistful of hay at him. "Which is why I'm going to say you have the best woman for you and I have the best woman for me. Beyond that, we're both entitled to our separate opinions."

"Even if you're wrong," Isaac promptly agreed.

"You're lucky I'm in such a good mood, or I'd have to make you take that back." Michael gave a contented sigh. "As it is, nothing can detract from the beauty of this day."

"Oh brother." Isaac rolled his eyes. "You're not going to wax poetic, are you?"

"No." Michael seemed oddly flushed. "I've learned I don't have the talent for it, so I'll leave it to men who don't actually have wives to keep them busy."

"You don't have a wife yet," Isaac pointed out. "Not that you'll be single much longer."

"Don't want to be." His friend pillowed his head on his hands, staring up at the roof of the barn. "Julia's supposed to talk with Nessa today, see if she'd mind having a double wedding."

"So you don't think you need to ask if I'd mind?" Isaac pretended to be insulted. "You take a lot for granted."

"What? I brought it up now, didn't I?" Michael bit back a laugh. "Not that it'll make much of a difference what you think once Nessa's all excited about sharing her wedding with her best friend."

"That's true." He chewed reflexively on a piece of hay. "There isn't much I'd deny Nessa if it'd make her smile."

"Now who's waxing poetic?"

"Watch what you say. I don't want to disappoint Julia by having you injured." Isaac stretched. "Besides, Nessa wouldn't like it if I 'accidentally' rolled you out of this hayloft and you sprained something."

"Does she know how violent you are?" Michael raised his brows. "She should be warned that you threaten other men."

"Only men who stand between me and my bride-to-be."

"Still itching a little over not having a man-to-man with Lawrence before he hightailed it?" Michael knew him very well.

"A little," he admitted. "Though it's not what God would have wanted, so it's a blessing the Hepplewhites packed up. I wasn't entirely sure I was ready to turn the other cheek after what Lawrence did."

"Can't say I blame you, but we're called to be stronger than we'd ever manage on our own."

"Think that's why God gave us such incredible women?" Isaac wondered aloud. "He knew we'd need extra help to become the men He had in mind?"

"I'd believe that's part of it." Michael rolled onto his side. "But I'd say a bigger part is His grace in giving us a reward we don't deserve. The sooner we get our women down the aisle, the better."

"Afraid Julia might realize she made a mistake?" Isaac scooted out of the way before Michael could grab him. "Hey, that was a joke. Won't happen again, I promise."

"It better not." Michael sat back down. "How long do you think it's going to take for us to become settled-down husbands, stuck in a rut we refuse to climb out of?"

"One of two ways," Isaac considered. "Either as soon as we're married and we have everything we ever wanted, or. . ."

"Or what?"

"Or it'll take Nessa and Julia an eternity to whip us into the husbands they deserve." Isaac grinned. "Is it wrong that I'm kind of hoping it'll be the second one?"

"Probably." Michael laughed. "But I hope so, too. I want every minute I can get with my wife-to-be."

"My thoughts, exactly."

Chapter 26

"Can I look yet?" Nessa fidgeted in the chair while Julia gave her hair a trim. "Please let me look. I know it's perfect."

"If you know it's perfect, then you don't need to look." Julia gave another judicious snip with the scissors.

"That's only because today everything will be perfect." Nessa paused and added as an afterthought, "Even if everything isn't, it'll seem that way to me."

"I know what you mean." Julia put down the scissors and held up the looking glass. "Now you can see."

"It is perfect!" Nessa fingered the newly trimmed tendrils framing her face and peered at the freckles barely discernible beneath a translucent layer of pressed powder. "In the real way, not the it's-my-wedding-so-it-has-to-be way," she clarified. "And our hairstyles even match!"

"I saw how much you liked mine, so I thought it would be a nice touch for our double wedding." Julia turned the looking glass and surveyed her profile to see the elegant sweep of curls falling from a simple twist high atop her head. "It is a pretty style, if the pins stay in."

Nessa admired her friend's willowy figure. "If you didn't say so, no one would know you were wearing your mother's dress. The lace you added to the bottom looks so sophisticated."

"Even if I hadn't mentioned it, everyone would still know, since Mama has told anyone who will listen." Julia bit her lip. "Do you think Michael will like it?"

"He'd have to be a fool not to, and we both know he's no fool." Nessa fingered the soft cream satin of her own wedding gown. "After all, he knows to marry you!"

"That's true. Have I told you how wonderful you look in your mother's dress?" Julia asked. "When you walk, it seems like you're floating on a whispering cloud."

"You have such a way with words." Nessa couldn't help but be pleased in spite of herself. "Julia, there's no one in the world I'd rather share this special day with."

"Except Isaac of course."

"It wouldn't be a special day without Isaac." Nessa affixed her veil while Julia did the same, finishing right as a knock sounded on the door. She hurried to open it. "Da!" Nessa relished his big hug as John Mathers went to embrace Julia. She noticed that her friend was having a soft conversation with her own father, so she was able to concentrate fully on the man who'd loved and raised her.

" 'Tis time," he rumbled. "Are you both ready to meet your fortunate grooms? Ach, anyone with a pair of eyes could see you're more than ready. Such a lovely set of brides I've never seen." He held out his hand, and Nessa took it.

"When have you ever seen a set of brides?" she teased. "I didn't know you'd ever attended another double wedding."

"Don't think your old da can't see what you're up to, Nessa." He shook his head. "Nothing you say will make it easy for me to give you away, not even to the man you love."

"Oh Da." Nessa rose on her tiptoes to kiss his cheek. "We're staying in Saddleback, so it's not as though you'll even have time to miss me!" In spite of the light words, tears sprang to her eyes. There was something bittersweet about leaving her family behind, even to be with the man she loved.

"Are we ready to go?" Mr. Mathers escorted Julia outside.

When both girls had carefully arranged the fragile skirts of their wedding gowns, the men closed the car doors and drove them the short distance to the church. In no time at all, Nessa stood beside her father before the double doors.

"I love you, Da," She whispered. "That'll never change."

"You'll always be my Nessa"—he patted her arm—"even after I give you away. You remember that you're not leaving us behind. We're happy to see you move forward. Are you ready?"

"Yes, Da." Nessa straightened her shoulders. "I'm ready."

⚭

This is it. She's probably right outside those doors, Isaac told himself as Alma struck up a processional on the piano. *She's arranging those gauzy things women wear at weddings, taking her father's arm, and starting to walk down the aisle now.* He blinked and opened his eyes, hoping to see her appear. She didn't.

Any minute now, he revised. *Aaannnyyy minute.* He wiped a bead of sweat from his brow as the doors stayed closed. *She wouldn't come to her senses and realize she deserves better than me now, right, Lord? Not on the day of our wedding. I promise I'll be the best husband I can possibly be, if only Nessa marries me today. . .*

The doors opened to reveal Nessa, escorted down the aisle by her father. Ewan Gailbraith may have been a big, burly blacksmith, but Isaac could only see his bride as she breezed down the aisle, a vision in white. *Thank You, Lord.*

When she reached him, she gave a smile so bright that it couldn't be hidden beneath her veil. Isaac eagerly accepted her hand as Ewan formally gave away the bride. He reveled in the warmth of her soft grip as Julia made her way down the aisle and Michael sucked in a sharp breath, much the way Isaac had when he'd seen Nessa.

In the blink of an eye, all four of them stood before the pastor, ready to be wed. The man of God welcomed everyone to the joyous occasion, and the ceremony began in earnest.

"Before I begin, there is a request I must fulfill." Rev. Mathers unfolded the sheet of paper Isaac had slipped him that morning. "The grooms have asked that I read this quote and promise before the vows are exchanged."

Isaac nodded as Nessa tilted her head in silent question. She looked ahead as the pastor began to read.

"A famous man once said, 'Love does not consist in gazing at each other but in looking together in the same direction.' Isaac and Michael both wanted Vanessa and Julia to know that, though they'll find it difficult to look away from the beauty of their wives, they're blessed to have found women who will look to God to guide them through marriage."

Nessa gave Isaac's hand a tight squeeze, and he squeezed back.

The next few minutes passed in a blur of "I do's" as Isaac and Nessa, then Michael and Julia repeated their vows. Isaac slowly drew off Nessa's white glove, sliding a gold band onto her left ring finger. He didn't pay attention to the others, but Michael must have done the same for Julia.

"I now pronounce you man and wife," the pastor proclaimed. "You may each kiss your bride."

Isaac didn't need any further invitation. He lifted the gauzy fabric concealing her face, tossing it away. Then he batted it back as it fell improperly. Then he gathered her in his arms, tilted her back, and gave her a kiss filled with all the promise of his love.

When he straightened up, her lips were rosy from contact with his, her eyes sparkling with tears. She opened her mouth and laughed.

The joyous sound was irresistible, and Isaac found himself joining in with chuckles of his own as he held her hand in his and took her up the aisle.

"This," he told her after they'd left the church, "is the first day of our life together and the beginning of the joy and laughter we'll share."

"I love you, Isaac Friemont." She leaned forward to brush her lips against his. When she moved to draw away, he pulled her back.

"I love you, too, Nessa Friemont."

"Isaac?" she murmured after their next kiss. "I was right."

"About what?"

"I finally caught you."

Epilogue

Montana, 1920

I'd say our family reunion has officially outgrown our home," Dustin Friemont told his wife, who nestled so sweetly at his side. "What do you think?"

"The Lord has blessed us beyond what we ever could have hoped for." Delana surveyed her family with obvious satisfaction.

Brent, Marlene, and Isaac all had their spouses and children present. The Gailbraiths and Horntons, joined by happy marriages, mingled with everyone. Delana's old friend, Kaitlin MacLean, sat with a blanket over her lap, surrounded by children.

"I never would have thought God would see fit to give us so many loved ones. Or that the spread I was so focused on proving up would be the beginning of an entire town." Dustin leaned back. "We've seen so many good years under the Montana sky."

"And so much growth." Delana took a sip of water. "From covered wagons, to the railroad, to private automobiles, Saddleback has kept pace with progress."

"I'd say we stayed ahead of the curve." Dustin gave a groan as he got to his feet then reached to pull his wife up beside him. "Because we always had the one thing technology could never improve upon."

"Love," she agreed, resting her head against his chest.

Her golden hair had faded to white, her skin held the lines of laughter, and his wife was more beautiful to him than on the day they'd met. "Love," he agreed, looking out on the many blessings of God's love and the love shared among their family. "And time."

" 'To every thing,' " his wife began, " 'there is a season.' "

" 'And a time to every purpose under the heaven,' " he joined her. " 'A time to be born, and a time to die; a time to plant, and a time to pluck up that which is planted; a time to kill, and a time to heal; a time to break down, and a time to build up; a time to weep,' "—he looked into her eyes, seeing his own happiness mirrored there—" 'and a time to laugh. . . .' "

Kelly Eileen Hake received her first writing contract at the tender age of seventeen and arranged to wait three months until she was able to legally sign it. Since that first contract over a decade ago, she's fulfilled twenty contracts ranging from short stories to novels. In her spare time, she's attained her BA in English literature and composition, earned her credential to teach English in secondary schools, and went on to complete her MA in writing popular fiction.

Writing for Barbour combines two of Kelly's great loves—history and reading. A CBA bestselling author and member of American Christian Fiction Writers, she's been privileged to earn numerous Heartsong Presents Reader's Choice Awards and is known for her witty, heartwarming historical romances.

If You Liked This Book, You'll Also Like…

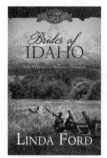

Brides of Idaho by Linda Ford
Three historical romances from bestselling author Linda Ford take readers into the rough mining country of Idaho. The three independent Hamilton sisters struggle to make a home and livelihood for themselves, and they don't have time for men they can't trust. Can love sneak in and change their stubborn hearts?
Paperback / 978-1-63409-798-7 / $12.99

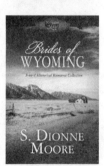

Brides of Wyoming by S. Dionne Moore
Author S. Dionne Moore takes readers onto the Wyoming rangeland of the late 1800s. In this historical romance collection, three strong men work ranches against the untamed forces of nature, outlaws, and feisty women. Can faith and love grow where suspicion and greed roam the range?
Paperback / 978-1-63409-799-4 / $12.99

Brides of Georgia by Connie Stevens
Author Connie Stevens travels back to 1800s Georgia during pivotal changes in the history of the Old South. In this historical romance collection, three men are on the verge of losing all hope for their futures, until they meet women who profoundly affect their hearts and faith.
Paperback / 978-1-63409-800-7 / $12.99

Find These and More from Barbour Books
at Your Favorite Bookstore
www.barbourbooks.com

BARBOUR
PUBLISHING

JOIN US ONLINE!

Christian Fiction for Women

Christian Fiction for Women is your online home for the latest in Christian fiction.

Check us out online for:

- Giveaways
- Recipes
- Info about Upcoming Releases
- Book Trailers
- News and More!

Find Christian Fiction for Women at Your Favorite Social Media Site:

 Search "Christian Fiction for Women"

 @fictionforwomen

---

WITHDRAWN